Kim ten Tusscher

BOUND IN DARKNESS

THE LILITH TRILOGY, BOOK 1

ALTEREGOPRESS.COM

Published in The Netherlands in 2010 by Zilverspoor
English edition published in 2014 by Alter Ego press

Cover illustration & design by Studio Zilverspoor
Designed and typeset by Studio Zilverspoor
Edited by Jos Weijmer
Translation by Rianne Stolwijk, www.spelledout.nl
Copy Editing by Studio Zilverspoor

www.kimtentusscher.com
Facebook: kimttee
Twitter: @kim_t_tee

www.alteregopress.com
info@alteregopress.com
Facebook: alteregopress
Twitter: @AlterEgoPress

ISBN 978 94 9076 747 1

Alter Ego Press is an imprint of Zilverspoor, www.zilverspoor.com.

1

A dull blow to her head caused Lilith to wake up. By reflex she tried to jump up, but the ropes around her wrists and ankles prevented her from doing so. She moaned and lay back down in resignation. Over the past few days, Lilith had been fruitlessly fighting her ties and, therefore, knew that she couldn't free herself. Lemuel's knots were just too tight.

Lilith looked around carefully. As a result of the blow, a sharp pain surged through her head whenever she moved too quickly. She expected that Pavel had awoken her and was looking for his silhouette in the semi-dark. The two men had taken her captive and the younger of the two had been the least patient with her. She was, however, the only person in the covered wagon.

Lilith did see a white stone, the size of a fist, lying next to her head. It glistened because it was wet. She knew it was hail. That was the word she had picked up during the first storm they had run into after she had been overpowered. She had also learned that it was made of ice. But how these stones could fall from the sky was a great mystery to her. In Lilith's native country the weather was usually dry, and the drought was only ever interrupted by short showers. Suddenly she spotted the hole in the hood. Hailstones were thrumming on the roof of the wagon and more stones ripped the canvas. Some hit her. Lilith tried to shift into a different position, but again the ties got in the way.

All of a sudden the wagon creaked and turned to the right. She rolled over, bumping her hip and elbow hard on the side board of the wagon. Lilith cursed. There wasn't a spare ounce of fat on her body to cushion the blows, and the jolting wagon gave her more and more bruises. Then the horses pulling the wagon came to a halt. The hailstones were no longer bashing the hood, but Lilith could still hear the thrumming sound. Apparently the men had found another spot for them to take shelter.

The canvas at the rear of the wagon was pulled aside and a blanket and a piece of bread were thrown in by Pavel. Behind him, Lilith could see that the storm was still raging violently. The canvas fell back down. While listening to Pavel's footsteps, she looked at the food lying well out of her reach. She twisted to get a bit closer but soon gave up as it cost her too much energy.

Lilith heard Lemuel ask something to his son . She couldn't understand what they were saying, but by now she knew which voice belonged to which man. The elder one usually spoke in a calm voice and swallowed the end of his words. Pavel had the same accent but his voice was shriller.

"I'm not going to any more trouble for her. That woman can take care of herself. She ought to be happy that we're giving her anything at all," he ranted.

The response was unintelligible. The canvas moved aside again, but this time Lemuel appeared in the opening. He climbed into the wagon, covered Lilith up, and moved the piece of bread close to her face.

"Can you reach it like this?" he asked, sounding slightly concerned.

"It's hard to eat with my hands tied," Lilith tried.

But the man shook his head. "Do you really expect me to untie you after what happened?"

Lemuel apparently didn't expect an answer, because he brought the waterskin to Lilith's lips. After that, he jumped out of the wagon.

"I hope that other group of travellers has found shelter as well," he called out to his son while he remained where he was. " It isn't a fit night out for man nor beast."

Lilith's heart skipped a beat. She strained herself to be able to hear the rest of the conversation. Could Lemuel be talking about her pursuers? He had to be, hadn't he? It was unthinkable that anyone would travel in this cold without having a very good reason to do so. Even Pavel and his father had debated the wisdom of waiting for the weather to improve before bringing her to the capital to put her on trial. And now there was a group of travellers – plodding through the unremitting storms – taking the same road they were.

"We haven't seen them for a while," Pavel answered. "Come,

let's go inside. I'm yearning for a nice fire to warm myself and I could do with some food."

The cracking sound of their footsteps in the snow faded. Lilith wanted to scream that they shouldn't leave her all by herself, but instead she suffered a bad coughing fit. When she had finally caught her breath, the only sound that remained was that of the horses shoving their food around on the bottom of the buckets as they were eating. It was too late. If the men showed up now, there would be no one to protect her. Then all would have been in vain.

The five men she feared had been pursuing her for several weeks and were sent by her master. In a fit of despair, Lilith had fled from him, from his suffocating authority and the horrible tasks he had imposed upon her. Running and creeping across savannahs and through forests, she had finally arrived at the mountains, hoping to shake off her pursuers there. But unfortunately the echo of laughter between the rocks spoke of the confidence of her pursuers, seemingly confident and in high hopes of finding her soon. Those sounds had made her even more wary. Under no circumstances did she want to fall into their hands again. This proved to be a great motivation; her fear had outweighed her fatigue and had kept her going.

Now that her heart was finally beating more slowly, Lilith tried to eat the piece of bread. She sucked on it until it dissolved in her mouth. It took her a long time to eat the small lump. After that, she fell asleep again, in spite of her worries. Thanks to the second blanket she was at least a little bit less cold.

All of a sudden someone pushed against her shoulder. The next instant she was lying face down in the snow.

"No, Seraph, don't. Help!" Lilith cried, with her nightmare fresh in the back of her mind. She kicked around wildly until she hit someone. Only when she was pushed onto her back, did she stop kicking. Pavel was standing beside her. His eyes were glowing while he pulled her up by her clothes.

"Are you starting again?" he hissed. Then he let go of her. Lilith couldn't stop herself from falling backwards and bumped her head on the wagon. "You're going for a little walk."

"I don't want to walk. Just take me there quickly," she begged, all confused, while she looked up at Pavel.

"Are you that eager to be punished?" he asked bewildered. "Or do you think the king won't punish you for what you did to us?"

"I'm not afraid to be judged. I've done nothing wrong."

"My brother was more dead than alive when we left him," he snarled at her, kicking her in the ribs at the same time.

"I never meant for that to happen. I only wanted to take some food and clothes and then leave again. But because you all threw yourselves on me, I had to defend myself."

Pavel snorted. "That didn't give you any reason to draw a knife."

"I'm really sorry about that, too," Lilith whispered, pulling herself up.

But just like after the fight, the man wasn't listening. "You're a filthy murderer," he hissed.

That remark stung.

"I don't even know how to kill someone with a knife. I'm truly glad I never learned *that*," she whispered, for which she received a blow to the side of her head. Pavel was raising his hand again when Lemuel joined them.

"The woman will be tried by lord Yvar. This is not the way," he said, stopping his son.

Pavel nodded reluctantly and they both disappeared from her sight. When, not much later, the wagon started moving again, Lilith had no choice but to walk alongside it. Her wet clothes stuck to her body, and the cold wind rose again. Lilith sneezed. She envied Pavel, who was wrapped in a warm cape and could take shelter under his hood. He rubbed his waist with his left arm. Concerned, Lemuel leaned towards him and whispered something inaudible. The answer was drowned out by another sneezing fit.

As she wiped her nose on her shoulder, Lilith let her gaze wander along the horizon. The snow had turned the landscape nearly as white as the sky. Nevertheless, she could distinguish a thin, grey line indicating the horizon. To the left there was a group of trees, but there was nothing else to be seen. Trying to wrap her blanket closer around her body, Lilith heaved a sigh of relief. There was no trace of her pursuers.

"I hope that's not another hail storm," Lemuel muttered as he peered into the distance. Lilith now also noticed the dark clouds gathering again.

"I hope so, too. There aren't many farms around here where we can take shelter," his son answered.

Lilith quickened her pace to get alongside the coach-box in order to catch the conversation. She picked up enough words to piece together a story, which turned out to be a reiteration of a conversation they had held a few times before.

"What a year," the old man sighed. "Do you think this is a punishment of the Gods?"

Pavel shrugged. "What makes you think we should be punished? Even if the Gods would exist. Sometimes I think the Gods were invented only to keep us docile."

Lilith was amazed that someone could think that Gods didn't exist. It had never even crossed her mind to doubt Jakob's existence, let alone question the truth of everything she had been told about Him. She thought about it but quickly dismissed the idea. Her master had had other ways to make her obey.

"I know our faith means a lot to you, father. But people seem to be just as capable of creating things as the so-called Gods are, and there's no proof of Their existence."

"There's plenty of evidence, but we're just not intelligent enough to recognize the signs. Therefore, some people say it's all nonsense."

"The miracles performed by the Gods? Those are just stories written a long time ago, so no one knows what really happened any more. I'm convinced there's a logical explanation for everything, including the harsh winter that sweeps over Merzia right now."

Lemuel shook his head disapprovingly. "Maybe people like you are to blame for the Gods bringing this winter upon us. You, who favour scientists...", Lemuel pronounced the word with contempt, "... over the Gods. All these so-called men of learning have only led us astray from that which is important."

Suddenly Lilith slipped on the snow. She slammed head first into the ground and was dragged along by the leash for several yards before Lemuel could bring the horses to a halt. In the meantime Pavel had jumped off the coach-box. Lilith was trying to scramble to her feet, but the man picked her up and shoved her back into the wagon. Then he cautiously climbed in as well.

"Does it hurt a lot?" she whispered. Pavel looked surprised but didn't say anything. "I'm really sorry that I did that to you. Honestly."

He glared at her furiously and tied the ropes around her ankles even tighter than he normally did. Lilith groaned, but he ignored her. Before he left he snarled at her, "What good are your excuses to me? Do you think they'll make me forget what you did to me and my brother? I'm glad you'll be sentenced soon and I hope the punishment will be severe."

Pavel walked away, leaving a sorrowful Lilith behind. She felt a stabbing pain in her temples. This was what her master had always warned her about; people wanted to capture her, hurt her, kill her. *And only because I...* Lilith pushed the thought aside, scared that the two men would somehow pick up on it. It wasn't even true to begin with; these people weren't holding her captive because of what she was, but because of what she had done. As far as she knew, they had no idea what was hidden behind her emaciated, weak appearance.

She struggled to get under the blanket but eventually gave up. For the first time since they had started their journey, she was worried about what the king would have in store for her.

It was as bad as they had feared. They failed to find a farm to spend the night that evening, so they stopped at a clearing in the woods. While Pavel got Lilith out of the wagon, Lemuel built a fire. The sky had cleared up, holding the promise of a night that would, at least for the most part, be dry.

"I have to pee."

Lilith turned to face Pavel and nodded at her bonds. The man reluctantly untied the ropes. The leash around her waist, however, stayed where it was. Before Lilith could disappear between the bushes, Pavel ordered her to remain within sight. She reluctantly squatted down on her hunches. How humiliating it was to do this with Pavel's eyes watching her back.

Apparently he thought she was taking too long, because all of a sudden Pavel gave a tug on the leash. Lilith groped around, but her hands didn't find anything to hold on to. Lying on her back, she reached out for the gold necklace she was wearing. Had he known whom he was dealing with, the man would certainly treat her differently. Lilith smirked as she imagined him begging for mercy before she took her revenge. But then she dismissed the plan, she couldn't use the power of the necklace.

Walking back, Lilith observed the situation at the camp closely. Lemuel was paying no attention to her and was still sitting at the fire, which was burning fiercely by now. She extended her arms to give the impression that she would obediently let them be tied again, but as soon as Pavel tried to put the rope around her wrists, she jumped towards him. He screamed when she hit him in the waist, and they were both knocked down to the frozen ground. They were tumbling all over each other. Then she hit him on the temple and Pavel stayed down, stunned.

Lilith crawled towards the edge of the wood as fast as she could, but Pavel had recovered and jumped on top of her. His weight pressed her into the dirt.

"You shall not escape your punishment. I won't let you," he hissed in her ear.

"We'll see about that," she gasped in reply, pushing him away from her.

Lilith jumped up and ran towards the bushes. Her heart was pounding in her ears, drowning out all other sounds. She was nearly there. Just a few more yards and she would be able to escape. Only one more yard and the bushes would protect her.

Suddenly she felt a sharp pain in her calf. Her strength dissipated and she fell face down in the bushes. The sounds returned: the men were shouting and the fire was roaring. Lilith tried to get up, but her right leg wasn't cooperating. Bewildered, she noticed the blood oozing down her calf. Then she looked at the two men, who were running towards her, and yelled that she surrendered.

Lemuel aimed his bow at her again to ensure she wouldn't do anything. Meanwhile, his son fastened the ropes around her wrists so tightly that they cut into her flesh. Lilith tried to ignore the pain by focussing on Lemuel's arms. They were shaking because he had kept his weapon drawn for too long.

Only when his son had dragged her towards the fire, did Lemuel put the bow away. Lilith gritted her teeth when he pulled the arrow out of her leg. After he had tied her ankles back together, he threw a blanket over her. It slid halfway down her shoulders, but this time the old man made no effort to cover her up properly.

"What are we to do with you? I'm glad we can hand you over to the king tomorrow."

Lemuel shook his head disapprovingly. Lilith looked away.

Without heeding her any more attention, the two men sat down at the other side of the fire where the flames hid them from her sight. Lemuel spoke softly to his son, who from time to time responded in a loud and angry voice. Lilith knew they were talking about her but she didn't want to hear it. Instead, she listened to the crackling flames.

When the fire was beginning to die down, Lemuel got up to gather his cooking gear. Pavel was staring into the flames. His legs were crossed and his shoulders hunched. Lilith studied his face, which was bruised and swollenswelling up around his temple. She didn't feel sorry for him, given that he had done the same to her. Her jaw was throbbing because his fist had hit it full force, and she was hurting in other places as well. Every time she moved her arms, however slightly, the ropes cut deeper into her wrists.

As if he sensed she was staring at him, Pavel suddenly looked straight at her. His eyes blazed with an anger that stirred up even more because she kept staring back. He roughly poked the fire with a stick, causing it to flare up again.

"Easy, son, otherwise you won't be getting anything to eat for a while."

Pavel threw away the stick. It missed Lilith's shoulder by an inch.

The clattering of pans and spoons preceded the delicious smell of roasted meat and vegetables. Lilith became aware of her hunger through the loud growling of her stomach. Expecting that the men would share their food with her, she sat up. Pavel kept moving his spoon in her direction before taking a bite. Lilith licked her cracked lips, following the spoon with her eyes.

"You've cooked excellently again, father. I was really starving, too," he said with his mouth full.

Lilith curled herself up in agony.

The elder man just nodded. Lilith grew nauseated from the rumbling feeling in her stomach. The men filled their plates a second time. When they had finished those plates as well, Pavel picked up the pan and said to Lemuel, "There's still something left, did you want some more?"

"No thank you, I'm full."

Pavel glanced at Lilith before he got up and walked in her direction. "I'm full too."

Expecting to get the leftovers, Lilith sat back up again. Pavel, however, walked past her.

"I'll bury it at the edge of the wood, so it won't attract wild animals."

At first Lilith thought the man was provoking her, but soon after he returned with an empty pan. He really did rather throw it away than give it to her. Defeated, Lilith lay back down. Pavel gave her a self-satisfied grin. A voice in the back of her mind told her that all of this was her own fault.

For the remainder of the journey, Pavel and Lemuel wouldn't let her walk any more. In the morning, Lilith was given a single piece of bread, and that had been all. The men clearly were in a hurry now that they were so close to their destination. In spite of a new storm, they didn't stop for shelter. Snow fell through the torn hood and formed a small layer on the floor of the wagon. Lilith licked it up to quench her thirst. She immediately realized that she had made a mistake; her mouth became even dryer and she felt even colder. With a great deal of effort, she turned to her other side when the wagon bounced over a bump. She slid down to the back and was pressed against the tailboard. Lilith tried to crawl back but she kept sliding down.

Out of curiosity she propped herself up a little to peek through the fluttering flap. To the right was nothing but a thick snow screen, but to the left there was a sheer cliff along which the path ascended. As soon as they turned the corner, Lilith could make out another rock pillar. When it dawned on her that they were nearing their destination, Lilith lay back down, feeling apprehensive.

It took forever for the path to level out again. The horseshoes clattered on bridges and grew silent again on firm rocky soil. The snow muffled all sounds.

Suddenly the wagon came to a halt. The flap was pushed aside and Pavel pulled Lilith out. With the first step, pain surged through her leg, but she managed to fight it off while the men dragged her to a building in front of them. They pushed her inside through a huge gate. Amazed, Lilith took in her surroundings. The walls were painted a dark green, and lamps, giving out a static white light, were suspended from the ceiling. It looked completely different from what she had been used to, because in the caves where Lilith had been raised, torches and candles had been used for illumination. The light had, therefore, been orange and forever moving because of the draught in the tunnels.

The walls in this palace were decorated with tapestries, but because of the speed with which Pavel dragged her along, Lilith couldn't make out what was depicted. There were many people in the palace. The Merzians made way for the trio and broke off their conversations.

Lilith received inquisitive looks but she didn't take notice. She counted her steps and tried to remember which corridors they took in case she would be able to escape.

After a while they reached a less crowded part of the palace. When they turned another corner they encountered a soldier of the Royal Guard. He regarded both men closely and then rested his gaze on Lilith. The soldier frowned for a second. "What brings you to Nadesh?"

"We wish to speak to our king," Lemuel answered calmly.

The soldier opened his mouth to ask another question but before he could say anything Pavel pushed Lilith forwards.

"This woman broke into my house and attacked me and my

brother. My brother is badly injured. That's why she deserves to be punished."

The soldier looked at Lilith again. Her thin clothes couldn't conceal the emaciated state she was in and she barely reached Pavel's shoulders, even though he wasn't all that tall himself.

"She did all that?" the soldier asked incredulously.

Lilith bowed her head to conceal her smile and let out a sob. Maybe she could use the ignorance of these humans to her advantage.

"All right," the man said. "This, indeed, sounds like a case the king should handle."

Another soldier joined and they led the way to the chambers of Merzia's ruler. Lilith stopped hiding the fact that her leg was hurting and followed obediently. It would be to her advantage if the king was to take pity on her. It was good to have a plan and she felt confident.

The soldiers escorted them to an elongated room that smelled of sweet herbs. There were large windows on one side. The curtains were open, but only a little light came in. This room was also illuminated by the cold light that Lilith had noticed before and it made her shudder. There were paintings on the other wall. Portraits of kings and queens preceding the current ruler looked down on her. Some faces were friendly but they all emanated determination and authority. Their eyes followed her while she walked on.

Now her gaze was drawn to the king. He was sitting on the far side of the room, close to the fire that was burning fiercely. The closer Lilith came, the warmer she felt, but she kept shuddering all the same. The king leaned back and regarded the approaching group with fascination.

Her confidence suddenly dissipated. Of course nobody would plead her case, especially not the king. Humans were her enemy. She tore herself loose from Pavel's grip. She was immediately grabbed on two sides. Lemuel and Pavel dragged her forwards until the king gestured they weren't allowed any farther. She struggled to break free, but Pavel forced her to her knees. The two men made a deep bow and Pavel pushed Lilith's head all the way down, until her forehead touched the cold tiles. She furiously looked aside.

After the guard had introduced them, it was again Lemuel who spoke.

"Lord Yvar, our king. Thank you for making time for us. This woman broke into my son's house. We beg you to punish her."

"Did she steal anything?"

Hearing his voice for the first time, Lilith looked up. Even though Yvar's question was directed at the man, he looked straight at Lilith. The resemblance to the pictures on the wall was striking. King Yvar had the same piercing eyes and his demeanour radiated both inner peace and power. He held her gaze for a few seconds, during which it seemed as though he could look into her very soul.

"Food and clothes."

"Was that all?"

Lilith finally managed to avert her eyes.

"She was also extremely violent when we caught her in the act."

It was of course Pavel who brought this to attention. He took out Lilith's dagger and made a step forwards. One of the guards immediately jumped between the man and the king. Pavel started back. Stammering his apologies, he handed the weapon to the soldier. The king ignored the entire incident.

Then he addressed Lilith, but she kept avoiding his gaze.

"What's your name?"

She replied almost inaudibly.

"Why did you want to steal food and clothes?"

"I hadn't eaten for days and I was cold," she snorted. Why else would she even go near his species?

"She nearly killed my brother, lord." Pavel related what had happened.

"Do you deny this?"

Lilith shook her head but remained silent.

"Wouldn't you like to say something in your defence? Don't you realize that I'm going to have to punish you and that this is your only chance to tell your side of the story?"

"I didn't mean for anyone to get hurt," Lilith sighed. She wondered if anyone would believe her. "All of a sudden two men threw themselves on me. I don't remember grabbing the knife, I just suddenly had it in my hand. I'm sorry."

There was a brief silence before she continued in a soft voice, "Honestly, I didn't want to use violence. You must believe me."

"Lord Yvar," Pavel interjected agitatedly and pushed her away from him. "She fought like a lunatic. She could have surrendered but instead she became violent." Pavel pulled up his clothes. A red stain on the bandages around his upper body emphasized his words, "She used the knife very efficiently."

"Is there anything else you want to say, woman?"

"There's nothing to add."

The king sighed deeply, thinking hard.

"The woman is to be punished for theft and assault by means of flogging."

Pavel was mumbling contentedly, which worried Lilith. She didn't understand the meaning of the words the king had used, but during their journey the man had repeatedly wished that Lilith would be punished severely.

"Furthermore, I will award you, Pavel and Lemuel, a sum of fifteen gold pieces in damages. The woman will repay me this sum by working for me."

There was another moment of silence. Cautiously, Lilith looked up at the king. She hoped his eyes would give away a hint on what was going to happen to her, but she saw nothing. Then Yvar addressed his guards.

"Take these loyal citizens to the kitchen where they can eat something. Bring the prisoner to the flogging room and notify everyone."

The two soldiers pulled Lilith to her feet.

"What are you going to do with me?" she whispered. She didn't receive an answer. She glanced over her shoulder at the king. He was bent over his papers again. "What's going to happen?" Lilith wrestled herself free and turned around. Without looking up, the king motioned for the soldiers to take her away. "This isn't fair. Tell me what's going to happen," she growled.

The men grabbed her by her shoulders to drag her away. Lilith realized that this would be her last chance to escape. She sized the men up. Obviously they were big and muscular, but that wasn't necessarily an advantage. If she could only surprise them... Lilith slid her gaze farther down. The men's swords were temptingly close at hand.

Almost immediately it dawned on her that this plan was doomed to fail. Even before she could obtain a weapon, one of the soldiers would have worked her to the ground, and the other would be pointing his sword at her. They might even kill her on the spot. To die was her biggest fear. Lilith believed that her Creator would punish her severely in the afterlife. It was best to go along willingly. Whatever punishment the king had imposed upon her, it clearly wasn't the death penalty. After all, he had said that she had to work for him. It was her only hope.

In the corridor they passed a tapestry that caught Lilith's attention. It depicted a yellow, grassy plain with a cloudless, clear blue sky in which brightly coloured birds were flying. Near a pond stood some trees, and animals were trying to quench their thirst. A zebra looked at her and drew Lilith into the world she knew so well and almost longed for right now. At least she knew what to expect there.

Lilith had halted for a second, but now the soldiers urged her on. Soon they reached another wing of the palace. The soldiers opened a door and, after having pushed her into the room, closed it with a muffled bang. She was alone.

Lilith looked around the room suspiciously. On the walls there were pictures of people engaged in horrible acts. They were tumbling over each other to kill others or to get away after having raped and robbed a woman.

But there was something else that drew her attention as well. The red-tiled floor sloped down towards the middle of the room, where there was a large pillar surrounded by a gutter. Lilith hesitantly approached it. There were four metal shackles on chains riveted to the pillar. Even more anxious, she again wondered what flogging was and she had a deep sense of foreboding. A text had been chiselled at the top of the pillar. She made it out letter by letter and whispered the words: "My blood for my sins."

That didn't bode well. She turned around and limped towards the door. She rattled the door handle and pounded on the wood. When the door suddenly opened, she fell headfirst. Two masked men caught her.

"If you don't cooperate you'll only make it harder on yourself. It's your choice," one of them warned her.

Lilith, however, kept fighting to break free.

A third soldier loomed up in front of her. "Need a hand?" His face wasn't covered and his eyes glistened with amusement.

"Of course not, we can handle a little lady like her. We have done this before," was the irritable answer.

The men dragged her backwards into the room. Lilith didn't get a chance to regain her footing. She tried to bite an arm, but one of the men immediately pulled her head back by her hair. Now she noticed that the ceiling was painted as well. The people behaving shamelessly on the wall were punished in the outer ring by creatures with strange faces. They were as void of any expression as the masks of the two men dragging her along. In the middle ring, twelve men and women sat on thrones with their backs to one another. Some were talking to each other as though there was nothing going on around them, but most of them were looking attentively at sentences being carried out. Then she recognized the God Jakob. He was pointing at a man who was tied to a wheel.

"Please help me, Lord!" she prayed. "Please!"

The two men didn't stop until they reached the pillar. Now that Lilith could stand again, she kicked the soldier on her left in his crotch. He lashed at her, cursing. His fist hit her jaw in the exact same spot where Pavel had hit her before.

"If you think that hurt," hissed the other one while she groaned, "then wait until we're finished with you."

Next, he undid the ropes around her wrists. Lilith didn't hesitate for even a second and pushed him away from her. She grabbed her amulet. "Qi ga ullar brut i-qi libèr..." Her hand was pulled away and a man put a metal band around her wrist. Her other arm was grabbed as well, in order to secure it. Nevertheless, she sang the final words, "...qi ouander i-a drag!"

The chains rattled when the men pulled them in until Lilith was pressed tightly against the pillar. In spite of this, she smiled. They wouldn't be able to stop her in a few seconds. But when the men fastened the shackles on her ankles, Lilith understood that she hadn't been fast enough. Now it had become impossible to draw on the power inside her. She desperately started to pull on the chains, but they wouldn't yield.

Suddenly Lilith felt something cold beneath her clothes. With a tearing sound, the back of her tunic was cut open. She begged the man to stop, but he didn't listen. She felt the blade on her arms when the man cut her sleeves. After that, he did the same with her trousers, so Lilith was hanging naked in the shackles.

"What are you going to do to me?" she gasped.

The other man appeared in front of her. He took an object from his belt and held it in front of her face. Tied to the end of the wooden stick were three leather thongs. "This is a scourge. Do you know what that is?"

Lilith shook her head.

"In a few minutes you will." He let the thongs slide over her arm. The metal beads on the ends felt as cold as ice. He stopped when the door opened again.

Judging by the sound of the footsteps, a big group now entered the room. Lilith couldn't see them until they were well into the room. Pavel and Lemuel were following two soldiers. The son was smiling contentedly at her as he took up the seat that he was directed to. A veiled woman looked at her with concern but then averted her head like the other women.

Suddenly the king appeared in front of her. In a clear voice he informed her of her punishment. "Woman, because of your wrongdoings against Lemuel and his family, I sentence you to fifty lashes with the scourge."

He gave her one final stern look, as if he was waiting for her to say something. Then he turned around and sat down next to the veiled woman.

"The punishment shall be carried out now."

Before Lilith could prepare herself for what was coming, she heard a crack and felt a blow against her back that slammed her into the pillar. The ensuing sharp pain spread through her spine and radiated to the rest of her body. All her muscles contracted briefly. Another blow immediately followed the first, but this time she was hit on the other side. Now Lilith understood what her punishment was.

The executioners counted each blow they inflicted and after the third one Lilith started to groan. She pulled at the chains with all her might. Time and again the scourge swished and the thongs cracked, resulting in excruciating pain. This was cruel: the men were beating her up while she couldn't even defend herself. Lilith shook her head wildly because it was the only part of her body she could move.

It wasn't long before Lilith felt blood seeping down her body. "Seven." Crack. Pain. "Eight." More swishing and more pain. She couldn't do anything to cushion the blows. She knew when the scourge was going to hit her, but it was impossible to be prepared for it.

At nine she started to pray. "Lord, give…"

"Ten."

"…me the… strength… to get… through… this… Please… help me." Her words kept being interrupted by new blows to her back. "Jakob!"

Lilith pulled forcefully at the chains. Suddenly her left hand was free.

She started pulling at the other chain. The next blow curled around the side of her body.

Then the executioners walked up to her. Her hand was pulled away, but Lilith yanked herself free. She lashed out wildly at one of the executioners. Her nails scratched his mask before her fingers got a hold on it. Lilith pulled it down so fiercely that the laces on the back snapped. Her hand was grabbed again.

"It's no use resisting," the executioner whispered. His eyes flashed with anger. Lilith spat at him in response. "Vixen, you're asking for it." The man wiped the phlegm off his face while his companion tied her hands together with a rope. After that, the men walked away again.

"Twenty."

He had aimed for the back of her knees and had hit even harder than before. Lilith's knees gave way and all of a sudden the chains had to carry her entire weight. When her wrist broke, she didn't feel the scourge any more for a brief moment. Lilith started screaming and clenched her right fist around the chain in an attempt to get her weight off the shackles.

By now, she could feel the difference between the two executioners. The strands of one scourge lashed the spots that had already been ripped open, while the other one unfailingly found the most sensitive parts of her body.

"Twenty-seven"

The man groaned while he put more speed into the whip. Lilith looked at the people watching from the side line. The smile on Pavel's face had disappeared and he looked deathly pale. Lemuel blinked with each blow.

Sweat dripped down Lilith's forehead and stung her eyes. She closed them, but she couldn't stop screaming. Her screams reverberated against the walls but couldn't drown out the sound of the scourge. The swishing, the cracking, it was deafening.

"Please, lord Yvar, make them stop."

Lilith opened her eyes when the words registered. Her vision was still blurred, but she could see that the veiled woman had turned to the king. He, however, ignored her.

"Please, she has been punished enough."

Despite the woman's pleading, the blows kept landing on Lilith's ripped skin. Sweat was stinging the wounds. Her feet slipped on the mixture of blood and sweat on the tiles. Lilith kept looking at the woman, who was shrouded in an orange, trembling glow. "I have scorched her," Lilith thought deliriously. She wasn't aware of the counting any more. "And the flames have spread to me. I have become the victim of the fire that I lighted myself."

This flogging was justice, even though it could never undo what she had done. Pavel's brother had survived, but many others hadn't survived an encounter with her. She had no right resisting this punishment.

So Lilith stopped screaming. The leather thongs swished through the silence; the metal beads slammed into her body. She felt all three of them, but not even a sigh escaped her lips. Almost immediately the whistling sound returned. She pressed her cheek against the cold stones.

"Thirty-eight."

The executioner yanked the beads out of her flesh. Her shoulder was starting to hurt because it was carrying her entire weight. She thought it was weird that she noticed this now. The rest of her body was hurting so much more. Nevertheless, she tried to pull herself back to her feet, only to immediately get hit in the back of her knees again.

"Enough."

The word quietly seeped through the sounds of violence. The ensuing silence was instantly supplanted by her own gasps for air.

"That was enough," the king repeated.

It slowly started to sink in. It was over: no more swishing. The scourge wouldn't tear her apart any further. The executioners walked up to her. They were panting as well and their red tunics stuck to their bodies due to the sweat. Lilith heard the king say that Pavel and Lemuel would be compensated for the six remaining lashes she hadn't received. This meant she would have to perform more duties, but she was happy that it was over for now.

Without speaking, the executioners released her from the chains. Their touches were soft compared to what they had done to her earlier. Lilith cast a final glance at Pavel and Lemuel before they left the room. The son held his head bowed and was visibly shaken by what he had seen. Lemuel wasn't responding to anything, so a soldier had put a hand on his shoulder and was guiding him outside. Suddenly she felt a hand on her cheek and her head was turned sideways. Lilith was carefully laid down on the floor. The tiles were delightfully cold.

Then the veiled woman appeared in front of her. "Good Gods, she's still conscious," she stammered.

"She's very strong. Let's try to relief some of her pain first," somebody who Lilith couldn't see answered. At the same time something was pressed to her lips. Lilith would have recognized the scent anywhere.

"No," she whispered powerlessly, even though she had actually wanted to scream it out loud.

"It's all right, this will help you sleep."

The veiled woman carefully stroked her hair while the other woman poured the liquid into her mouth. Lilith tried to spit it out, but somebody pinched her nose and covered her mouth, forcing her to swallow. When they released her, she growled once more.

"It's for your own good. Soon you won't feel anything any more."

The words sounded farther and farther away. The woman's voice was distorted as the world around Lilith became blurred. She didn't feel the hands that were taking care of her any more. She only heard her own heart beating in her temples. A stab of pain went through her body when somebody touched her wounds. She held on to the pain in an attempt to stay awake. Eventually, she had to let go and then there was nothing.

Ghalatea stroked Lilith's sweat-soaked hair again. She wondered what this young woman could have done to deserve this. The king never told her why somebody had to be punished and she always assumed that he was just, but this girl... When Lilith finally closed her eyes, Ghalatea looked up at Betrys in relief. "She's asleep."

The other woman nodded and continued taking care of the marks left by the whip. It was nice that she had taken the initiative to dress the worst wounds, no questions asked. This allowed Ghalatea to focus on Lilith's left hand, the flesh of which had been stripped off when she had pulled it out of the cuff. While the Ancilla Princeps bandaged the hand, she realized that the wrist was probably broken, so she splinted it. After that, she washed the woman.

"It looks as though she hasn't had much luck in her life so far," the Ancilla Princeps whispered while her fingers traced the scars on Lilith's arms and legs. "She's extremely undernourished and scarred. What on earth has happened to her?"

Ghalatea immediately rearranged her veil to conceal the scar on her own face even more. Betrys briefly looked at her and then glanced at Lilith. Then she shrugged. She'd always been a bit indifferent, but then again, maybe it only appeared that way because she didn't speak much.

After a while they wrapped Lilith in a blanket. Putting her on the stretcher wasn't any trouble at all because she hardly weighed anything.

Ghalatea felt the knot in her stomach tighten as she watched the two soldiers carry the stretcher out of the room. Betrys followed them, and Ghalatea remained behind alone. The king wished to speak to her. He had told her so before he had left the flogging room. Ghalatea knew very well why he had demanded this. She should have kept her mouth shut, like she always did.

Ghalatea looked around one more time. The floor was still covered in blood. Servants would clean the room later, but the Ancilla Princeps knew that the stench would remain. It was as if the pillar absorbed the smell of blood, sweat and pain of everyone who was punished here, mixed it and poured it out again. Their screams slumbered in the silence. Lilith's screams, however, were drowned out by other voices. Memories of her youth forced themselves upon Ghalatea and she ran from the room.

Breathing deeply, she stood still in the corridor but she couldn't calm down. Even though the memories of the baptism ritual she had undergone in the name of the Goddess Margal when she was a sixteen-year-old girl always lingered in the back of her mind, the Ancilla Princeps was perfectly capable of keeping them at bay. But not today. Lilith's flogging had opened the floodgates, and images, sounds and feelings washed over her. Ghalatea sought support against the wall and buried her face in her hands. Through the fabric of her veil she felt the rough edges of her deep scar. The acid that had been used in the ritual had eaten away the flesh on her temple and cheek. She quickly pulled her hands away. Servants came by, so she started walking aimlessly. The king would have to wait a while longer, she had to calm down first.

Suddenly Ghalatea found herself in the flower greenhouse that was an outbuilding of the palace. The flogging room with its harsh, smooth walls wasn't very far from the greenhouses, but the contrast couldn't be bigger. The atmosphere was warm and humid, and even in the middle of winter the air was heavy with the sweet scent of flowers. Flights of steps led the Ancilla Princeps down and she walked underneath arches of honeysuckle and passion flower. But today she was blind to their beauty.

"Good afternoon, my lady…"

Only when she had passed the two men, did Ghalatea realize that they had greeted her. Even then, she didn't bother to turn around. This wasn't a good day anyway. Why had the king thought it necessary for her to attend the flogging? Why couldn't she have stayed in the kitchen, where it was safe? Then the doors to her memories wouldn't have been wrenched open this violently. Then her friends' screams wouldn't be drowning out all other sounds right now.

Ghalatea fell to her knees near a bed of lavender and whispered their names, "Ghudrun, Marougha, Eligh…" Tears ran down her cheeks now that she saw their faces before her. She pulled a twig off a lavender bush and held it to her nose. It gave off a fresh scent that she had never smelled before she had come to Merzia. She rubbed on the leaves to intensify the scent. It helped her to suppress her memories of the things that had happened a long time ago, and she thought back to the flogging of that afternoon. Who was this woman who had appealed to Jakob so desperately?

She was startled from her thoughts.

"Ancilla Princeps, have you noticed? The peonies are in bloom!"

Vester shared her passion for flowers and he looked elated while he walked up to Ghalatea. She shook her head and got up, happy for the distraction. "This early?" she asked, quickly wiping away her tears.

The man led her to the rear section of the greenhouse where there was a bed filled with large flowers. Double peonies grew next to single peonies and the colours varied from almost white to a dark purple. It was wonderful to see these plants in full bloom while outside the winter still held the world trapped under a blanket of snow. Vester took a sharp knife from his belt and handed it to Ghalatea.

"I'm sure you would like to cut a bouquet of peonies for lord

Yvar."

The Ancilla Princeps, however, declined. It was high time to call on the king. She might come back later.

"You spent a lot of time on the woman," the king said, at long last breaking the silence. Ghalatea had stood in front of him for several minutes.

"To be honest, my lord, I didn't come here straight away," she confessed nervously. "There were a lot of things I needed to think about."

His expression was gruff. "Do you understand why I want to speak to you?"

"Of course I do, my lord. I'm sorry that I spoke during the execution of the punishment. I shouldn't have interfered."

Yvar gave a satisfied nod and rose to his feet. He put his hand on her shoulder and led her to a windowsill. There he scrutinized her with a penetrating gaze. Ghalatea had often witnessed how other people told him things they actually didn't want to tell him, only because the king looked at them this way. She smiled, he had been like this since childhood.

"Tell me, why did this specific punishment affect you so deeply? You've witnessed floggings before."

The smile immediately vanished from her face and Ghalatea heaved a deep sigh. It didn't matter how many floggings she attended, she would never feel anything but abhorrence for this form of punishment. For a moment she wondered whether she should say this out loud but she decided to remain silent on the subject. "The screaming got to me. It brought back memories of the day that my friends and I were maimed."

"I thought as much."

Yvar put a hand on hers. Again his gaze penetrated her, but this time his eyes were full of compassion. It was just like thirty-seven years ago, when he had sat by her bed as a young boy after she had just arrived in Nadesh. While his mother was looking after the refugees, the young prince had sat by her bed and had held her hand. Ghalatea nodded, of course he understood.

"How did your friends fare afterwards?" Yvar asked her.

"Eligh was chosen to go with Margal to Emek Jaryi. Other than that, I can't remember much of what happened after the Purifications. I was scared of being left behind because I didn't have a family any more, so I followed the other refugees. Sometimes I think I remember at least one of my friends coming with me, but Ghudrun never reached Merzia. She probably died from her wounds during the journey, so we may have left her behind."

Ghalatea bowed her head and dabbed her eyes with a corner of her veil. Yvar got up but returned moments later with a glass of water that he pushed into her hands.

"I think we just left them where they fell down, because nobody cared about anyone else. That's what's eating away at me, maybe I could have saved her. I should at least have stayed with Ghudrun when she died and given her a final resting place."

"There was nothing you could have done, Ghalatea. I clearly remember that you were in an extremely bad shape when you arrived at the palace. The only thing you could do was make sure you reached Merzia. If you had let anything distract you from that goal, you would have died as well."

Ghalatea nodded and drank some water. She knew all this, but it didn't feel that way. All she felt was guilt, because she had left her friends in the lurch.

Yvar gave her another look of concern, but then his expression grew stern. In a cautioning tone he raised the subject of the flogging again.

"Next time I expect you to not interfere with the punishment. You forced me to let the flogging continue longer than necessary. I wanted to tell them to stop, but what kind of king would I be if I followed orders from my Ancilla Princeps?"

Ghalatea's hand flew to her mouth in shock. She was responsible for the prolonged duration of Lilith's punishment.

"Let this be a lesson for the future."

"Certainly, my lord. It will never happen again."

He nodded approvingly. "I never doubted that. I hope you understand why I'm telling you this."

Ghalatea took another sip of water. By reprimanding her, he had resumed his role as king. The transition was big and unexpected.

"What else has been weighing on your mind?"

Ghalatea put her glass down and told Yvar about Lilith's scars.

"Some of them were the result of cuts that she scratched open numerous times, but others were clear evidence of deep wounds, and on the inside of her right wrist there was a thick line. The wounds were administered with terrifying precision." Lost in thought, Ghalatea shook her head. "Maybe it's a religious ritual," she suggested. "I've read about certain tribes where scars are a part of their faith."

The king gave a vague answer as if he didn't really care. That changed when Ghalatea said, "There is something else. The woman said a prayer during the flogging."

"You could understand her?"

Ghalatea nodded. "I think she spoke Naftalian. It closely resembles the language of my people. There are only a few differences in pronunciation. She begged Jakob for help."

There wasn't much else to say about it, but the Ancilla Princeps knew that this was important. Deep in thought, Yvar stared at his hands for a while before he told her she could leave. Ghalatea jumped to her feet and curtsied.

"I want you to take good care of our prisoner. She still has a debt to repay. If you find out more about her, I want you to inform me."

"Of course, my lord, I will."

2

Nadesh was already shrouded in darkness when the gates opened. The man slowed down his horse, but as soon as the metal-bound doors had opened wide enough, he rode through at full speed. The sound of the pounding hoofs on the bridges cut into the silence of the night, but he didn't care about that. He purposefully rode on to the only single-storey building among the blocks of flats. Given that the capital was built on rock pillars, it was a sign of great wealth when a building didn't exist of more than one storey.

A stable hand was waiting and took the horse from the nocturnal traveller who hurriedly jumped off the animal. Subsequently, he rushed up the palace stairs and moments later found himself in the king's room. He had entered without knocking.

Yvar wasn't surprised by this late-hour visit. He put down the book he had been reading and welcomed the visitor, "Good to have you back, Ferhdessar."

Dozens of candles illuminated the room with an orange glow. All other sources of illumination were turned off. This made Ferhdessar smile. He had provided the capital with electricity, but whenever Yvar took some time for himself, he hardly ever used it. Yvar preferred the atmosphere of candle light to the static artificial light. Not so lifeless, he had explained once when Ferhdessar had asked him about it.

"I'm also glad to be back," the sorcerer answered while he took off his cape. He had walked straight to the fireplace. He glanced at the large vase with peonies that stood in the centre of the mantelpiece. "I don't think we've ever experienced such a hard winter. The hailstorms are horrible, I had to take shelter several times. One would almost say it was a mistake to leave the palace, but my journey wasn't a waste of time."

"Have you discovered anything new about the situation in Naftalia?"

"Pontifex Peschi is dead."

"Murdered?"

Nodding, the sorcerer brushed the snow out of his short hair. "His entire city is destroyed."

Ferhdessar only wore his hair longer on the sides. The ends of two plaits hanging in front of his pointed ears caused wet spots on his chest. Two other plaits hung behind his ears and reached past his waist.

"First the Pontifex Maximus and now he," the king muttered, frowning.

Ferhdessar nodded again and took the kettle off the stove. He swirled it to see if there was anything left. "I hadn't expected the battle between the pontifices to take this long. Peschi's odds of becoming Maximus were pretty good. It looks as if someone has eliminated a rival." In the meantime he held up the kettle and looked questioningly at Yvar, who gestured that Ferhdessar could have the last drops of tea. Warming his hands on the glass, Ferhdessar flopped into a chair. The king sat down as well but remained silent.

As Ferhdessar took a sip, he contemplated the situation. The events in Naftalia worried him and he feared that the next Maximus would target Merzia in his hunt for new followers. This meant it was vital to stay abreast of all developments. He tried to get to the bottom of every rumour – no matter how far-fetched – to find out the exact truth behind it. Unfortunately, information coming in from Naftalia was few and far between. Nevertheless, he was convinced that Peschi would have crossed the borders into Merzia if he had seized power.

"It's a relief that he's dead," he therefore exclaimed, "but there are others who can be just as dangerous."

Ferhdessar shuddered at the thought of how the pontifices had attracted followers in the name of Margal. Ghalatea was a living example of their practices.

Yvar nodded, "I'm glad the mountains separate us from Naftalia."

"Let's hope they'll keep protecting us in the future," Ferhdessar said with a hint of doubt in his voice.

They fell silent once again, both lost in their own thoughts.

"A prisoner was brought in today," the king said, and he related what had happened with Lilith. "She's probably from Naftalia."

"What makes you think so?" Ferhdessar asked.

"Ghalatea suspects so. The woman said a prayer during the flogging. The Ancilla Princeps could understand her."

"Who was she praying to?"

"Jakob."

Ferhdessar was surprised. Why would the woman pray to this God? One would expect her to beg Ischa or Trudh for saviour or strength. When he said this out loud, the king answered, "That's not what confuses me the most. Don't you think it's strange that a woman from Naftalia believes in our Gods instead of Margal?"

Ferhdessar had to agree. The power of the pontifices was great and they wouldn't allow anyone to believe in any other Supreme Being than the Goddess. Perhaps the rumour about the new prophet was true after all. Ferhdessar had once heard about a man who, in the name of Jakob, had set his sights on Naftalia as well. But when he had been unable to find out anything more about this prophet, he had discarded the rumour as nonsense. Maybe he had been wrong. He definitely had to look into this.

"I'll talk to the prisoner tomorrow. How far am I allowed to go?"

Yvar shrugged. "You know the rules, Ferhdessar. You can only use customary magic on prisoners, unless they pose a direct threat to you or give their consent."

Ferhdessar gave a disappointed shrug. During his journey he had acquired a magical key that he would have loved to try on this woman.

Lilith was awakened by the lights turning on. She was lying on her stomach. The pain in her body grew more intense with the slightest of movements, and instantly reminded her of what had happened the day before.

There was a light-green, plastered wall right in front of her face and she could just make out the bottom of a tapestry depicting plants and birds. She carefully turned her head the other way. The first thing she saw was a simmering fire, but then she spotted the man entering the room. He was dressed in a stately, dark-red robe that hung from his shoulders in many folds and emphasized his height.

He looked at her closely as he calmly walked towards her. "So, you're awake. That makes things easier."

Lilith shuddered. What was going to happen to her? The king had ordered her to work for him, but surely he hadn't meant right away? She could hardly even move. She stared back to hide her fear. Her left nostril quivered.

The man sat down next to her on the bed and said in an emotionless voice, "You're Lilith, right? I'm Ferhdessar. Sorcerer and…"

Lilith didn't wait for him to finish his sentence. A sorcerer! Groaning, she moved her arms and legs under her body to get up. She wanted to get as far away from him as possible. She was fed up with these men.

He, however, put his hand on her shoulder and pushed her back down on the bed. "Hold on, that doesn't seem wise. You're supposed to rest. Apart from that, there's nowhere you can go anyway."

Ferhdessar put his hand back in his lap, but the pressure on Lilith's shoulders remained. She twisted to shake off the feeling, but it only got worse.

"You'd better not do that, it's counterproductive," Ferhdessar confirmed her suspicion. Now Lilith was absolutely sure that he hadn't come with good intentions.

That impression was reinforced when he pulled her right hand towards him and shoved a wristband around her arm. The sorcerer mumbled some words which made the metal shrink until it closed tightly around her wrist.

"What is that?" Lilith asked anxiously. She tried to pull the band off.

Ferhdessar explained coldly, "This is something all prisoners get and it won't bother you unless you try to escape. It won't even do anything if you leave the palace." He leaned forwards and lowered his voice, "Put so much as one foot outside Nadesh, however, and you'll feel that you've made a huge mistake."

Lilith felt a shiver run down her spine. She started to pull even harder. "Get it off! Get it off!"

She took a swing at Ferhdessar, but he caught her hand. Despite her attempts to pull free, Lilith couldn't prevent him from putting a second wristband on her arm. A stabbing pain surged through her arm and up to her shoulder. It hurt so much that it felt as if her wrist had broken again. She couldn't hide the pain.

"Calm down, Lilith."

"No, I won't calm down. Why should I?" she ranted.

The pain was increasing and expanded via her neck until it pressed behind her eyes. What was this man doing to her? Hadn't she been punished enough?

"The pain will disappear when you calm down."

She reluctantly followed his advice. The pressure did, indeed, subside. She looked at him again, still gasping and fighting her anger.

He didn't look like the other sorcerer she knew. Or… Lilith took another good look at him. Apart from his pointed ears, in which three silver earrings glittered, and the deadpan expression on his youthful face, he did wear the same sort of clothes as her master, with strange symbols along the borders. But her master usually hid them underneath inconspicuous outer clothing.

"What are you doing to me?"

Ferhdessar shook his head. "At first I was hesitant about doing this to you, but you gave me no other option. I think it would be best if you controlled your anger somewhat. You now know what this band does, so next time think before you lose your temper."

"You're all the same," she hissed. Instantly her arm started to hurt again. So she took a deep breath. "What do you want from me?" she growled. The band burned, but she could bear it. She wouldn't allow him to tame her completely.

"There are some things I'd like to know about you. First tell me where you're from."

"That's none of your business."

"Why the secrecy? It would be best if you just told me everything I want to know, I'll find out…"

Before he could finish his sentence, the door flew open and the veiled woman stormed into the room.

"What are you doing here?" she snarled at Ferhdessar.

"Lord Yvar ordered me to talk to the prisoner," he answered agitatedly. "She presumably has important information."

"And the king ordered me to take good care of Lilith. So that's what I'm going to do. She's much too weak to answer your questions right now."

Ferhdessar snorted. Then the woman noticed the metal wristbands.

"Was that really necessary?" she asked, pointing at Lilith.

"You know we do this to all prisoners. There's no reason to make an exception for her."

The woman waved her arms dismissively. "As long as you don't use her for your creepy experiments. Now, get out!"

To Lilith's surprise, but also relief, the sorcerer got up. Nevertheless, she felt even more scared now. What important information did Ferhdessar hope to get from her? And the experiments the woman had spoken of alarmed her as well. Lilith hoped she would never have to learn what they entailed.

"We'll continue our conversation another time, Lilith. I'm looking forward to it."

"Leave," the woman hissed again.

When Ferhdessar had left the room, the woman carefully lifted the sheet. She clicked her tongue and removed the bandages from Lilith's buttocks.

Lilith succumbed to the soft, caring hands that applied new bandages and tucked her in again.

"Are you cold or are you afraid?" the woman asked in a soothing voice when Lilith shivered.

"Both."

The bed moved when the woman got up, and the fire flared up high when she threw on new logs. After that, she opened the curtains. A pale light entered the room, but the woman didn't turn off the lights.

"Who are you?" Lilith asked suspiciously.

Nevertheless, the woman answered calmly as she sat down next to her again and plucked away a few hairs that were stuck to Lilith's lips: "You're right. My name is Ghalatea. I'm here to take care of you."

Lilith nodded and glanced at the door. After Ferhdessar had left, two soldiers had taken up post in her room. She sighed. It had all been for nothing. Her escape hadn't gotten her far and she hadn't found the freedom she had sought. Feeling overconfident because of the potions her master had given her and the fever that had set her body ablaze, she had chased a dream which – now that the anaesthesia had worn off – turned out to be nothing but an utopia. Her master had warned her about this so many times.

"Netaligha?"

Lilith was startled. Ghalatea had asked her almost in her own language if she was all right. She hadn't expected that, and it made her hesitate.

"Do I look all right?" she finally snapped at her.

The woman just nodded understandingly while she laid a cloth underneath Lilith's face. Then Ghalatea held a spoon in front of her mouth. Lilith started to eat greedily. It had been an entire day since she'd had her last small bite of food. The plate was empty much too soon.

"Don't you have more for me?"

"You'll get some more later. It's unhealthy to eat too much at once."

Ghalatea pulled the cloth away and used it to wipe Lilith's mouth clean. Then she folded it and put it on the serving tray. All her movements were so calm that Lilith started to think that maybe this woman did have her best interests at heart.

"Are you from Naftalia?"

She was immediately on her guard again. The Ancilla Princeps asked the same questions as the sorcerer, but Lilith didn't intend to answer them. It didn't matter where she came from any more, she wanted to forget about all of that as soon as possible.

"How was your night? Have you slept well?"

"That's a bit hard when your body is aching all over," Lilith snorted.

Ghalatea nodded and took a little glass bottle from her pouch. She removed the cap and held it to Lilith's lips. Even though her nose was stuffed up, Lilith recognized the heavy scent. So she pressed her face into the pillow.

"It will help you sleep, so you won't feel your pain," Ghalatea tried to persuade her.

"I don't ever want to drink that stuff again." The pillow muffled her words.

"It's just a mixture of herbs."

Lilith looked to the side, but kept her lips pressed together.

"I only wanted to relieve your pain a bit," the Ancilla Princeps tried again while she capped the bottle.

"I don't know what you people want from me, but I do know what this potion can do. And it won't ever do that to me again!"

"In that case I'm afraid there is nothing more I can do for you. I'm truly sorry. I'll come back later to give you something more to eat."

She gave a few more tugs on the sheet that covered Lilith and threw another log on the fire before she addressed the soldiers, "I want you to make sure that the fire keeps burning brightly."

The men nodded and followed her out of the room.

"If there's anything wrong with the prisoner, I want to be notified immediately," she added before she closed the door.

Lilith kept staring at the door for a while and wondered what to think of Ghalatea. The woman seemed very friendly, but at the same time she asked the wrong questions. She had to be careful, because this woman might be more dangerous than the sorcerer. She wouldn't reveal anything to him, but when the Ancilla Princeps was around she dropped her guard, increasing the risk that she might let something slip.

3

Ghalatea folded a pair of trousers and smoothed it down. In the background the rustling sound of paper could be heard. It was Yvar, who was working in the other room. The door between the two rooms was open, because her presence never disturbed him.

After she had put the trousers in the wardrobe, she picked up the next piece of clothing from the basket. She could feel that she was getting older. Her duties cost her more energy these days than they used to and now that she had been combining her normal duties with the care of Lilith for several days, she was feeling tired. Of course it didn't help that she was having difficulty sleeping lately. Lying awake because she was afraid to go to sleep, she brooded about what the prisoner's story could be. How alike were they? Nevertheless, Ghalatea didn't ask her. She had noticed straight away that Lilith didn't want to be reminded of her past and she respected that.

Ghalatea looked over her shoulder. Through the doorway she could see the king. He was absorbed in the text before him and he was tapping his fingers on the table top. After a brief hesitation she walked up to him.

"Lord, can I ask you something?"

When he looked up, his gaze was caught by the tunic she was holding. His finger rested at the sentence where he had stopped reading.

"Is that a new one?"

She nodded.

"Beautiful embroidery."

Ghalatea smiled and looked at the stylised flower vines she had stitched along the borders. It was nice that the king noticed her work.

"What did you want to ask, Ghalatea?"

"I've heard that Ébha has come to Nadesh. Can I send for her so she can treat Lilith?"

"You want to bring a healeress into the palace? You'll have to come up with a very good reason for me to agree to that."

Ghalatea heaved a sigh. In her opinion there wasn't much difference between women who could heal with their hands and sorcerers. She therefore thought it was hypocritical that the Merzians did accept sorcerers but not healeresses.

"Is it really so strange that only women have this power? It was a Goddess who gave life to the first humans."

"No one should interfere with illness and healing in such a way, especially women." Ghalatea opened her mouth, but Yvar continued, "I'm not in the mood for a religious discussion, Ghalatea. I believe in the written word."

Such as befits a monarch, she completed the sentence in her head. She clenched her fist around the tunic. Of course she understoodthe king had to set the right example, but she interpreted her religion differently. Her parents had taught her to respect the healeresses.

"How is the prisoner doing?"

"She's recovering slowly. It could take a while before her wounds are healed. She sleeps a lot, but even sleep doesn't deliver her from her pain."

"You can give her something for the pain, can't you?"

"She doesn't want to take anything, lord."

She had hoped that the king would take pity on Lilith but the exact opposite was the case.

"So that's her own fault then. Am I right to presume that her life isn't in danger?"

"It isn't, lord, but..."

"Then I don't understand why you brought up your request. There's no need for a treatment and I don't want to give my people the impression that I associate with such women. The prisoner deserved to be punished. This is part of her punishment. She has to suffer the consequences of her actions."

"But Lilith was already wounded when she arrived here," Ghalatea objected. "That had nothing to do with her punishment. It would do her good to be treated for those wounds because then the other wounds will heal faster as well."

The king didn't respond and returned to his paperwork. Ghalatea hesitated for a few seconds but then asked, "Don't you think that Lilith has been punished enough?"

Yvar finished reading his paragraph and didn't even take the trouble to look up. "I'm not accountable to you, Ancilla Princeps."

Ghalatea made a deep curtsy and indignantly turned around. She had been reprimanded as though she were a new maid who had only been in the palace for a day. She didn't deserve to be treated like that. After all, she had taken care of the king when he was a child. She wanted to walk away but before she could leave the room Yvar asked, "Do you know what the woman was convicted for?"

She reluctantly turned back to face him. "No, lord. I'm never told why people are punished."

He let out a grumpy sigh. "I don't even know why I'm telling you this, but perhaps I'm hoping you will understand my point of view when you hear this. Not that it makes any difference, but anyway… This prisoner nearly killed a man and she wounded someone else."

That came as a shock. Ghalatea couldn't imagine that slightly-built woman doing such a thing. Not without a reason, at least. "I'm sure she had good reason…" she said, speaking in defence of Lilith.

"I'm surprised to hear you say that, Ghalatea. Do you really think that under certain circumstances it's all right for someone to brandish a knife? That's not like you."

Ghalatea shrugged weakly. The king was right, but it was different with Lilith. When she said that out loud, the king replied, "No, it isn't. This prisoner is no different from other criminals. She's not one of your friends who need to be saved by you, Ghalatea. She brought this on herself. She doesn't deserve your pity."

Fighting her tears, Ghalatea walked back to the other room and threw the tunic into the wardrobe. But before she walked away she changed her mind. She picked up the piece of clothing and hung it on a hanger. She didn't, however, smooth out the creases on the shoulders.

After that, she made her way to the kitchen. The servants were working as well as chattering. They greeted the Ancilla Princeps with a nod.

"Raja, when you're finished with your doubtlessly important conversation, I'd like you to pluck the pheasant," Ghalatea ordered, pointing at the fowl hanging from the arm rest of a chair.

The girl turned around with a start. Her cheeks were red and she made a quick curtsy. "Of course, Ancilla Princeps, as you wish, Ancilla Princeps."

Everyone in the kitchen went quiet. The girls got stuck into their work, hoping not to draw attention to themselves. The silence was only interrupted by the sounds of plates being rinsed down and vegetables being chopped.

Ghalatea looked around contentedly. At moments like these she would sit down by the fire to observe the girls. That always made them even more industrious. But today the Ancilla Princeps decided to go to bed for a little while. Maybe she could make up for the wakeful hours of the previous night.

As she walked down the corridors, Ghalatea realized that she had been much more brusque with the maidservant than usual. The conversation with the king had made her irritable. She felt ashamed when she realized that she had almost been thankful for the opportunity to reprimand the girl. It had been a nice diversion.

A big bang released Ghalatea from the claws of her nightmare. The wind, howling around the building, pounded against the window a second time. Tears were streaming down Ghalatea's face and she thanked the Gods that she had woken up.

She had been dreaming about the Purifications again. After all these years, she still didn't really understand what that meant, being Purified. The Goddess said that all shapeshifters and their offspring were descendant from the devil. Evil blood ran through their veins, but the ceremony remedied that. But what had exactly changed since her Purification? Ghalatea didn't know the answer, she only knew that she had been scarred for life.

"Stop thinking about it, just stop thinking about it," she told herself in order to distract her thoughts. She looked at the little clock on the mantelpiece that she could only just see from her bed. The hands indicated that it was a little past five.

"The perfect time to check whether the servants have set lord Yvar's table properly. After that, I'll bring Lilith some food again. Let's see, where did I put my shoes?"

She said everything she was doing out loud to stop herself from thinking about her dream.

Ghalatea scraped the plate with a spoon and held the last mouthful in front of Lilith. Even though quite a few days had passed, the woman was still wolfing down her food. She had a bit more meat on her bones now, and the bruise on her face had finally started to disappear. The Ancilla Princeps put the plate on the bedside cabinet, and Lilith followed it with a disappointed gaze. Smiling, Ghalatea brushed the hair out of the young woman's face.

"I also brought you some fruit purée." She grabbed a bowl out of her basket and removed the cloth.

The first bite made Lilith groan in delight. For the first time she ate slowly, as though she was trying to savour every mouthful as long as possible. "Will you stay?" she asked when the fruit purée was gone.

"Would you like me to?"

The prisoner nodded.

"I'll stay with you until you fall asleep."

Ghalatea was prepared for Lilith's request. She took a green veil out of her basket. After she had moved the hoop, she embroidered a little flower with quick and precise stitches.

"Don't."

Ghalatea looked up. Lilith was having a nightmare again.

"Stop it, please!" This was followed by a scream. Lilith was shielding her head with her arms and tried to crawl to the wall. Her body was twitching and each twitch was followed by a moan. It seemed as if an invisible person was beating her up. "Please, stop!" she begged.

Ghalatea tried to calm her down but didn't succeed this time.

"Do whatever you want, master," Lilith eventually whispered.

She screamed but after that she finally calmed down.

Ghalatea stared at her, thoughtful. This was the clearest nightmare Lilith had had so far. Normally she would growl without uttering intelligible words. Other times her body would only twitch.

She thought back to what the king had said about this woman having attacked two men. The words of the king didn't leave room for doubt that Lilith would have murdered them if she'd had the chance. But that seemed inconsistent with what just happened. What the king had said, therefore, couldn't be true.

"I'll take care of you, dear," she whispered.

The prisoner coughed a few times without waking up. At the same time she moaned.

"I'll be back with help," Ghalatea promised as she wiped away the mucus around Lilith's mouth.

All was quiet in the corridors of the palace, because it was the servants' dinner time. Once she got outside, Ghalatea pulled her hood farther over her head. It was snowing softly. The cold wind effortlessly cut through the thick wool of her clothes. It wasn't wise to leave the palace in such nasty weather, but Ghalatea was determined to fetch Ébha. So she hurried across bridges and slithered along narrow stairs between high buildings. The buildings sometimes offered protection from the wind, but it wasn't long before Ghalatea was chilled to the bone. The Ancilla Princeps knocked on a door, relieved that she could get out of the cold. The door opened to a crack.

"What do you want?" Two eyes regarded her suspiciously. The eyes were all that could be seen of the person standing behind the door.

"I've heard that lady Ébha is here. I need her help."

The door opened a little wider. The woman looked her up and down.

"It's not for me," Ghalatea rushed to tell her. The warm air emanating from the house touched her cheeks invitingly, but the woman didn't seem to have any intention of letting her in. She even stepped forwards and looked around. The street was deserted.

Then she swung the door open more widely and motioned for

Ghalatea to follow her. The Ancilla Princeps stamped the snow off her boots and hung her cloak on a hook.

"We have to be very careful," the woman explained in justification of her behaviour as they walked to the living room. Ghalatea nodded understandingly. "People who want to hurt Ébha could also come at the door, this has happened in other cities." She shook her head and gestured at the couch. "Have a seat, the lady is busy."

The group of Merzians that had gathered in this house mainly consisted of women. They all looked up when Ghalatea entered, but after they had examined her, they relaxed. Ghalatea sat down next to a woman who had her arm in a sling. Her other neighbour was one of the few men in the room. He was shivering incessantly.

The door at the back of the room opened. A woman appeared. She didn't wear any jewellery and was clothed in a brown dress. That had to be Ébha. There was nothing that indicated her powers, but at the same time her appearance, being as plain as it was, screamed healeress.

The contrast with the way sorcerers dressed couldn't be more striking. They embroidered symbols on their clothes and wore rings, pendants and bracelets to increase their powers. It was almost as if the healeresses were trying to provoke the sorcerers with their appearance: they didn't need all those trinkets to be able to use their powers.

Ghalatea chuckled to herself. Ferhdessar probably wouldn't agree with her.

Ébha noticed her and walked up to her. "Welcome. May I enquire why you're here?"

Ghalatea guided the healeress to a corner of the room, as far away from the others as possible. She lowered her voice. "There's a young woman in the palace who could really use your help. I want to ask you to come with me."

"Of course I will. I'm occupied here for a few more hours, after that I'll come with you."

The Ancilla Princeps shook her head. "There's more you should know about her. This woman is a prisoner of the king. She was flogged." The healeress frowned. "Lord Yvar hasn't given me permission to ask you for help. I think you should know that, so you can decide for yourself."

For a brief moment Ébha's eyes flared with anger. "You're only giving me more reasons to come with you. Wait here for me, I need to help the others first."

Ghalatea nodded, and Ébha returned to the backroom to resume her work. Ghalatea attentively observed all the people who entered the room. Some were even carried in because they couldn't walk any more. When they came back out, they all looked much better. They were happy and relieved that the treatment provided immediate results. Ghalatea saw this as confirmation that she had made the right decision in coming here.

"Wake up."

Ghalatea's voice woke Lilith from her nightmare. The haze in which the past few days had gone by had only been interrupted by a few lucid moments. Lilith had a strong suspicion that someone was putting something in her food to keep her numb, but in spite of that, she hadn't been able to refuse the food. She was much too hungry.

Even though Ghalatea was the only one bringing her food, Lilith didn't suspect her of being the one tampering with it. The Ancilla Princeps was often there when she woke up. She would be embroidering by the window or holding Lilith's hand when she jolted awake from a nightmare. Her calm voice soothed her, but Ghalatea never asked what her dreams were about. That was why Lilith had decided she could trust the woman.

Even before she had opened her eyes, she heard another woman say, "You can stay outside. The girl can't do anything anyway, she's in too bad a shape."

That had to be directed at the soldiers who always entered the room when someone came to take care of Lilith. She only saw a brightly lit rectangle before the door closed.

Ghalatea lighted some candles. Another woman appeared before Lilith and carefully put a hand on her shoulder. At first Lilith got angry, but she soon relaxed. The woman's touch was really gentle. It was a pity that she almost immediately took her hand away again to tie her hair back.

"I'm Ébha, a healeress. The Ancilla Princeps asked me to treat you."

Lilith nodded meekly. When the woman held her hands above Lilith's head, the pain slowly disappeared. To Lilith's relief, it didn't make her any less clearheaded.

"Very well, I'll get started," the healeress said while she pulled the sheet away. "I'm not going to touch you, but you will notice that I'm doing something. If you want me to stop, just say so."

Lilith was surprised that the healeress consulted with her and even gave her control over what was happening. That had never happened before. She had never had a say in anything. Ébha was holding her hand above her back. Lilith felt a warm glow spreading through her body. Ghalatea had seated herself next to the door. She was nervously plucking at her skirts. Without saying it out loud, Lilith mouthed a thank you. The Ancilla Princeps gave her an encouraging nod.

"How does this feel?" Ébha asked Lilith.

"Nice."

"That's good. I feel that your body was working hard at healing itself already, but I'll lend it a hand."

"Thank you," Lilith whispered.

"Close your eyes and surrender to the treatment."

Without hesitation she did what the woman asked. Moments later Ébha's hands moved to her wrist. The warmth got even more intense and it felt as if little jolts of energy shot up and down her bones.

"Right, this shouldn't bother you any more."

Lilith opened her eyes when the woman removed the splint. Completely amazed, she moved her fingers.

Ébha had a proud smile on her face. As she took some herbs from her bag, she said, "I've done a lot today, so I'm too tired to give you a full treatment. I've closed your wounds but they are still very fragile. I'll apply herbal compresses to speed up your healing process. Contrary to my powers, the powers of herbs are never exhausted. If I accidentally hurt you, please say so."

Then Ébha got out some other things. She hesitated for a second when she pulled out a leather roll but decided to put it away again. Ghalatea fidgeted, causing the healeress to look at her over her shoulder.

"I don't think there's much time left," Ghalatea whispered in clarification.

"He'll have to wait," was Ébha's determined answer.

While Lilith was still wondering who they were talking about, the door flew open.

"What's going on here?" Ferhdessar roared.

Lilith screamed. Since that first day, the sorcerer had paid her a few more visits. He had asked his questions but hadn't pressed Lilith for answers. Sometimes, when she had pretended to be sleeping, he had just stared at her from the doorway.

Lilith knew that he was determined to get her to talk, but his silence terrified her just as much. She couldn't guard herself from it and she lived in fear of another confrontation with him. The question wasn't if but rather when it would happen.

"Please, let Ébha carry on, she's almost ready," Ghalatea begged as she tried to stop him.

But Ferhdessar pushed her aside and stormed towards the bed. "You spawn of the devil, I should have you taken prisoner," he growled.

Ébha calmly turned around. "I would very much appreciate it if you'd let me finish my job first. After that, we'll go somewhere nice and quiet to discuss whatever it is you dislike about me. My patient doesn't need to witness this."

"This woman is a prisoner, not a patient."

"She's hurt and she needed my help."

"She brought this on herself."

Lilith cringed when she felt his finger on her back. Ferhdessar slowly traced the lines left by the scourge. The healeress pulled his hand away.

"You people are criminals yourselves for doing things like this to others. How can you condemn violence if you inflict punishments like that. How do you justify that?"

The sorcerer didn't respond and instead kneeled beside Lilith. He was so close that she could feel his breath on her cheek. "Now that you're restored to health, the Ancilla Princeps can no longer keep me from talking to you. We'll meet again soon."

He laid his hand on her hair, but Lilith withdrew her head. The sorcerer got up and walked to Ghalatea.

"I don't think the king gave you permission for this," Lilith heard him say to the Ancilla Princeps, who averted her head before straightening her back.

"I won't allow you to hurt Lilith."

"And how exactly are you going to stop me? I think it would be best if someone else took care of the prisoner from now on. As of tomorrow, you're no longer allowed to see her and she'll be in my hands."

He laughed and Ghalatea stood aghast. Lilith could hardly hear her response because the Ancilla Princeps spoke very softly.

"You can't just decide that, that's up to lord Yvar."

"Of course I'll confer with him first, but I'm pretty sure he'll follow my advice."

Lilith knew this to be true, because Ghalatea bowed her head. She suddenly noticed that her fists were clenching the sheet. She let go but didn't succeed in relaxing. Ébha didn't fail to notice.

"I'd appreciate it if you'd leave the room, wizard," she said without looking up.

Ferhdessar grabbed Ghalatea by her arm and dragged her out of the room, at the same time sending the guards in.

"Good, now I can at least finish my work in peace," Ébha mumbled.

When she was finished, she pulled up a chair and sat next to Lilith. She lowered her voice, so the soldiers couldn't hear the conversation. "If it was up to me, I'd come back for another treatment, but I don't think that's possible. Nevertheless, I hope we'll meet again in different circumstances. I'd like to get to know you better. I think there's something hidden inside you…"

That gave Lilith a fright. Why did everybody think she was hiding something?

"Calm down. You're an extraordinary woman, in the good sense of the word. That which lies hidden, however, is tucked away deeply and I don't have time right now to examine it more closely. There's someone who'd like a word with me." She made a meaningful gesture at the door and rolled her eyes. "Don't forget that everyone has good in them, Lilith. You may have known nothing but pain, but I think underneath all of that something very beautiful has managed to grow."

As Ébha got up, Lilith was still trying to get her head around what she had just said. The words were a riddle but held great promise. Before Ébha could leave the room Lilith said, "Thank you for everything. I hope this won't get you into trouble. Or Ghalatea…"

"Don't you worry. We both knew the risks involved and we're prepared to accept the consequences. I wish you well, Lilith. It might not seem that way right now, but I truly believe things will get better for you."

The soldiers blew out the candles and left the room as well. Until then Lilith hadn't realized that it was the middle of the night. Her body was still glowing from the treatment. It was miraculous that people could carry such power inside them, constructive instead of repressive like the power of the sorcerers she knew. She dozed off, soothed by the knowledge that tonight she wouldn't be haunted by images from her past.

4

Ghalatea was humming quietly as she spread out the herbs on the floor. The treatment had done Lilith much good and she was proud of that. Even though it was still hard for her to move, the prisoner had walked around her room a little bit this morning.

Of course Ferhdessar had been livid. He and Ébha had been arguing in the corridor for a long time. The argument had claimed all his attention, so Ghalatea had come away unscathed. She, however, didn't know for how long. The sorcerer was bound to confront her sometime. That couldn't be helped. Ghalatea felt that she'd had no choice but to bring in Ébha.

On top of the thin layer of grey-green sage, she now strewed decorative lines of purple lavender. The herbs filled the room with a wonderful scent that was reinforced each time someone walked over the dried leaves and bruised them. In the middle, she created the symbol of Merzia out of dandelion leaves. They were scentless and chosen for their colour.

Because she didn't want to disturb the pattern, Ghalatea walked around it to the door. She started when the king appeared in the doorway. He stopped and inhaled the scents while Ghalatea curtsied. She hoped he would be smiling when she looked up, but he wasn't. He gave her a displeased look and walked on. He apparently had already been informed of the events of the night before. This made things a little bit easier.

"Lord, I'd like to ask you to reconsider Ferhdessar's judgement."

"Which judgement?"

"That I'm no longer allowed to go near Lilith."

"Absolutely not, the decision is completely justified." He shook his head disapprovingly. "I'd never imagined you would do such a thing. For almost thirty years you've done what Merzia's rulers asked of you. You haven't once ignored my wishes. Should I ascribe this to a fit of insanity?"

"It was so hard to decide what was right in this case."

"That was my decision to make, all you had to do was follow my orders."

At that moment Ferhdessar entered. His clothes left a smudge on the herb carpet. "I'm about to pay our prisoner a visit, Yvar," he said.

"What is it you want from her!" Ghalatea suddenly yelled. Yvar raised his eyebrows. "Just leave her alone. She's been punished and she's going to work to repay her debts. She doesn't owe Merzia anything else!"

Only now, did the sorcerer look at her. "The prisoner can tell us more about the situation in Naftalia. Maybe she knows something about the attack on Peschi's city. I'm sure you understand how important it is for us to get that information," he said in a patronizing voice, as if he were talking to a child.

Because Ghalatea didn't know how to hide her discomfort, she folded her arms. Yvar joined in on the conversation.

"Forget her, Ghalatea. She isn't your concern any more."

"Forgive me for saying this, but I think you're making a huge mistake by handing her over to the sorcerer. She won't tell him anything."

"I have means to make her talk," Ferhdessar said smilingly.

"And I wouldn't be surprised if she was able to withstand them. Please, give me another chance, lord Yvar. She trusts me, I can get her to talk."

This was the only way to keep Ferhdessar away from Lilith. Unfortunately, it meant that she would have to do what the sorcerer wanted, but everything was better than letting Lilith fall into his hands. Ferhdessar snorted, but the king seemed sensitive to her arguments. So Ghalatea upped the ante.

"The most obvious assumption is that this woman is on the run from Margal's priests. That means I have something in common with her. Maybe she'll talk once she realizes we're not like the Naftalians."

"You might be right. Fine, I'll give you one last chance. Get the prisoner to talk. If you fail to do this within a reasonable period of time, Ferhdessar takes over."

"Thank you, lord," Ghalatea said. She had great difficulty repressing a smile.

Ferhdessar was staring straight ahead with a sour expression on his face but suddenly he turned his gaze to Ghalatea. "Maybe lord Yvar is right. Tell Lilith she'd better tell you her story, Ghalatea. It might be an incentive to know that she'll have me to deal with if she doesn't."

Ghalatea shook her head in irritation.

"Has the treatment been successful?" the king suddenly changed the subject. Ghalatea told him that Lilith had been out of bed for a little while that morning. "Good, then she can start paying off her debt today."

Ghalatea wanted to object but decided it would be wiser to keep her mouth shut, so she agreed.

Lilith was intrigued by the movements of the Ancilla Princeps, who was filling a washbasin with hot water. All Ghalatea's actions were carried out at an even pace and when their eyes met, the woman gave her a reassuring smile.

"I thought I wouldn't see you again," Lilith remarked.

"Thankfully, the king realized that Ferhdessar made the wrong decision. He, however, did decide that you have to start paying off your debt this afternoon."

"That's fine."

Ghalatea turned around in surprise.

"I feel well enough, as long as I don't have to bend over."

To prove she was ready, Lilith let her legs slide off the bed. She used the edge of the bed to push herself up. Then she staggered towards the Ancilla Princeps, who was shaking her head as she was observing Lilith.

"I'll help you wash," Ghalatea said.

Lilith used her hands to scoop water out of the bowl and wash her face, while Ghalatea washed the rest of her body.

"How did you get those scars?" the woman asked totally unexpectedly.

Lilith grew rigid. Of course she hadn't been able to hide them from Ghalatea, but the woman had always kept silent about her scars, until now. Lilith had been so relieved to think she would never mention them. She searched for a fitting explanation but before she could stop herself she snapped, "That's none of your business."

She felt her face freeze into a stiff mask. She also saw Ghalatea flinch when she looked up at her.

"You shouldn't feel ashamed of them."

"That's rich, coming from you," she snarled.

Ghalatea looked away. Lilith hadn't meant to hurt her but she hadn't known how else to silence her. Her plan worked, because the Ancilla Princeps helped her into a loose-fitting, beige dress without saying another word.

After that, Lilith walked to the mirror. She saw herself for the first time since her escape. Ghalatea had cut her hair above shoulder length the other day, because she hadn't been able to disentangle it without pulling clumps of hair out of Lilith's head. The result was disappointing.

"I've never thought of myself as beautiful," she said out loud.

She touched the mirror with her hand. The glass was cold and hard to the touch, which corresponded with the image she saw in the mirror.

"Maybe I expected to look different now. Maybe I thought that I'd really left everything behind. It's strange how one can fool oneself. I can't run away from the past, I will always carry it with me. It's written on my face *and* my body. These scars are a diary, they recount exactly what my life has been like. But no one understands which words they are forming."

"But your eyes reveal the person who's hidden behind the hard exterior," Ghalatea added.

Lilith closed the shutters of the mirror, so she didn't have to look at the cold, angry face any longer. "There aren't many people who are willing to look that far," she answered. Then she turned around and grabbed hold of Ghalatea's hands. "I'm sorry. Just like you, I feel uncomfortable when someone sees my scars. I'm not proud of them."

Ghalatea smiled in relief, but her face darkened when she whispered, "People who do these things to others are scum."

Lilith nodded and limped to the table. Leaning on a chair, she looked at the food that was set out. For the first time since her arrival she was given something other than porridge. On one dish big pieces of fresh bread were laid out and on another lay a variety of dried fruits. Steam rose up from a decanter. When she cautiously leaned forwards and held her nose in the steam, she smelled the faint resinous scent of herbs. She grabbed a glass and poured herself some tea. Then she took a piece of bread and shovelled it into her mouth; it was still warm and deliciously soft. She immediately shoved in a piece of fruit as well. Because her nose was still stuffed up, she started to chew with her mouth open.

Lilith was confused. Even though the food on the table was very simple, she hardly recognized what everything was. Almost her entire life, she had eaten porridge and sometimes a piece of stale bread on the verge of growing mouldy. But she had also seen what the prisoners' food had consisted of. It was never much and always worse than what she got. But here she was a prisoner herself and she was given a meal fit for a king. She didn't understand it, but when she made a remark about it to Ghalatea, the woman asked, "Is there anything the king should know about you, Lilith?"

"Such as?"

"I don't know, but I can imagine him being curious about you. About how you ended up in Merzia for instance. Or why you left your own country and came here, in the middle of winter, without any possessions. Why are you so skinny and frightened?"

Lilith looked at her with fear in her eyes. Then she looked away and said softly, "I wanted to start over." She sighed before she continued, "But I don't seem to be able to put that which I escaped from behind me. Where can I hide? Where in the world will I be safe? Here? How can I believe that, after the reception I've been given? But apart from that, a group of men followed me. I heard them when I crossed the mountains. How long will it take them to discover that I'm here?"

"Who are after you and why?"

"I can't tell you," Lilith whispered.

"If they are followers of Margal, you don't have to be afraid. You're safe here, no one in Merzia will help them. Many people who live here fled from the priests as well."

Lilith frowned and shook her head.

"What did happen then?" the Ancilla Princeps asked.

Lilith shrugged and contemplatively stared into the distance. Images of burning villages entered her head and she heard people screaming in terror. She felt her own fear which had taken hold of her the moment she had decided to leave everything behind and which hadn't disappeared since.

"It's too awful," she whispered. It was hard enough to admit that much, let alone relate in detail what had happened.

"It would be best if you started talking, Lilith. The king thinks you have important information for him."

"What does he want to know?"

"Everything you can tell him about Naftalia. Ferhdessar thinks you know more about the struggle for power going on there."

Lilith staggered and sought support from the table. How did the sorcerer know she was involved?

Ghalatea caressed her upper arm. "I don't really want to ask you all these questions, but if I don't ask them, he will come to drag the answers out of you. I'm sorry, I don't want to scare you but…"

Lilith stood aghast. The Ancilla Princeps didn't finish her sentence but continued, "It's hard for me to force you. I know I'm Ferhdessar's puppet right now, but I have my back against the wall. He has me exactly where he wants me. I don't want him near you, so I have to find out what's going on with you. But actually it's none of my business, is it?"

Lilith's wristband started to glow. "I'm sorry that you keep getting into trouble because of me, Ghalatea."

The Ancilla Princeps shrugged.

Lilith turned away. She pressed her hands to her eyes. "It hurts so much," she sighed.

Ghalatea reached out to comfort her, but Lilith froze up as soon as she touched her.

"This isn't right," Ghalatea sighed. "I'll leave you in peace, Lilith.

I'll listen to your story when you're prepared to tell it. I'm not going to keep asking you questions that make you nervous, but you're going to have to make a decision soon. I don't know how long the king is willing to wait before he gives Ferhdessar a chance to interrogate you."

Lilith nodded gratefully. "What kind of work do I have to do?"

"There's always laundry that needs folding. I think you'll be able to do that. For today at least. When your health improves, you'll be charged with other duties as well."

"Let's go then. I want to pay off my debt as soon as possible. The sooner I'm out of here, the better it is for everyone," Lilith said as she walked to the door.

"Shouldn't you eat something first?" Ghalatea called after her.

"I've had enough." Then she turned around. "How long will it be before I've repaid my debt?"

"That's up to the king to decide, but it could very well take two years."

"That long?" Lilith sighed, crossing the threshold. Ghalatea joined her, and the two guards followed them at a distance. Lilith briefly glanced at them, but then decided to accept their presence.

The Ancilla Princeps walked slowly, so Lilith could easily keep up with her. Lilith was intrigued by everything she saw and took it all in. She raised her arm but lowered it when it was only halfway up.

"Where does that light come from?"

"Ferhdessar invented it. It has something to do with water falling down the rocks on which Nadesh is built." Ghalatea shrugged. "I don't understand how it works. Water that doesn't extinguish fire but fans it? He claims it's plain science, but I think there's magic involved. There must be."

"Science? My master told me that science is bad. It moves people farther away from God."

"God?"

"Lord Jakob," Lilith nodded.

"And the other Gods?" the Ancilla Princeps asked intrigued. Lilith gave her a suspicious look. Ghalatea apologized, "I didn't mean to interrogate you. It's just that I'm very interested in religion."

Lilith smiled in relief, "What other Gods do you mean? Not Margal?"

In the mean time they had reached a bridge to another part of the palace. It was covered but moved slightly because of the powerful wind that had free play at this height. The windows on the left side were snowed shut, but Lilith could see the blue sky through the windows on the other side. It was one of the rare moments that it wasn't snowing.

"Goodness, no. I mean Gaia, Phoibos or Ischa, to mention a few."

"I don't know them. Do you believe in that many Gods?"

"I believe there are twelve Gods, all with their own tasks."

"I only serve Jakob, I know that He's the one true God."

"Is He a good God to you?"

Lilith stopped and stared into the depth below her. There wasn't much to be seen there.

"To be honest, I'm not really sure," she confessed. She silently prayed for forgiveness. It felt wrong to doubt Him, but at the same time she had so many good reasons to do so. Her master was driven by his faith in Jakob and he had used her in His name. "Do you believe in Jakob as well?"

"Yes, Jakob is one of the twelve Gods. Everything we can't explain or isn't the domain of the other Gods falls under Him. Apart from that, Jakob has helped the other Gods with many of their tasks. Gaia gave life to all creatures, but Jakob created mankind and the animals. Phoibos is the Goddess of purity. Water is an important element for Her, but Jakob was the one who created riverbeds and craters for seas and lakes, so the water doesn't sink back into the ground where we can't reach it."

"Jakob created the world and its inhabitants," Lilith agreed.

They had crossed the bridge and now entered the washing room. The air was warm and humid. The room was tiled, causing the sounds of the machines and voices to reverberate shrilly off the walls. When the maidservants noticed the soldiers they fell silent and closely observed Lilith. Some girls leaned into each other and started whispering. They weren't as yet pointing at her, but it was obvious that they were talking about her. Ghalatea had given Lilith the impression that everything was normal, but of course she was still a prisoner. The Ancilla Princeps yelled some orders over the loud thumping of the machines and gave the maidservants a penetrating gaze. Everybody immediately went back to work.

Ghalatea guided Lilith farther along the washing machines that were driven by waterpower. They consisted of cylinders of several yards in length with various loading doors. As long as they were spinning, nobody needed to pay attention to them. Therefore, the maids were occupied with other duties: mangling the sheets, which also largely happened with the help of machines, or hanging out the damp laundry. Along another wall stood a row of tables where women were ironing and folding. Ghalatea halted there.

Lilith inquisitively eyed the young woman who was folding laundry next to her. She estimated her age around the mid-twenties, only a few years younger than she was herself. The woman stared back. When their gazes locked for a second, Lilith was struck by the contempt in her eyes. She quickly turned around. Ghalatea reached down past her and pulled a sheet from the pile.

"Again, Aida," she ordered as she unfolded the sheet. There was a double crease all the way down. "You know I don't approve of this."

"Of course, Ancilla Princeps. My apologies, Ancilla Princeps."

Lilith observed the girl from the corners of her eyes. Her cheeks were glowing red and the contemptuous look in her eyes had disappeared. She hurried to the ironing table while Ghalatea pulled two sheets from the basket. Lilith paid close attention to what the Ancilla Princeps did. She didn't want to be reprimanded like Aida. So she meticulously imitated every movement, earning a proud nod from Ghalatea.

The days after that, Ghalatea took Lilith to the wing where the Royal Guard was housed. Lilith's main task was sweeping the long corridors. She wasn't able to perform any other duties without help yet. Ferhdessar sometimes came by to observe her, but whenever Ghalatea stopped by to check on Lilith, he disappeared.

The soldiers treated her with contempt. It was no secret that she was a prisoner who needed to be watched. The men constantly got in the way, forcing Lilith to step aside. They also often dropped things in places she had already swept and then she had to start all over again. But nothing was worse than their remarks. They called her names and laughed at her. Sometimes Lilith thought that she recognized the voice of one of the executioners, but she was never sure. Even though she had seen the face of one of them, she couldn't call it to mind any more.

A group of soldiers came out of another corridor. Lilith wanted to step aside but tripped and fell flat on her face. The men started to laugh.

"Watch where you're going!"

She tried to get back up, but it felt as if her wounds had been ripped open again. The men kept laughing. Furious, Lilith banged her fist on the tiles.

At that exact moment Ghalatea appeared. "Lilith, what's happened?"

The Ancilla Princeps gave her a worried look and glared at the soldiers, who walked on. Then she carefully helped her back up. Lilith moaned.

"Are you all right?"

Lilith shrugged. "Why do they think they have the right to treat me like that? Why is it always like this?"

"You're not only referring to the soldiers now, are you?"

Lilith leaned against the wall and took a deep breath. She started to tell her story with her eyes closed.

"Where I grew up there were many servants as well. They made a sport out of tormenting me every single day. They started when I entered the dining room for breakfast and didn't stop until I went to bed. At least, that's what it was like for the first years of my life. When I grew older, they became a bit more cautious." It was safe to say this. But the fact that her tormentors hadn't been human, was something she didn't have the heart to tell.

Ghalatea put a hand on Lilith's arm. Lilith heaved a deep sigh and thought back to something that happened almost every day. After waking up, she would reluctantly make her way to the dining room. Only she and the servi would eat there. She didn't know where the master and his five human followers ate.

The servi were big and fast. They moved around without making any noise. Their eyes were big and dark, slightly slanted and they stood far apart. They had no auricles and no eyelids, but sometimes a transparent fleece covered their eyes. It was their equivalent of blinking. They used charcoal to draw black lines around their eyes, which made their gaze even more piercing. It gave Lilith the impression that they were always watching her, even when they were sleeping.

The servi could be divided into two groups: the slaves, who were simply called the servi, and the warriors, who preferred to be called Muircadh. The primary difference between them and the slaves was their long, razor-sharp fingernails.

Each morning was the same. There were never any plates left, so Lilith scooped up her porridge with her hands. Before she could leave the dining room, a servus would trip her up. The creatures all looked so much alike that Lilith never had been able to find out if it was the same servus who tripped her up every single day. She could only distinguish the slaves from the warriors. "Watch where you're going, ynfytyn," the slave would say.

Lilith didn't know what the word meant, but the way the servus spat it at her – as if he had something dirty in his mouth – spoke volumes. Each morning she would flee the room amidst howls of derision.

"They made sure I hardly got anything to eat. Most times my breakfast consisted of the chunks left on my clothes after they had made me trip."

"Didn't anybody do anything about it? Your master for instance?"

Lilith gave a wry laugh. "As if he cared. What he did to me was even worse."

"So there was nobody to help you?"

"There was. Seraph sometimes made sure the tormenting

stopped for a while."

Lilith opened her eyes. Her gaze was caught by yet another tapestry from Naftalia that covered the walls of the palace corridors.

"Clearly there are no lions around, because the giraffes and the oryxes are much too calm."

Ghalatea gave her an inquisitive look and studied the tapestry.

"Seraph taught me about these things when I was allowed out of the caves for the first time. My master had always told me that I couldn't stay inside forever, so I had been looking forward to that day for a very long time. But at the same time, I was afraid. My master had made it clear to me that I had to beware of people. When I left the caves for the first time, however, I couldn't imagine there being anything worse than what his servants did to me every day."

"But was he right?" Ghalatea whispered.

Lilith nodded. Then she stared at the scar that wasn't completely covered by the veil.

"Seraph and four other men I know are marked the same way. I always thought they had been involved in an accident. But they weren't, right?"

Lilith raised her hand and brushed the veil aside, revealing more of Ghalatea's face. The Ancilla Princeps allowed this for a brief moment but then she pulled the veil even closer around her head.

"No, it wasn't an accident."

Lilith noticed the pain in Ghalatea's eyes and felt conscience-stricken.

"I'm really sorry. I shouldn't have done that."

Ghalatea nodded. "I suppose it's okay for you, because I've also seen your scars. In a way it's only fair you saw mine. Even though I know very little about you, I have a feeling that we have much in common."

Lilith couldn't imagine that, but it did put her mind at ease. It meant that the Ancilla Princeps had no idea what really had happened.

"Did those men wear a veil as well?" Ghalatea asked.

"Seraph only wore one when he went to the villages in the desert. But almost all villagers wore blue scarves around their heads, so

I don't know whether he was hiding his scar or trying to blend in."

"You've been to the Kel Cornu? They're my people."

"I found them scary." Lilith waited to see how Ghalatea reacted. To her surprise the Ancilla Princeps nodded. "But the journey out there was amazing!"

"That's the first time you've been enthusiastic about your past. Would you like to tell me more about it?"

Lilith carefully sat down on the windowsill. "I thought it was going to be a day like any other. The servants had chased me out of the dining room again. In tears, I had fled to the cave entrance. When I heard a horse whinny, I quickly wiped my tears away. Seraph, Nander and Ghideon were leading four horses through the tunnel.

As the men were busy talking to each other, Nander opened the doors. The light came in through a small gap, driving the deep darkness of the cave farther and farther away. I held my breath as I looked outside. But all I could see were silhouettes of more rocks against the bright blue sky. The light blinded me and I hadn't noticed that my master had joined the three men. Only when he began to speak, did I realize that my presence had been noticed.

The master ordered Seraph to take me with him. The Purified one's hesitant gaze went back and forth between me and my master. But then a smile appeared on his face. I immediately forgot about my grief and threw myself into Seraph's outstretched arms. With a big sweep he lifted me into the saddle. When I looked back, the master had already disappeared. The men crossed the threshold and the doors closed behind them."

Lilith smiled. She had fond memories of that morning.

"I didn't know where to look. Everything was so different from what I knew. The rocks stretched out as far as the horizon, sometimes forming deep valleys but more often rising to great altitudes. In places where shrubs had managed to take root on the hard surface, the grey world was interspersed with green. In the distance a few clouds drifted through the otherwise blue sky. The wind blew through my hair.

Everything looked so wonderful to my eyes. It made Seraph laugh. He assured me that the savannah was even more beautiful. I asked him what that was, but he told me to be patient."

"You must have a very good memory, being able to remember so many details."

"My youth was pretty uneventful. So anything that deviated from the ordinary made a big impression. Still, I wish my memories were less vivid."

Ghalatea gave a sympathetic nod. "What happened next?"

"Ghideon had guided our group around the rocks to a path that winded down. I looked back but couldn't tell for sure where we had emerged from the rocks. I heaved a sigh of relief. For a brief moment my excitement had given way to fear. I hadn't forgotten my master's warnings.

Wherever possible, the horses picked up speed. The farther we descended, the more vegetation we saw. By now, the plant growth was no longer limited to bushes clinging to the rocks, there were trees as well. Their roots kept the little amounts of sand together that had been carried there by the wind. Everything was new to me.

When we rounded a corner, I couldn't believe my eyes. We had left the rocks behind us and in front of us an entirely new world loomed up. A grassy plain stretched out as far as the horizon. Large groups of trees grew in the shadow of the rocks, but because of the sweltering heat of the sun, vegetation became scarce again in the distance. The grass waved in the wind. Among the branches of the trees, rustling sounds of animals could be heard and birds were singing, but however hard I looked, I couldn't see them.

The horses were now put into a trot. Ghideon was still leading us. He had a bow in his hands and kept a close eye on our surroundings. Nander was holding a spear at the ready. I wondered if they were afraid of humans, but Seraph put my mind at ease. Humans wouldn't hurt me.

Reassured, I leaned into him but pretty soon I sat up straight again to have another good look at the savannah. It seemed as if the world was deserted, until Seraph ordered Ghideon to stop. He pointed at a group of trees in the distance where some giraffes were eating." Lilith gestured at the tapestry. "At first I thought they were predators, because that was what Ghideon and Nander were on the alert for. But Seraph shook his head and explained that the savannah was too quiet, so there probably weren't any predators out hunting. He caressed my shoulder and then pointed in another direction. He explained that the striped horses were zebras, quenching their thirst at a pool. We kept watching a little while longer, but then Ghideon urged us to get going again."

"I'm glad to hear that someone was nice to you and took care of you."

"Seraph was indeed nice to me but he hardly ever had time to hang out with me. At least, less time than I would have liked. And he's one of the men following me now."

Ghalatea looked taken aback, but Lilith wasn't sure if it worried her any more. Lately she had been dreaming about Seraph turning up at the palace. He was going to rescue her and they would both escape from the master. Deep down, however, she knew this to be vain hope. It was a fairy tale that only naive children thought up. "My master sent him. No one can defy my master."

Nevertheless, Lilith held on to the longings of that naive little girl. They offered a glimmer of hope that kept her going. Seraph had saved her before, why wouldn't he do it again? Lilith leaned on the broom. A shiver ran down her spine.

"After we had arrived at the village, Seraph told me they had business to take care of and that I could go wherever I pleased, as long as I stayed in the square. I was grateful for this opportunity to discover the world. Very soon, I couldn't tell the three men apart from the rest of the blue crowd any more.

A woman addressed me. She kneeled in front of me and put a hand on my shoulder, stopping me from walking away. She regarded me closely. I started to feel trapped. I hastily looked around but I didn't see Seraph anywhere. It felt as if I had made a huge mistake. The master had told me to beware the people, but I had placed myself among them anyway.

Cautiously I looked at the woman again. She looked me up and down. She shook her head as her eyes rested on the leftovers sticking to my tunic. Her one hand was still on my shoulder but the other moved across my body. That didn't feel right and I wanted to step backwards. The woman, however, had a firm grasp on me. She mumbled that she could take me with her and that she would take care of me." Lilith looked at the Ancilla Princeps. "Maybe you know her, her name was Maraghon."

Ghalatea shook her head. "I lived much farther to the east."

"Maraghon was determined to take me with her. She told me she would be like a mother to me. She had such a penetrating gaze that I averted my head to escape her bright blue eyes. Her hand rested on my ribs. She said I was too skinny for a six-year-old girl. But I snarled at her that I was already nine. She looked at me in dismay, which felt like a victory. Then she grabbed my hand and started to walk. I resisted, but Maraghon dragged me along."

"That must have been really scary."

"It was. But looking back, she could have been my saviour. If I had known then what my future was going to be like, I wouldn't have resisted."

"I doubt if that would have been any better. A woman who kidnaps children just like that…"

Lilith shook her head violently. "I didn't run away for fun! What happened after that encounter was much scarier."

"What happened?"

Lilith shook her head again.

"How did you manage to escape from her?" Ghalatea asked.

"Seraph returned only just in time. He tore me loose from Maraghon and carried me away. I asked him if all people were like that, but Seraph didn't answer. I took that as a yes. A little while later he apologized for having left me on my own. He held me even tighter and promised me it would never happen again. He kissed my neck.

When I looked up, I saw that Ghideon and Nander were already waiting with the horses. The fourth horse was packed with new supplies. We mounted. I was glad that we were riding away from the village at great speed. We were back home before dawn."

Lilith dropped the broom and hid her face in her hands. Ghalatea put an arm around her.

"Does this bring back too many memories?"

Lilith nodded. "Nightmares haunted me for a long time after

that. Until I dreamed that I defeated the woman myself."

"That must have been a good feeling."

"Yes, back when it was only a dream."

Ghalatea was appalled. "You don't mean... Lilith, did you do something to her?"

"To Maraghon? No, I never saw her again."

Lilith looked Ghalatea in the eye. Had she revealed too much?

The Ancilla Princeps smiled, however. "It isn't right to take revenge. But fantasizing about it can be a great relief."

"Have you ever wanted to take revenge on the people who maimed you?"

"In my dreams I caused them all sorts of harm," Ghalatea confessed rosy-cheeked. "But I've never had the urge to put those plans into action. At first I thought I lacked the courage, but now I know that revenge isn't the answer."

Lilith wasn't sure about that. Revenge and anger were emotions that gave you an overwhelming feeling of power. It was an addictive feeling. When she thought back to the dream in which she had defeated Maraghon, she felt the same emotions all over again. Just like Ghalatea, Lilith knew it wasn't right to take revenge, but Lilith had never been strong enough to resist those feelings. She shook off her thoughts. "I wish I had never even dreamed about it."

"Oh well, you shouldn't feel guilty about that."

"I actually meant that the dream gave my master yet another reason to punish me."

"So that's what your last nightmare was about. He maltreated you."

"He only punished me for being disobedient. I deserved it." That was what her head told her, but in her heart she felt differently. The beatings from her master had been far less painful than the humiliation and helplessness she had felt back then. Those feelings still haunted her, whereas the bruises had long since disappeared.

Ghalatea shook her head disapprovingly. "Why did you say in your dream that he could whatever he wanted to you?"

"Did I say that?" Lilith wondered what else she had said. How much had she given away unawares? "Begging him to stop never helped. He punished me to show me who was in control. It would be a sign of weakness if he stopped when I asked him to. I learned this pretty soon. I knew the master wouldn't stop unless I told him to keep beating or kicking me. Because then the roles were reversed.

You might think those are only words and that I would scream them even before he started hitting me, but I never did. Only when it really got too much, did I beg him to go on. Then he would hit or kick me one last time and stop."

"What a pig. Someone should beat *him* up for a change." Ghalatea clenched her fists.

"But I asked for it, didn't I? How can I blame him for what he did when I asked for it?"

"Oh, Lilith..." Ghalatea grabbed her shoulders and gave her a good shaking. She couldn't find the right words. Then she let go of Lilith. "And you also got punished because you dreamed about defeating that woman?"

Lilith shook her head. In her dream she had changed. Up until then, her master had been the only one who knew the words to set the transformation in motion, but when Lilith woke up she could still hear the incantation in her head. She was convinced that she could change of her own accord now.

So she had sneaked past the sleeping servi into the great hall, where she had caressed the amulet her master had given her and she had spoken the words that were echoing in her head. She had longingly awaited the fire she always felt when her master made her change. But nothing had happened. So she had tried again, louder this time, but there still hadn't been any sign of her starting to change.

In the end she had sunk to her knees in tears. She had realized that this part had also been nothing but a dream. She had been furious for not being able to control her own body. Then her master had come and he had taken his frustration out on her.

"My master was afraid that I could take his power away from him."

"But you were only a child. What on earth could you have done?"

Kill him, perhaps, but Lilith didn't say that out loud. It wasn't even true. She had never been strong enough to kill him. "The worst thing that could happen was that I wouldn't obey him any more. At least, that's what I think he was afraid of. But I was always too weak to resist his will." Lilith shivered and whispered, "It was my own fault that he battered me."

"No, Lilith. You must never think that!"

"You don't understand! My master went to a lot of trouble to protect me. And I repaid him with disobedience. He was very disappointed in me. I knew he was quick to anger, but there were ways to prevent that. That night I just hadn't tried hard enough."

"And you still believe that?"

After some thought Lilith shrugged. "The stupid thing was that I didn't even intend to disappoint him. I was scared and that was the reason why I wanted to feel the strength hidden inside me. It had nothing to do with him."

Ghalatea shook her head. "It doesn't matter what you did, he should never have punished you like that. You were a child! He had no right."

"But he felt really bad about losing his patience with me. He always made it up to me."

Ghalatea snorted. "I wonder how he did that."

"The next morning, one of the servants came for me. He brought me to my master's chamber. Of course I was afraid of more punishment, but my master immediately got up and told me he was sorry. He explained to me that I had made him really angry, and I understood why. I promised I would behave the way he wanted me to. It wouldn't happen again."

"No, you clearly had learned your lesson."

"My master gave me something to drink and sat beside me on the couch. When my glass was empty, he gave me a piece of cake. He observed me approvingly as I ate every last crumb of the delicious treat."

Ghalatea shook her head and gave Lilith a look of compassion. "Was that all he did to make things right?"

"It was enough," Lilith lied. She couldn't tell her what else had happened.

Her master had told her that he had thought things through. He had reached the conclusion that it would be best if Lilith could control her transformations herself too. His powers extended far, but she would have to go outside increasingly often and she could end up in situations where she needed to be able to change of her own accord.

As the master caressed her hands, he once again warned her of the humans. He told her they wanted to kill her, just because she was different. Humans were afraid of her and despised her, because they realized that they were lesser creatures than she was. She would never be safe in their world.

Lilith thought of Maraghon and believed him.

Then her master spoke the incantations. He patiently taught Lilith the words until she mastered the pronunciation completely. Then he took her to the hall. That had been the first time she had changed all by herself. He was proud of her for learning so quickly. He put an arm around her and gave her a brief hug. *Together we can take on the world, Lilith. No one can stop us.*

Everything that had happened was forgiven and forgotten. She was important to her master and that was exactly what Lilith needed to hear. She would do anything for him, as long as he was proud of her.

"Fortunately, it's all bygones now," Ghalatea interrupted her thoughts. "I can well imagine why you fled from him. It's a miracle you stayed with him for such a long time."

Lilith shook her head. Ghalatea knew so little of her life. The Ancilla Princeps had already been shocked by her story so far, but much worse things had happened. This hadn't been the reason why she had escaped.

"Are you going to tell the king about this?"

Ghalatea thought for a moment. "I don't see how this information is useful to him. But if he asks me about it, I do have to tell him."

"I understand. It's all right."

"Maybe it would be best if lord Yvar knew you're a victim. Ferhdessar seems to work under the assumption that you're a perpetrator. I'm not sure what he suspects you of, but it can't be much good."

It was best to not respond.

"Now I understand why you wished you didn't have such a good memory. It's almost like you're reliving it all."

"Exactly. That's what's making it so hard." It was nice that someone understood her so well. "What about you?"

"I've repressed everything. Now and again I remember bits and pieces, just like after your flogging. It brought back many memories but they are all just fragments."

"Nevertheless, they hurt too much."

"Yes. More details would only make them unbearable."

Lilith put an arm around Ghalatea. "I understand."

"Merzia gave me a new life. It will give you the opportunity to start a new life as well."

"Who knows." Lilith picked up the broom. She thought about what kind of life it would be. "When I'm released, I'll go live in a little house. Will you come and visit me?"

"Of course. And I'll bring freshly baked cake."

Lilith nodded and started sweeping again. Ghalatea followed her.

"I would grow lavender underneath my windows," Lilith fantasized out loud.

"You should plant sage. It signifies that a woman is in charge in that house."

Lilith chuckled. "Very well, I'll plant sage."

"An added advantage is that sage keeps evil at bay. You know what, I'll bring you some to keep in your room."

Lilith stopped sweeping and put a hand on Ghalatea's shoulder. "I'd like that very much, thank you."

The Ancilla Princeps nodded and disappeared in the opposite direction. In good spirits, Lilith raked the dust together. She glanced back at the Ancilla Princeps one more time and started humming. She envisioned a bright future for herself. But first she had to pay off her debt to the king. Maybe he would be willing to set her free sooner if she worked harder.

Farther down the corridor she turned right. A man approached her from the opposite direction. He was alone but he clearly wasn't a soldier. When he glared at her, Lilith noticed his absent expression. The man scratched his head, causing his sleeve to slide down. His wristband revealed him to be a prisoner as well. He nodded at her before he disappeared through a door.

Lilith started sweeping faster. She was curious to know where the man had gone. She cautiously stuck her head around the doorpost. With a start she recognized Ferhdessar. He stood with his back to her. The man stood in front of him. He had uncovered his arm, which he held extended to Ferhdessar. The sorcerer uttered a few words and removed the band.

The man instantly transformed from an obedient person into someone with unprecedented rage inside him. Screaming, he ran at Ferhdessar.

"Who do you think you are! What gives you the right to oppress me!"

He raised his arm and flexed his muscles. Ferhdessar was the taller of the two, but the prisoner looked much stronger. His absent expression had given way to a blind rage. His arm came down.

Lilith was surprised that the sorcerer didn't even move. It seemed as if he was waiting for the moment the man would hit him.

Suddenly the man went down on his knees. His movements were slow and he had difficulty forming his words. "You were only just in time, lord sorcerer."

Lilith was surprised at the sudden changes. What had Ferhdessar used to cast a spell on him? The man extended his arm so Ferhdessar could put his wristband back on. The man's submissive behaviour disgusted Lilith. In her mind she encouraged him to jump up and strike the sorcerer down. He wasn't expecting it right now.

"Tell me, Lilith, did you enjoy that?"

Blood rushed to her cheeks. Ferhdessar hadn't even turned around. How did he know she was there?

"Impressive, isn't it, how I can control someone so well with such a small object?"

He finally turned around. He held out his hand to her. Between his fingers he was holding a little piece of wood.

"What did you do to him?" Lilith hissed.

"I was told that this is a splinter of the yoke used by the Gods to submit the devil to Their will. Judging from what I just saw, I believe it wasn't a waste of money."

She clenched her fists. Ferhdessar's gaze slid down to her wristband. "It hurts, doesn't it?"

Lilith shrugged and she averted her eyes.

"It's good to know you can take the pain so well, maybe I should readjust the band. Bareld, could you explain to her what just happened? I think she values your words more than mine. Lilith could perhaps benefit from the same treatments."

"Treatments?" sneered Lilith, "That's nice window dressing for something Ghalatea calls creepy experiments. Are you insulted when I say her description is more fitting?"

The man cut in. His voice was void of emotions, just like his face. "Ferhdessar is helping me to control my anger. I detest not being able to do it myself and I'm grateful that he can help me. I wear the same wristband as you, but it still hurts a lot. So we're looking for another solution."

Lilith snorted in disbelief. "You're nothing more than an object for him to test his tricks on. He doesn't care whether it helps you or not. He only wants to increase his power."

"How can you say that? You don't even know me," Ferhdessar said.

Lilith ignored him. "How can you allow him to do this to you?"

The sorcerer answered the question, "Some prisoners are offered a reduction of their sentence if they help me with my research. It's their own choice to participate or not. I'm sorry you were never offered this choice, Lilith, but I'll ask the king if I can make you such an offer. Then you can buy off part of your sentence."

"I'll never allow you to perform such experiments on me," she said, stepping backwards.

Bareld cut in again, "It's not as bad as you think. Ferhdessar treats us well."

Lilith shook her head disdainfully and her voice trembled. "He has total control over you. You aren't yourself in any sense."

"If anything, I'm much more myself. Now that my anger no longer dominates everything, there's more room for the rest of me."

"I don't believe you. My eyes tell me a completely different story. I know what sorcerers are capable of. You have no free will any more, he has complete control over you. It only makes it worse that you think this was your own choice. The only thing that sorcerers want is to control others."

"You aren't talking about me, are you?" Ferhdessar concluded, scrutinizing her attentively. "Which other sorcerer do you know, Lilith? What has he done to you?"

"I am talking about you," Lilith screamed in panic. She turned around and left the room. She didn't start sweeping again until she had put several corridors between herself and Ferhdessar.

5

The door to her room opened when she came out of the lavatory. Ghalatea and Ferhdessar entered together.

"I'm sorry, Lilith. I can't hold him back any longer. You'll have to go with him today. Unless you're willing to answer his questions," the Ancilla Princeps said. The red blotches on her neck were evidence that she hadn't given in without a fight.

The sorcerer smiled smugly.

"I was expecting this, Ghalatea," Lilith sighed. She slipped her feet into her shoes and took another bite of an apple. "What are you going to do if I don't want to tell you anything?"

"You'll see. In any case, you're going to work for me. Why not combine your punishment with my assignment?"

Lilith followed him reluctantly. "What do I have to do?"

"You'll find out soon enough."

A few minutes later, Ferhdessar opened a door for her. When she hesitated, he pushed her into the room.

As Ferhdessar sat down behind his desk, Lilith looked around the room. There were books on the shelves, and models of strange machines stood next to them. There were also jars, containing things that looked like animals. Lilith shuddered. More flying machines were suspended from the ceiling. There was one wall without any shelves. It was covered from floor to ceiling with drawings of wings and skeletons. Other sheets of paper had texts and schematic drawings, explaining thermals, scrawled all over them. Pretty much everything was untidy, except for the desk the sorcerer was sitting at right now. It was empty, except for a few pencils, a sheet of paper and a pile of books.

"Can you read?" he cut into the silence. Lilith nodded, so Ferhdessar tapped on the pile and said, "Put these back on the shelves, in alphabetical order."

Was this why he had brought her here? She shuffled forwards an picked up a book.

"If you put away only one book at a time, it'll take much too long. I have other things for you to do."

Lilith sighed and piled more books on her arm. This man intended to play a game with her to break her, but she wouldn't let that happen.

There was a long silence. Even when Lilith had put away all the books, Ferhdessar didn't look up straight away. He calmly continued on with his work. His ruler moved across the paper and his pencil drew lines with quick strokes. As Lilith was watching him, she suddenly saw her master before her. The sorcerer she had served her entire life had always been busy writing. Ever since her childhood, she had been told to clean his room without disturbing him in any way.

"Great, you're finished. There's a bucket in the corner. I'd like you to empty the shelves and clean them."

Lilith did as he asked. She was holding the books that she had just put back on the shelves for a second time. She was convinced he had done this on purpose, but she didn't complain. After the books, she started with another shelf. She carefully picked up the jars. Horrified, she took a better look at the animals in formalin preservation. She couldn't understand why anyone would want them in their room. And there were so many of them. After she had wiped the shelf clean, she put everything back exactly as it had been. That was also something she had learned as a little girl. Finally, she picked up one of the scale models.

When she turned around, Ferhdessar suddenly stood in front of her. Lilith tensed up and backed away. To her dismay, the sorcerer came closer again. He put his hand against her cheek. His skin was warm, but there was a sense of coercion in his touch. Then his hand slid down to her neck.

"That's an extraordinary necklace you're wearing..." he mumbled. "You could use it to pay off your debts to the king outright."

Panicking, Lilith slapped his hand away. At the same time she dropped the model. It smashed to pieces on the wooden floor.

Ferhdessar looked at her in amazement. "So, the king was right when he said you're stronger than you look. Tell me, Lilith, where do you come from?"

His voice now almost sounded commanding.

"I'll never tell you."

She pulled her collar tightly around her neck, so Ferhdessar could no longer see her necklace. At the same time, she walked to the other side of the room. She tried to keep him at bay by casting furious glances at him, but he didn't seem impressed.

"What are you hiding from me?" he asked.

Lilith snorted. The pain in her arm increased, but she welcomed it. It helped her keep a clear head.

"It's going to take more to get me to talk," she said provokingly.

"So that's how you want to play this game? Have it your way." Ferhdessar removed an object from his belt and showed it to her. "The king has given me permission to test this on you."

Lilith started to shiver. "What is it?" she squeaked.

"This is the key of truth. You might as well start talking, Lilith."

She yanked the door open. The door handle, however, slipped from her fingers and the door slammed shut. Her breathing became faster. She tried to open the door again but it wouldn't budge. She turned around slowly. Ferhdessar stood five steps away from her and his hand was extended towards her. Puzzled, she looked away.

Suddenly she ran straight at him. After three strides she felt a blow as if she had run into something. Utterly surprised, she stood still. She didn't see anything other than Ferhdessar, who now had both hands raised. She reached out with her hands and felt along the invisible wall that Ferhdessar had put up.

"Where do you come from, Lilith?"

As he asked this, he moved the key in her direction. Lilith braced herself to resist the urge to answer, but to her astonishment she didn't feel an irresistible desire to tell him anything.

"It looks as if it's not working, Ferhdessar," she scoffed.

"Of course it's not working. I haven't even used it yet. I was only showing it to you, so you can think about my proposal to have your debt remitted in exchange for helping me."

Lilith was confused. When he pointed at the model on the floor, she really didn't follow any more.

"Aren't you going to clear that up?"

"You made me drop it."

Ferhdessar's hands hardly moved, but Lilith felt something brush along her face before it pressed down on her shoulders. The pressure increased for a moment, but then it disappeared again.

"Aren't you going to clear that up?" he repeated.

Lilith nodded, feeling nauseated. Fighting off the pain, she sunk to her knees.

The sorcerer looked down at her with contempt. "Oh, Lilith. I don't understand you. You force me to hurt you even though I ask so little of you. Just answer my questions and I'll leave you in peace."

"You've given me no reason to trust you."

"What is it that I've done?"

"You're a sorcerer…"

"That can't be the only reason." He knelt down beside her, whereupon Lilith moved away. "Tell me the name of the sorcerer that you're so afraid of."

"Fine, I'll answer your question."

Ferhdessar's eyes briefly glowed with expectation.

"His name is Ferhdessar."

"Vixen!"

His face darkened and he shoved her aside. Lilith rolled over the floor. She squealed but wasn't sorry that she had brought this on herself. She felt empowered for being able to stir up such a response in him. She would never have dared to do something like that to her master, but she wouldn't let this sorcerer control her.

Ferhdessar stood up straight again. "Get up."

Lilith turned to her stomach, but before she could raise herself up entirely, Ferhdessar dragged her up by her arm and pulled her against him.

"This has gone on long enough. What can you tell me about pontifex Peschi?"

"What…? How…?" Lilith felt the blood drain from her face.

Ferhdessar was clearly surprised by her reaction. He briefly loosened his grip on her arm and scrutinized her.

"So you do know something about him," he muttered, "and even more than I expected."

"I have no idea who you're talking about." Lilith tried to sound indifferent.

"I should have known. You arrived in Merzia at the same time that the news of his death reached me," he said, wrapped up in his own thoughts. But then he turned to Lilith: "What do you have to do with his death?"

Lilith shook her head in despair. She didn't know how to respond. "I'm not responsible for that," she finally said. At the same time she was cursing herself. Why had she lost control?

"But who is?" the sorcerer continued.

Lilith's thoughts were all over the place. How could she get herself out of this predicament? "My master," she answered truthfully when she couldn't think of anything else to say.

"I want to hear a name."

"I don't know. Please, believe me. I don't know his name," she whispered. *Pull yourself together!* But she couldn't.

"All right, I believe you. What else can you tell me?"

"Not much, he wants to convert the world to his religion."

"Merzia as well," Ferhdessar mumbled with a tone of concern.

Lilith was trembling. It was hard to keep upright. Ferhdessar's grip immediately grew tighter. He guided her to a chair. She didn't sit down but gratefully grabbed hold of the backrest.

"Were you serving a pontifex, Lilith?"

She shook her head in denial. Her throat clamped shut. She didn't want to tell him anything, but now that he had discovered so much already, she couldn't stop answering his questions.

Ferhdessar was talking to himself, "Indeed, that wouldn't make sense, seeing that she believes in Jakob. It's becoming more and more likely that the rumours about the prophet are true." He looked at her again. "Is there really nothing more you can tell me? Surely there must be something."

Lilith had closed her eyes and was concentrating on her breathing in an attempt to calm down. To her astonishment the sorcerer said, "I think we're going to have to leave it at that, for now. But I'll definitely return to this subject, Lilith. You're the only one who can tell me everything about this prophet. It's important that I know more about him."

He pushed her out the door. She fell back against it in an attempt to stay on her feet. Using the wall for support, she made her way through the corridors, but Lilith had no idea where to go. Her fingertips alternately brushed along the texture of the tapestries and the smoothness of the plastered walls. People were looking at her, but nobody made an attempt to help her.

Suddenly Ghalatea grabbed hold of her. "What happened?"

For a brief moment, Lilith was tempted to tell the Ancilla Princeps the full story, but then she changed her mind. If she did so now, the sorcerer would have won. She had already told him too much.

Ghalatea eyed her inquisitively. Then Lilith fell into her arms. "Help me, please." It had dawned on her that there was another reason not to tell Ghalatea what had happened. If she told the truth, she would lose her. And then she would be all alone again.

6

Ghalatea had awoken with a knot in her stomach, and now it was being pulled even tighter as she entered the king's room. It was dark inside. A single lamp on the far side of the room spread a yellow light that only barely reached the figure sitting hunched up in the chair. Yvar had buried his face in his hands and nothing suggested that he had noticed the Ancilla Princeps entering his room.

Today was the anniversary of his wife's death.

Ghalatea turned around and chased the maidservants out of the room before they had so much as crossed the threshold. After she had softly closed the door, she walked up to the king. He was wearing a pair of leather trousers and a white shirt, but he hadn't bothered with the buttons. Ghalatea kneeled at his feet.

"Lord…"

In response, Yvar put his hand on her shoulder. When she looked up, her eyes met his smiling face. She was surprised.

"It has been twenty years since Caliste died, but at the same time it feels as if we got married yesterday."

"It was a wonderful day."

"It certainly was. In my memories she always looks the way she looked then."

"I'm sure that's how lady Caliste would have wanted you to remember her. She was always so strong, even when death drew near."

Yvar's expression turned grave and he averted his head. The weak light emphasized his features. Deep creases ran from his nose to the corners of his mouth and he had his eyes half-closed.

"Alas, very shortly after our wedding she fell ill and she suffered such a long time." Yvar turned his head back to Ghalatea and gave her a penetrating gaze as he grabbed hold of her hands. His thumbs caressed her fingers. "I'm grateful for what you did for us back then."

Ghalatea had trouble concealing her uneasiness and pulled her hands free. "Let me help you get dressed," she said and started buttoning up his shirt. Next, she walked to the wardrobe and got out a purple overcoat. She held it up behind Yvar, so he could put his arms through the sleeves.

They shared their grief in silence. Caliste had been a beautiful woman and Yvar had loved her greatly. She had been his true love.

Ghalatea had also loved the queen very much. She had found it very hard to take that such a strong and young woman like the queen had fallen so ill. With Yvar's knowledge, she had gone out at night to call in healeresses, but they hadn't been able to help Caliste. So many years after her death, time still hadn't healed all wounds. The king, undoubtedly, felt the same way.

Ghalatea wished she could hold the man standing in front of her in her arms, like she had done so many times when he was just a boy. Instead, she stroked his shoulders with her hands. It was meant to be comforting, but could also be interpreted as an innocent touch of a servant smoothing down his clothes. It would be inappropriate to go any further.

She went to stand in front of the king and crossed the coat fronts before tightening a belt around his waist. Then she looked up at him.

"Please be seated, lord, so I can help you with your boots."

She put the soft-leather boots on his feet and laced them up. While she walked to the wardrobe to get his cape, the king got back up. Ghalatea was draping the green fabric around his shoulders when somebody knocked on the door.

"Enter!" Yvar called.

The head of his Guard entered the room. "Your Guard is ready to take you to the temple, lord," Harald said. He held his hands to his heart and bowed his head slightly.

The king put on a golden headband before he walked towards him. He held his head high and his strides were powerful. His emotions were safely tucked away.

A tear ran along Ghalatea's face, but she immediately regained her composure. She rearranged her veil and wiped the tear away in one and the same motion. Then she hurried to join up with the group.

In the porch of the chapel they were joined by the priest and his altar boys, and they entered the main hall in procession. All those present rose when the king and his retinue walked along the middle aisle to the statue of the Goddess on the far side of the chapel. The bells that invited the people to join the service were still tolling.

This temple was devoted to Gaia. Not all Gods occupied equally significant roles in the faith of the Merzians, but the Goddess of Life and Death was very important. Therefore, Her shrine was the biggest in all of Nadesh. Every piece of this temple was decorated with colourful paintings. Contrary to the other temples, the main hall wasn't screened off from the gallery by walls. The demarcation was formed by a row of columns, behind which hundreds of people were gathered who wanted to attend the mass as well.

To Ghalatea, Gaia was the most beautiful of all the Gods. Her statue was breathtaking. Her facial expression seemed to change every second; sometimes She looked happy, then again comforting. The next moment, Her expression would be sad as if She was mourning the dead.

Gaia was holding an hourglass in Her left hand, and two flowers, one blooming and one withered, in Her other hand. The pedestal underneath Gaia's feet was always strewn with flowers of the worshippers. Today, vases had even been placed next to the statue. Yvar put his offering in the only vase that was still empty. He arranged the flowers as he murmured a prayer.

Ghalatea stood still for a minute as well. She laid a purple rose among the other flowers. It had been Caliste's favourite flower. After that, she hurried to the pews on the left side of the altar. She found herself a seat in the back row.

When the priest had said the first prayer, everybody sat down. The man held a welcoming speech in which he mentioned the queen. Ghalatea had her head bowed, but peeked through her eyelashes at the king in the front row. Outwardly, he didn't show any signs of being overwhelmed.

Then the priest invoked the Goddess in a melodious tone, "Gaia, give us guidance in our lives!"

Everyone in the temple replied to the priest's words, "Gaia, have mercy upon us."

"Gaia, stand by us when death draws near!"

Again, everybody replied, "Gaia, have mercy upon us."

Ghalatea whispered the sentences and let the words sink in. As always, they had a calming effect on her. A few years after she had arrived in Nadesh, she had joined this religious community. She had heard others speak about the Gods and had gone to a few services before she had decided to let herself be initiated. It had been her own choice, nobody had tried to force her like Margal's followers had. Even though Ghalatea bore the signs of that faith, she had never set foot in their temples. The ritual that should have drawn her in, had driven her away.

Margal had been the first God she had ever learned about. Her own people, the Kel Cornu, didn't believe in any Gods. To them, life wasn't set in stone. After all, they had come into this world without any help of the Gods; it had been the sorcerers who had given the shapeshifters their abilities. The Kel Cornu only believed in one thing: themselves. The rest of the world was hardly of any interest to them.

There was a brief hush before the choir started to sing. They sung Caliste's favourite song. The queen had quite often sung it herself. Clear as a bell at first, but breathy and with a rasp in her voice towards the end of her life. Ghalatea looked at Yvar again. His head was bowed and his hands were clenching the arms of the chair. She was sitting too far away to be able to do anything.

Ferhdessar was sitting next to the king, but he was looking straight ahead. A maternal anger welled up in the Ancilla Princeps. The sorcerer was sitting close enough to do something; he could whisper something comforting or put a hand on Yvar's hand, but he didn't do anything. She didn't understand how the sorcerer could be so heartless.

The choir had stopped singing and now the priest's voice filled the chapel on its own. He sung the verses in a clear voice. It looked as if Yvar shivered briefly, but Ghalatea wasn't sure she had seen it right. Maybe her observations were clouded by her own emotions. She bowed her head. At moments like these she was glad she wore a veil, at least now nobody could see that she couldn't hold back her tears any longer.

When the priest said another prayer, Ghalatea's thoughts went out to the king. She prayed for him, but just before the prayer came to an end she asked the Goddess to look after Lilith as well.

After the final song everybody rose. Ghalatea followed the king to a staircase leading down to the crypt, which housed the tombs of the royal family. On the far side of the vault there was a statue in commemoration of Thibauld, the first king of this bloodline. A family tree was painted on the wall behind him. Not all the old kings and queens were buried here, but in this way they were all remembered in the same place.

Yvar walked to his parents' twin tomb and kneeled before it. Next to them lay his elder brother. Yvar also whispered a few words to him. Then he looked at Caliste's tomb. The likeness of the bas-relief on the stone lid was striking. The queen looked peaceful and almost happy. Her clothes had been painted, but her face and hands were bare stone.

Ghalatea kept a close eye on the king as he walked towards the tomb. Yvar put his left hand on the stone pillow next to Caliste's cheek and let his gaze slide over the sculpture. Then he bent forwards and whispered something. His forehead briefly touched hers before he walked on. He stroked his wife's stone hand in passing. At moments like these, the king was unable to hide his grief, or at least, to hide it from Ghalatea. Tears welled up in her eyes again.

The procession made its way back to the king's chambers. A group of maidservants came walking towards them, but before they were close enough to see her swollen eyes, Ghalatea said, "You're not needed."

She was the only one who followed the king into his room. Yvar lit the candles, but as soon as he had done that, he turned around and looked at her. She knew he couldn't fail to notice that she was still crying. The king walked up to her. Ashamed, she averted her eyes.

"Thank you for crying for her, Ghalatea," he whispered as he wiped away her tears. "I couldn't cry today, not in front of everyone."

Once again, Ghalatea felt the need to hold him in her arms and whisper to him that it was all right to cry, just like she had done when he was a little boy. Instead, she clenched her fists and smiled at him.

Yvar took off his cape, and Ghalatea caught the garment before it could fall on the floor.

"Is there anything I can get you, lord?" she asked after she had put the cape away.

Yvar had walked over to the bookcase but turned around again. "No, thank you, Ghalatea. You've done enough for me."

She curtsied to him. Even before she stood upright again, he said, "I admire your ability to comfort people and put them at ease. That was the reason why I chose you to be my Ancilla Princeps. Please, don't ever feel ashamed about being such a caring person, not even if you're being held accountable for it."

Ghalatea wasn't sure how to respond, so she curtsied once more. "I'll remember that, lord. Thank you."

As she left the room, Ferhdessar entered.

He waited until the door was closed and then said, "Five men have arrived and they want to speak to you." Yvar wanted to wave Ferhdessar away, but the sorcerer continued, "They're here about the prisoner."

"Lilith?"

Ferhdessar nodded.

"Have you explained to them that I have other things on my mind today?"

"Not in so many words, but I gave them to understand that you weren't seeing anyone today. They say it's extremely important. They want to buy off her debt, so they can take her with them."

Yvar looked up in surprise.

Ferhdessar had been amazed as well. The men had seemed eager to find the prisoner and take her with them. He had only spoken with them briefly, but the conversation had aroused his curiosity.

"Maybe they can answer our questions," he suggested, and the king agreed to see them.

Ferhdessar led the king to the hall where he had left the five Purified men. At the recommendation of the sorcerer, Yvar was accompanied by twenty members of the Royal Guard. In view of the information that Lilith had come up with the day before, it was smart to give the outside world the impression that Merzia was very powerful.

The five strangers bowed deeply when the king entered. Harald gave some instructions, and the soldiers lined up along the walls. They unsheathed their swords a few inches. Ferhdessar followed the king to the throne and stood next to him. Only now, did the men look up again.

It didn't escape Ferhdessar's notice that their leader's eyes darted back and forth nervously. The man, however, almost immediately regained his composure. He made another deep bow.

"I would like to thank you very much for receiving us, lord Yvar. I apologize for showing up unannounced and at such an inopportune time. My name is Seraph." He subsequently introduced the others. "We're looking for the woman who destroyed our lives. Her trail has led us to Nadesh. Her name is Lilith, but that might not mean anything to you. She's small and skinny, has dark hair and a pinched face."

"What has this woman done that caused you to go looking for her?" the king asked.

"Even though her small stature might lead one to believe otherwise, there is a very powerful side to her. She destroyed our city, and not many people escaped her wrath. Therefore, I no longer have a family."

Seraph bowed his head and fell silent for a moment.

"We have to find her to get even," he added, looking up again. "I'm sure you'll understand my need to avenge the death of my wife and children." His voice wavered, but he quickly regained his composure. Seraph gestured at the others and said that they had all lost loved ones too.

Yvar gave a sympathetic nod and was genuinely interested when he asked what had happened exactly.

"She came in the middle of the night and spread fire everywhere, so it wasn't long before the entire city was ablaze. Awakened by the fire, we fled outside with our children tucked under our arms. But Lilith snatched them away and murdered them. She threw the babies into the fire, and the mothers jumped in after them, trying to save their children. It was all in vain, the only thing they found in that heat, was death."

Yvar raised his eyebrows. "And she did all of this on her own?"

"That's what's so misleading about her. No one suspects what's hidden inside her."

"She tells us a totally different story," Ferhdessar interfered. "The prisoner says she serves a master. Probably a sorcerer."

He looked hard at Seraph, who lowered his eyes. He opened his mouth, closed it and briefly glanced at the man he had called Nander. It was as if he was looking for help. Then he said, "If that's the case, then she's hiding her true self from you."

"Do you live in Peschi's city?"

Seraph raised his eyebrows. Then he nodded. "Lilith has killed our lord."

Ferhdessar knew that some of the Purified people were Margal's most fanatical followers. But it still baffled him.

Seraph continued, "I'll never forget the night that Lilith showed up. It's like a festering on my heart. The pain grows with each passing day and there's only one way to deliver myself from this agony. Lilith will have to pay." Seraph's voice became more and more agitated. "She took away everything we had. Everything that mattered."

His face had turned red and he was snorting. His fists were clenched. Nander walked up to him and put an arm around his shoulders. He whispered something that helped Seraph relax.

"Ferhdessar told me that you want to pay off her debt," Yvar stated when the man had calmed down a bit.

Seraph nodded. "We were told that Lilith owes you twenty-one pieces of gold. I offer you two hundred pieces of gold in exchange for her."

Ferhdessar's confusion rose. Nobody was worth that many gold pieces, especially this prisoner if she had done what this man was accusing her of. He leaned towards the king but before he could say anything Yvar asked Seraph, "What is it you want to do with her?"

"We want to execute her."

Ferhdessar shook his head. It was insane to pay so much gold for someone who was going to be killed. So he asked, "Don't you need the money for the reconstruction of your city?"

"Gold is not what's most important to our community. We want compensation for what she did. Not one person who died because of her would have it any other way."

This sounded plausible. The men were dressed in fine wool and silk. Their costumes fit perfectly, and it was clear that they looked after themselves. They clearly were wealthy.

Yvar thought for a long time. Then he said, "I feel for you and I'll see what I can do to ease your suffering. This woman, however, resides under my supervision, so I'll give her a chance to respond to these allegations."

Seraph turned red in the face again and raised his voice. "She'll only tell you lies."

"Don't you deem the king wise enough to see right through her lies?" Ferhdessar asked in irritation.

"Of course I do, lord sorcerer." Seraph addressed the king, "I'm sorry if I've offended you, that wasn't my intention."

Yvar gave a nod of approval. "There's no need to rush this. The woman isn't going anywhere. I'll keep your interests in mind when I make my decision."

"Of course, my lord, as you wish."

Yvar got up and Ferhdessar followed him. In the corridor the king said, "It's high time the woman told us her story. Make sure she understands this."

Ferhdessar nodded and left for Lilith's room.

Lilith was standing in front of the fireplace to warm herself on the fire. When Ferhdessar came in, she turned around. She had been expecting him.

"Seraph is here."

Lilith nodded and smiled. She had seen him while she was at work. She was convinced that the Purified one had come to rescue her. Now she would finally be able to leave this dreadful palace. She gave the sorcerer a hopeful look. "Does he want to take me away from here?"

Ferhdessar squinted. "Yes, he wants to take you with him. He has told the king that you killed his family and that he wants to execute you."

Lilith hadn't expected that. Her lower lip started to quiver. She paced around the room and knocked over everything in her path. But it didn't calm her down. Eventually, Lilith smashed her fist into the wall with great force.

"What had you expected?"

Lilith shrugged. How could she have been so stupid to think he was coming to save her? She knew full well he was going to return her to her master. She was going to be punished for her disobedience and then she would have to continue carrying out her abhorring tasks. If she fell into her master's hands again, her future would be even more awful than her prospects in this palace.

"I can't go with him. It will be years before I've paid off my debt by working for the king." She triumphantly put her hands akimbo.

Ferhdessar gave her a pitying look. "Seraph has thought about that. He's willing to pay two hundred pieces of gold for you. Don't forget that your work here is largely symbolic. It's not like your work will get the king his money back. The offer is very tempting."

Lilith was taken aback.

"You must have done something really bad if he's willing to pay so much gold for you. The king is seriously considering handing you over."

Lilith turned around and rested her face against the wall. She drove her nails into her arm until it started to bleed.

"I don't want to go with him."

"I can imagine that. The flogging was a stroke with a feather compared to what's awaiting you now."

"He's told you lies. You can't hand me over to Seraph."

Ferhdessar nodded. "As just as lord Yvar is, he has decided to give you a chance to defend yourself. You're going to have to tell us what really happened."

This was so confusing. Could she be sure that the king wouldn't punish her? *Of course not, you fool.* Maybe Yvar's punishment was even worse than what her master would do to her. At least her master needed her alive. The king would probably have no choice but to sentence her to death. *But you don't know that for sure,* a voice whispered inside her head, *maybe...* Lilith silenced the voice. What was the use of guessing? Her wristband was starting to irritate her.

"Leave me alone!" she screamed as she pulled at the wristband to get it off. It didn't work and the pain only fuelled her anger. Suddenly she realized there was a third option.

Lilith tasted sulphur in her mouth and she knew her eyes were glowing dangerously. This always happened when she got angry, and once she had discovered that, she had made ample use of it to scare away the servi. Ferhdessar, however, didn't let her scare him off. Quite the contrary, he walked up to her. Before he could say anything she whispered threateningly, "Leave me alone, or else..."

"Or else what? What do you think you can do to me that should make me afraid of you?"

Lilith hesitated briefly but then she rose on tiptoe to look Ferhdessar in the eye. "I'll destroy you, I'll destroy this palace and all its inhabitants."

"And you think I'll let you?"

Ferhdessar shook his head condescendingly, but when her hand reached for her amulet and she started to whisper the incantation, his expression became suspicious.

As she felt the power flow through her body, Lilith realized she had been longing for this feeling. She was stronger than the humans. She felt the scales press through her skin. Anger and feelings of revenge took hold of her emotions and she grew in size. Ferhdessar would be the first to burn, and then the entire palace would go up in flames.

The sorcerer was casting counter-spells to prevent her from changing completely, but Lilith fought to keep the change going. Nothing could stop her. She screamed the incantation again, "Qi ga ullar brut i-qi libèr qi ouander i-a drag!"

But then the Ancilla Princeps walked into the room. She yelled something at Ferhdessar and turned towards Lilith, who thought she saw a trace of disgust on Ghalatea's face. It made her waver long enough to give the sorcerer the upper hand.

Lilith fell on the floor as a woman. Panting, she pressed her face against the tiles, fighting her feelings of powerlessness. Someone knelt beside her and put a hand on her shoulder. With a jolt, Lilith sat up straight and pushed the person away. Ghalatea let out a yelp when she fell against the table.

Lilith hadn't meant for that to happen. She looked over her shoulder and saw that the Ancilla Princeps was rubbing her arm. Whispering apologies, she crawled towards Ghalatea. But Ferhdessar stopped her, so she started to scream, "I'm sorry, Ghalatea! That wasn't supposed to happen!"

The Ancilla Princeps got up and took a step in her direction. Ferhdessar stopped her as well.

"Let her be. This woman is a murderer. She has killed thousands of people."

Confused, Ghalatea looked from the sorcerer to Lilith. Then she backed away a few steps. Lilith hit her own throbbing head with the palm of her hand.

"I didn't have a choice," she stammered.

Ghalatea stared at her with wide open eyes. Then she stepped sideways so that Ferhdessar's body shielded her. Lilith moaned because her headache was getting worse. She cursed Seraph for showing up. Now she had lost everything.

"I was only a child," she whispered in defeat. "A child who did everything he asked of her, because she didn't know what else to do. She had learned that it was best to obey. How could I understand the implications of what he asked of me? How could I have an opinion about it? I only knew what he had told me and I was only twelve when I destroyed the first village."

She was down on her hands and knees and looked up through strands of her hair to see how the others reacted. Ghalatea was trembling, Ferhdessar seemed unmoved.

"Is Seraph your master?"

"No, but he was involved. The sorcerer told me what I was expected to do. He controlled me. Seraph was his right-hand man." Lilith was now standing upright. "I didn't mean to hurt you, Ghalatea. I hope you can believe that."

The Ancilla Princeps looked away. "But you do admit that you're guilty of the things you're being accused of?"

"I wish I could tell you that I'm innocent, but that would be a lie," Lilith sighed.

"Don't you feel any remorse?"

"You have no idea how terrible I feel. But who can I beg for forgiveness? Those who have the right to judge me are no longer alive. I have to live with the knowledge of what I've done. That's my punishment: knowing that I'm a monster and knowing that I didn't have a choice. But I don't blame you for not understanding."

Ferhdessar shook his head. "Nothing but a bunch of lies. I think you wilfully agreed and now you're trying to justify yourself."

Lilith shrugged feebly.

"You should tell them the rest of the story as well," Ghalatea urged her.

"I know," Lilith answered.

Suddenly she felt completely calm. She was going to tell her story in the hope that Ghalatea would understand, but also in the hope that the king would decide against handing her over. Ferhdessar put his hand on her shoulder.

"Before we go to the king, I want to have your amulet."

Lilith wanted to object but she knew his demand was warranted. Even if she promised that she wouldn't use it, Ferhdessar wouldn't believe her. And why should he? Lilith raised her hand, but the sorcerer pulled her arms behind her back.

"Ghalatea will take it from you."

The Ancilla Princeps was reluctant to touch the necklace.

"It won't hurt you, Ghalatea," Lilith whispered.

"How do I open it?"

"There's a little switch underneath the dragon's head."

Lilith turned her head to give the Ancilla Princeps more room.

When the gold jewel slid down her neck, Lilith instantly felt weaker. It was as if her power had disappeared along with her necklace. Ferhdessar produced a metal chain and fastened it around her waist. Her hands were shackled, but they weren't bound nearly as tightly against her body as Lemuel had done. Lilith didn't put the strength of the metal to the test.

"Now we're ready to go to the king."

Ferhdessar was holding the end of the chain and pushed her towards the door. The two guards were somewhat surprised when Lilith stepped outside, but when Ferhdessar and Ghalatea followed, they were reassured.

Yvar was pacing in front of the window but immediately looked up when the sorcerer entered with the prisoner. Ferhdessar said curtly, "She's willing to talk."

The king nodded. Ferhdessar pushed Lilith farther into the room and secured the chain to a ring in the floor. Yvar sat down in a chair at a safe distance from Lilith. He looked at her expectantly. Ferhdessar remained standing and leaned against the mantelpiece. Lilith couldn't see Ghalatea. She had kept her distance after she had taken the amulet.

"Have you found out if and how she did what Seraph is accusing her of?" Yvar asked Ferhdessar.

Ferhdessar nodded but when he handed Yvar the amulet, Lilith said, "Why don't you ask me directly? I'm a dragon."

Yvar regarded her with surprise. "You're a shapeshifter?"

Lilith nodded as she fought her resurfacing anger. "Yes, I'm a monster. Are you going to kill me now?" she asked rebelliously.

Yvar shrugged. "I won't make any decisions until I've heard your story. But the fact that you can change into a dragon doesn't automatically make me think that you're a monster."

Lilith was taken aback.

"You know what Seraph is accusing you of?" the king asked her.

Lilith nodded. "The murder of Peschi and the destruction of his city."

"In that case, I would like to hear your side of the story now."

"Where should I begin?"

"Just tell us everything. What's the first thing you can remember?"

"My earliest memory is of a dark shadow falling over my cradle. Icy hands lift me up and I feel his cold breath on my cheeks as he talks to me. He takes me away from a soft, warm world where light and darkness take turns, to a dark, cold world underground."

She briefly stopped talking. The king nodded at her. His expression was kind and encouraging. When Lilith continued, the words started to come faster and faster. Finally she could tell someone the full story. She gave an elaborate description of the world she had lived in, and recounted everything that had happened. Meanwhile, she thought of Ferhdessar's accusation that she had participated wilfully. Could she blame him? Her fingers traced the thick scar on her wrist and she thought back to the day that she hadn't had the courage to take her own life.

7

Lilith had retreated to her room and kept banging her head against the cave wall. All the while she was screaming, "I don't want to do this any more, I can't do it any more. I hate it, everything. I hate myself."

She had just returned from destroying a village, but contrary to all the other people she had killed, these villagers hadn't tried to run away. They had looked up at her in awe and they had seemed elated. Lilith had burned everyone with one devastating sigh, because she knew that if she didn't end it at once, she wouldn't be able to complete her assignment. Up until the very last moment, the people had been overjoyed at her presence. She had flown back home in a state of utter confusion. She felt terrible, because she knew that her master's words didn't hold true for these people. They hadn't been afraid and they hadn't attacked her. Lilith didn't understand why the master had wanted them to die or why she had killed them without any mercy.

She hadn't noticed that the sorcerer had entered her room. She kept banging her head against the wall. Blood streamed down her forehead, but she didn't notice that either. Lilith only felt the pain that emanated from her heart and spread through her entire body. When the master spoke, she didn't look up.

"I want you to destroy another village, Lilith. Tewarsum lies to the north. Go there now."

She knew that he didn't accept "no" for an answer, but Lilith was worn out. Her inner voice had often told her that what she was doing was wrong. She had always been able to ignore her conscience. But now her inner voice was screaming at her and she could no longer silence it.

"I can't do it any more, I can't. I hate…"

"Do you hate me? Think carefully, Lilith, I'm all you've got. You're nothing without me. I'm your friend and, therefore, your enemy as well. You might not want to be around me, but at the same time you can't do without me."

As he said that, he pulled her away from the wall. She fell and as she lay on the floor she looked aghast at the man towering over her. His eyes flashed with anger and his mouth was set in a thin line. He squatted down beside her. He produced a dagger from the sleeve of his dark red underclothes. The dagger glittered threateningly in the dim light of the sole oil lamp that illuminated Lilith's room. "Here you are, Lilith, this is your only way out."

She tentatively took the dagger from him. The cold metal was wonderful to the touch. It dispelled the burning pain somewhat. Lilith was still in a panic and couldn't think straight. She felt her blood flowing through her veins like boiling lava and she thought she could use the knife to cool it down. She felt the need to let the blood flow from her body, not realizing that would kill her. But it didn't really matter anyway. Anything would be an improvement over the way she was feeling right now. She twisted the dagger around. The cold metal touched her skin and she pressed down harder until the knife cut through it. Blood immediately started to seep along the metal and down her arm.

The master reached out at high speed and grabbed hold of Lilith's wrist. Now she couldn't continue cutting her wrist open, but she couldn't pull the blade out of her flesh either. The blood started dripping to the ground faster and faster. It didn't calm her down, if anything, it only made her even more afraid. The master spoke with an icily calm voice.

"You know that Jakob will pass judgement on you when you're dead. Can you be sure He'll embrace you? Or is He going to punish you for the way you lived your life?"

The master got up and left the room. Lilith stayed behind, unable to do anything.

During the days that followed, nobody came to see her. Lilith felt like a prisoner of the caves, of her master and of herself. She tried to decide which was the lesser of the evils, but couldn't reach a conclusion.

At times, Lilith thought that, no matter how horrible her life was, whatever was waiting for her after death was probably much worse. At other times, however, Lilith felt like nothing could be worse than the life she was living right now. Her death wish grew until she realized once again that her fate was unbearable either way. She could either live and suffer through it all, or die and end up in the exact same misery. It was an impossible choice to make.

At long last, her agonizing thoughts slowly faded into the background as they were replaced by pangs of hunger. Lilith sat up but had to remain seated for quite some time before she was able to stand up. She staggered to the dining room, but when she went inside the servi were just getting ready to leave, and all the food was cleared away. She didn't dare say anything. In her present emotional state, there was no way she could stand her ground against the others.

Lilith supported herself on the cave wall as she walked back to her room. To her relief she encountered the master and Seraph. Lilith whispered that she was hungry, but the two men walked by without so much as glimpsing at her. She yelled after them, but neither responded. Defeated, she lowered herself down to the floor and continued on hands and knees.

Lilith spent the next day in her room. Her hunger increased and her mouth was dry. She licked the moisture off the walls but it wasn't enough to quench her thirst. All of a sudden she realized that she was going to die if this went on any longer.

She heard her master's voice. "You'll go to hell, Lilith. Are you sure you want to die?"

Lilith turned in his direction and she could even see him sitting there. Full of despair, she crawled towards him, but then she saw that there was no one in her room.

"No," she whispered, "I don't want to die."

She repeated the words several times until she was screaming them.

"No!"

Jakob had every reason to punish her; for the things she had done or for doubting Him. As long as she was alive, there was a chance she could rectify her sins. She looked at her wrist and rubbed the scab that covered the spot where she had cut herself.

"For my life", she whispered, "and for hope."

In an all-concealing darkness she destroyed Tewarsum. She didn't see any people, only buildings, which she burned to the ground. They were lifeless objects that were easy to attack. The people died in their sleep. Lilith didn't reflect on it, because that was the only way she could survive.

Early in the morning, the door to Lilith's room opened. A servus motioned for her to follow him to her master's chambers. Lilith tried to walk tall but she nevertheless stumbled every now and then.

The master was having breakfast. Lilith regarded the food he was gobbling down with hungry eyes. Grease dripped down his fingers. She wanted to lick them clean. She'd do anything to alleviate her hunger.

Without looking up, the sorcerer threw her a half-picked bone. She sunk to her knees and gratefully ate the little amount of flesh that was still on the bone.

Finally the sorcerer said, "Sit down."

She pulled herself up as quickly as she could. The master gave her a plate and nodded as a sign that Lilith was allowed to eat. As she filled her stomach, her mind became empty. She washed the last of her worries away with big gulps of water.

"I thought you died, but apparently you've come back from the dead."

She didn't fail to notice the sardonic look in his eyes and she knew that he enjoyed having so much power over her. It didn't matter.

The previous night, Lilith had found a way to shut down her emotions. They didn't serve any purpose. She had resolved to never feel anything again: no fear for others, no grief about what was happening, and no happiness either. Ever since she had started her destructive flights, she had hardly ever been happy anyway. She wouldn't trust anyone any more, she no longer had the ability to do so. The only feeling that remained was the need to survive.

After she had eaten, the master sent Lilith back to her room.

She fell into a dreamless sleep that was only interrupted when she had to throw up. After having been empty for such a long time, her stomach just couldn't hold the large amount of food.

"Why did you escape in the end?"

Lilith was startled from her thoughts. It had turned dark outside and she wondered where she had left off with her story. Her thoughts had distracted her from the story she was telling.

"What happened that finally made you leave?" Ferhdessar repeated.

Lilith bowed her head and stared at the glass in her hands. She couldn't remember getting it, but it was almost empty, so she must have drunk from it.

Ferhdessar was asking her about the moment when she had decided to escape. After the attack on Tewarsum she had simply obeyed the master's wishes for quite some time. She had become an emotionless machine that did what others told her to do. The master had used her to violently force entire regions to convert themselves to Jakob's religion.

Lilith had been schooled in this religion since her early childhood. The master had often said he was "preparing" her. But she still didn't know exactly what he meant by that. Preparing her to help him bring people together in this faith? Or preparing her for Jakob's return to this world? Because that was her master's goal. Jakob had abandoned the world during the Second Era, but now He had promised the master that He would return. First, however, harmony had to be restored to the world. The divide that had begun during the Second Era and had widened during the Third, had to be undone. In the end, the master had even allowed Lilith to move out of the caves to assist him in fulfilling his task.

"One day I found a boy who was being attacked by a lion…"

"You've already told us about Myar," the king said, "and then you told us about the inn you worked at for a while."

Lilith nodded. She had saved Myar and he had been grateful. Unlike everybody else, he hadn't had any preconceptions about her. This had never happened before. The encounter with the boy had planted the first seeds of doubt in her heart since her attack on Tewarsum.

After that, she had worked at an inn for a while. This experience had taught her that her life could be very different. The people at the inn had always treated her with respect. But it was a hot summer afternoon when she finally decided that enough was enough. Lilith drained her glass and started talking again.

"I was in bed with a high fever. My body felt like it was on fire and every movement cost me too much energy. The master came by and ordered me to take flight and destroy Peschi's city.

His words slowly sank in: I was going to have to move house again, and I'd be back to square one. I begged him to postpone his plans, because I truly was too ill to even get out of bed. His voice, however, became more commanding. I tried to get up but collapsed, feeling exhausted. I couldn't find the strength to get back up again. With great strides my master walked up to me and dragged me outside by my hair. I was even too weak to scream for him to stop. Outside he cried out the incantation.

I reluctantly flew to the city. From the sky, I saw that the servi had already begun their attack on the ground. I wanted to go back to bed as soon as possible, so I immediately destroyed the pontifex's palace. He came running out, and when I hit him he was turned into a little pile of smouldering ashes. The fever rushed me and heated my body, but my heart was cold.

The master observed everything from a nearby hill. As soon as the city was destroyed, he turned around contentedly and left the area.

Then it hit me that this was my chance to escape. It would be days before he came looking for me, because he was busy with other things. He was expecting me to find a new place to live, and so I did. Only not the way he thought I would.

Extending all my energies, I managed to fly east. Exhausted, I looked for a place to hide. My illness was getting worse and in my delirium I thought I heard his voice. But he didn't find me, and I recovered.

I decided not to change any more. Even though I would be faster as a dragon, it would also mean that the master would know where I was. So I plodded on. Pretty soon, I noticed that I was being followed by a group of men. I couldn't take on all five of them, so I did my utmost to stay ahead of them. I crossed the mountains in the south and ended up in this country."

Now that her story was finished, Lilith looked up at the others. The king and Ferhdessar looked at each other but didn't say anything. Ghalatea's cheeks were wet with tears. Lilith wondered if it was disgust or pity showing on her face. The Ancilla Princeps was still keeping her distance. Lilith couldn't blame her but she longed for Ghalatea's embrace. She needed it now more than ever.

Suddenly the king broke the silence. "This was definitely not what I was expecting. I will address both you and Seraph tomorrow and pass my judgement. I take it that Ferhdessar already explained to you why the five men have come."

Lilith nodded. "I beg you lord, don't hand me over to them. I'll do anything you ask. You can make me work here for the rest of my life." Then she looked at Ferhdessar and whispered, "I'm even willing to participate in your experiments. As long as I don't have to return to my master."

There was another prolonged silence. The king was staring into the fire. Then he said, "I can't make any decisions right now."

Lilith sighed. Two soldiers entered and undid the chain from the ring in the floor. Then they escorted her from the room.

"I swear that I ran away to never have to do anything like that again. I want to make amends, lord Yvar," she yelled over her shoulder.

Ghalatea followed her. Lilith was surprised that the Ancilla Princeps even came into her room. But when she raised her hand to touch her, Ghalatea started back.

"I would never hurt you, Ghalatea. It was a mistake that I attacked you before. I was convinced it was Ferhdessar who was touching me."

The Ancilla Princeps gave an uncertain shrug.

"Do you know what's going to happen next?" Lilith asked, sounding scared.

"Lord Yvar and Ferhdessar will deliberate on what to do. I have no idea what their decision will be."

Lilith bowed her head and sat down on the bed. "And you, do you think I'm a monster now?"

Ghalatea pulled at a piece of thread from her veil, but when she noticed that she was unpicking the embroidery, she stopped. "I have no idea what to think of you."

"Will you stay with me tonight? I don't want to be alone."

"I can't."

Lilith nodded her understanding. Of course Ghalatea wouldn't want to be alone with her. Her fears had come true: she had lost everything. Then she pulled herself together, it had always been that way, this wasn't any different.

She buried her head in her hands and clasped her hair with her fingers. She heard Ghalatea leave. The soldiers freed Lilith from her chains, but she didn't look up until the door had closed. She was alone, even the soldiers had left the room. She sunk to her knees and started to pray:

"Lord Jakob, why have You deserted me? I need Your help now more than ever. All I wanted to do was to stop everything. Why did Seraph find me? You could have sent him in another direction, couldn't You? Was I really carrying out Your will when I murdered all these people? Did You really choose me to serve You like that? I found that hard to believe, but if this is what You want from me, then please give me a sign and I will obey You. However difficult it might be. Lord Jakob, help me! Give me clarity!"

Shivering, she rolled on her side and slowly fell asleep.

Hours later she jolted awake.

"Seraph!"

She cast a quick look at the door, but it was still closed. She flinched when she heard the same loud bang that had woken her up. Just when she had convinced herself that it had been the wind, she heard footsteps in the corridor.

"He has come," she whispered.

She hid herself behind her bedside cabinet and heard the door open. She cautiously peeked around the cabinet. In the doorway stood Ferhdessar, who was regarding her intently. Lilith wasn't sure whether she should be relieved or not.

"What has lord Yvar decided?" she squeaked.

"Nothing yet," he answered curtly and left again.

Trembling, Lilith got up and pulled open the curtains. There were frost flowers on the windows. She breathed on them and wiped away the ice to be able to look out through the tiny glass panes.

There was no indication that dawn was approaching. The almost full moon shone on the snow far below her. The moon was like a silent friend in the night. Her only friend, and the one who had almost always been with her during her most painful moments. Lilith rattled the windows but wasn't surprised to find they were locked. She looked down once more. How nice it would have been to step out into the night. To feel the cold wind on her body as she fell faster and faster until she hit the ground. Would there be pain or would a pleasant nothingness await her in death? She banged on the window with the flat of her hand. What was the use thinking about it when she couldn't escape anyway?

Lilith walked to the table but changed her mind when she was about to sit down. She threw the chair into the window. The glass shattered. The room was immediately filled with cold air. The soldiers came rushing in. They cast one look at the window and then at her. Lilith was already down on her knees. She had seen at a single glance that the frames had remained undamaged. The two men deliberated briefly and then one of them walked towards the window. When he had made sure there was no way for Lilith to escape, the soldiers picked up the biggest shards of glass and left the room.

Not much later Lilith crawled in the direction of the wall, feeling her way around. She had such a severe headache that she couldn't see clearly. Then her fingers touched a cold piece of glass. She sat up straight and jabbed it into her wrist. The pain cleared her head. Her headache receded and she looked at the blood trickling down her arm and onto the floor. In the moonlight it looked like a black stripe running down her white skin. She realized that suicide wasn't the answer, but nevertheless jabbed the shard into her arm a few more times. More blood dripped onto the floor. Her mind was freed from all emotions. Feeling completely empty, Lilith eventually fell asleep on the floor.

She didn't wake up until her door opened. Ferhdessar took one look inside and turned back to the soldiers.

"Why didn't you warn me?" he roared.

As the men were defending themselves without much conviction, a woman slipped past the sorcerer. Lilith sat up when she kneeled beside her. The woman didn't say anything but shook her head disconcertedly as she took hold of Lilith's arm to have a better look at the cuts. Ferhdessar came in, lifted Lilith up and laid her on the bed.

"Do you have any other shards anywhere?" he asked sternly.

Lilith hadn't even considered using them as a weapon, so she shook her head. "It must be somewhere on the floor."

He briefly glanced at where she had lain and then said to the woman, "Get her ready to see the king."

"Where's Ghalatea?" Lilith asked warily.

"She has decided that she doesn't want to see you any more. Betrys is taking over her duties."

Lilith sighed. The woman now grabbed hold of her other hand. There were cuts on the inside. Lilith hadn't even noticed that she had injured herself there as well.

Ferhdessar kept a close eye on her. When Betrys had helped her out of her clothes and Lilith was standing beside the bed naked, Ferhdessar walked around her. She bowed her head and closed her eyes. When the sorcerer had ensured himself that she wasn't hiding any shards of glass, he addressed the soldiers. He once again grumbled at them that they should use their brains next time.

"She's ready," Betrys finally said.

Ferhdessar turned around. After he had put Lilith in chains again, he motioned that both women should follow him to the throne room. Betrys supported Lilith, because her legs had gone weak now that she was about to hear the king's judgement.

Only when her chain was secured to a ring in the floor again, did Lilith look up. Rays of light fell through the high windows and onto the still empty throne. On both sides of the room, ten soldiers stood against the wall. A few yards away stood the five Purified men. They started talking to one another quietly when they saw her. Seraph monopolized the conversation and kept staring at her intently. If it was Jakob's wish, she would soon be leaving the palace with him.

"This, indeed, is the woman we're looking for, lord Ferhdessar. She has killed our families."

The sorcerer walked on and didn't even look up. Betrys also left Lilith's side. Now she was standing all alone in the middle of the room. She shook her head in response to the allegations.

"Just you wait, woman. You'll soon be coming with us and then we will punish you."

Lilith looked at Ferhdessar in despair, but the sorcerer was ignoring them. Anger welled up inside her. Maybe the king believed these men.

"You're all just as responsible for what happened as I am," she snapped at them.

"I don't know what you're talking about, Lilith," Seraph answered confidently. He walked towards her, but before he had gone as far as three paces, Ferhdessar called out, "Stay away from the prisoner."

Right at that moment the king entered, escorted by several members of his Guard. The soldiers lined up behind Yvar when he sat down. Lilith instantly threw herself on the floor.

"Lord Yvar, I beg you to not hand me over to these men. I swear that I've told you the truth. I deserve to be punished, but they are not the right people to execute my punishment."

She cautiously looked up. The king glanced at her arms and leaned towards Ferhdessar, who told him what had happened the night before.

"Woman, stand up," the king eventually ordered.

She obeyed as quickly as she could.

Seraph shook his head scornfully. "Don't be taken in by her politeness, lord. Don't make the same mistake we have."

Yvar gave him an angry look and the Purified one fell silent. The men quickly bowed.

"Woman, do you know these men?"

Lilith told the king their names. She ended with Seraph. "He was almost always accompanying my master."

"Come on, you don't believe a word of that do you, lord Yvar?" Seraph said in defence and threw his hands up in the air.

The king addressed him. He related what Lilith had told him the other day about the attack on Peschi's city.

"They're all lies," Seraph called out.

The king nodded. Lilith wanted to say something, but Ferhdessar's gaze made her think twice. Yvar continued, "There's something that's bothering me, but maybe you can help me out, Seraph. How is it possible that this woman knows you all so well? And it seems you know her, too. How can she know your names if she came to the city like a thief in the night to destroy it?"

"At night? It was in broad daylight," Lilith stammered.

"That's not important right now," the king said. But he did seem to be smiling to himself. "I'd like a satisfying explanation, Seraph."

The man took a minute to come up with an answer. "She lived among us for a while. We trusted her. Who would you believe, a victim or a murderer?"

The king was getting annoyed. "It's a dead certainty to me that the woman is a murderer. But I have my doubts about your claim of being her victims."

He looked at Ferhdessar, who was standing next to him. The sorcerer nodded. Lilith's heart started pounding when Yvar continued, "All right, it's time for my judgement. I think that your story is a lie, Seraph. The prisoner knows you too well and you know more about her than you're letting on. Maybe you mixed up your memories of your Purification with what you saw the woman do. I'm highly offended that you chose yesterday, of all days, to come forth with your story, because I'm convinced you knew exactly what day it was. It hasn't done you any good." Seraph opened his mouth, but Yvar raised his hand. "I don't believe that the prisoner made up her story. The only thing she put forward as a defence today, was that you were lying about the time of day the attack on Peschi's city took place. That's not typical behaviour for someone who's trying to exonerate herself, so I believe that the woman's story is the truth."

"You're making a huge mistake, lord Yvar."

The king nodded. "You are to leave my palace and Nadesh today. I don't have any authority over you, so there's nothing else I can do. Maybe *that* will turn out to be my mistake."

"And the woman, is she coming with us?"

"The prisoner is indebted to me. She is going to repay her debt and will stay in the palace while doing so."

Lilith's heart skipped a beat. She couldn't believe what she was hearing. She made a deep curtsey and whispered a thank you, directed at both the king and Jakob. Yvar nodded and signalled at the soldiers standing along the walls.

"Accompany these men to the fortress. A group of soldiers will be waiting there to escort them to the border."

"There's no need for that, lord Yvar," Seraph objected.

"It would be rude to send you away unaccompanied in this weather," Yvar brushed aside his objections.

The soldiers turned the five Purified men out of the room. Lilith felt a jolt of relief when the door closed behind them.

"And now back to you." Yvar got up and paced up and down in front of the throne. Lilith immediately felt scared again. "I'm sure you understand that I can't ignore your story. I'm going to have to make a decision about you."

She nodded timidly.

"Every single one of your actions is a huge crime on its own and your actions need to be punished severely. You committed your crimes under extenuating circumstances, but is one to take that into account in a case like this? That's one of the questions that have kept me occupied."

Yvar fell silent for a while. The room started to feel more and more oppressive. Lilith stood in front of the king with her head bowed. His words crashed into her skull. Her vision became blurred because it felt as if her eyes were being pushed out of their sockets. She moaned. The red tiles seemed to be moving like a bloody mass. Her heart was in her throat.

"Woman, the crimes that you've described didn't take place in my realm and, therefore, I've decided that I can't punish you for them. This means you will continue working for me."

"Really?" Lilith smiled and closed her eyes. "How can I thank you?"

"Wait until I've finished. You might change your mind. From now on, you'll be spending more time with Ferhdessar. There's much he can teach you, so try to control your temper. I hereby give the sorcerer my permission to use his gift to keep you under control. Let this be a warning."

It was all fine by Lilith. She couldn't believe that everything had turned out this way, this outcome was beyond her wildest dreams.

"Ferhdessar, I take it that you will do as I wish."

"Of course."

"Good, take her with you. I'll let you decide how much time she spends with you and how much time she spends working."

8

Lilith left her room and walked through the corridors. After a while she reached the tapestry that depicted her native country. As always, she briefly studied this carefree world and compared it to her own memories. As calm and peaceful as the world looked on the tapestry, as harsh it had been in real life. The pond at which the zebras were trying to quench their thirst probably largely consisted of mud and would soon dry up, forcing the people of the savannah to move away and search for another water source. The people in Naftalia didn't have an easy life and they always had to work hard. Everything in Naftalia revolved around survival, and it hadn't been any different for Lilith.

Over the past few weeks, Lilith had built up enough trust with Ferhdessar for him to allow her to walk to and from work by herself. She had kept her temper under control, as the king had advised her to do, and because of that the sorcerer seemed to have become a bit more lenient. She was on her way to the kitchen. She hoped that Ghalatea would be there to tell her what her duties were for the day.

Ever since Lilith had told her story, the Ancilla Princeps had kept her distance. But each day Lilith hoped that Ghalatea would smile at her again and propose to forget all about the past few weeks. It didn't look like that was going to happen any time soon though, because when Lilith opened the door she saw that Ghalatea wasn't in the kitchen.

Aida immediately walked up to her. She had a satisfied smile on her face. Lilith didn't like her; the maidservant enjoyed provoking her. One time, Aida had locked the door when Lilith had gone outside to throw something away. She had stood in the rain for hours and had been soaking wet and frozen to the marrow by the time someone had let her back in again. After that, she'd had a cold for an entire week. To add insult to injury, the Ancilla Princeps had punished her for not having finished her duties on time. Lilith hadn't been given a chance to explain. Ever since, she had tried to steer clear of the maidservant.

"Hey, prisoner, Ghalatea has given you the task of cleaning all the cupboards."

Luckily that wasn't a rotten chore. Lilith shrugged and wanted to walk to the corner where the buckets were. The maidservant, however, stopped her.

"I'll get you some water."

Lilith was surprised, but she soon understood what Aida's plan was. There was a bucket of water boiling on the fire. The maid dropped a cloth in the water and dragged the bucket towards Lilith.

"Here you are."

To provoke Lilith even more, she kept standing in front of her. Lilith shook her head and wanted to walk around Aida to get cold water, but the maid blocked her way. "You're going to use the water I just gave you," she hissed.

Lilith shook her head again. The other maids in the kitchen had all stopped working and were staring at them. Lilith knew they weren't going to help her, so she pushed Aida aside. The maid staggered for a second but quickly regained her balance. She grabbed Lilith's arm and pulled it down. Steam rose up past Lilith's fingers, but she didn't offer any resistance. If she stayed calm and just let it happen, it would probably be over soon.

But when her fingers touched the boiling hot water, Lilith exploded. She hadn't expected Aida to go that far. She pulled her arm back and knocked the maidservant to the ground. One of the girls screamed and Aida eyed Lilith furiously.

"You're going to regret this," the maid growled as she jumped back to her feet.

Lilith flew at her and gave her a few more punches. This girl was a sadist, her torments were worse than what the servi had ever done to her. Aida fought back; she pulled at Lilith's hair and tried to bite her. Lilith could no longer control her anger. The maids screamed. Aida started to cry because she didn't have any energy left to fight back, but Lilith couldn't stop any more. She gave her tormentor a good pummelling. That would teach her to stop treating her like dirt.

Suddenly someone grabbed Lilith's shoulder and pulled her away from Aida. Panting, she stared at the woman lying curled up on the floor. Blood was trickling from her nose and one eye was beaten shut. Slowly her own feeling returned. She looked at her fingers. The blisters had burst open during the fight. She flapped her hands, hoping it would cool them. Then she looked at Aida again. Several girls were kneeling beside her, dabbing her face with wet cloths. Then they helped the maidservant back on her feet.

"You're both coming to the Ancilla Princeps with me," a man's voice said. Lilith hadn't realized until then that a soldier had pulled her off the maidservant.

Ghalatea was pacing the room. Lilith had never seen her like this before. She kept clenching her fists, and Lilith saw that the Ancilla Princeps didn't really know how to deal with the situation. Finally, she looked at Aida, who had been allowed to sit down on a chair.

"What happened?"

"I don't know, Ancilla Princeps", the maid sobbed. "I only brought her some water, so she could get to work, but then she lost it."

Ghalatea shook her head sharply. "Don't play me for a fool. I know what you're like." Then she turned to Lilith. "What do you have to say for yourself?"

"Aida brought me boiling hot water and when I refused to use it she immersed my hand in it. I defended myself."

Lilith wanted to show Ghalatea her burned fingers, but the Ancilla Princeps didn't look at them.

"That's always your excuse, isn't it. You were defending yourself?" She pointed at Aida, but Lilith didn't look up. She knew how badly she had beaten up the girl, but the little vixen had deserved it. "This is taking it a bit far if you're only defending yourself, isn't it?"

Lilith opened her mouth.

"No, Lilith, I don't want to hear it. Others have already told me what happened. You attacked her. If Harald hadn't pulled you off her, you might have beaten her to death." She shook her head once more. "It's disgusting."

It was starting to dawn on Lilith what she had done and she bowed her head in shame.

"You will take over Aida's duties until she is fully recovered and I'll ask Ferhdessar to readjust your wristband."

Lilith was shocked. She knew how much Ghalatea hated it that Ferhdessar used magic on the prisoners. But now the Ancilla Princeps suggested this of her own accord. Before she could say anything, Harald dragged her out of the room and through the corridors. He had a short, whispered conversation with the sorcerer and then left them alone.

Ferhdessar gave her a penetrating look. "And you were doing so well," he said, shaking his head. He got up and grabbed her hand. "But apparently Aida is no saint either."

Lilith nodded enthusiastically. Finally, someone who understood her. She started to relate what had happened.

Ferhdessar interrupted her, however, "The fact that Aida is a mean little vixen, doesn't justify your behaviour." He pointed at the water jug. "Go ahead and cool your hand with water."

Lilith rushed to the corner of the room and poured water over her fingers. The cool liquid was a great relief and she closed her eyes.

"Ghalatea wants me to adjust your wristband. Do you think that will help?" he asked after a long silence.

Lilith shrugged. Ferhdessar grabbed hold of her hand and started to bandage it. He wasn't gentle about it, but Lilith didn't flinch.

"I don't think it will make any difference. You don't respond to pain the same way as other people do. Pain only seems to increase your anger. It means something to you that I can't comprehend."

"So you're taking it off?" she asked hopefully, extending her hand towards him.

Ferhdessar laughed at her. "Of course not. There's no harm in you feeling that you're doing something wrong." He opened a drawer. "The king informed me this morning that he wishes to speak to you. After what happened today, I think it wise to take some precautions."

"I would never hurt lord Yvar," Lilith stammered, startled by his distrust.

"I can't take that risk, Lilith. You lose control much too easily. Could you bare your back, please?"

Lilith hesitantly pulled her tunic over her head without taking her arms out of the sleeves. She clenched the fabric in front of her chest. When Ferhdessar rubbed something cold between her shoulder blades, she couldn't suppress a shiver. It felt as if he was writing something, but she couldn't feel which letters he was forming.

"What are you doing?" she whispered.

Instead of answering her, the sorcerer murmured a few unintelligible sentences. With the last word, something entered her body. It found its way to her neck and stopped just below her skull. It didn't really hurt, but it didn't feel comfortable either, as if it was serving as a warning. Lilith decided to take that warning to heart. She didn't really want to find out what this ritual could do to her.

Only when Ferhdessar had washed his hands, did he give her an explanation: "I could have put you in chains again, but that seemed unnecessarily humiliating. So I administered a temporary, but very powerful, shackle."

"But why on my back?" Lilith rolled her shoulders. They were still itching.

"You can't reach there, so you can't rub it off and undo its effect. All right, you're ready to go."

Ferhdessar took her to the room where she had been taken on her first day. Lilith cast a quick glance at the painted portraits. The sun was shining so brightly that the translucent curtains had been drawn to dim the light. She curtsied a few feet away from the table where the king was sitting.

"Come closer."

She hesitantly did as she was told. The king motioned for her to walk up to his table.

"I want to show you something."

There was a box on the table. Yvar's hand briefly stroked the woodcarvings before he lifted the lid. Intrigued, Lilith leaned forwards and stood on tiptoe. The king picked up an object that was wrapped in rags and handed it to Lilith without saying anything. Ferhdessar was keeping a close eye on her.

"Where did you get this?" she asked in astonishment when she had unfolded the rags. She was holding a figurine.

"Someone called Kasimirh sent it to me. What can you tell me about it?"

Lilith knew the figurine all too well. This was the God Jakob. Or rather, a stone image of Him. His grave features, however, were life-like. The folds of His stone robe fell smoothly around His body. His arms were wide open and Lilith had always felt that God would embrace her if she needed to be held. She'd just never had the courage to ask Him. A man-sized version of the figurine stood in the chapel where Lilith had attended hundreds of services. She had often had the feeling that God was truly present in the statue. At those times she had prayed with even more determination.

The figurine she was now holding in her hands also seemed to radiate life. She stroked the little stone face. Her fingers were trembling.

"Was it my master who sent you this?" She looked up and followed Yvar's eyes, which were staring at Ferhdessar. She hoped the sorcerer would shake his head, or at least tell her that they didn't know for sure.

"We indeed assume it was. I believe that Kasimirh is your master."

Lilith's hope that someone else had sent the figurine was shattered. She tried to figure out what this meant for her, but the king interrupted her thoughts.

"What can you tell us about the figurine?"

"This is Jakob, the one God. What else can I tell you about it? I was forced to strike terror into people and attack their villages in His name." Lilith stepped forwards and rested her hand on the edge of the box. "May I?"

The king nodded his assent. She felt around in the box and came up with a pouch containing three small stones. Her fingers tingled when she touched them and she felt the need to pray. So she took the yellow stone in her right hand and pressed it to her heart. She murmured, "I hold this stone in my hand. I press it to my heart and hear Your voice. The message You give me helps me to remember. You turned us into who we are and taught us to live in harmony with You by our side. I'm grateful for the reminder and show You my gratitude by not forgetting again."

Then Lilith picked up the black stone and repeated the ritual. This time, however, she held the stone to her forehead.

"I hold this stone in my hand. I hold it to my forehead and hear Your voice. The message You give me helps me to learn. You kept taking care of us, but we turned our backs on You and went our own ways. I beg You to show me the right path once more, so I can learn as I walk in Your shadow."

Lilith held the third stone – black with gold veins all over its surface – to her lips.

"I hold this stone in my hand. I press it to my lips and pledge to You that I will live in Your light. I will honour everything to which You gave life. Full of desire, I will follow Your orders to show you that I'm worthy. Full of desire, I will wait for the day when You return to teach me."

Lilith handed the stones back to the king. "There are many different stones and each has its own prayer. The prayers for these three stones are about the promise that Jakob made to the people."

The king rolled the stones around in his hands before putting them back in the pouch. "Ferhdessar told me that Kasimirh has cast a spell on them."

Lilith nodded. Now she understood the irresistible desire to say prayer. This, however, didn't ruin the pleasant feeling she was having.

Next, the king produced a book from the box and gave it to Lilith. The cover told her all she needed to know, but she opened it anyway. She immediately recognized her master's elegant handwriting. He was always working on these books. Whenever she was summoned to him, she had to wait until he put down his pen. He often had ink stains on his fingers, even when she encountered him in the tunnels of the cave.

Lilith had once owned a book just like this one. As a part of her lessons she had copied it herself. She had always been proud of the book, because the master had often praised her for her neat handwriting. Unfortunately, she'd had to leave it behind when she ran away.

Lilith told Yvar and Ferhdessar what they could expect if they read the book. The king took it from her and thumbed through it. He stopped at a page that was richly decorated. Some details were even coloured in with gold leaf.

"He has sent you a special copy. My master didn't decorate all of them. I think that the village chiefs who followed him only received text copies."

Yvar examined the page more closely. Lilith leaned forwards to be able to get a better look as well. With much eye for detail, small people had been depicted who were slaughtering other small people in a huge battle. Demon-like figures, representing false Gods, were seated on the shoulders of the leaders of both parties, whispering commands in their ears. Among the fighting men and women there were also objects to be seen: telescopes, to tell whether the stars were aligned favourably, and strange machines that generated lightning. Several men were even armed with rifles that wiped out large groups of opponents with a single shot. Lilith wondered if this was possible in real life, but the symbolism behind it wasn't lost on her: people would keep pushing boundaries to satisfy their lust for power, risking their own lives in the process.

"This part of the text is probably about the Second Era and the reasons why Jakob severed ties with the world," Lilith explained out loud.

"Interesting," the king mumbled. "I'll do your master a favour: I'll definitely read it."

"Is there anything else?" Lilith asked.

The king shook his head. "Not in the box, but there is something else I'd like to know."

He got up and walked to the wide windowsill. Before he sat down, he opened one of the curtains so that he could look outside.

"Was your master planning to attack me?"

Lilith nodded. "If Merzia joins his cause, we will be one step closer to world peace. My master is convinced that Jakob will return once everyone in the world is a follower of His faith. God has personally promised him this."

Yvar rubbed his chin. Because of the bright sunlight Lilith could only see his dark silhouette. "Has he ever mentioned anything about how he wanted to conquer this country?"

"He never discussed things like that with me. I was only given commands to destroy villages and towns. But it isn't hard to imagine how he would operate. If Merzia doesn't voluntarily surrender to God's will, my master will employ other methods to ensure harmony is restored to the world."

"One way or the other, Kasimirh is going to make sure a new Golden Era begins."

Yvar looked at her. A cloud covered the sun, so Lilith could see his face more clearly. Lilith noticed that he had a worried look in his eyes. She wished she could take his worries away, but then she would have to lie to him. She nodded wordlessly. That was enough.

"What will happen if I join him voluntarily?"

"You'll be initiated in Jakob's teachings. Not much else. My master will gain dominion over Merzia, but since he has to concern himself with other things, the reality will be that you keep your position. At least, that's how things usually went in the towns and villages where I used to live. The master came to initiate everyone and then he left again. Life went on, unless there were signs of people doubting Jakob. Then my master would return to restore order."

"War or peace, it makes no difference to him, as long as the outcome is the same." The king drummed his fingers against his lips. He heaved a sigh.

"There's nothing horrible about following Jakob. It's just that my master isn't a benevolent leader. It's best to stay out of his way." Suddenly Lilith realized what she was suggesting. If Yvar surrendered to her master, she would fall into his hands again. She gave the king a startled look.

"Don't worry, Lilith. We'll make sure that he doesn't get you back. After all, it's also in Merzia's interest to keep you away from him."

Lilith heaved a sigh of relief.

"When is he planning to invade this country?" Ferhdessar asked.

"I don't know."

He regarded her closely while running his hand over the key on his belt.

"He never told me about his next move or when it would take place! He only informed me when he needed me."

"How much time do you think he'll give us to contemplate his offer?"

"I really don't know, Ferhdessar."

She averted her head and stared at the box. "What are you going to do now?" she whispered. "Are you going to join my mas... Kasimirh?"

The king shrugged. "It would help if we knew how much time we have to answer him."

"I'm afraid that I can't help you with that. And I also don't know what his next move will be." She wished she knew, because then she would be able to prepare herself for what was coming as well.

"In that case you may leave." Yvar averted his gaze.

Lilith hesitated briefly but then asked the question burning on her lips: "Can I have the figurine?"

Ferhdessar gave the king a disapproving look. After some thought Yvar asked, "Has Kasimirh put any spells on it?"

"No, he hasn't," the sorcerer answered, "but..."

The king didn't wait for him to finish. "Then she can have it. Give it to her." Ferhdessar shook his head but did as he was told.

Lilith carefully wrapped her fingers around the figurine. "Thank you, my lord."

After Ferhdessar had escorted her from the room, he returned to the king. Shaking his head, he sat down on the windowsill across from Yvar.

"Having her in this palace worries me greatly," the king said. "Especially now that her master has his eye on Merzia. We're going to have to get rid of her."

"I fully agree, but how? I don't know of any place where we can take her to. I don't think any other sorcerer is anxious to take her in, but at the same time only a sorcerer can keep her safe."

"Can't you take away her ability to change? That would render her useless to Kasimirh."

"The only thing I can do is destroy her amulet. But her master will make a new one, so that won't help."

They remained silent for a while. Below them, a horse and wagon moved through the fallow fields, but Yvar didn't seem to notice.

"In that case, I want you to keep a close eye on her. And if the situation requires it, you're going to have to kill her."

Ferhdessar nodded. "I will. But she might yet be of use to us. If I can persuade her to attack Kasimirh, all our problems will be solved at once."

He didn't anticipate many problems. Lilith had more than enough reasons to hate her master.

Yvar's eyes started to shine. "That's a good idea. His own creation will be used against him. Lilith might even thank us for this opportunity."

Back in her room, Lilith was looking for a nice place to put the figurine that she was still holding in her hands. When she had come to a decision, she carefully placed it on her bed and emptied her bedside cabinet. After that, she burned a little bit of sage to create smoke. She murmured a prayer, "I'm sorry, Lord, if I gave You the impression that I deserted You. That was never my intention, but I couldn't continue on the path set out by my master. I still genuinely believe in Your promise to return and I will resume living my life according to Your teachings."

The smoke had disappeared when Lilith ended her prayer, but the scent of sage was still very noticeable. It made her feel safe.

She took off her clothes and examined her back in the mirror. Even though her skin had healed, the welts caused by the scourge were still clearly visible. They would probably never disappear completely, Lilith thought as she ran her fingers over the rough scars. Then she washed off the sign that Ferhdessar had painted between her shoulder blades. The itchy feeling immediately disappeared.

Lilith put her clothes back on and nodded at Jakob before she left her room. There was much to do now that she had to perform Aida's duties as well.

9

"Lilith, I need you."

She turned towards Ferhdessar, who came walking down the corridor.

"I want you to come to the library with me. Maybe you can show me where Kasimirh lives and I hope you can tell me how big the area is that he has converted."

She nodded obediently and Ferhdessar led the way.

"What is the library?"

"It's the place where all of Merzia's knowledge is stored. The library houses the king's collection of books and documents."

Lilith recognized this concept. The walls in her master's study had been covered with books. Over half of them were written by Kasimirh himself as a result of Jakob's teachings, the other books had been bought by her master because he had been interested in their subjects. He had once told Lilith that his collection encompassed the truth and that she had to be extremely careful with it for that reason. Now she was to discover Yvar's truth.

Ferhdessar knocked on a door and was greeted by bumping noises. A short, plump man appeared in the doorway, but as soon as he saw the sorcerer he went back inside to get a bunch of keys. He crossed the corridor to a handsomely wrought door that was the same height as the wall.

"Couldn't you for once come during opening hours, like everybody else?" the man grumbled as he unbolted the door and turned the key. When he looked at Lilith, however, she noticed that his eyes were shining.

Ferhdessar didn't say anything and patted the man on his shoulder as he walked past him.

Overwhelmed by the vastness of the room, Lilith stopped short on the threshold. Along the walls and in the middle of the room there were many bookcases filled with books and scrolls of parchment. Finely-carved wooden spiral staircases led visitors to various balconies, where even more books were to be found. Chandeliers were suspended on rafters protruding from the third floor. The semi-dark above the rafters concealed another two storeys.

Paintings, indicating the subjects of the writings, hung between the bookcases. Lilith walked to a painting of plants. She carefully took one of the books from the shelf and opened it at a random page. She saw a picture of a red flower with a seed pod next to it. There was a description of the plant, which was followed by an explanation of its effects: *The opium poppy can be used for several purposes, but is most often used as a remedy for insomnia. The milky juice has an analgesic and tranquillizing effect. Known side-effects are: overconfidence and recklessness. It prevents anxiety, depression, apprehension…*

"Lilith, where are you?"

She immediately closed the book and put it back in its place. She could see Ferhdessar through the bookshelves. He was standing next to a gigantic orb that represented the earth. He motioned for her to come join him on the little platform. There was a brass keyboard in front of him.

A click sounded whenever Ferhdessar struck a key. It didn't take Lilith much time to realize that he was typing the word "Naftalia". When he had typed the final letter, he pulled a handle. The platform rose silently. The orb started turning.

Small trees growing along river banks were hanging their roots in the water. The deserts were composed of yellow sand dunes, and the silvery snow on the north pole glittered. When everything stopped moving, Naftalia was right in front of them, illuminated by a spotlight.

"Can you point out where Kasimirh lives?"

Trembling like a leaf, Lilith studied the globe. She was looking for the river she usually followed when she flew back to the caves where she used to live. But the lifelike representation of the world stirred up many emotions. It was almost as if the master had sent her on one of her destructive flights again. So she looked away.

Ferhdessar turned around. "What's wrong?"

"It's just… I've looked down on the world from this angle much too often."

Her voice was trembling. Lilith was trying to focus on Ferhdessar's face, so she didn't have to look at the grassy plains. But every time she did look at them, she thought she could see the shadow of a dragon passing over the plains. The zebras seemed to be running away from it, just like they had run away from her in reality. When Lilith blinked, the shadow disappeared, only to reappear somewhere else on the globe.

Ferhdessar had been regarding her with raised eyebrows, but now he said, "All right, I will show it to you another way. Follow me."

He tapped a key and pulled the lever again. As the platform descended, the globe turned back to its starting position, with the spotlight on Merzia.

They climbed the stairs together. At the third floor Ferhdessar picked up a lantern.

"The upper two floors house the books that are consulted the least," he explained. "We also keep the atlases there because most people use the globe. I hope a two-dimensional map will have less of an impact on you."

Lilith nodded.

It took Ferhdessar several tries before he found the right book. He carefully wiped the dust off its cover and turned around.

Lilith, however, was nowhere to be seen. An unpleasant sense of foreboding came over Ferhdessar when he saw a shadow moving along the bookcases on the other side. In a faraway corner of the library, the controversial books were to be found. Hardly anyone took the effort to read them, but if they fell into the wrong hands, they could be highly dangerous.

Ferhdessar ran to the other side, but he was too late. Out of all the books in the library, Lilith had chosen the single one that she should never had laid eyes on. It was a book in which Margal had recorded her views about the human race, which, in her opinion, was superior to all other races. The Goddess had described in elaborate detail how the world could be Purified. Ferhdessar didn't want Lilith to know anything about this religion, because he was convinced it would drive her back into her master's arms.

Lilith was holding the book in such a way that the little light that reached this dark corner of the library fell onto the pages. She was clearly straining her eyes to be able to read the words. Only when Ferhdessar pulled the book out of her hands, did she look up. Her eyes were burning with hate.

"So my master was right after all," she hissed. "Why haven't you killed me yet? What are you planning to do with me?"

"No, Kasimirh wasn't right. And neither are you. You weren't meant to see that book."

"Obviously not."

She turned around and ran down the spiral staircase. Ferhdessar stepped forwards but wasn't able to grab her.

"Lilith, don't run away! It's not what you think," he yelled.

She didn't stop, so he focussed on the door. It slammed shut and was locked with loud clicking noises. Lilith pulled on the door handle but when she couldn't open the door, she kicked it, infuriated.

Ferhdessar didn't hurry. It was better to let her cool down first. Squatting down on her hunches, Lilith kept banging on the door as if she could shatter the thick wood.

"Lilith, stop making a spectacle of yourself. There's no use. You're only hurting yourself."

She glanced over her shoulder. When she saw him coming closer, she started to scratch on the door. She called out for help, but there was no one who could hear her. Ferhdessar had made sure of that. He couldn't run the risk of the librarian suddenly opening the door. It would give Lilith a chance to escape before he'd had the opportunity to speak with her.

"Lilith, hear me out," he said when he stood next to her.

"Why? You all think I'm a child of the devil."

Lilith had stopped trying to escape. She sat with her back against the door and was resting her head on her knees. Ferhdessar squatted in front of her, but she turned her head away to avoid his gaze. Despite her stubborn attitude, he tried to explain it to her.

"King Yvar has kept these books to remind himself of how dangerous certain people can be."

"You mean the shapeshifters?"

Lilith's voice sounded offended and Ferhdessar heaved a deep sigh.

"No, I mean the people who wrote those books and believe what's written in them."

She snorted sceptically. "Why did I think I could trust you people? It's always the same, no matter where I go, but this was the last time."

Ferhdessar gave an annoyed sigh as he rose to his feet. He wanted to help Lilith back up, but she pulled her arm away. They left the library in silence.

When they reached her room, they both went their separate ways. Lilith laid her hand on the door handle and watched Ferhdessar walk away. Without meaning to, he had warned her about the king and she was grateful to him.

The book hadn't told her anything she didn't know already; humans thought shapeshifters were dangerous, possessed by the devil and always out to do evil. Humans were the chosen ones who had to vanquish the spawn of the devil. Everything her master had told her was true; humans really did want to kill her. By running away, she had abandoned the only place where she was truly safe.

Ferhdessar had long since turned the corner when Lilith decided she would leave the palace. There was no reason to stay here any more. Sooner or later, these people would show their true nature, but she wasn't going to wait for that to happen.

After she had gathered some of her belongings, she pulled a blanket off the bed. Wrapping it around her shoulders, she looked around the room one more time. The small room had become her home and she had felt safe here. She'd never expected that everything could change this abruptly.

But then again, do you ever see through anything? her inner voice scoffed. Lilith could only agree. She didn't understand anything of the world and every time she thought she had caught on, it turned out that she couldn't be farther away from the truth.

Embittered, Lilith left her room. She hurried through the corridors. She was scared someone would stop her, but nobody paid her any attention, not even the soldiers. At the end of the corridor she saw the door to the outside world. She would soon be leaving the palace and its inhabitants. She might even return to the only other country she knew. In Naftalia she could continue fighting against the humans. It was the logical thing to do.

When she opened the door, she was greeted by a cold wind. Lilith wrapped the blanket tightly around her and crossed the threshold. She halted for a moment. A strange feeling of freedom came over her. But you're not out of the woods yet, she sternly reminded herself. She started walking again.

The city looked very different from when she had been brought to the palace. That day, the unremitting snowstorms had covered Nadesh in a white blanket, which had made it difficult to discern the outlines of the buildings. But now the streets were clean.

Lilith stopped on the corner of a street to take a good look at her surroundings. The sun, shining palely in the bright blue sky, was reflected in the smooth bricks. As a result, the upper storeys of the buildings seemed to dissolve into thin air. The houses all looked very much alike. Block after block, they were built in the same slender, plain style. The repetition, however, wasn't boring. It added to the beauty of the city.

Just like the palace, the houses had large windows. Lilith couldn't stop herself from looking inside. The people of Nadesh personalized their interiors by painting the walls in bright colours. Some people had plants on their windowsills. Other houses had sculptures on display or paintings and tapestries hanging on the walls. Now and again a resident looked up and waved as Lilith walked past, making her feel as if she was caught doing something illegal. She bowed her head and quickened her pace.

Throughout the town, narrow staircases and bridges connected streets and squares with each other. Whenever she had a choice, Lilith followed the paths that led down, but more often than not, those paths started to climb again after a while, forcing her to stand still to find her bearings. After having wandered around the city for hours, Lilith finally reached a bridge leading to another rock pillar.

She crossed it with a sigh of relief.

As the night fell, it started to rain. The lights in the houses were lit and Lilith saw people eating their dinner. A few hours later the people closed their curtains. When the lights in the houses had long since been turned off, Lilith finally arrived at the city gate. She hid in the porch of a shop. It was a good vantage point to keep an eye on the soldiers guarding the city.

"What a beastly night!"

A man stepped into the porch.

Lilith nodded a greeting and stepped aside. What did this man want?

"It doesn't look like it's going to clear up anytime soon, so maybe you should just continue your journey. I hope you don't have much farther to go."

Lilith shrugged. The man produced a key from his pocket and opened the door. "Either way, I wish you a pleasant evening."

"Likewise," Lilith answered. She laughed to herself. Because she was trying to escape, she thought that everyone in the city was trying to stop her. But this man had seen nothing but a woman taking shelter from the rain. She looked at the gate again. Would the soldiers also mistake her for a regular passer-by?

There weren't many people leaving the city at this time of night, but those who did make their way to the gate were stopped. Lilith couldn't hear what was being said, but after a short conversation the people were allowed to proceed. It started to dawn on Lilith, however, that the small door in the big gate wouldn't be opened for her. So many hours had passed since she had left the palace that, by now, Ferhdessar had undoubtedly told the soldiers to be on the lookout for her.

Now what? Lilith considered finding another way out but she doubted that there would be one. Tomorrow it might be busier at the gate, increasing her chances to escape unseen. The longer she thought about it, the more convinced she became, so she stepped out of the porch and turned into a side-street.

Not much later she found a little space underneath a staircase. She curled herself up in an attempt to get warm. Clutching the figurine of Jakob to her chest, Lilith fell asleep.

Lilith had been watching the gate for quite some time. During the morning, the soldiers were occupied with traders who wanted to enter the city, but people leaving the city still had to undergo a thorough check.

It wasn't until late morning that it started to get busier. Lilith realized that circumstances wouldn't get much better than this, so she stepped out of the shadow of the building. Pretending that she had every right to leave the city, Lilith walked towards the gate. She joined a group of travellers with a horse and wagon. They slowly advanced in the direction of the gate. Lilith pulled her blanket up so that it covered part of her face. She focussed on her hands in an attempt to get them to stop trembling. It only made her more nervous, because it reminded her of what she was about to do.

Two soldiers went to stand in the middle of the road. Lilith slowed her pace until she was walking behind the wagon and waited for what would happen next. Even though she heard two men talking to each other, she couldn't understand what was being said. She nearly had a heart attack when a soldier suddenly turned up next to her. She bit down on her blanket only just in time to muffle a squeal and quickly turned away from the soldier. After the man had glanced into the wagon, he yelled to the people in the front that they were allowed to walk on. He even wished them a pleasant journey.

So far, everything was going according to plan. The group started moving again and Lilith quickened her pace to join the people in the front. The arch that housed the gate was supported by pillars that were carved out of the rocks. Lilith touched her wristband as her eyes searched for a symbol that indicated how far she was allowed to go. But there didn't seem to be any sign: no marking in the stones, no way-marker posts along the road, absolutely nothing. She wondered what would happen if she went too far, but she wasn't really scared. Ferhdessar had said that she endured the effect of the other wristband too well, so maybe it would be the same with this one.

I'm free! Lilith took her final step, but as soon as her foot touched the ground, she felt some kind of pressure on her throat. She told herself that it was just nerves, but when she took another step, the pressure increased. She tried to suck in air, but her breathing was laboured. At the same time, she was doing her utmost to conceal the fact that there was something wrong with her. She didn't want to draw any attention to herself, not now she had managed to escape. She draped the blanket more loosely around her shoulders and pulled at the neck of her tunic. With every step it became harder to breathe.

"Are you all right?"

A woman came to walk next to her and gave her a worried look. Lilith wanted to answer, but she couldn't voice any words, so she just nodded. The woman walked on but glanced over her shoulder one last time. Lilith raised her hand to wave her thanks and tried to smile.

When she had rounded the corner, she stopped. She threw her shoulders back and tilted her head. That didn't help either. She wasn't about to admit defeat just yet. Maybe she just had to cover a certain distance. So Lilith started to run, but she couldn't keep that up very long. Her throat was squeezed tighter and tighter. Wheezing, she sucked in small amounts of air as she banged her wristband on a sharp ledge. There wasn't so much as a scratch on the metal. Her final blow was powerless.

Lilith realized that she couldn't go on, because it would mean certain death. She reluctantly walked back to the city. The pressure on her throat instantly disappeared when she walked through the gate. She greedily breathed in big gulps of air. She was sorely tempted to keep standing there for a few minutes to draw some deep breaths, but she walked on regardless. A soldier appeared before her. When Lilith wanted to walk around him, he barred her way again.

"Get out of my way," Lilith said hoarsely. Her mind was already working hard to come up with another plan to escape.

"I want to know what your business is in Nadesh."

"Get… out… of… my… way." Lilith scowled at him.

The soldier made a gesture with his hand. Lilith was immediately grabbed from behind. She pulled herself free with a single movement and turned around. Just before she could hit the man, her arms were twisted behind her back and she was forced down on her knees.

"We have orders from the palace to bring you back," said the man who had stopped her.

"I'm not the woman you're looking for," Lilith said and she wriggled to break free.

"Pull the other one. We've been watching you since last night." She looked up at him in surprise. "Lord Ferhdessar wanted you to attempt an escape first."

Of course, Ferhdessar wanted her to understand the effect of the wristband, so that she would never try to escape again. He had simply waited for her to return of her own accord.

"I have to admit that you got pretty far, we were about to come after you," the soldier continued as he motioned to another soldier. "You're not the first person to attempt an escape, but most people turn around after their first step out of the gate. There has been only one occasion where we had to carry someone back because he had passed out."

A small wagon pulled up in front of her. Lilith was pushed in, a soldier climbed on the wagon and they rode off. Lilith cast a final glance at the rapidly shrinking gate. Even though her prison cell was as big as the entire city, a feeling of claustrophobia washed over her as though she were locked away in a small dungeon.

It wasn't long before they arrived at the palace. They had only just entered, when they ran into Ghalatea.

"You're late," she said sternly. Then she shook her head. "You look a mess."

Ashamed, Lilith dusted some sand off her clothes, but it didn't make much difference. There was mud on her trousers. Apparently she had lain down in some mud last night, but she hadn't even noticed.

"I'll take her from here," Ghalatea said to the soldier and she escorted Lilith to the kitchen. "You're going to get yourself something to eat first. After that, lord Ferhdessar wishes to see you."

Ghalatea pushed a bowl of soup into Lilith's hands and motioned impatiently that she was to eat it right away. Lilith gratefully took a mouthful. Again, the woman gave her a searching look.

"Have you spent the night outside?"

Lilith nodded as she chewed on a piece of potato. There was an irritated look in the Ancilla Princeps' eyes and she called Lilith a foolish woman. Then she grabbed herself a chair and, to make sure the other servants wouldn't understand her, said in her own language, "Ferhdessar has told me what happened yesterday. You couldn't have been more wrong. My mother was a unicorn shifter. The people who wrote that book killed her for that reason. Mine was a lesser sin in their eyes, so they *only* maimed me. I wouldn't be here if the king worshipped Margal."

Drinking the last sip of broth from her bowl, Lilith looked the Ancilla Princeps in the eye. Her story sounded plausible, so she nodded. Then she got up. "What are my duties for today?" Her voice was still sounding hoarse.

Ghalatea also got to her feet. "You'll have to go to lord Ferhdessar first. Wash yourself before you go to him, because you reek. You're going to wash your clothes in your own time. If the stains don't come out, you'll have to pay for your new clothes yourself."

The other women in the kitchen sniggered softly. Lilith lowered her eyes and wordlessly grabbed a bucket. She wanted to fill it with hot water but there wasn't any left. A large cauldron was suspended over a fire, but it had only just been hung there. When Lilith commented on it, the Ancilla Princeps grabbed the bucket from her hands and filled it with ice cold water that came directly from the waterfalls. Lilith shivered at the idea of having to wash herself with it. Nevertheless, she left the kitchen without protest. It probably wouldn't be too bad if she stayed close to the fire.

Thirty minutes later, Lilith walked into the garden behind the library. The garden had been laid out on the ledge of the highest rock peak and overlooked the west side of the city and the fields at the foot of the rocks. Ghalatea had told her that Ferhdessar was to be found in the shed that was built against the palace.

The big doors were open. The sorcerer was busy stretching thin, black fabric over the frame of his aircraft. He was so engrossed in his work that he didn't even notice Lilith entering the shed. Lilith was amazed to see a life-size version of the models she had seen in his room.

"I didn't know you also had a big aircraft."

Disturbed at his work, Ferhdessar looked up. "Why are you here?"

"Ghalatea told me you wanted to talk to me."

"Hmm, is that what she said? And you don't think it necessary for us to have a chat?"

Lilith wondered what he wanted to hear. "I'd like to apologize. I should have stopped to think before getting angry."

He observed her thoughtfully. "I don't know how much your apology is worth. If you hadn't been wearing that bracelet, you'd have been gone. Maybe these are just empty words to soften me up."

"I assure you they are not. I've thought things through and I've changed my views."

Wiping his hands clean, Ferhdessar walked to the workbench. He handed Lilith a book. "To make sure that you understand we don't live according to the rules in that book, I'd like you to read another passage."

Lilith opened the book at the leather bookmark. She skimmed the page.

"Read it out loud," he commanded as she looked up in shock.

Lilith swallowed before she read out, "At least as dangerous is the race of sorcerers. With a single word or gesture they can exercise power over any other creature. Some of them pose as missionaries of the Gods who want to help the human race. This is a deception. The superior race doesn't need help. If we give them our trust, we will be destroyed. We should no longer close our eyes to the truth, instead we should fight against this evil. Only then…"

Lilith wanted to read on, but Ferhdessar interrupted her in exasperation.

"I've heard enough, it makes me sick. Unfortunately, some people still attach importance to these ideas."

She nodded her understanding. Apparently this palace housed

130

many people who had ample reason to hate Margal's followers. Everything was so confusing.

"I understand what you're trying to tell me Ferhdessar. I'm sorry about yesterday. I should never have doubted you. I truly am sorry. Shall I show you where I used to live?"

"Later. I've stuff to do right now."

He got back to his aircraft. Lilith seated herself on the workbench. They both remained silent for a long time. Lilith watched how he glued the wide strips of fabric onto the aircraft. She couldn't imagine that thing ever taking flight.

"Can I ask you something, Ferhdessar?" Lilith cut into the silence.

"It's my task to answer your questions." His voice oozed unwillingness.

"Was my master right? The book that I found did say that people hate what I am? And they attacked Ghalatea. Were my actions justified after all?"

"This is what I was afraid of."

Lilith looked at him uncomprehendingly.

"That you would find a reason to justify your master's behaviour. What if I told you he was right? Will you go back to him then?"

He squinted as he looked at her. Shivering, Lilith shrugged.

"I don't know," she whispered. It was hard to admit to that, but she didn't want to lie either. "Do you think he was sincere, Ferhdessar?"

"If I were to tell you now that it was all right to attack the Naftalians, I would be just as bad as your master."

Lilith despondently bowed her head. "That's almost the same as openly admitting that you agree."

Ferhdessar went to stand right in front of her. "No, it's not," he said sharply. "In my opinion there's no justification for what Margal has done, but I don't know if it's sufficient reason for revenge. Many people would agree with you, but others would admire it if you chose a different path. It's for you to decide what's the right thing to do."

"But it's so hard. I'm sure you have an opinion about it."

There was a long silence before Ferhdessar admitted, "I do. I condemn what the Naftalians did. But what your master made you do – and especially what he did to you to make you obey him – is worse in my book. So if you want to take revenge on anyone, it should be Kasimirh."

Lilith bowed her head and started to tremble.

"Where would you have gone if you had managed to escape?" he asked.

Lilith averted her head. Ferhdessar held the key under her nose. "You know what the king has said."

"I think I would have returned to my master. That's what I wanted…" Ferhdessar shook his head. "But I probably would have changed my mind," she added quickly.

"That's why I brought you back. Of course you being a prisoner was part of the reason, but my main goal was to protect you from yourself."

Frowning, Lilith looked at him. Could it be true that he was concerned about her even though he was hurting her? She decided that was impossible.

For a minute it seemed as if Ferhdessar wanted to walk away, but then he turned back to face her. "Where does your anger come from?"

Lilith had to think about that. "I can't stand it if someone tries to corner me."

"Does it make you feel strong?"

Lilith nodded. "At those moments, I want others to show me respect. They don't realize who I am, but they should be afraid of me. I know that I'm stronger than they are. Aida knows this now as well." Lilith knew that this conversation was also about her fight with the maidservant, so she might as well bring it up herself. "But at the same time, I'm not as strong as I'd like to be, because whenever I release my anger, I lose control. I have to be forced to stop. Either by someone else or by the fact that there's nothing left to destroy."

Lilith looked outside through the open doors. It was so hard to admit that this was who she was.

"Did your master take advantage of your anger?"

"I think so. He told me to beware the people, and I suppose he taught me to hate humans. When I change into a dragon, anger is the first emotion that I feel." She had never thought about it like that. "You know what it is, Ferhdessar, anger is an easy emotion. Much easier than grief or fear. It's easier to hate someone than to love them. At those moments, anger justifies everything. It can become so overpowering that it impairs your ability to think, and sometimes, no most times, that feels really good."

Ferhdessar didn't respond. To Lilith's amazement she didn't see disapproval on his face, whereas to her mind it was loathsome that it worked that way. She wanted to use her anger to feel strong, but in reality she was a weakling. She was shocked to realize she despised herself for this.

"Maybe you should use your anger to make everything right," the sorcerer interrupted her train of thought.

"What do you mean?"

"You can use your anger to eliminate Kasimirh."

"I don't know if I can," she whispered.

That clearly did displease Ferhdessar. "Wouldn't it feel good to fight against him? To know that you're stronger than he is? You can do it, Lilith. And you're the only one who should do it."

Lilith shrugged. "I really don't know. I know that I should hate him, and that should make it easier to destroy him, but..." She shook her head.

It was too hard to admit that, in spite of everything, she still looked upon her master as some kind of father. Kasimirh had often told her that he was proud of her. She needed that kind of validation. He had acted as her patron. She had been grateful for that, despite the things he had asked her to do. Now that she had been separated from him for so many months, his protective side dominated her memories. It sometimes seemed as if the man she had ran away from only existed in her nightmares.

"Will you protect me if I can't hurt him when the time comes?" she asked.

Ferhdessar gave her a reassuring smile. "I'll make sure that you'll never fall into his hands again."

"Thank you."

His gaze wandered for a second and his face darkened. Suddenly he grabbed hold of her chin, forcing her to look him in the eye. "But it would be best if you did it yourself." A shiver ran down her spine as he regarded her closely to see if she understood him. "It would be best if you did it yourself," he mumbled again and then he let go of her.

Lilith lowered herself down from the workbench and walked outside. When she looked up, she saw the blue banners flying in the ever present wind. With the sun shining through them, they were hardly visible. She stared at them for a while and then walked to the edge of the garden. Lilith forced herself to think about her master.

"I hate you!" she shouted against the wind.

The three words didn't mean anything. She heaved a disappointed sigh. Why was it that, when it came to him, she couldn't call up the one emotion that was always so near the surface? Whenever she so much as thought about the servi – or Aida – her muscles tightened and her body shivered with the desire to hurt them. But whenever she thought about her master, she felt small and insignificant and she became scared. She could feel the anger, but if she actively tapped into it, a scorching heat devoured her, causing her to quickly let go of her anger and hide away in a corner of her mind, shaking, until she had comforted herself with the lie that her master had always protected her.

Lilith was resting her elbows on the wall and supported her head with her hands. She was searching for a memory to fuel her anger. It wasn't long before she thought of Myar. She had rescued the boy from the claws of a lioness. At the time, she hadn't understood what had gotten into her, but she had taken the boy with her to her cabin and she had taken care of him. The boy had had absolute confidence in her. Her care had helped him recover quickly and he had been deeply grateful to her. Even now, she could still feel how confusing that had been. Myar had been the first human who hadn't been afraid of her. He had judged her on what she had done for him.

The people, however, though that she had bewitched the child.

To exorcize the devil, they had put him on a ridiculous diet, which had eventually killed him. But the people had blamed her for Myar's death. In a state of fury, Lilith had flown out. She had killed the priest who had been responsible for the boy's death.

This had played havoc with her master's plans. So he had returned to restore order and had promised the people that he would slay the dragon. They had acted out a fight during which Lilith hadn't been allowed to fight back, even though her master had wounded her several times.

Kasimirh had laughed out loud each time that the crowd had roared. It had been a long time before that laugh hadn't haunted her nightmares any more. Lilith had always told herself that his excitement – just like the fight – had been an act, but part of her suspected that this wasn't true. In reality he had probably enjoyed hurting her.

Still shivering, Lilith opened her eyes. *You deserved it. You had to be punished for your disobedience.*

"No, he could have solved it differently, but he deliberately humiliated me," she whispered to herself. Then she straightened her back and screamed, "I hate you, master!" She clenched her fists, but that didn't help to give the words any weight. She shook her head in defeat.

All of a sudden Ferhdessar stood next to her. He gazed at the southern horizon before he looked at her.

"I think we want the same thing. I want to defeat Kasimirh to protect Merzia, and you still have a personal vendetta to settle. If we work together, we can both achieve our goals."

"No, I want to stay as far away from him as possible."

"Don't you understand that he'll keep following you forever if you keep running away? As long as he's alive, you'll never be free. You have to end this. Let's make a deal: I'll help you and you'll help me. By working together, we can defeat him."

Lilith squinted. Could she trust him?

"I won't lie, I'm not doing this for you. My objectives are protecting the king and this country. But I don't have any reason to hurt you. I promise you that, as long as it doesn't stop me from obtaining my objectives, I'll protect you, but I don't see any reason why protecting you would get in the way of achieving my goals."

He looked her straight in the eye. Lilith couldn't fathom what was going through his mind, so she shrugged. "With you by my side I may find the courage."

Ferhdessar extended his hand and she shook it. "In that case, we have a deal, Lilith. I truly believe we will all benefit from this."

10

Ghalatea guided her horse down the path leading out of the city and onto the plain. Now and again she encountered people on wagons leaving the city or coming from the opposite direction. Some greeted her. The Ancilla Princeps enjoyed the ride, because the view of the sloping landscape and the trees in the distance was magnificent.

The sun was powerful enough to warm the air, but the temperature on the shady side of the rocks was low enough to make her shiver.

After a while she reached the foot of the rocks. Ghalatea spurred on her horse and hurriedly rode in the direction of the army camp, situated to the right. She was elated to see her husband again, even if it was to say goodbye.

She had to wait for the gates to open, but as soon as she rode through them, two guards walked up to her.

"Ghalatea, are you here to say goodbye to your husband?" one of them asked cheerfully.

She could immediately tell by his walk that it was Olav. His leg had been wounded during a mission and now he was a guard of the fortress. Ghalatea gave him a friendly smile and asked if he knew where Rogan could be found. Olav nodded.

"He's probably at headquarters."

Ghalatea rode on.

"He'll be pleased to see you again, Ghalatea!" he called after her.

She turned around and waved. "He's not the only one."

Ghalatea rode past the barracks, which were unoccupied at this time of the day. She smiled as she remembered the time when Rogan was also still accommodated in one of these buildings. Back then, it had always been a challenge to find a place where they could be alone for a little while. Fortunately, her husband had a room of his own now where they could retire to whenever she came to visit him.

Even though she couldn't see the shooting ranges behind the barracks, the loud bangs told her that the soldiers were busy training. Rifles had been introduced into the army not all that long ago, and her husband had complained that they were much too inconvenient. He, and many other older soldiers, preferred the sword to weapons that had to be reloaded after each shot.

Rogan was commander of a fighting unit and Ghalatea would have liked to see him use a rifle. Because that would mean he could hide in some bushes and take out the enemy from a great distance without running any risks himself. When she had said this to him, however, Rogan had sneered, "Right, and then every enemy in the wide vicinity knows where I am, and they can all throw themselves at me at the same time." Ghalatea had been sure that he was overreacting, but she had dropped the issue.

At the fortified headquarters she was again greeted by a soldier. This one was still very young and she didn't recognize him.

"My lady, what brings you to this fortress?"

"Could you please inform lord Rogan that his wife is here to see him?" she asked as she dismounted.

This clearly aroused the young man's curiosity and he observed her closely. She noticed his gaze lingering on her veil. Ashamed, Ghalatea briefly averted her eyes. But then she looked him straight in the eye and snapped at him, "At once!"

The man flinched and quickly bowed before he walked inside. The other guard chuckled, but Ghalatea gave him an angry glare. The soldier immediately went back to staring straight ahead.

Ghalatea let her gaze wander across the vast square. Nothing indicated that the soldiers were preparing to leave the fortress. The square was empty. The four watchtowers soared high above her and stood out against the blue sky. The guards inside the towers walked around calmly, everything was quiet.

Ghalatea turned around to the sound of doors opening. Rogan came walking out. His grey hair glittered in the sunlight. He wore the same uniform as the Royal Guard, but being commander of a fighting unit, the colours of his clothes were brown and green. The golden symbol of the Merzian kingdom was clearly visible on his chest. Below the symbol he wore the emblem of his unit: a white mare without a horn. It was an homage to Ghalatea. Yvar allowed his commanders to pick their own emblems, because he was aware of the power that could radiate from them. Ghalatea was proud that her husband had insisted on this symbol for his unit's emblem.

This, however, wasn't the uniform Rogan wore on missions. This was his ceremonial uniform. Her husband wouldn't often be seen wearing his battle gear while he was in the fortress, because it was worn-out and dirty due to the blood that was soaked into the fabric. His eyes were beaming and he kissed her.

"Rogan…"

Ghalatea blushed and pointed at the two guards. They were pretending not to have seen anything. The young soldier's cheeks were still red.

"Ghalatea, the entire world can know that I love you. It has been way too long since we saw each other last."

He put her arm in his.

"Are you busy?" she asked as they walked away. Her horse would be brought to the stables by another soldier.

"Most of the preparations have been taken care of, so I can spend the rest of the afternoon with you."

"That's nice," Ghalatea said, smiling.

After Rogan had closed the door of his room he asked, "What did you do to that young guard? He was shaking like a leaf when he came to tell me you were here."

Ghalatea shrugged. Rogan walked up to her and took her in his arms. His beard pricked her forehead and she could feel his body-heat and his muscles through his clothes.

"He stared at your face too long, didn't he?"

She nodded.

"When will you finally understand that men look at you because you're beautiful and not because of your scar?"

"Rogan, he could have been my grandson!" she called out in dismay, "You can't fool me any more."

"You look much younger than you really are, and I think you're gorgeous."

Ghalatea looked up at him, smiling. Rogan was the only one who could say that and make her believe he was sincere. He caressed her face and gave her another kiss.

"I was hoping you would come."

Ghalatea sat down next to Rogan when he seated himself on the sofa. "I couldn't let you leave without saying goodbye, now could I," she said.

"Will you stay here tonight? We're leaving in the morning."

"I'd love to stay, Rogan. The palace will be so empty the coming months. Even though I can't see you regularly, I often look down, because I know you're at the fortress. It's different when I know that you're not here."

Rogan smiled. "I do the same thing. Sometimes I even think that I see you. And who knows, maybe I do."

They talked some more about how they were both doing and then Rogan asked, "Do you know anything about lord Yvar's prisoner? I was told that she served the man who's now threatening Merzia."

Ghalatea told him a few things about Lilith. She still got angry when she thought about everything the woman had done. But what annoyed her most, was that her faith in the prisoner had been unjustified. She had been deaf to what others had been trying to tell her, because Lilith had seemed so helpless. Her husband clearly picked up on her frustrations.

"The way I see it, she's a soldier who followed orders. She's well trained."

"But you wouldn't do things like that if you were asked to, would you?" she asked horrified.

Rogan thought about that for a moment. "If this Kasimirh were to attack us next week, I would have no qualms about fighting back. If the king orders us to attack him on his own territory, I will do that. Is that any different from what Lilith has done?"

"She has killed so many people."

"Because she is so much stronger. A soldier carries out his commander's orders. A soldier doesn't ask questions."

Ghalatea stared at her hands and shrugged. Her husband's words made her question her feelings. "You fight against other soldiers. There were innocent people among Lilith's victims: women and children. People who never so much as touched a weapon and didn't stand a chance against her."

"I'm not saying that what she did isn't horrible. But did she have a choice?"

Ghalatea shrugged and thought about Aida. The bell on top of the building started to toll.

"Time to eat."

Ghalatea nodded. They walked arm in arm to the dining room. They were again greeted by Olav. He grabbed a few rolls of bread from a dish and put them on the plates in front of them. He also served them some vegetables and meat. Before they started their meal, however, they folded their hands and Rogan led in prayer.

"Tomorrow you'll return to the place where you first met her, Rogan," Olav said with his mouth full, after they had eaten in silence for a while.

Ghalatea gave a bashful smile. Her cheeks turned an even deeper shade of red when Rogan answered, "I knew from the very first moment I laid eyes on her that I would love her forever."

His hand briefly touched her arm and she nodded. Teasingly she said to Olav, "I had no choice but to marry him. His letters were very clear about that."

Olav laughed and Rogan pretended to be offended, "Unbelievable, I go out of my way for her and this is what I get in return."

"That's true, Ghalatea, he was punished with many extra chores because his mind was occupied with you instead of with the threat posed by Margal," Olav said.

"That's what I meant, I had no choice," Ghalatea winked. "But I wouldn't have it any other way. I couldn't wish for a better husband than Rogan."

Her husband gave a satisfied smile. Ghalatea thought back to thirty-seven years ago. She didn't have any recollections of their first meeting, but she had heard many stories about it. First from the nurses, but later also from soldiers and from Rogan himself.

Ghalatea's flight from Margal's followers had led her to the southern fortress. Severely weakened, she had collapsed upon reaching safety. Rogan had caught her and carried her to sick-quarters. He hadn't left her bedside until she was brought to Nadesh with the other refugees.

Ghalatea hadn't come to until she was in the palace. The stories about Rogan, and the letters he wrote her, were a small ray of hope that had kept her going. She had fallen for Rogan even before she had seen him.

"We teased him a lot," Olav said.

Rogan protested, but Ghalatea laughed. "Still, I was told that you took over many of his duties, so that he could stay with me during those first few days," she added.

"I won't ever forget that," Rogan said gratefully.

Olav shrugged. "You would have done the same for me."

As they continued eating, laughter could be heard coming from their table time and again. The two men had been best friends for many years. Even during the war started by Margal, their friendship already went back quite a few years. Later, Ghalatea had also developed a strong bond with Olav. So he had been best man at their wedding.

The next morning Ghalatea woke up in Rogan's arms. He softly caressed her shoulder and whispered, "It's always wonderful to have you here with me. This will keep me going for months. Which is not to say that I won't miss you."

Ghalatea sat up and kissed him. "I know."

Then she got up to get dressed. She washed in front of the mirror. As always, she turned her head away so she only saw the undamaged side of her face. Rogan got up as well and went to stand behind her. He grabbed hold of her head and turned it in the direction of the mirror.

"Rogan, don't..." Ghalatea whispered.

"Will you just look at your bright-blue eyes and the lovely shape of your lips? Everything about your face is equally beautiful. You're not a spark less attractive than before the Naftalians dropped by. You've grown a bit older, but that only makes you even more beautiful, my love. Your eyes undoubtedly look wiser, but you hardly have any wrinkles and your flowing hair is just as brown as when I first met you. In spite of everything you went through, the lines around your mouth aren't grim. Instead, it seems as if there's always a faint smile on your lips."

Ghalatea had closed her eyes. Tears were streaming down her face.

"Why can't you see that? It's such a small part of your face that's gone."

She opened her eyes and looked in the mirror. She tried her hardest to see what Rogan described, but she couldn't. All she saw was the hole in her skin. Even if she turned her other cheek towards the mirror, she still only saw her ruined appearance. So she closed her eyes again. Rogan let go of her head and went to stand in front of her. Then he wrapped his arms around her.

"I hope you're not mad at me for doing this," he whispered in her ear.

Ghalatea shook her head. "I know why you do it, Rogan. And I wish I could see things the way you do." With a deep sigh she rested her head against his chest.

Then Rogan handed her back her veil. She wrapped it around her head and her husband secured the left side on her right shoulder.

After a quick breakfast it was time to say goodbye.

"Will you be careful?" Ghalatea whispered. Now that they were truly saying goodbye, she was starting to feel anxious. She always felt that way when her husband was sent on a mission, one could never be sure that a soldier would return.

"Of course, always."

The light-heartedness in his voice calmed her down somewhat. They hugged each other once more before they walked outside. Rogan had a final meeting in the main building, where the king would address him and the other commanding officers.

Ghalatea would await the soldiers' departure in the square with the other women who had just said goodbye to their husbands as well.

It was busy in the square today. Wagons were being packed and lined up at the last minute. There were steel wagons among them to transport the ammunition and rifles. The horses were whinnying nervously and pulled on their reins. It was nowhere near the entire army that was assembling to go south, but nonetheless, no fewer than a thousand soldiers were assembled in the square. They were to join the army that was permanently stationed at the southern fortress. Some ten thousand soldiers would stay behind in Nadesh.

All the preparations were making the women nervous. It had been decades since an army of this capacity had been mobilized. The women kept telling each other that it was just a precaution. Merzia had to be ready in case of an attack. There wasn't any real threat yet, so everything would probably blow over. But looking at all the tense faces around her, Ghalatea knew that it wouldn't make any difference. She was glad that the king held Lilith captive. If she had still been a part of the enemy forces, this army might not have stood a chance.

At long last, the commanding officers came out, followed by the Royal Guard with Yvar and Ferhdessar in their midst. As one, the soldiers lined themselves up in orderly rows.

The king let his gaze pass over the army before he started to speak, "My heart fills with pride when I see you all standing here. You are the chosen ones who are going to defend this country and I know that we can rely on you. Go with the protection of the Gods and in the name of Merzia."

The soldiers responded to these words with a salute and, as if someone had given a sign, the one thousand soldiers bowed as one.

The king had said that the soldier's task was defensive, not offensive, but still some of the women started to cry. Ghalatea had never done that, because she knew that it would make it even harder for the soldiers to leave. When Rogan was seated on his horse and had joined his unit, Ghalatea walked up to him. The men guided their horses to form a circle around her.

Ghalatea said a prayer, "Wigg, protect these men during the battle that might come. Give them the courage and strength they need to return home safely."

"We put our fate in your hands," the men said together. "We trust in you."

Ghalatea gave Rogan a little pouch. This was a custom she had adopted from the Kel Cornu. Women gave men such gifts when they were to be separated for a long period of time. Ghalatea had filled the pouch with protective herbs and a few talismans. She had selected them with care. Rogan kissed the pouch and hung it around his neck. Then Ghalatea handed the other men a pouch as well.

One of the scouts accepted it with the words: "I couldn't imagine setting out without this gift. It means a lot to me, to all of us."

"I'm glad I can offer all of you some support in this way."

The man nodded and tucked the pouch under his tunic.

"This reminds us of what we want to return to. I'm convinced that it gives us strength," another soldier said.

Ghalatea smiled. In the beginning of their marriage, Ghalatea had only made pouches for Rogan. When he became commander, however, his soldiers had objected. Ever since, she had gladly made pouches for all of them. On their safe return to Nadesh they sacrificed the pouches to the Gods to say thanks for their protection. This was a ritual of their own making, the Kel Cornu didn't do that.

The column of soldiers started to move. Rogan bent towards Ghalatea and kissed her hand. There was nothing left to say, they had already said their goodbyes that morning. Dwelling on it would only make it harder to hold back her tears.

The king stayed behind at the top of the stairs, but the women accompanied the soldiers until they had left the fortress. The tread of marching feet was the only sound that broke the silence. This showed how well these soldiers had been trained. The women waited at the gate until the last wagon had passed. Ghalatea mounted her horse and started on her journey back to the palace. She stopped halfway between the fortress and the city. She could still see the column of soldiers, but they had covered quite a distance by now. She kept watching until the trees swallowed them up and they disappeared from sight.

"Come back safe, Rogan," she whispered as she wiped away her tears.

Another woman dabbed her eyes as well and nodded at her. They continued their journey together.

11

Lilith wiped the sweat from her forehead and bent forwards again. She was holding a pot pressed between her knees. One of the maid-servants had let the food get burned, and of course Lilith was the one who had to clean the pots again. Her arm was hurting from all the grating.

Even though she could only reach the bottom of the pot with great difficulty, Lilith didn't dare stick her head in it any more. When she had done so before, someone had forcefully hit a spoon against the side. Her ears were still ringing. Everyone had laughed at her, so Lilith hadn't said anything. She was a prisoner, so she was the one who got the lousy chores, that's how it was. Her confrontation with Aida had taught her that there was no use complaining. The Ancilla Princeps didn't care about what happened to her.

Fortunately, she was almost finished. Lilith sprinkled some new sand on the black stain. Meanwhile, she listened to the others.

"Aida, how are you doing?"

Even though Aida didn't have to work because she wasn't completely recovered yet, she did visit the kitchen regularly. She lowered herself down on a chair near the fireplace, groaning dramatically. One of the girls immediately responded by bringing her something to drink.

"I'm healing very slowly," Aida whined and she listed all her aches.

Baby. Lilith didn't dare say this out loud.

Not much later the pot was clean. Lilith got up and stretched the stiffness out of her back. She wiped away the sand and rinsed the pot. Then she put it away. Aida instantly picked it up to inspect her work. Lilith smiled when the maid put the pot back down in disappointment and limped out of the kitchen. Of course she hadn't been able to find the tiniest of flaws, Lilith had made sure of that. Now she only had to clean the worktop and clear out the ashes in the fireplace, and her duties would be finished. After that she could get started with Aida's duties. Lilith sighed, it was going to be a late one again.

She briefly looked up when Ghalatea entered the kitchen and she made a small curtsy. "Shall I make you some tea, Ancilla Princeps?"

"Yes, please."

Lilith hung a small kettle over the fire and continued with the dishes. As she was rinsing the plates, she kept a close eye on the kettle to see if the water was boiling yet. More and more maidservants were leaving the kitchen. By the time that Lilith handed Ghalatea her cup of tea, they were the only ones left. Lilith kept working as hard as she could, because the Ancilla Princeps was keeping a close eye on her. She wanted to say something to break the suffocating silence, but she didn't know what. Maybe she could say something about the book she was reading. Lilith had found a very interesting book about Merzia's history in the library. Nevertheless, she kept quiet.

When the chair creaked, Lilith looked over her shoulder. The Ancilla Princeps seemed lost in thought. Lilith didn't dare ask her what was on her mind, so she dried the last few plates and put them in the rack.

"Will you make sure that the kitchen is tidy when you leave tonight?" Ghalatea asked as she got up to leave Lilith to it.

"Of course, Ancilla Princeps," Lilith replied.

The clock over the fireplace showed that it was nearly midnight when Lilith had finally completed all her duties. She turned off the lights and stepped into the corridor.

At this time of night, the palace was usually wrapped in silence. The green glow of the night lighting gave the building a strange atmosphere. Lilith had become fond of this world where she was all alone. At this time of night, the palace was hers. On most nights, though, she was too tired to walk around a little while longer, and today wasn't any different. So she decided to go straight to bed.

Suddenly Lilith heard a shuffling sound. But there was no one to be seen. She hurried to the nearest intersection of corridors. Now she could hear footsteps. A feeling of inquisitive excitement welled up inside her. She had forgotten about her fatigue.

In the green light she spied the silhouettes of people clad in long, wide robes that were trailing along the ground. The sleeves covered their hands and the big hoods of the robes covered their faces, making their height their only distinctive feature.

Lilith frowned and wondered what this meant. Should she warn someone? She shook her head, surely the presence of these people was known. A group like this could never enter the palace unseen. There had to be something else going on.

Lilith decided to follow the almost noiseless procession. Nobody noticed her when she slipped through a door just before it closed. The king was waiting in a room that was lighted by too few candles. His dark clothes were modest. His gold headband glittered.

The ceremony was performed as noiselessly as the procession had moved through the corridors. One by one, the people came forwards. Lilith stole to the left to better see what was going on and hid behind a pillar.

The people presented the king with gifts, but nobody took down their hood or said a word. The king accepted the gifts with a friendly nod and handed the gift giver a pouch in return.

Lilith observed the ritual incredulously. She stole even closer and could now hear the contents of the pouch chinking as it changed hands. What in the world was going on? From this vantage point she could also see the gifts that the people gave to the king. They were manifold; some people had brought food – predominantly bread – or an ordinary piece of clothing that the king would never wear. But others gave the king nothing more than a single flower that could probably be picked by the side of most footpaths. Still, Yvar made no distinction in what he gave in return. Everyone who visited the king at this nightly hour left the palace with equally sized, chinking pouches.

When the next gift was handed to the king, Lilith caught a glimpse of a woman's hand. She gave the king a bracelet made of plaited straw, decorated with dried wildflowers. When Yvar gave her a pouch, she fell to her knees and stammered softly, "Thank you, lord. Now I can finally give my children a decent meal again. Thank you, thank you."

She humbly bowed her head, but the king got up and kneeled before her. His guards became nervous and moved forwards, but the king didn't take any notice of them. He put his hand on the woman's shoulder. She warily looked up. Then he said softly, but still loud enough for everyone to hear, "Lady, you force me to thank you in the same way. It isn't hard to share when you have great wealth. Compared to your gift, mine is but small. You give me something of yourself, which is the biggest gift anyone can give."

Yvar was still holding the bracelet, but now he slipped it around his wrist instead of putting it aside with the other gifts. Then he helped the woman back up. When he had seated himself on his throne again, the ceremony continued in an orderly manner and in silence.

The king's words kept reverberating in Lilith's head. They puzzled her. There was no doubt in her mind that the king possessed great wealth, but Lilith would much rather own glittering jewellery and gems than a trinket made out of straw.

She was suddenly roused from her thoughts. She couldn't explain her sudden vigilance, but she decided not to ignore the shivers that were running down her spine. What looked like a man, judging from his height, came forwards. He made a graceful bow, but Lilith couldn't keep her eyes off him. She straightened herself to better see what was going on. The king received a pouch that was made of seaweed and decorated with shells. Lilith was shocked when she recognized it, and from the corners of her eyes she saw more people moving to the front.

"Muircadhi!" she screamed, jumping up.

The servus pulled down his hood and dived forwards. But because of Lilith's scream, the king was now standing upright as well. Therefore, the creature's claws came nowhere near Yvar's throat – which was what the creature had been aiming for – and only dug into his arm. Nevertheless, the king let out a cry of pain.

Harald jumped forwards. He pushed the king aside and drove his weapon into the servus. The creature sank to the floor, lifeless.

It was as if everybody else only now began to realize what was happening. Everybody started to scream and move around. Because of the tremendous chaos, Lilith couldn't see what happened to the other servi.

The fight ended almost as quickly as it had started. The people were escorted to another room, but Lilith dropped to her knees, shivering. Now that the room was almost empty, she had an unobstructed view.

Three servi lay dead on the floor. Two others were being held at gunpoint by soldiers. Harald was examining the king with great concern. The sleeve of Yvar's tunic was torn at the shoulder and there was a bloody wound underneath. The Muircadh's nails had driven into Yvar's arm and had torn loose a big chunk of flesh. One of the soldiers pushed the king against the armrest of the chair to make sure his knees wouldn't give way.

"I told you this was a bad idea," Harald grumbled before he turned around.

He bent over one of the bodies and picked up a hand. The Muircadh's long, hornlike nails were filed into sharp points. Harald tried to bend one of them, but the creature had reinforced it with something. Harald let out a curse when he scraped his finger. Then he looked at the rest of the body. The fabric of the robe couldn't hide the creature's muscular build.

Kapow!

Harald dropped the hand to the floor and quickly turned around as the sound of the shot died away. Lilith's heart was beating in her throat. One of the Muircadhi was lying in a pool of blood and red spatters formed an irregular pattern on the wall. The soldier that had been guarding him lowered his rifle. He said almost apologetically, "He made another attempt to attack the king."

The only remaining servus was dragged out of the room by two guards. Harald ordered four others to follow them. When the door opened again, a chirurgeon entered the room. He rushed to the king and started taking care of him.

Harald walked up to Lilith and pulled her to her feet. "Why are you here?" he snapped at her.

Lilith gave him a frightened look. She didn't know how to explain her presence.

"How did you know that the servi were here today?"

"I recognized the gift. They all wear pouches like that."

"But how did you know they would be in the palace today?"

"I didn't," she stammered.

"Rubbish. Why else would you be here?"

"I was just curious," she whispered, and she explained how she had run into the group of people in the corridor.

"Bring her over here," Yvar whispered.

Harald tightened his grip on Lilith's upper arm and wanted to drag her with him.

"Let go of her," the king commanded, suppressing a groan.

Hesitantly, Lilith came closer. Harald was walking right behind her. He was so close that she could feel his rasping breath on the back of her head. Instinctively she knew that he was holding a dagger and was ready to strike if she made one wrong move. The mistrust hurt her feelings, but there was nothing to be afraid of. She would never even dream of hurting the king.

Yvar smiled at her, but immediately after that he winced in pain because the chirurgeon had begun stitching his wound. The man apologized and started to apply bandages.

Harald was the first to speak, "This prisoner has to be involved, my lord. She shouldn't have been here."

"If it hadn't been for Lilith, things would have turned out much worse. Because of her warning, these monsters couldn't do what they came for," the king growled, partly in anger, but undoubtedly also from the pain he was feeling.

"We killed them, lord, and took them prisoner."

"But would you have been just as fast if you'd had to respond to the movement of one of the servi?" Harald remained silent. The king shook his head in anger. "It was her scream that enabled you to defeat these creatures." More calmly he addressed Lilith, "That's why I want to thank you. I will give you a fitting reward tomorrow, but now I want you to leave. I'll let two guards accompany you, so they can search your room. That way, you can rest assured that there are no servi lurking there. The soldiers will also keep watch tonight. I hope this will make you feel safe enough to be able to sleep."

Lilith was surprised that the king would think of her well-being under the present circumstances. She curtsied and thanked him. Harald picked out the two men who were to accompany her.

They walked past another room, and when Lilith cast a quick look inside she saw that the people in the long robes had been brought there. Maidservants had been woken up to take care of them, because some of these people had been wounded as well. They were still visibly shaken and it was deathly quiet in the room. The Ancilla Princeps gave her a brief glance and then quickly continued with her duties as Lilith walked on.

12

Lilith was lying on her bed and she was following the movements of a little spider that had almost finished spinning its web on the ceiling.

Suddenly the door flew open, causing Lilith to jolt upright. Ghalatea entered. She had a dress draped over one arm, and a basket hung from her other arm. The door slammed closed behind her and they awkwardly stood across from each other for a little while.

"The king has asked for you. I will help you get ready."

Lilith nodded. That morning, a soldier had informed her that she was to wait in her room until the king was ready to see her. Of course he had other things to take care of first, but the long wait had made her nervous. By now he'd had ample time to change his opinion about last night.

"How's he doing?"

"He's doing well, but I was told that he could have been killed if it hadn't been for you." Suddenly the Ancilla Princeps grabbed hold of Lilith and hugged her. "I'm sorry that I've kept myself aloof from you. I needed distance to be able to think everything through."

Lilith froze up for moment, but then she wrapped her arms around Ghalatea in great relief. "And what did you decide?"

"That I've been too hard on you. I may have been too kind at first, but after that, I was too hard. The truth lies somewhere in the middle." The Ancilla Princeps pushed Lilith away and grabbed hold of her still bandaged hand. "You have to get undressed, we don't have much time."

After Lilith had stripped down to her underwear, the Ancilla Princeps pushed the dress into her hands. Lilith held it in front of her with her arms outstretched and examined the garment from all directions. The sleeves of the purple dress were embroidered with gold thread and glass beads. She had never worn anything like it. The bodice looked too tight to step into, so she decided to pull the dress over her head. The skirt consisted of three layers of thin fabric. She struggled to find the sleeves and had difficulty slipping her head through the neck opening. She smoothed down the skirt that fell wide around her legs, and then fastened the buttons on the bodice and the sleeves. To her great relief the sleeves fit tightly around her underarms and were long enough to cover part of her hands.

Ghalatea gave her a delighted look. "You look so pretty!" She plucked at the dress, mumbling, "It's a perfect fit, I knew it would be."

Lilith was blushing. "It feels strange to wear this. Why can't I just wear my normal clothes?"

Ghalatea put an arm around Lilith's shoulders and guided her to a chair. "You can't face the king in your working clothes, now can you? It's time to do your hair."

She started brushing. After a few seconds Lilith asked, "What was going on last night?"

"You mean the ceremony?" the Ancilla Princeps asked as she started to plait Lilith's hair.

Lilith nodded.

"Unfortunately, not everyone in Merzia is rich. Some people hardly get by. The people you saw last night, are the poorest in this country. The king gives them an allowance to help them make ends meet. Could you hold these for a second?" The Ancilla Princeps gave her a few pins to hold and then continued plaiting. Lilith felt small tugs on her hair. She was holding her hand up, so that Ghalatea could pick up the pins when she needed them to attach the plaits in loops to her head.

"But why in the middle of the night, concealed underneath wide clothes?" Lilith asked.

"Not everyone is open about their situation, even though many of them are poor through no fault of their own. They are peasants whose crops failed, or elderly people who don't have any children who can take care of them. Everyone has their own story, but they all share the shame that goes with being poor. That's why the kings have invited them in the middle of the night for centuries, so nobody sees the people who are summoned to the palace. And that's also the reason why they wear robes that make it impossible to recognize anyone by their external features."

Lilith thought about the humble gifts that the people had brought. She now understood the nature of the gifts, but she still didn't know why people brought them. When she asked her about this, the Ancilla Princeps clarified, "These people may not have much, but they haven't lost their pride. You shouldn't look upon all this as a rich man giving alms to a beggar. Even though the tradition is aimed at relieving the needs of Merzia's poorest, the ceremony focuses on the exchange of gifts. By bringing the king something, these people preserve their dignity." There was a hush as the Ancilla Princeps tied long ribbons of the same colour as the beads on Lilith's sleeves into Lilith's hair. Then she asked, "Do you really not understand what you witnessed last night, Lilith? It was an exchange on equal terms. Everyone shared on the same level. The value of the king's gift might be somewhat bigger, but to someone who owns nothing, the one flower growing next to their front door can be an equally valuable gift."

Now Lilith was starting to understand what the king had meant and she felt great respect for him.

Ghalatea patted Lilith's shoulders. "Go and look at yourself in the mirror."

Lilith got up. She stared at herself, baffled.

"Is that me?" she whispered.

Ghalatea went to stand behind the mirror and nodded.

"I don't even recognize myself any more," Lilith said cheerfully.

This was what she had been longing for. The woman in the mirror looked reassuringly unfamiliar. Lilith thought she even looked pretty, something she had never thought about herself before. There was a smile on her lips and her eyes were beaming. Even though she had gained weight, her cheekbones were still prominent, but that only added to her beauty. She looked at Ghalatea.

"Thank you so much for coming. I'm glad that we can be... normal around each other again."

The Ancilla Princeps nodded and walked to the door. "Come, we have to go. You can't keep the king waiting."

Lilith threw on her boots and hurriedly joined the Ancilla Princeps, who was waiting with the two soldiers.

On the way to Yvar's chambers they encountered many soldiers. They were going in and out of rooms and they were searching the corridors. Even though they were clearly busy, the men did find the time to turn around and stare after Lilith. Ghalatea leaned in to her and made a remark about it. Lilith started to blush, but it made her smile as well. After a little while they reached Yvar's office.

Lilith gave a self-confident knock on the door. Ghalatea's words had made it clear to her that the king hadn't changed his mind, and she was looking forward to her reward. It wasn't long before she was called in. She looked at the Ancilla Princeps, who gave her an encouraging nod, before she opened the door and entered the room.

Yvar received her in full regalia. There was a crown on his head, and a richly decorated, velvet cape was fastened on his shoulders with two gold clasps. His attire contrasted strongly with the way he had been dressed the night before. The king wasn't alone; Ferhdessar was also present.

"I hope you were able to get some sleep," the king began. He held his arm pressed against his side, but otherwise he looked well.

Lilith nodded. "I lay awake at first, but I eventually drifted off. And you?"

The king laughed. Lilith realized how inappropriate her question was. She hadn't meant to ask it like that. She awkwardly fidgeted with her skirts. "I meant," she hurried to say, "how is your arm doing?"

There was a flash of pain in his eyes when he shrugged. "It will heal. But let's talk about why I asked you to come here. You might very well be the reason why I survived yesterday's attack. Of course it was my Guard that defeated the servi, but I don't want to downplay your part in this matter. Therefore, I think it only right to remit your sentence."

Lilith's mouth fell open and she didn't know what to say. Yvar's words only truly started to sink in when Ferhdessar removed her wristband. This was more than she had expected. Of course the possibility had crossed her mind, but she had pushed that hope aside for fear of being disappointed.

"Thank you, lord," she stammered, rubbing her wrist. The impression of the band was still visible on her skin, but it was a huge relief to no longer be wearing it.

The king nodded. "You're no longer a prisoner, so that wristband is no longer necessary. You will keep wearing the other one though, until you decide to leave the palace."

Lilith preferred to have both wristbands removed, but she understood why both men thought this was best.

Harald entered with five guards. Their eyes were tense, and their swords were partly drawn. Lilith had not seen them wearing rifles before. Harald gave Lilith a suspicious look before he addressed the king, "All is in readiness."

Yvar got up and motioned for Lilith to follow him.

"Lord, I see it as my duty to once more advise you against taking her with you," Harald objected.

The king burst out in anger, "We've discussed this before. The woman is part of our company."

"But…"

"I don't want to hear it. I'm convinced that Lilith won't hurt me. I might even be safer with her around, because she at least spotted the danger."

"I was the one who advised you not to hold the ceremony in the first place, exactly because of…"

"Enough!" Yvar raised his hand as a sign that his bodyguard now really had overstepped the mark.

"I'm only doing my job," Harald mumbled offended.

Right at that moment a panel in the wall slid open. Lilith had been looking at it only a minute ago, but she hadn't noticed that it was a passage. Two guards disappeared through the opening. Ferhdessar went next, followed by Harald and the king. Lilith was escorted by the three remaining soldiers.

The passage was narrow, forcing them to walk in single file. The air was stale, but there were no spider webs and the floor had been swept. With a grating sound, the wall slid back into place. After several bends they arrived at a fork, but they didn't go into either passage. Another stone panel slid aside, revealing a staircase. Lilith saw soldiers standing on the landing below them, but the party went upstairs. Then they had to wait until Ferhdessar said they could proceed.

Even though the sun had already sunk behind the buildings, Lilith blinked against the light when she suddenly found herself outside. The balcony was only just big enough for four guards, the king, Ferhdessar and herself. The other two soldiers remained behind on the stairs. A crowd had gathered in the square in front of the palace. It looked as if they were standing behind a wall of glass. Lilith saw her own reflection and that of the six men hovering above the railing. Just when Lilith started to wonder if she was seeing things clearly, the sorcerer turned towards her.

"I've created a shield. We don't know for sure if the five servi we caught are the only ones who have come to Nadesh. That's also the reason why you're here and not somewhere in the crowd."

This was the first time that Lilith was thankful for Ferhdessar's magic.

The crowd had started cheering when the king had walked onto the balcony. He took it all in with a smile on his face. When he raised his hand, everyone became quiet.

"Fellow countrymen and women, I'm glad to be able to stand before you today. Yesterday, five servi broke into the palace. Thanks to a few brave people, my life wasn't at risk for even one second. The intruders were discovered on time and the attack was thwarted before it had even started. Let yesterday and today be a warning to all our enemies. Merzia is strong!"

Everybody started cheering again and in the meantime the remaining Muircadh was led into the square. The people backed away nervously. They, undoubtedly, had never seen a creature like him before. Some boys were more courageous and spat at the prisoner. When the Muircadh tried to tear himself loose, however, the boys took to their heels.

Lilith suddenly spotted the gallows that was put up on the other side of the square. She started to smile when she realized what was going to happen. Ever since last night, all the feelings of hatred inside her were fighting to be released, but now those feelings gave way to satisfaction. Finally these creatures would get what they deserved, even if it was only one of them. She was startled for a second when she saw the masked executioner, but almost immediately the feeling of elation got the upper hand again.

As if sensing she was staring at him, the Muircadh suddenly looked up at her. She grinned at him but wasn't sure if he could see that from this distance.

Goodbye, fish face. Now I have the last laugh.

He bowed his head when the noose was put around his neck. The executioner looked up at the balcony. When the king gave a nod, the servus was pushed off the platform.

How quickly a life could end. Moments before he had been walking through the crowd, now his lifeless body was dangling from a rope. It was almost disappointing that the Muircadh had gotten off so easily.

The Merzian crowd apparently didn't agree. The people in the square had been silent for a little while, but now there was an outburst of noise. Someone started to sing Merzia's national anthem. More and more people joined in and soon everybody was singing. Impressed, Lilith looked at the king. She saw a shiver run through him, but he was smiling. She felt a stab of jealousy and bowed her head. She wished she was the one being cheered and sung at by the crowd. For a tiny second she believed that she was entitled to it: she was the one who had saved the king's life. But then she understood that there were no reasons to applaud her. She had already received her reward.

The body was taken down from the gallows and put on display in a cage while Lilith followed Ferhdessar back into the palace. Halfway down the stairs, the king and his guards disappeared into the passage behind the wall again, but the sorcerer turned around to face Lilith. "There will be a party tonight, to celebrate Merzia's victory over this threat. Go find Ghalatea, she can take you with her." He pointed downstairs.

It was clear that he wasn't going to attend the party himself, so Lilith became nervous. Ferhdessar gave her a reassuring nod. "The soldiers have searched every room in the palace twice. There's no need to worry."

Not entirely at ease, she descended the stairs.

"Oh, Lilith, one more thing." He waited for her to turn around. "I want you to keep quiet about what you saw yesterday."

She reluctantly agreed. She had wanted to brag to the other maidservants about what she had done, but now her chance to gain some respect was taken away.

"It's important, Lilith," Ferhdessar said.

"I understand. I'll pretend I wasn't there."

"Great."

Lilith walked on to find Ghalatea. The Ancilla Princeps was now wearing a light blue dress with shining dark blue stitching. Her veil was the same colour blue. Ghalatea had used kohl to draw black lines around her bright eyes, making them the centre of attention.

"Are you looking forward to the party?" she asked Lilith as they walked on together.

Lilith shrugged, she had no idea what to expect.

A buzz of voices greeted them as they crossed the threshold to the Great Hall. Many of the people who had previously been in the square had gathered here. They were illuminated by patches of light in various colours. Amazed, Lilith looked up. High above her, eight ribs were joined together in the shape of a dome. The planes between the ribs contained stained-glass windows. The light falling through the windows was very bright.

"What time is it?" she asked Ghalatea with surprise in her voice.

The Ancilla Princeps briefly looked up as well and said, "The dome is illuminated from the outside, but the sun is, indeed, setting."

Lilith couldn't keep her eyes off all the pictures. The Merzians seemed to have a fondness of plants because, just like the tapestry in her room, the dome was mainly decorated with flowers. But there were animals hidden among the flowers as well. She saw eagles, wolves and unicorns, and the longer she looked, the more animals she discovered. She, however, didn't pay attention to where she was going.

Someone grabbed her shoulder when she bumped into him. Lilith apologized, blushing. The man smiled at her and disappeared in the crowd. Ghalatea guided Lilith past a music group who were just starting a new song. At the first tones, Lilith stopped dead in her tracks and turned around. A woman was standing behind a musical instrument, stroking the strings with her fingers. She had her eyes closed and was leaning her head almost lovingly against the wood. Her face was beaming. She clearly enjoyed her own playing.

"What is it?" Ghalatea asked as she came back to stand next to Lilith.

"This sound is so familiar."

"Did someone you grew up with play the harp?" the Ancilla Princeps asked, sounding surprised.

At first Lilith hesitantly shook her head, but then she was sure that this hadn't been the case. Still, the sound of this instrument was reassuringly familiar to her. The strange feeling disappeared when the other musicians joined in and the tempo increased. Lilith turned around. "It's a beautiful instrument."

Ghalatea nodded. "But personally I like the violin better."

They made their way through the crowd of people who were talking to one another. Towards the middle of the hall some people were dancing. Ghalatea and Lilith both got themselves a goblet of wine and found a place to sit in one of the many alcoves. Lilith leaned back into the brightly coloured cushions lying on the floor. The noise was a bit less loud here.

Pretty soon, Ghalatea engaged into conversations with other people. Lilith kept aloof because they were talking about the attack on the king, and she wasn't allowed to say anything about that. Then she spotted Aida. She was sitting a bit farther down and was carefully resting her arm on a cushion. It looked as if she had accentuated her black eye with some powders. She wasn't wanting attention of men; they went out of their way to get her more cushions to support her back and to bring her drinks.

Lilith thought the maidservant was putting up an act, which annoyed her. *She should actually be grateful to me, otherwise she would never have gotten that much attention.*

"I want to go dance."

Ghalatea was already on her feet and she was waiting for Lilith to join her. But Lilith rather observed the dance floor from a distance, so she shook her head. She followed Ghalatea with her eyes until the Ancilla Princeps disappeared in the crowd. Now and again she had to laugh because some people were starting to behave increasingly boisterous. Someone came by to fill up her goblet, but she refused. The wine hadn't agreed with her, and she was feeling a bit drowsy.

"Is it all right if I join you?"

It was the man she had bumped into before. Lilith nodded. He held out his hand and introduced himself as Chrys. He had long, light brown hair that was tied back into a ponytail. A little piece of yellow fabric stuck out from under his bright green tunic. He sat down and folded his legs underneath him.

"What's your name?" he asked.

Lilith told him her name and anxiously awaited if he had heard stories about her

"Why is it that a beautiful lady such as yourself is sitting here all alone?" he asked.

Lilith blushed. But at the same time she became angry. How dare he make a fool out of her?

"I'm serious. I was scared to come and sit next to you. To pluck up some courage, I told myself that it couldn't have been a coincidence that we bumped into each other." He smiled shyly.

Lilith carefully glanced at the man next to her. Chrys seemed to be genuinely shy. Then she looked around the room. She was expecting Aida to be watching her from a distance. Or maybe someone else had sent this man over to hurt her.

"Has someone sent you?" she therefore asked.

"No, why?"

"Forget I asked."

Aida was much too occupied with the men hanging around her, so she probably didn't have a hand in this, and Lilith didn't see anyone else who might be involved.

They sat in silence for a while. Lilith was secretly sizing him up. Chrys was rather handsome and he looked cheerful. When he noticed that she was looking at him, his cheeks turned red. She liked that as well. She hated it when she blushed herself, but it made him look attractive.

"I haven't seen you here before, have you been in Nadesh long?"

Lilith hesitated briefly, but then she said, "For several months. I work in the royal household."

"You're a bit old to be a new maidservant," he observed inquisitively. She decided not to respond. "And what happened to your fingers?"

Lilith covered the bandages with her other hand. "I burned myself on boiling water."

"Ouch…"

Judging by his face, he could almost feel the pain right then and there. That made her smile. "It's fine now," she reassured him. She wasn't like Aida, and she didn't need to put on an act to get attention from this man. "It happened a week ago."

"I'm glad to hear it."

Lilith looked up at the ceiling again.

"It's lovely, isn't it? It's thousands of years old." Chrys was looking at the ceiling too.

"That old?" Lilith asked incredulously.

"Well, that's not entirely true. The design was never changed, but broken panels have been replaced over the years. There's probably nothing left of the original dome any more."

"You know a lot about it. Most people here don't even look at it. But maybe they've seen it too often."

"I doubt if they ever had a good look at it. But I've spent hours here. You get the best view if you lie down on the floor in the middle of the hall."

Lilith laughed. "And I guess you've done that."

He nodded.

"But why?"

"I'm an archaeologist. Right now I'm involved in the excavation of the Nicasian ruin in the south, which of course has the same origin as this window, so that's why I've studied it extensively."

The way he said it made it seem as if everybody would know

what he was talking about. Lilith hesitated briefly but then said, "I don't really understand what you mean. Who are the Nicasians?"

"I'm sorry. This is my profession, but I shouldn't assume that everybody knows these things."

"You could teach me..."

Chrys shook his head. "I would only bore you with dull stories."

"Try me."

She moved a bit farther back to escape the noises coming from the hall. Chrys did the same.

"All right, but I warned you." He cast a quick look at her and then dreamily stared off into the distance. "This story takes place over four thousand years ago."

Lilith wrapped her arms around her knees. She kept looking at him as the story unfolded.

"Back then, the region that we now call Merzia formed one big country together with Naftalia and even the desert. The mountains were much lower and still overgrown with grass and trees, and the desert was less hot. Only Naftalia hasn't changed much since then. That entire area was called Nicasia, and its inhabitants were the Nicasians. Despite being subdivided into tribes, the people formed a unity because of their way of life. They were satisfied with what they had, even though it wasn't much. In other words: the Nicasians were a happy people.

But all that was about to change. Another people sailed across the ocean in big sailing ships and came to Nicasia. These Hurath were wealthier and more civilized, but at the same time they were never satisfied. Unfortunately, the Nicasians didn't know this.

During the first few days, everything went well. The strangers were given a hearty welcome, and the Nicasians shared their food and even their houses with them. Relatives went to live under the same roof to give the newcomers a place to stay. Among themselves, however, the Hurath spoke about the Nicasians with contempt. They found them inferior and decided that they had the right to rule over the them. The Nicasians could never have suspected the changes that were to be brought about by the coming of the sailing ships. Pretty soon they were turned into slaves who lived by the grace of the Hurath. They had to give up all their possessions and they only got food when the new rulers decided that they deserved some. And trust me, that wasn't very often."

Chrys took a short break when someone came by to fill up his glass. Lilith seized the opportunity to ask a question.

"Didn't the Nicasians offer any resistance?"

Chrys shook his head. "Violence wasn't part of their nature and they quickly learned that negotiating only made matters worse. So they reconciled themselves to the new situation."

"Just like that?"

Chrys shook his head again and his eyes started to shine. "No, there was a small group of people who did offer resistance. Thibauld and Hadumar had been friends for a long time. They had different plans for the future than to serve as slaves to the Hurath, so they gathered a group of likeminded men and women around them. Overt resistance led to violent reprisals, so they operated under the cover of darkness. They didn't book many successes, but that was no reason for them to stop. They would go on till the end.

Then the sorcerers came to Nicasia. They secretly supported the resistance fighters, but the effect of their attacks was still negligible. So the sorcerers convened another, even more secret, meeting. That night, Thibauld and Hadumar, and all other men and women who had fought against the Hurath from the very beginning, were given the ability to shapeshift. As the leader of the group, and because he had risked his life to save others on several occasions, Thibauld was given the ability to change into a dragon."

Lilith heaved a sigh. She hadn't expected that this story would be about shapeshifters.

"See, I'm boring you," Chris said. He was insecurely playing with his bracelet.

"Not at all. I never knew that this was the history of the shapeshifters. I think it's a wonderful story. Thank you so much for sharing it with me."

He gave her a look of surprise. "I have to know all of this because I concern myself with the heritage of the Nicasians, but otherwise it's just a dry piece of history."

"But it's my history. I'm a", Lilith had wanted to say that she was a dragon, but she changed her mind, "a shapeshifter."

She immediately regretted having said that. How could she be so stupid? She hardly even knew him. It must have been the wine, she told herself. Someone had filled up her goblet again and she had unwittingly emptied it.

"Of course," Chrys said. "Such a beautiful woman, what else could you be. What kind are you?"

Lilith shook her head.

"A unicorn?" When Lilith didn't say anything he listed a few other races.

"Do you really want to know?" she whispered at long last.

Chrys moved closer. Lilith sighed. "You can't tell anyone. I'm a dragon."

His jaw dropped with surprise.

Lilith shook her head in confusion. "I shouldn't have told you," she said, trying to get up.

Chrys, however, pulled her back down. "Please, don't leave. I... I can't believe that I'm sitting right next to you."

Lilith lowered herself back down into the cushions. "Why not?"

"Shall I tell you how the story ends?" She nodded. "So, Thibauld became a dragon. Hadumar was a scout and had to be able to rely on a keen eye. So he became the first eagle man.

As you might imagine, in its new form the resistance was much more effective than before. It wasn't long before the Hurath – chased by unicorns – were driven out of Nicasia. According to the story, they never even got the chance to board their ships. Instead, they ran north for days before they jumped into the sea." He gave a short laugh.

"What happened next?" Lilith asked. "Did everything go back to normal?"

"No, too much had happened. The Nicasians had become one as slaves and now that they were free, they were unified as a people as well. Thibauld was elected king and his descendants have ruled over Nicasia, and later Merzia, for centuries."

"Yes, I read about that."

He smiled briefly. "When Merzia became smaller and smaller, however, the shapeshifters were no longer the ones who became king. No matter, back to King Thibauld. During his rule, and that of the sovereigns who succeeded him, large buildings were erected." He made a wide gesture at the hall. "This is one of those buildings."

"Has Thibauld lived here?"

"No, he hasn't. It is said that Nadesh used to be a religious centre. Priests and monks used to live here. Furthermore, this building is thought to be of later date. Thibauld lived to a very old age, but he won't have seen this dome. There are, however, signs that there was a building here prior to this one, so it is possible that he visited this location."

Lilith closed her eyes as if trying to sense the presence of the first dragon man. The story filled her with pride. She was a descendant of this brave man, who was held in high esteem by everyone. Chrys carefully touched her hand. She opened her eyes. He pointed at the ceiling. "Do you see the dragon?"

Lilith leaned forwards and followed his finger. Now she noticed that the black spot she had thought to be the night sky had the shape of a dragon. She hadn't noticed before, because this creature was depicted much larger than the other animals.

"Was he black?" she whispered.

"Thibauld?" Yes, he was a black dragon. The sorcerers gave him that colour so he would be even less visible during the night.

She smiled because he voiced what she had been thinking. Maybe the artist who had painted the window had given the dragon man the illusion of the night on purpose. It also affected her for another reason: she was a black dragon herself.

"It feels to me as if I'm sitting next to a queen."

Lilith laughed. She, a queen? She did like the thought of it, though. Being cheered at by a crowd, like Yvar had been on the balcony that afternoon, was something she would like very much. It had to be an incredible feeling to know that people looked up to you for the right reasons.

"I'm sure you were joking when you said you're working in the royal household," Chrys cut into the silence.

Lilith shook her head. "I really am a maidservant." It wasn't a lie. After Ferhdessar had removed her wristband, she and the king had agreed that she would keep working at the palace in exchange for a small allowance.

"But lord Yvar is also descended from Thibauld. You're related to one another!"

Lilith laughed it off. "Aren't we all descended from the same person if we go back in time far enough?"

A bit farther down, people were laughing as well. Lilith looked up, but the laughter wasn't in response to her remark.

The music group started a new song. Many people started to clap. Men and women came out of the alcoves and rushed towards the dance floor. Chrys got up as well and held out his hand.

"Would you honour me with a dance?"

He made a small bow when she put her hand in his and then he pulled her up. As she walked beside him, she whispered bashfully, "I don't know how to dance."

"That's all right. There are no real rules."

Lilith looked at the other couples. The women held their skirts with one hand and they put their other arm around the man's shoulders. She copied that. She surrendered to Chrys's lead and she whirled past the other partygoers. She spotted Ghalatea, who was dancing as well. The Ancilla Princeps winked at her and then disappeared from view again. Lilith was having a great time. She twirled right in front of Aida a few times, but the maid didn't recognize her. After a few songs, Chrys led her back to one of the alcoves.

"What did you do before you came here?"

Lilith thought about this. Then she answered, "I used to work at an inn. That was after I had left my parental home."

It wasn't a lie, but it sounded better than it had been.

"Where did you live?"

"In a small village in… er… the south."

"The ruin that I'm excavating is in the south as well. In which village did you grow up?"

What was she going to answer? The only village she knew was the one where Pavel lived. That's why she said, "I'm from Kandar."

"I've been there occasionally."

Lilith was becoming nervous, but luckily Chrys said, "It's pretty close to where I work, but I don't go there very often."

"What kind of building are you excavating?"

"A palace. It's one of the biggest ever found and also one of the oldest. We've only searched a small part of the area, but rumour has it that there are tunnels leading all the way into the desert, or maybe even as far as Naftalia. It would be a dream come true to find them, because they should contain traces of the first shapeshifters."

Lilith shared his excitement. She would love to go there sometime. When she said this out loud, Chrys answered that he might take her with him one day.

Someone walked up to Chrys, and Lilith observed both men as they talked for a while. That was how she discovered that Chrys had come to Nadesh to collect information from the library. Chrys stared after the man as he walked away. "Funny, that's a friend of my father's. I hadn't expected to see him here." He turned back to Lilith and told her a bit about himself.

"Do you have any brothers or sisters?" he asked after that.

His inquisitiveness was getting on her nerves. How long would he continue to ask questions and how much should she tell him? There was no way in the world she would ever tell him what her real job had been. But what should she say?

"A little brother, Myar." Lilith winced as she said his name. It still hurt that he had to die. At the same time she was amazed at how quickly the lie had escaped her lips.

"You really miss him," he concluded, looking worried.

She nodded. "Shall we have another dance?"

"Good idea."

They danced a few more dances before Lilith told him that she was tired.

"Shall I walk you to your room?"

They left the hall with arms linked. Lilith quickly looked around for Ghalatea, but she hadn't seen her any more since the first dance. At the door of her room she said goodbye.

"Thank you very much for the lovely evening."

"In that case, I should to thank you as well. Will we see each other again?"

"I would like that."

Before Chrys could say anything in response, Lilith closed the door. She took off the dress and left it lying on the floor. Exhausted, she fell down on her bed.

When Lilith woke up the next morning she realized it was late. She splashed some water in her face to wash away the sleep and threw on her clothes. When she looked in the mirror she saw that the ribbons had made one big mess of her hair. The plaits had come loose in some places and tufts of hair were sticking out. She pulled out the pins and started to undo the plaits. She was grumbling because it didn't go as fast as she would have liked. Lilith brushed her hair once and then tied it into a pony tail. Next, she ran to the kitchen.

She quickly looked at the clock hanging over the fireplace. Even though she wasn't very good a telling the time, there were certain times that she did recognize, and she saw that she had almost been too late. She curtsied to Ghalatea and gasped, "What can I do for you, Ancilla Princeps?"

Ghalatea laughed. "Did you have a late one last night? I'd wanted to take you with me when I left, but you were having such a good time with that young man that I decided to leave on my own."

Lilith blushed.

The Ancilla Princeps continued, "You can go scrub the Great Hall. I'll send some of the other maids to help you in a little while. We have all morning, because the hall is closed to the public."

Lilith walked to a corner to get the things she needed. She put a tub on a cart and filled it with hot water. Then she grabbed a broom and a cloth and left the kitchen.

After Lilith had removed all the cushions from the alcoves, she threw buckets of water on the floor. She started scrubbing with her broom. The other maids came in, but they didn't show any intention of getting to work. They were still full of stories about last night's party. Then Lilith heard footsteps. Without looking up she knew it was Aida, she could always sense it when she was on her way.

"And what about you, Lilith, did you have a nice time as well?"

Before Lilith could answer, everybody started to laugh. In mocked surprise, Aida held her hand to her mouth. "Oh, how silly of me. Of course you couldn't go. I'm so sorry."

Lilith straightened her back and ignored Aida's remark. "Yes, I had a wonderful night, thank you."

"With the dishes, I'm sure," someone sneered.

"No, in the arms of the most handsome man at the party." That was how Lilith had heard the others talk about their dancing partners. "Unlike Aida, I was able to dance. It was wonderful."

Just as Lilith had hoped, Aida was astonished.

"You're lying," she hissed.

Lilith shook her head and went back to work. She felt the smile on her lips and that made her even merrier.

She was busy changing the covers of the dirty cushions when Chrys walked in. Lilith was flattered because she realized that he had come especially for her.

"Did you sleep well?" she asked him.

"Splendidly, I dreamed of you."

Her cheeks turned crimson. Then she saw Aida coming towards them. She was putting a surprising amount of weight on her left leg. Lilith had already been wondering why the maidservant had been limping the past few days. She was pretty sure that she hadn't hit her left leg. Apparently Aida had been putting up an act after all.

Lilith knew exactly what Aida was going to say when she opened her mouth. Before she could actually utter the words, though, somebody else called out, "Aida, look at you being up and about again. Do you think you can resume your work soon?"

Ghalatea entered the hall.

The maidservant immediately started limping again. "It really does still hurt very much, Ancilla Princeps. She beat me up badly."

To Lilith's great relief Chrys had his back to Aida, so he didn't see the maid pointing at her.

"In that case you should really take a rest. Come, let me bring you to your room."

Ghalatea carefully put her arm around Aida's shoulders and escorted her out of the hall. Lilith heaved a sigh of relief as she threw a cover into the laundry basket and turned a clean one inside out.

"Are you busy today?" Chrys asked.

"I have to finish this. And I was to stop by lord Ferhdessar this afternoon, but he just sent me a message that he won't have time for me."

Chrys looked surprised, but Lilith decided to not give an explanation if he didn't ask for it. The less she told him, the better. She pulled the fabric over a cushion and beat it against her knees a few times to fluff it up. Then she tossed the cushion into an alcove.

"I'll ask the Ancilla Princeps if I can take the afternoon off," Lilith said as she got ready to put the laundry basket on the cart. Chrys, however, beat her to it and she smiled gratefully.

"Will you wait outside for me? I'll drop this off and then I'll come out to tell you if I can be excused."

Chrys nodded and walked out of the hall with big strides.

Not much later, Lilith walked outside. Chrys was waiting a bit farther down. "I have no more obligations for today," she said as she joined him.

"Great, it's nice to be able to spend some more time with you. I'll have to return to the south pretty soon." He pulled her cape closed. Then he gave her a penetrating gaze. "You are so special. I keep worrying that I'll wake up to discover that it was all just a dream."

Lilith averted her head in embarrassment. Nevertheless, she enjoyed hearing him say things like that to her. He had done so last night as well, when they were dancing. It seemed as if he meant what he said.

"What are we going to do?" she asked him. She hadn't been out of the palace since she had tried to escape.

"Let's go for a walk."

She nodded, and he wrapped his arm loosely around her shoulders. They walked past the cage with the dead servus. His body was starting to smell already. Lilith glimpsed at it, but even now she found the creature intimidating. Chrys made a few remarks about the attempt on the king's life, but Lilith didn't respond.

They strolled around the city until they reached a small inn. The scent of freshly baked apple pie came drifting out an open window. Lilith stopped.

"That smells delicious."

"Perhaps we should find out whether it tastes just as good."

Chrys turned around and pushed the door open.

"I don't have any money," she objected.

"I'm inviting you, aren't I?"

The inn consisted of a small room, causing the tables and chairs to stand close to each other. The walls were painted orange-red. Lilith looked around while Chrys ordered for them both. There were a few groups of other customers, but it wasn't very crowded. On the far side of the room, a man and woman were whispering to one another. They were holding hands and their tea was growing cold. Lilith smiled and let her gaze wander through the room. All furniture was made of wood, there were tiles on the floor, and in front of the windows stood plants with big leaves and white flowers. The inn had a modest interior, but the delicious scent emanating from the oven gave it a homely feel. The oven was situated in one of the corners of the room. The pies were cooling down on the shelves over the oven.

"You used to work at an inn, didn't you? Did it resemble this one?" Chrys asked, pulling up a chair.

Lilith shook her head. This was one of the few subjects she had been truthful about, so she gratefully elaborated.

"It was bigger and less cosy. But I did enjoy my time there."

There was a brief silence when the tea and pies were served. Lilith took a bite of her apple pie. Her eyes started to gleam with delight.

"This is truly delicious!"

That made Chrys laugh.

"So, why did you leave?"

Lilith flinched. What was she going to say? One day her master had walked into the inn. She had known instantly that her carefree existence was over. She had reluctantly served him, and when he had paid her he had grabbed her hand and had ordered her to leave. Lilith had argued with him, because she had felt safe in that trading town where she didn't stand out. Kasimirh, however, had made it clear to her that it was an order, not a request. That same night, she had told the landlord and his wife that she was leaving.

"Is there something wrong?" Chrys asked when she didn't answer his question.

Lilith shrugged and looked at the pair of lovers behind them. They were still holding hands. Lilith did the same. "It was time to leave."

"Time to move on."

She nodded smilingly. It wasn't exactly the way Chrys thought, but it wasn't a lie either. He was caressing her hands now, but when his fingers moved in the direction of her wrists, she pulled her hands away and started eating again.

"Working at that inn, I'm sure you met quite a few attractive men."

"Never, I've never even met so much as one attractive man." She averted her head but kept looking at him. "Except for you, of course."

His eyes started to shine and his cheeks turned red. There was a wide smile on his lips. Lilith enjoyed being able to cause such a reaction in him. And it really wasn't all that difficult.

"Then I guess that I should consider myself lucky for ensnaring this demanding woman," he said earnestly.

Lilith swallowed the last bite of her apple pie and, disappointed, pushed the plate away. Chrys cut a piece off his pie and held it out to her. When she wanted to grab it, he pulled it away. He apparently thought this was very funny, but his laughter made Lilith angry. He held the piece out to her again. As soon as she opened her mouth to ask him what he was playing at, he shoved the pie between her teeth. His fingers softly touched her lips. Abashed, she put her hand to her mouth.

As if nothing had happened, he said, "I'll ask my superior if I can take you with me next time. Then we can also visit Kandar. It must have been a long time since you saw your family last."

Lilith stared into the distance without seeing anything. She wished he wouldn't keep bringing up these subjects, but she couldn't tell him that. He was much too curious and would surely ask why she didn't want to talk about it.

"You'll be able to see Myar again."

Lilith bowed her head in sorrow when Chrys said his name.

"Do you miss your little brother so badly?"

She nodded. Chrys got up and sat down next to her. He put his arm around her.

"I'm sure he's missing you too. Come with me, so you can spend some time with him again."

"I'll see if I can get some time off," Lilith answered weakly. All of a sudden the inn felt oppressive. "Shall we get going?"

Chrys chucked some coins on the table and draped her cape around her shoulders. "Come, I know a beautiful place. If you're up for a little more history, that is."

Lilith laughed. She knew that he wouldn't ask her questions if he could tell her stories. But she also simply was curious.

They crossed a narrow bridge, decorated with metal flower vines. Chrys stood still at the rail and looked hundreds of yards down. "Is this what it's like when you're flying?"

"The view is the same of course, but there's also the feeling of floating."

Lilith closed her eyes and felt the wind brush along her cheeks. She could tell by the smell of the air that it was going to rain later on.

"It must be wonderful to be able to fly," he said.

She shrugged. Flying had never been a pleasant experience for her. "You act as if it's extremely special that I'm a dragon." She turned around and walked on. Only when Chrys grabbed her arm, did she stop.

He looked at her. "But it is, isn't it?"

Lilith shook her head. "What's the use? If I were to change now, people would panic and run away from me. And that would actually be a good thing, because there's also a chance they'll attack me."

She could tell by the look on his face that he realized that this was true.

"Sometimes people are much too narrow-minded," he grumbled.

Lilith laughed but she didn't agree with him. She couldn't blame the humans for thinking that way about her species.

The rock peak they were now climbing was uninhabited. The branches of the mighty trees were creaking in the wind. There weren't many leaves left on them. A narrow track, which wasn't much more than a strip of flattened grass, indicated that someone had been here not too long ago. But that person had been the first visitor in a long time.

A bit farther down stood the remains of a temple. The ravaged columns were overgrown with climbing plants, but through the overgrowth Lilith saw strange symbols that wound their way up the column. She traced the relief with her fingers. Chrys explained that this was the script used by the first shapeshifters to pass on messages to each other. In later times, they had used the symbols to embellish buildings.

"I'd love to remove all these plants to decipher what's written here," he mused.

"Can you read it?"

"A little, but it's hard because these symbols are so weather-beaten. It would be so great to restore this temple to its former glory."

They walked across cracked tiles until they reached a low pillar. Water seeped over the edges into narrow drains and flowed out of the temple, quickly swelling into wider streams. Lilith put her hands in the ice-cold water and took a sip.

Meanwhile, Chrys had found a nice spot in the sun, and she went to sit beside him. He pulled her against him and before Lilith knew what was happening she felt his lips on her mouth. What was going on? His arms were holding her tightly, but she nevertheless managed to turn her head away. He whispered that he was sorry. Lilith shrugged and looked up at him. Then she closed her eyes and brought her mouth back to his.

Lilith was relieved when he let go of her, but she could tell from Chrys's eyes that he had enjoyed this strange business, which was nice.

He made a wide gesture at the nature surrounding them. "It's beautiful out here, don't you think?"

"It's gorgeous."

Lilith looked at the fountain again. Her eyes followed a stream that disappeared between the trees a bit farther down. She licked her lips. They still tasted a bit of Chrys. It wasn't disgusting, but she nevertheless rubbed her mouth as inconspicuously as possible.

"This is the Fountain of Origin," he said.

"The place where the world was created," Lilith responded.

She knew that name from the stories her master had told her. Jakob had let a fountain spring from His hands. When the water trickled down His fingers, the world had been formed. It had grown bigger and bigger, because wherever the water went, land had been created alongside it. This place was named after that fountain.

Chrys looked at her in amazement. "Only very few people know this story. Who told you about it?"

"My, er, father." She had a lump in her throat. Something inside her fought against calling Kasimirh her father, but she didn't see any other way out.

There was a prolonged silence. Lilith closed her eyes and felt the sun on her face. Birds were singing and the few remaining leaves were rustling. Lilith started to pray. The more words she directed at Jakob, the more she felt as if something warm was wrapping itself around her. The feeling didn't disappear when she opened her eyes. Lilith felt even more connected to Jakob than she ever had during a service. When she said this out loud, Chrys nodded.

"That could be right. In this place you're literally in God's Hands."

"What?" Lilith shook her head. "No, that's impossible. What do you mean?"

He started to explain: "Nadesh was built on ten rock peaks. Look, like this." He held his hands up as though he was holding a sphere. Then he extended his fingers. Lilith looked on in growing dismay.

"You mean that Nadesh looks as if it was built on fingers."

Chrys nodded.

"God's Hands," Lilith murmured. Then she jumped up and clasped her hands to her mouth. It all reminded her of something her master had often said.

"What's wrong?" Chrys asked. He had gotten up as well.

Lilith shook her head. "I can't explain, but I need to talk to Ferhdessar." She was already running and she shouted the last words over her shoulder. Chrys yelled for her to wait, but she didn't stop.

At the palace she almost bumped into Ghalatea. "Where's Ferhdessar? I must speak to him," she panted.

"He's with the king."

Lilith immediately turned around.

"You can't just go there," the Ancilla Princeps called after her.

Lilith didn't listen. This was too important.

On her way to Yvar's chambers, Lilith encountered several soldiers. Yvar's room was guarded by two members of the Royal Guard as well. Lilith threw herself between them and wanted to jerk the door open. One of the men grabbed her by the collar.

"I must speak with Ferhdessar," Lilith stammered. She tried to pull free, but the man tightened his grip.

"You're going to have to wait. Lord Yvar has indicated that he doesn't wish to receive anyone."

"It's highly important, why won't you understand that!"

A struggle ensued. Lilith kicked and hit everything around her. In the meantime she desperately shouted at the soldier to let her go. Suddenly she felt cold steel against her throat.

"Stop moving," the soldier who was holding the sword ordered.

Lilith stepped back and the man stepped forwards. Then the door was pulled open.

"What's going on here?"

Lilith grabbed Ferhdessar's arm. "I know what Kasimirh wants."

Ferhdessar looked surprised. Then he motioned at the guards that it was all right. Lilith followed him inside. She caught sight of the king and quickly curtsied. "Kasimirh... Nadesh is the centre. The fountain in God's Hands."

The king gave her an uncomprehending look. "What's going on?"

Lilith vainly tried to explain again. Yvar admonished her to calm down.

Ferhdessar pushed a glass of water into her hands. "First take a few deep breaths. This is about Kasimirh, that much I understand. But I'm sure it isn't so urgent that you have to throw it out all at once."

"It's extremely important," Lilith protested.

"We understand, but just drink your water first," the king ordered.

Lilith tried to do as she was told, but because she was so upset, she couldn't drink fast. With every sip, however, she calmed down a bit more. Ferhdessar took the empty glass from her and nodded, "Now you can calmly tell us what happened."

Lilith explained how Chrys had taken her with him and what he had told her. "My master often said something. It always sounded cryptic to me, but now I understand. In God's Hands lies the Fountain of Origin. The place where it all began will be the centre of the world once more."

There was a brief silence.

"That's why Merzia is so important to Kasimirh," Yvar mumbled.

"He is determined to conquer Merzia, but it won't be like in those other cities. My master will come to live here. Nadesh will never be the same again," Lilith whispered.

Ferhdessar nodded.

"Now what?" Lilith whispered in a worried voice. If the circumstances had been different, she might have been able to laugh at the irony of the fact that she had fled to the most important place in Kasimirh's plans. Instead, she was feeling increasingly anxious. She bowed her head and buried her face in her hands.

"You don't have to worry about all of this, Lilith. There's nothing you can do about it. You may leave," Ferhdessar said.

When she was halfway to the door, the king suddenly said, "Thank you, Lilith, for coming to tell us straight away."

"I'm sorry that I always bring you bad news," Lilith whispered in response, and then she looked at Ferhdessar. "I really want to help you prevent this from happening."

The sorcerer smiled and accompanied her to the door. "That

makes me very happy, Lilith."

The king waited until Ferhdessar was seated next to him again. Then he continued the conversation they'd been having before Lilith had interrupted them. The information she had given them didn't change much about anything. It only emphasized the gravity of the situation.

"All right, let's recapitulate," the king said. "What are our options?"

"Resist or surrender. Those are our options."

"And you think we should attack…"

"I don't look at it as an attack. Kasimirh has made the first move. Several moves, to be precise. If we were to go to battle now, it would be a defensive action." Ferhdessar shrugged, as if to indicate that it was an open-and-shut case. His voice even betrayed some irritation. "We've talked about this many times before, Yvar. My views haven't changed."

Yvar merely shook his head. "But what are the consequences of our choices?"

Ferhdessar raised his eyebrows. This question changed the course of the conversation. "If we resist, Merzia will remain the Merzia that many have fought for in the past. Your father even died defending the values and beliefs of this country.

If we were to surrender, Kasimirh will submit your subjects to his rule. And I don't even have to start about the consequences for you personally. Kasimirh has made your future under his rule abundantly clear. Lilith's words only confirm this."

"Is it really that simple?"

"Isn't war always that simple? You have two choices: you're either for or against. Everything in the middle won't get you anywhere. Neutrality isn't an option this time. Nadesh is Kasimirh's target."

They both remained quiet for a long time.

"It's not as black and white as you make it out to be, Ferhdessar. If only it were that simple. There are so many other things to consider. So much is uncertain. What if this man is truly serving Jakob?

The consequences would be incalculable. According to Kasimirh, Jakob will destroy the world if we don't follow Him."

"According to Kasimirh, indeed…" The sneering undertone didn't leave any doubt as to Ferhdessar's feelings about the other sorcerer's threats. "But if he's a false prophet…" he continued immediately.

"Exactly, uncertainties."

There was another silence between them. Yvar opened the book that Kasimirh had sent him and leafed through it without reading the words. Ferhdessar had read the book too. It hadn't convinced him that the sorcerer was telling the truth. Nevertheless, it was put together well, and he could imagine its appeal to gullible people. He hadn't expected, however, that it would make Yvar question things. The king slammed the book closed.

"What is religion?"

Ferhdessar looked up in surprise.

"What's the difference between what you and I believe and what Kasimirh believes?" the king clarified.

"I see quite substantial differences. We believe in multiple Gods who keep the world balanced. Kasimirh regards Jakob as the only God. One who can do whatever He wishes. Our Gods don't incite violence, Jakob, as the only God, apparently does."

"But we pray to Jakob as well. Isn't the only difference between all the religions in the world that we use different names? Couldn't it be that all our Gods are nothing but different names for the various character traits of one single God? We all believe in something that created the world and has the power to destroy it again. A power that created everything and gave us life."

"There are so many differences. The way that we experience our faith, the rituals we perform. I know of tribes who sacrifice people to their Gods. I'd rather compare them to the Naftalians than to us."

Yvar nodded. "But our rituals are imposed by people. Leaders within the religious community tell us to carry them out. I'm talking about the basic principles."

Ferhdessar reluctantly agreed. "But I repeat: is Kasimirh a true prophet or a man bent on power? Is he a crazy sorcerer that we need to put a stop to?"

"I don't know," Yvar sighed. He was leaning his elbows on the armrests and held the tips of his fingers against each other. He bowed his head until his lips touched his index fingers.

"I think it's the latter," Ferhdessar answered his own question. "It isn't Jakob who's behind all of this, it's a sorcerer who has gone astray. The Gods have nothing to do with this."

"I don't know," Yvar sighed again. "I'm not even sure which answer I hope for."

Ferhdessar banged his fist on the table. "Kasimirh can't be acting on the authority of Jakob."

This whole situation was getting him more and more concerned. Ever since Yvar had received the box, Ferhdessar was having dreams about Lilith's master. They were standing across from each other, saying nothing, and Ferhdessar had an overwhelming feeling that he knew the prophet. It was extremely frustrating to him that he woke up every time when Kasimirh was getting ready to pull down his hood to reveal himself. He was racking his brain to remember where he knew the other sorcerer from, but the answer kept slipping away from him.

"I'll ask Anukasan to come over. He might be able to discover more about what Kasimirh has been up to the past few weeks."

The king agreed, and they ended their conversation.

13

Lilith woke up from a soft knock on her door. She stretched and sat up. It was dark in the room because the heavy curtains were closed, and Lilith had no idea what time it was. There was another knock on the door.

"Come in."

Lamplight drove away the darkness as Ghalatea entered.

"Is there something wrong?" Lilith asked with concern, looking at the clock. It wasn't time to get up yet, but it wasn't much earlier either.

"I'm sorry to have woken you, but I came to tell you that you don't have to work today. I have a message for you." The Ancilla Princeps handed her an envelope and put the blanket, which had slipped down, back on the bed. "Maybe you'll be able to catch some more sleep."

Lilith turned on the light and studied the envelope. It had her name written on it in an unfamiliar but neat handwriting. She turned the envelope over, but there wasn't anything written on the back. Curious, Lilith opened the flap and pulled out the card. Her eyes raced to the final line. "Love, Chrys," it said.

It made her smile, but she also felt nervous. Lilith hadn't been in touch since she had left him behind at the fountain a few days ago. He must have been wondering why she had left in such a great hurry.

To her great relief he didn't mention the incident in his note. He only asked her to come to the Great Hall later that morning. Lilith looked at the clock again. She had three hours left. More than enough time to catch a couple more hours of sleep and get ready. After she had turned out the light, she soon fell asleep again.

Even though she'd had more than enough time, Lilith still needed to hurry when she woke up the second time. It was strange to walk through the palace at this time of day. Everywhere she looked, she saw servants who were hard at work, and on any other day Lilith would have been one of them. Normally, she would have been at it for several hours by now, and it would be time for a short break. But today she hadn't even had breakfast yet.

A surprise awaited her in the Great Hall. The light behind the dome was on, but apart from a few candles in the middle of the hall, all the other lights were off. There were also some cushions piled up next to the candles. Chrys immediately got up when she came in.

"Could you bolt the door, please?'

Lilith did as he asked. Chrys greeted her with a kiss on her cheek.

"Why didn't you come to see me again?"

"I was busy."

"That's what the Ancilla Princeps told me as well. But you do know that this is my last day in Nadesh, right?"

She nodded.

"I think we should talk."

"You're right." Lilith knew that they needed to talk, but that was exactly why she had been avoiding him. She didn't want to have to make up any more excuses.

"I'm glad you agree." He held her hand. Then he gestured at the breakfast that was waiting for them. "Let's eat. I'd like this to be a lovely day during which we can get to know each other better." There was a look of mischief in his eyes. "I've abused my authority somewhat. The Hall is closed today because I have to study the dome. So now we have the place to ourselves."

Lilith laughed.

While they were eating, Chrys asked, "What was it that made you take off so suddenly? Was it something I said?"

Lilith almost choked and shook her head.

"Was it the location or something that happened?"

"It wasn't you. It was everything at once. It made me remember something important."

"I've been worried about you." He caressed her hand and gave her a worried look.

"Really?"

"Of course."

"That's sweet of you, but there was no need."

Chrys bowed his head. He wrapped his fingers around her hand. "I have to admit that it bothers me that you don't trust me. Trust should be the foundation of a relationship. You should feel so safe around me that you would tell me anything, no matter how strange." He eyed her seriously. "I keep running into the same wall. Does it have anything to do with your past?"

Lilith felt sorry for him. "Please believe me when I say that I wish I could tell you everything. But you're right, it's about my past. I can't talk about it and that has nothing to do with trust. I do trust you, Chrys. But you won't be able to understand what happened. Can't we just focus on the future and leave the past behind us?"

"I don't know if that's the solution, but I am willing to give you some more time."

"Thank you for being prepared to do that for me."

"Can I ask you one last question? It's not about your past, it's about the present."

Lilith felt anxious, but nevertheless she answered, "I'll answer your question truthfully if I can. Otherwise, I'll tell you that I can't talk about it."

"That's okay."

He took hold of her left hand and rolled up her sleeve a little bit. Lilith closed her eyes and bit on her lip. It took great strength of will to not pull her hand back.

"You're trying so hard to hide this wristband, but I noticed it anyway. Why are you wearing it?"

There was a hush. Lilith wondered if Chrys knew that she had been a prisoner.

"Lilith? Is this a question that you don't want to answer?"

She opened her eyes and smiled. "Of course this is a question that I don't want to answer."

Chrys averted his head. Lilith touched his cheek with her hand and turned his head back so that she could look him in the eye. "But I am going to. I promised you that I would be honest if I could. It's not easy for me to tell you this, but..." She took a deep breath. "Ferhdessar put this band on my wrist to help me control my anger."

She searched his face for clues as to what he was thinking right now. Strangely enough, she primarily saw relief.

"I hadn't been able to come up with an explanation, and this was the last thing I expected. You seem so gentle."

"If you only knew."

"How does it work?"

"When I get angry it gives off a pain stimulus that doesn't disappear until I calm down."

"Does it need to do that often?"

"Less often than in the beginning, and it has never given off any stimulus when you're around."

"I'm glad to hear it."

"Do you think differently of me now?"

"I think you're brave for telling me this. It means a lot to me. But has it changed my opinion about you?" He pensively stared into the distance. "I don't know what answer I expected when I asked you this question. The prisoners working at the excavation also wear those bands, but the Ancilla Princeps already told me that you're not a prisoner. It would have been strange if you were, because then they would never have let you go to the party."

Lilith smiled in relief.

"But now that I know that it has to do with your anger, I can understand a little bit better why you don't want to talk about your past. There has to be a connection."

Lilith bowed her head. "You promised that you wouldn't bring that up again."

"You're right. I didn't mean to. But now I also understand why you prefer to look to the future. You have closed the book on your past. And you started wearing the wristband to better yourself. That takes a lot of courage. You're clearly someone who's willing to learn and look into herself. That's brave."

A smile formed on Lilith's lips. "If you only knew what it means to me to hear you say this. You're right, I want to get to know myself better. That's pretty frightening sometimes, so to hear you call me brave is a form of recognition to me. Thank you." She caressed his hand and leaned against him. Chrys wrapped his arms around her.

In a few days' time, her life had completely changed. She was no longer a prisoner and she had met a wonderful man. What had she done to deserve this? She listened to Chrys's heartbeat. If he knew what she was thinking, he would have told her that she deserved it for being who she was. He had so much faith in her.

I won't disappoint you.

She closed her eyes and pressed her face against his shoulder. She inhaled his scent, because she wanted to be able to remember it. He smelled fresh. It took her some time to recognize his scent as eucalyptus.

For the first time, Lilith was determined to become a dragon and fight one more time. Ferhdessar had already made her contemplate the possibility, but Chrys had given her a reason to actually do it. During that final battle, she would set straight everything that had happened in the past. Chrys would be so proud of her. That alone would make it worth the effort to become that which she feared most one last time.

She went to lie on her back. Thibauld was watching over all the animals depicted on the dome, but also over her and Chrys. "The dome really does look best from this point of view."

Chrys followed her example and put his arm under her head. "To me it looks even more beautiful than ever, because you're with me."

"Stop saying those crazy things all the time."

"No, of course I won't. They make you smile and then you look even prettier."

"You're sweet."

They looked at the dome in silence for a while.

"Forgive me if I'm asking you something that I shouldn't. But what was the reason you came to Nadesh? Was it to ask Ferhdessar for help?" Chrys asked.

"To be honest, I ended up here by coincidence."

"I don't really believe in coincidences. The reason might not be clear to you right now, but I'm sure there was one."

Lilith propped herself up a little and looked him in the eye. "Then it must have been because you were here."

"In that case you made an enormous detour," he laughed. "The excavation was much nearer to where you used to live."

"But you wouldn't have wanted to know the person I was back then."

Lilith lay back down again. It was quite a relief that she could say things like that. Chrys pulled her against him and planted a kiss above her ear.

For a while they pointed out the things that stood out to them about the dome. Chrys told a few stories about the first known shapeshifters.

"What are your plans for the future?" Chrys turned on his side and looked at her.

"I'll stay here until I've settled with my past once and for all. That's the most important thing. I once said that I was going to live in a little house after that, but now that I've met you I'm debating whether I wouldn't rather live in a larger house." She gave him a meaningful smile.

"But there isn't something in particular that you want to do?"

"I don't really know what I'm good at. I might find a job as a maid somewhere. Or I could go work at an inn again. But I'd rather do something where I can be of importance to others."

"There must be something. Maybe you could even use your dragon side for it."

"I can't really picture that. What would I be able to do as a dragon?"

Chrys shrugged.

"You told me about Thibauld. He was created to fight and that's the only thing I can imagine I could do. But I don't want that."

Well, except for one last time.

"No, I can imagine."

Someone rattled the door. They both jolted upright. Lilith felt her cheeks turning red out of embarrassment of getting caught. The door remained closed, however, and they both burst out laughing.

"Maybe you'll think of something one day," Chrys continued the conversation.

"Maybe. And if you come up with a good idea you should let me know."

"I will. That gives me something to think about while I'm away."

Lilith's hand searched his. "I'm going to miss you."

14

Lilith stood still for a while to inhale the scents carried on the wind. Ghalatea had sent her to the entrance of the palace to sweep the floor. The wind kept blowing the dirt back, but that didn't bother Lilith. It was nice to look out through the open doors and to smell the blossoms.

The mild weather had a positive effect on the people passing by. They all greeted her and some of them even stopped to have a chat.

Then she saw Ferhdessar. He was having a heated discussion with the man walking beside him. The stranger had a pointed nose and short, white hair that stood in all directions as if he'd been out in the wind too long. He wore a uniform that resembled the one worn by the guards in the palace, only his was grey blue.

"Lilith, this is Anukasan. He's a friend of mine," Ferhdessar said when they had reached her.

The man gave her an inquisitive look with his golden eyes. They were so bright that they seemed to be emitting light. Then he took hold of her hand and planted a quick kiss on it. "Lilith, at last we meet."

Ferhdessar explained, "Anukasan is also a shapeshifter. He is descended from the race of eagle shifters."

That got Lilith even more interested.

"Who could have thought that I would actually get the chance to meet you? I'm here on business, but Ferhdessar mentioned your name and I instantly knew that you were the girl whom I've been searching for such a long time. There's much that I want to tell you."

They went to the Great Hall to find a place to talk. In one of the corners a harpist was playing. Anukasan and Lilith could only see part of the instrument from the alcove where they had retired to, but Lilith was intrigued by the hands that now and again entered her field of vision.

"Your mother used to play the harp. She was very good at it and many prominent people invited her to come play for them."

"You know my parents?"

He nodded. "I met them shortly after you were taken from them. Not many people knew you were a shapeshifter, but I can proudly say that I can find most children of shapeshifters. Your parents didn't know for sure whether you were a dragon child either, because you inherited your gift from your grandmother. She was a dragon woman who married a human. Their son didn't have the power to change and he also married a human. They had one daughter, which is you. Your father is called Almor and your mother's name is Ludmilla."

"Are they still alive?"

Anukasan slowly shook his head. Lilith started to shiver. Ever since she had told Chrys invented stories about her family, she had been hoping to see her parents again one day. But now that hope flew right out of the window.

Anukasan pulled her against him to comfort her. Lilith felt his hands rub along her back, but it only made her grief worse. By acknowledging her emotions, he permitted her to feel the pain.

"I promised your parents that I would try to find you. But I never managed to discover your whereabouts, and I lost track of them. Your parents were grief-stricken because of the loss of their daughter. You mother never touched her instrument again. You father used to be a respected member of society, but he became listless. People accept that for a short while, but in the long term they expect you to get on with your life. Your parents weren't able to do that. They never stopped loving you until the day that they died." Anukasan abruptly stopped talking.

Lilith asked, "How did they die?"

His reluctance to answer her question scared her. Nevertheless, she wanted to know, she had to know! She grabbed his shoulders and gave him a rough shaking. "What happened to my parents!" Her voice pierced the room.

There was another brief silence. When Anukasan cautiously looked into her eyes, he saw her threatening gaze. He swallowed away the lump in his throat. "Your parents must have suspected what had happened to you. And your master must have known that your parents had moved. They had gone to Tewarsum."

The news hit her like a rock. Her fists were still clenching the fabric of his clothes and she fell back against him. Her short scream sounded like the cry of a wounded animal. She made no other sounds, but everybody looked in their direction. Even the music stopped. Anukasan had gone numb and didn't move.

The devastating truth had instantly struck Lilith. If her parents had moved to Tewarsum, she had been the one who had taken their lives. It felt as if her body was being ripped apart by a sudden force. The pain was unbearable but it couldn't find a way out. It was becoming harder and harder to breathe. Her head was pounding and the world seemed to be spinning. She wanted to cry to let the pain flow away, but she couldn't. Her tears had dried up a long time ago. She sat motionless and listened to the silence that was filling the room.

"Kasimirh felt threatened because your parents were closing in, so they had to die. He probably would have used it against you one day to make you even more dependent on him."

Lilith had recovered her voice but she was still sounding hoarse. "Why are you telling me all these lies? You're even worse than my master. He always had my best interests at heart. My parents probably came to find me in order to kill me. He did it for me, he wanted to protect me. I wasn't given a choice, but he did it to protect me. And you as well, Anukasan, it was to protect all shapeshifters. Humans want to kill us, therefore you have to eliminate them before they find you."

Lilith was telling herself the lies that the master had imprinted on her mind. By turning the story around, she could suppress her pain. This strategy had kept her going all those years that she had lived with Kasimirh. With her whole world collapsing, she sought solace in the only way she knew how.

Anukasan, however, didn't let her. He pushed her away and said softly, but also sternly, "Lilith, you know that's not true. Stop it. You didn't know, fine, but don't try to distort the truth."

Aggrieved, she glared at him from behind her hair. Her wristband started to irritate her and she was fighting her emotions. It didn't work. "Don't tell me that I didn't know!" Lilith suddenly screamed in anger. "I knew what the effects of my actions were, didn't I? I knew that people were dying because of me, that lives were being destroyed because of me." Anukasan wanted to say something, but Lilith kept on ranting, "There is no excuse. I can't hide behind ignorance. So don't ask me to do that."

Lilith tasted sulphur in her mouth and she knew that her eyes burned fiercer with every word she spoke. Anukasan opened his mouth again, but she made sure that he couldn't interrupt her. She knew she was being unreasonable, but it was good to feel the anger and let it out. Everything was better than giving the grief a chance to overwhelm her, because then she would drown in the tears she wouldn't be able to shed.

"I'm no longer the baby that was kidnapped." She got up and paced around the hall. She shoved aside everyone who got in the way. Right below the dome she turned around. "I knew very well what I was doing and I chose to rob thousands of people of their lives!"

Ferhdessar looked up expectantly when the eagle man entered his room.

"I should never have agreed to this," he ranted.

Ferhdessar knew enough. His plan to turn Lilith against Kasimirh once and for all had failed.

"So she didn't react as I thought?"

Anukasan shook his head angrily. "She blames herself. And me."

"I'm sorry that she offended you."

"That's not necessary, but you should be sorry that you made me do this."

Ferhdessar lowered himself into an armchair. When he had discovered that Anukasan knew the dragon woman, this plan had welled up in him. It had seemed like such a good idea to tell Lilith what had happened to her parents. Anukasan had argued to have it remain a secret, but Ferhdessar had been convinced that this was the way to fully win the woman over. How could it have gone so wrong? Wasn't it clear what Kasimirh had made her do?

"This whole plan has left Lilith even more vulnerable," Anukasan ranted. "In order to deal with the murder of her parents, she relapsed into her old habits. You should leave her alone. You should make sure that she stays as far away from that guy as possible. Your plan will drive her right back into his arms. Tread with care, Ferhdessar. When she finds out what kind of game you're playing with her, she'll start wondering how different your actions really are from those of her master."

Ferhdessar jumped up. "Don't you dare compare me to him! I have her best interests at heart. And Merzia's."

"This Kasimirh probably thought the same thing." Anukasan gave him a contemptuous glare. "In any case, I should have stayed out of this. I really regret telling her. What was the use? All we did was cause her even more pain. She should have remained ignorant."

"I didn't mean for it to go this way," Ferhdessar grumbled.

"You never even stopped to think about what this would do to her. All you wanted was for her to jump up and fly straight to Naftalia to put an end to your problem."

Ferhdessar didn't get a chance to respond, because Anukasan opened the window and flew away.

Of course it wasn't long before everybody in the palace knew what had happened in the Great Hall. In the kitchen the servants were talking about it disbelievingly. Aida dominated the conversation, "I told you. That woman can't be trusted."

"Stop it."

Aida turned around with a start. Ghalatea had entered the kitchen.

"You have no idea what Lilith has been through."

Everybody fell silent. Ghalatea picked up a basket and laid some fruit in it. Then she grabbed two mugs and a large jug of tea. As she walked out of the kitchen she snatched the bunch of keys hanging to the left of the door off the hook.

Not much later she was standing in front of the door to Lilith's room. She wasn't surprised that it was locked. She quietly knocked on the wood, but she didn't get a response. She knocked again, a little bit louder this time, and now she heard a muffled voice say, "Please, go away."

"Lilith, it's me, Ghalatea. Please, open the door."

"Go away!"

Ghalatea, however, got out the keys and unlocked the door. She stopped on the threshold and looked around the room. Only when she stepped forwards, did she see Lilith sitting in front of the fireplace. The poker that she was stirring the fire with was red hot. The scent of scorched meat entered Ghalatea's nose, but she didn't see anything that could give off that smell, so she chose to ignore it.

A few more paces into the room she could see Lilith's face. It was set tight and she looked ghostly pale. The Ancilla Princeps sat down next to her on the floor. She carefully stroked Lilith's hair. "I'm sorry about your parents."

She had expected Lilith to start crying, but she didn't. Ghalatea pulled her against her and wrapped an arm around her. "It's all right to cry."

Lilith shrugged. Ghalatea didn't understand this response so she waited.

Suddenly Lilith whispered, "Every time I think that I'm on the right track something happens that turns everything upside down again. Why, Ghalatea? Why?"

The Ancilla Princeps shook her head and sighed. "I don't know, Lilith. I wish I could guard you from all the misery."

"Why wasn't it enough to know that I was responsible for the death of so many people? Why do they have to have names? Why do they want me to know that I killed my parents?"

There was nothing that Ghalatea could say. Lilith bowed her head and buried her face in her hands. Ghalatea held her even tighter and kissed her hair.

"How can I ever forgive myself? How can I ever look in the mirror and feel proud of myself again?"

"You have so many reasons to be proud of yourself, Lilith. Please don't forget the good things you also did. The things that you did because you wanted to do them and that you did out of your own free will."

She remained silent to give Lilith a chance to let the words sink in. Then she continued, "Don't be too hard on yourself. During the first years of your life you never had a choice. All you could hope to do was make life a bit more bearable for yourself. Not even much better, only a little bit better, and everyone in your situation would have jumped at that tiny chance. But time and again the pain found another way to eat away at you, forcing you to find a different way to survive. You're no lesser person than we are. You just had a much worse start in life."

Lilith stared pensively into the fire and shook her head. "You say I did it to save myself, but don't you think that's unreasonable? How can I convince myself that my life was worth all those victims? I refuse to do that."

"Of course, but wasn't that why you fled? When that truth finally sank in and all other reasons became less important, you decided to put your own life on the line."

"I don't know, Ghalatea. It sounds too good to be true. Right now I can't believe it. I don't deserve your forgiveness." Lilith pushed Ghalatea away and got up. She opened the curtains and looked outside. "Margal's followers are right, I am a monster. It would be better if I were dead."

Ghalatea had remained seated, but now she turned around with a start. "Lilith, please…"

"Don't worry, I'm too cowardly to take my own life. That's what I've always been: a coward. You say that I didn't have a choice, but that's not true. I had a choice, but I was too scared to make it. I'm nothing but a coward."

Lilith rested her hands on the windowsill and leaned her forehead against the window. The lines in her face were hard, her countenance was deathly pale. Her hunched shoulders touched her ears. Ghalatea was powerless. She couldn't console this woman.

Lilith suddenly turned around and pulled up her sleeve. She held her right fist in front of Ghalatea's face, so that the Ancilla Princeps was forced to look at the rugged scar on her wrist. "See, this is proof. If I had simply gone through with it, my parents would still be alive. All I had to do was drive the dagger in farther. I did have a choice!"

Ghalatea felt tears running down her cheeks. One big drop fell on Lilith's scar and followed the contours before it rolled to the other side of her arm. Lilith took a step back and wrapped her arms so closely around herself that her hands touched her shoulder blades. Her chin was resting on her chest, so her arms were almost completely hiding her face, except for her eyes.

"But I made the wrong choice. I chose to protect the monster that didn't deserve to live."

Then her hair fell forwards, making her entire face invisible. Ghalatea brushed Lilith's hair out of her face. Next, she lowered Lilith down on a chair. The young woman was rubbing her wrist and seemed to be miles away with her thoughts.

Ghalatea knew how terrible it could be to carry around so much guilt, even if there was nothing to reproach yourself with. It wasn't her fault that her parents and her friends had died, but still, maybe she could have tried harder. If this and if that. It didn't get you anywhere, but Lilith would be going through the same process right now. The thought that it would have been better if she had killed herself would haunt her for a very long time.

As Ghalatea looked at Lilith's hands again, she suddenly realized that Lilith wasn't rubbing the scar. Her scar was on her right wrist, but she was rubbing her left wrist. Ghalatea pulled the hand towards herself and was appalled by the big burn mark. She gave Lilith a rough shaking. "What have you done?" There was no response.

A cool wind rushed along Lilith's body. It sounded as if there was a harp playing softly somewhere. Below her, she saw her own shape reflected in the water, and in front of her a village loomed up. Even though it was pitch-dark, she could easily discern everything.

The village was deserted, apart for two people standing in the square. They were waving at her. Lilith felt her heart fill with love. These people had been waiting for her. She wanted to commence her landing, but then she noticed her master on the other side of the square.

"Kill them, Lilith."

Without any hesitation, she did as she was told. A fiery, orange beam was aimed at the man and woman. The sounds of the harp morphed into a sickening scream. There was a hand protruding from the fire. It belonged to the man. And then there was nothing any more. Satisfied, Kasimirh looked up at her. "Those were your parents, Lilith."

Gasping for air, Lilith jolted awake. Ghalatea was immediately there. She comforted her, but Lilith started shaking more violently. She couldn't get the images of her parents out of her head.

She was crying inside. She was nothing but a vessel filled with grief. The water had reached her lungs, making it hard to breathe. Why didn't Ghalatea leave? Maybe she could let the water flow away then. And after that, she could make sure that the only thing she felt was pain. Because that was an emotion she could deal with. She'd never learned how to cope with grief, so how was she going to come to terms with this?

"Where did you get this?" Ghalatea rolled up Lilith's sleeve.

Lilith looked at the burn. She absorbed the pain, but it was immediately extinguished by the water flowing through her body. She shrugged.

"Did you do this to yourself with the poker yesterday?"

"This is what they went through because of me. Have you any idea how terrible it is, how painful it is to be burned?" Lilith didn't notice that Ghalatea's hand briefly disappeared underneath her veil. "It's horrible. I've tried to do it to myself, but even this small burn was too much for me."

And even that amount of pain hadn't been enough to calm her down. It hadn't vaporized her tears. It was going to take a whole lot more to achieve that.

"How can you forgive me, Ghalatea?" Lilith asked.

"Because I've been able to see the real you from the beginning. There's a little girl hidden underneath that hard, battered shell. I can often see her when I look into your eyes. Maybe that little girl hid herself on the day she was taken. Maybe she put up thousands of protective layers around herself because of everything that was done to her. And later on she might have added thousands more when she had to start working for her master." Lilith opened her eyes but didn't seem to see anything. Ghalatea was sitting on her knees in front of her. "But that girl is still in there. Sometimes she pulls away a few of those layers, like a flower that opens itself, but whenever something unexpected happens, she closes herself off again and puts up new layers. I know that you don't believe me right now, but I know that Ébha saw this as well. She told you that, didn't she?"

Lilith nodded. Ghalatea held her face with both hands and pressed a kiss on Lilith's cheek.

"Cherish who you are, Lilith. Don't forget about that little girl. Cherish her, until the day that you're strong enough to cast off your shell and present yourself to the outside world."

Lilith bowed her head and curled herself up. Ghalatea wrapped her arms around her. The old woman's tears rolled down Lilith's neck and back. They sat in this embrace for a while.

When the bells started to toll, Ghalatea jumped up.

"The alarm bells," she exclaimed in shock, and she rushed out of the room.

Lilith remained curled up for a little while longer, but then she got back to her feet. She picked up the poker and raised her arm to strike. After some hesitation she threw the poker away. She knew it wouldn't help her drive away the pain. Even if she cut her entire body open, it wouldn't be enough to forget about the pain in her heart.

Without knowing what she was going to do, Lilith left her room an hour later. There were lots of people milling around in the corridors. Servants were rushing past, carrying baskets filled with vegetables or sacks of flour, and maids were running around with bedclothes in their arms. Lilith hardly noticed them. Only when someone bumped into her, did she become aware of all the people around her.

"I'm sorry," Aida stammered, picking up the bedclothes she had dropped. "Please, don't hurt me."

"Why would I hurt you?"

Lilith was taken aback by the fear in the maidservant's eyes. When she took a step forwards, Aida backed away. Shaking with fear, she picked up the last cloth and ran off. Lilith stared after her.

She could never have expected that it would affect her so much to see Aida this afraid of her. A few days ago she had even wished that Aida would be scared of her, because then the tormenting might finally stop. But right now, the maidservant's eyes were a mirror that showed her how others saw her: as a scary monster, a murderer. Maybe it felt so bad because what Aida thought of her was the truth.

A group of servants walked by. Lilith stepped backwards. Some of the women sneaked a surreptitious glance at her and when they were a bit farther down the corridor they started to whisper to one another. They might as well have been screaming, though. "She's dangerous, do you know what she's done?" As one of them related what had happened in the Great Hall the other day, two men looked over their shoulder. They immediately cast down their eyes when they met Lilith's gaze.

Lilith suppressed the urge to stop them and tell them the full story. There was no use, none of the servants would understand. Not even Ghalatea had understood it at first. Only the king and Ferhdessar had comprehended what had happened. Maybe it was best to go looking for the sorcerer now.

No one answered when she knocked on the door to Ferhdessar's room, so she tried to push it open. The door was locked, however, so she walked back to the soldiers who were guarding this part of the palace. When she asked them where she could find Ferhdessar, they answered that he was in the garden. Lilith had an anxious feeling that she had to be quick, so she ran through the corridors. People jumped out of the way and she yelled apologies at them.

When she found Ferhdessar, he was just pushing his flying machine to a ramp that was placed at the edge of the rock pillar.

"What in the world is going on?" she panted.

Vexed, the sorcerer looked up. "We received a message that one of Merzia's seaport towns is under attack."

"From Kasimirh?"

"I think so."

So it had begun, Kasimirh had taken the next step. Lilith came even closer. "Are you going there?"

Ferhdessar nodded.

"Are you flying?" Lilith asked incredulously.

"Why not? This is the perfect opportunity to test this machine and there's no faster way to travel."

Lilith let her gaze pass over the aircraft. Ferhdessar had painted the light metal of the body a shiny black and then he had wrapped it in transparent, black fabric to give the flying machine a better shape. The sorcerer's relatively slow pedalling would be converted by means of gear wheels into faster wingbeats. Lilith shook her head. She couldn't believe that Ferhdessar was really going to ride off the ramp and plunge into nothingness in the hope that his machine would carry him.

"You'll grow tired pretty soon if you have to pedal the entire way."

"I'll manage, one way or the other. There's no alternative. I need to get to Havv'n as soon as possible. I might still be of help."

Lilith pushed her misgivings about the aircraft aside. "Will you take me with you?"

"That's much too dangerous. You're better off staying here."

"As if I have a life here. They're all giving me the cold shoulder," she complained.

"Yeah, well, that's your own fault. You're the one who shouted your crimes from the rooftops."

"I did have other things on my mind than to think of the consequences of my actions, thank you very much."

Ferhdessar gave her a penetrating gaze before he walked up to her. "Anukasan has told me what happened yesterday. I was astounded by your reaction. Your master killed your parents. You should be angry with him, not with yourself."

"I was the one who did it." Lilith viciously tapped her finger on her chest three times, while repeating the word "me". "Nobody else."

Ferhdessar heaved a deep sigh. "That's why I can't take you with me, Lilith. I'm working under the assumption that Kasimirh will still be in Havv'n when I get there. You're a long way from being ready to meet him."

Lilith bowed her head. She wanted to get away from Nadesh so badly.

"Fine," she suddenly said resolutely and held out her arm to him. "I want you to take off my wristband. It's time for me to leave the palace."

"And then what?" Ferhdessar had been getting ready to board the plane, but now he turned back around.

"Then I'll fly to this town that you're talking about and I'll go help the people there."

Ferhdessar shook his head disapprovingly. "It isn't that simple."

Lilith nodded. She knew that her plan wasn't perfect. As soon as she changed into a dragon, Kasimirh would enter her mind. It wasn't going to be a pleasant flight.

"I want to at least try to do this. So I'd like you to take off my wristband and give me back my shapeshifting amulet. And should Kasimirh still be there, I'll help you defeat him, like we agreed."

Ferhdessar uttered a brief laugh, as if she was making a joke. Then he shook his head. "I don't think it's wise. But, at the same time, I can't stop you." He looked at his machine. "Seeing that you're going in that direction anyway, could you perhaps take me with you? I'm sure you're faster than my aircraft."

Lilith grinned. "That wouldn't be a problem."

"Great, I'll notify the king."

"That gives me the opportunity to gather some things and say goodbye to Ghalatea."

Side by side they walked back into the palace. Lilith was glad that she would be travelling with the sorcerer. As long as she was near him, nothing could happen to her. It made her a bit less anxious about seeing the master again.

Lilith wrapped the figurine of Jakob in a cloth. It was the last item she put in the rucksack that Ghalatea had given her. Then she turned around to face the Ancilla Princeps, who was sitting on the edge of the bed.

"I'm going to miss you Ghalatea. You've taken such good care of me and I know that I can trust you. Your insights have often helped me when I didn't know what to do any more."

"I'm honoured that you think of me like that."

"I'm sure there are more people who feel that way. You didn't become Ancilla Princeps for no reason."

Laughing, Ghalatea rose to her feet. "I'm going to miss you too, but I'm so proud of you. It's good that you're going to do this." They hugged. "Will you be careful?"

"Of course I will. And Ferhdessar is with me, so you don't have to worry."

A deep sigh escaped Ghalatea's lips. "Be on your guard around him. He's not interested in your well-being."

Lilith shrugged. "I know that you never trusted him, but I do. He promised to help and protect me."

"He's capable of much more than you think, Lilith. When push comes to shove, he'll do what he thinks is right and he won't take your best interests into consideration. It scares me to think of all the ways he could hurt you."

"I'll remember that, Ghalatea. And I'll be careful. I can stand up for myself, you know."

"Lilith, he has..." Then Ghalatea changed her mind. She had wanted to say that Ferhdessar had urged Anukasan to tell Lilith what had happened to her parents. But she feared that it might have an adverse effect.

Luckily, Lilith didn't ask what she had wanted to say.

"If Kasimirh is still in Havv'n, I will destroy him with Ferhdessar's help! That's all I'm going to do. Please, don't worry, I'll be back before you know it." Lilith conjured up a smile. Nevertheless, she didn't feel half as confident as she made it sound. "And then nobody will call me a murderer any more. Instead, I'll get a hero's welcome!"

The biggest reward, however, would be that she could finally come clean with Chrys. If she had done away with Kasimirh, Chrys could no longer hold her past actions against her.

Ghalatea shrugged resignedly and handed Lilith a little pouch. "Maybe this will offer you some protection. You're leaving in a bit of a hurry, so I had to gather this rather quickly. I hope it will make you come back safe."

Lilith was surprised by the gift. She tucked it away underneath her clothes. "I hope it will lead me back to Chrys."

They walked to the Great Hall. Lilith had arranged to meet Ferhdessar there. They didn't have to wait long before the doors were opened and a group of people walked in. Accompanied by a few members of his Guard, the king entered together with Ferhdessar. They stopped in front of Lilith, who made a deep curtsy.

"Thank you, Lilith, for going out there to help my people."

She didn't dare look up, but Ferhdessar encouraged her to come with him. She whispered, "Where are we going?"

"The garden is big enough for you to change."

"What will the people think when they see me?" she asked, horror-stricken.

The king gave her a reassuring smile. "It might help that they see you coming from the capital."

"Are you coming with us?"

"I'd like to see you change. I've never seen a dragon before," Yvar said. "Or do you have any objections?"

Lilith bowed her head, "Of course not, my lord."

Ferhdessar drew forth her amulet from his pocket and hung it around her neck. Hesitantly, Lilith looked from Ghalatea to Ferhdessar.

"I'm scared. This reminds me of how my master prepared me for my missions. Shapeshifting is unpleasant and I fear my master. What's in store for me?"

"Nothing can happen to you, Lilith. I'm with you."

She nodded at the sorcerer and began her change. Ferhdessar watched Lilith go through the transformations that he had witnessed before. But now the scales replaced the human skin completely, and Lilith grew even larger. Both transformations happened at the same time. Ferhdessar couldn't tell which happened first, Lilith growing bigger or Lilith changing into a dragon. Suddenly she was a dragon and it seemed as if she had never been a woman. Her black scales gave off a red glow.

Ferhdessar was keeping a spell prepared to restrain Lilith the second she showed any sign of wanting to attack him or the king. But he was also full of admiration for the creature standing in front of him. Even though she towered over him by several feet, the sorcerer knew that Lilith was small compared to other members of her species. Her long tail was wagging gently. The spikes on her head and back sometimes stood up, but they also went down again. Ferhdessar could clearly see her teeth underneath her lips. Her face was delicate but radiated danger at the same time. There was a coldness in her deep-black eyes.

Lilith lay down and ordered Ferhdessar to mount. He went to sit between her shoulders. She carefully got back up.

"Are you ready, Ferhdessar?"

"Let's go! You know I've been dreaming about flying for a very long time."

The dragon bowed deeply in front of the king and smiled at Ghalatea before she took a great leap and flew away.

Lilith dived into the abyss. The wind soared around her body as she followed a waterfall that was hurtling down from one of the rock peaks. This was the waterfall that put the wheels in motion which provided Nadesh with electricity. Drops of water spat up against her belly. Ferhdessar was pressing his knees into her shoulders. He had nestled against her neck and his yells of excitement sounded close to her ears.

Several feet from the ground, Lilith changed direction. She flew into the circle between the ten rock peaks and circled back up. With smooth twists and turns she avoided the bridges and the thick cables that ran between the city and the plain to supply the surrounding villages with electricity. She skimmed along tall buildings. It was lovely to behold the city from this point of view. Lilith flew over the palace garden once more, saw that the king and his guards were still watching her, and headed north.

15

Kasimirh raised his arms and closed his eyes before he called upon Jakob. He waited for several minutes, but nothing happened. After that one period – so many years ago – God had never appeared to him again. Back then, Jakob had given him his assignment and had disappeared for good. Kasimirh bit back his disappointment. He knelt and started to pray.

"Lord Jakob, give me the strength to fight in Your name one more day, so that I can do what You desire of me. The battle for Merzia has begun. You taught me that this country, and Nadesh in particular, was pivotal to Your initial plans. That's why it hurts me that the Merzians, of all people, have strayed farther away from You than anyone else. But that's going to change!" Kasimirh heard wet footsteps behind him but he wasn't ready yet. "It won't be long, Lord Jakob, before this country belongs to You again." Then he whispered, "I would very much appreciate receiving a sign from You, just so that I know that I'm on the right track."

He ended his prayer. He had difficulty getting back up. It drained one's energy to be using magic, and he had been at it for more than twenty-four hours on end.

The Muircadh bowed deeply. "Your plans?"

After all those years, Kasimirh still wasn't used to the way the servi spoke. They always sounded so curt. He knew, however, that it wasn't a sign of disrespect. Kasimirh simply hadn't been able to teach the amphibians more of his language.

"The same as yesterday. Hopefully we'll succeed in defeating the Merzians today. It's safe to say that it won't take much longer."

He studied the creature's face. The servus seemed to fully understand what he meant.

"We ready," the Muircadh said. Then he turned around to dive back into the water. Kasimirh caught a final glimpse of his silhouette that quickly disappeared below the choppy water.

The Merzians hadn't been expecting an attack from the north.

The element of surprise had helped Kasimirh in his attack. When the first and largest tidal wave had struck them, the Merzians had thought they were dealing with a natural disaster and they hadn't yet been aware of what was hidden in the waves.

Nevertheless, it had all taken much too long. This seaport town should have fallen in a few hours' time, but the servi didn't have much more to show for their actions than the destruction of the wooden houses on the beach and of one of the two lighthouses. The big gate that was to be their entrance into Merzia remained an unassailable barrier at present. Even from this distance, Kasimirh could see how the gate sparkled defiantly in the light of the morning sun.

Kasimirh waited a little while longer before he extended his hands towards the water. As he chanted, the water accumulated around the little island. The waves reversed direction and were no longer rolling towards the beach.

From the second that Kasimirh started to call up the magic, he didn't feel his fatigue any more. Water was life, and now that he was connected to the first thing that Jakob had given to the people, he felt more alive than ever. The servi and their boards popped up between the crests on the waves. Everything was in readiness. Kasimirh reluctantly released the power that he had built up. The servi paddled until they moved fast enough to jump on their boards. Kasimirh didn't notice it any more; there was something else that attracted his attention.

"Welcome back, Lilith!" he yelled across the water, feeling delighted. He silently thanked Jakob for giving him a sign after all and then focussed on the dragon woman. There could be only one reason why she had changed: she was coming back to him.

Lilith shivered briefly when the master suddenly entered her mind. She decided to ignore him.

"Are you coming back to me?"

She was surprised to hear that he was almost pleading. Nevertheless, she remained quiet.

"Lilith, answer me!"

She was startled, because he had suddenly raised his voice. She shivered again. Ferhdessar had to hold on tight to keep from sliding off her back. He yelled something at her, but his words were lost in the wind howling around them.

"He has noticed me," she growled in answer to the question he had probably asked. "And he's getting less friendly by the minute."

Ferhdessar's hand stroked her scales, which reassured her for the time being. She tried to focus on the landscape passing below her. Over the past centuries, rain and wind had shaped the surroundings of Nadesh into what it was now: a rolling terrain with hills that were covered with forests. The waterfalls had flowed together into wide rivers.

After Lilith had left the capital behind her, she had flown over fields of grain. From this altitude, the water mills that grinded the grain with the help of the fast-flowing river had looked like minia-ture models. Full of admiration, Lilith had gazed down upon the enormous fields of flowers that the Merzians had cultivated in the hills to supply themselves with the pigments they needed for all the colours they used in everyday life. She had descended some-what and the air displacement caused by her wings had released the lovely scents of the flowers. Upon approaching a village, she had re-gained height.

"Who are you talking to?" Kasimirh asked.

Lilith decided not to answer him. Below her she saw a long line of wagons. The horses snorted wildly when her shadow passed over them, and their riders had great difficulty holding them in check. Some people shouted at her in excitement.

"Very well, you might not be alone any more, but are you sure that this person is strong enough to protect you from me?"

"This sorcerer is the best there is," Lilith snarled at him.

Kasimirh groaned. "How can you say that? Everything I know I've learned from Jakob. There's nobody who knows more than He."

Lilith shook her head and peered at the horizon. The sun stood directly above her, but she was sure that she was flying in the right direction. She had left the wagons far behind her, and the fields of flowers had given way to vast fields of grain that were interspersed with stretches of woods.

"Dear Lilith, please return to me. Let's finish what we once started. You're an important part of Jakob's plans. Have you never understood that?"

"How could I understand when you never explained anything to me?"

Lilith immediately regretted that she had let herself be tempted into giving an answer.

"Back then, I thought you knew, but now I know that I was wrong to think that. You were too young to understand. I realize that now, but back then you seemed so mature that I kept forgetting you were a child. You always carried out Jakob's tasks with such determination."

Lilith swallowed. "That was a mask, because you never allowed me to think about what I was doing."

"I understand that, my child. Please come back, and everything will be different. I'll prove to you that I've learned from my mistakes. I'm not mad with you for leaving, but it has grieved me." Lilith was having doubts. The master had apparently noticed this, because he begged, "I'm sorry for all the times that I hurt you. I'm sorry that I didn't do enough to soften the pain. But please, give me another chance, Lilith."

"How can I be sure that you really have changed?"

The master answered, but Ferhdessar drew Lilith's attention. He was leaning forwards and yelled, "Maybe we should take a rest somewhere."

Lilith nodded and searched the landscape for a place to land. She saw nothing but trees below her, but suddenly she spotted a small clearing to the right. She changed direction and commenced her landing.

"What's going on?"

Ferhdessar gave her a worried look, but Lilith averted her eyes.

"We're talking." She shrugged as if it meant nothing.

"I can only hear your side of the conversation and because of the wind I can't even hear everything you're saying, but I can't escape the feeling that he's winning you over."

"No! He'll never control me like that again!"

Several minutes passed. Staring into the distance, Lilith was angrily pulling pieces of grass out of the ground. Then she bowed her head. She dropped her voice to a whisper and admitted that the sorcerer was right. "Now that he's not in my head any more, it feels so stupid. I don't even understand it myself, but when I hear him talking, he is so convincing. He sounds so sincere." She shook her head.

"I thought as much."

"That's why you made me land…"

"I can't allow him to get a hold of you again. And by now, I know that you don't want him to either."

Lilith nodded. "Thank you. We have a long journey ahead of us. Shall we get going again?"

"Are you ready?"

He regarded her closely. Lilith curled the corners of her mouth up, but it wasn't a genuine smile. She knew that Ferhdessar wouldn't buy it. She shrugged and changed back into a dragon. The master immediately entered her mind again.

"I was afraid you had disappeared again. It would have broken my heart. Fortunately, you're back."

"I'll never come back. I still don't regret my decision to leave. It's the only good thing I ever did while I was with you."

"How dare you turn your back on me again?" His voice was suddenly shaking with anger. Lilith had to exert every ounce of will power to refrain from answering him. "Lilith, I won't allow you to ignore me!"

He can't force me to talk to him. He is so far away, what could he do to me?

"You can't run away from the plans that Jakob has for you, Lilith. I'll be waiting for you in Havv'n and it won't be long before you'll return to me. It doesn't matter that you ran away. I'll even forgive you for what you just said to me. You don't have to be afraid. I'll welcome you with open arms."

Lilith didn't say anything. She told herself that his flattering tone was feigned.

"You can't escape me, Lilith. I've always known that I would get you back someday. And it seems I don't have to wait much longer."

Now she was sure. With every word his voice sounded more threatening.

"Talk to me! Don't make me angry. You know you should never make me angry, don't you? If you behave the way I want you to, nothing bad will happen to you! Answer me!"

Lilith shivered. The landscape below her became blurred. She squinted to focus, but the pressure in her head was too intense. In the distance she saw a few trees. She had wanted to keep flying but she really needed to rest.

The landing was rough because she hadn't judged the distance to the ground right. Ferhdessar was hurled off her back. Lilith was relieved to be able to change back into human form. She was lying on the ground, gasping for air. The sorcerer knelt down beside her and looked worried.

"Are you all right?"

"How can I win this fight? He keeps trying to make me change my mind." Then she whispered, "I'm not strong enough to resist him. This was a mistake."

"I knew this would happen," Ferhdessar mumbled as he lifted her up. He laid her down beneath the shelter of the trees and built a fire. Lilith couldn't find the nerve to respond to his remark.

"Do you want to go on?" he asked her.

Lilith banged her fist on the ground. She was going to prove to both sorcerers that she was strong enough. As she sat up she said resolutely, "Absolutely. You have to go and help the people up north as soon as possible."

Now that Lilith was back in human form, her master couldn't reach her. That made her feel safer. It was already getting harder to imagine why resisting him cost her so much effort. But her fatigue was proof of how hard it had been.

Ferhdessar produced a small kettle and boiled some water. After that, he handed her a mug.

"What is this?"

"It's just tea."

Lilith gratefully drank her tea and looked at Ferhdessar. He stared back at her. There was something in his eyes that she hadn't seen before. Was it concern? Then Ferhdessar broke a piece off the bread that Ghalatea had given to Lilith.

"Could you teach me how to pray to Jakob?" he asked to Lilith's utter surprise.

"Don't you have a different religion?"

"Jakob is part of the most influential religion in Merzia. And I'm starting to have second thoughts now that I've read Kasimirh's book. The way that he's preaching Jakob's message may be wrong, but the faith itself appeals to me. Just like you, I don't think it's Jakob who's wrong in this battle, it's Kasimirh." Ferhdessar avoided her gaze. He seemed somewhat shy confessing this, but Lilith could never really tell what he was feeling. It could just as easily be the opposite. "Anyhow, I'd like to learn more about Him and it seems to me that you are a much better teacher than Kasimirh."

The fact that Ferhdessar wanted to learn from her made her feel good. It was almost as if they were equals. Lilith said a prayer to thank Jakob for the food. Ferhdessar repeated her words.

They sat beside each other in silence for a while, until Ferhdessar broke the silence again. "Have you ever thought about the possibility that Jakob is still guiding you?"

"What do you mean?"

"It's one of the reasons why I started to have doubts. What are the odds of you ending up in the one place that is the most important in Kasimirh's plans, without even knowing it?"

Lilith shrugged. Chrys had also talked about how he didn't believe in coincidences.

"Maybe it's Jakob's will that you fight against His prophet. He might be offering you a chance to redeem your sins."

"I don't know whether I should believe that, but it doesn't really matter. I don't think I can redeem my sins – too much has happened – but I can try to counterbalance them with positive actions. The best way to do that is to fight Kasimirh. Come, let's get going. We have to reach Havv'n before it's too late to put a stop to Kasimirh."

Lilith walked onto the field and let her gaze wander along the horizon. Her hand touched her neck, but she held back from saying the words. Her fear for the master had increased tremendously, and she was dreading getting in touch with him again. Unresolved, she turned around to face Ferhdessar. He was standing in the shadow of the trees, watching her. Then he nodded at her.

"I'm not afraid of you," she whispered before she murmured the incantation to set about the change. She hardly noticed Ferhdessar climbing on her shoulders again, because she was immediately plunged into the struggle to shut out her master as much as possible.

As Lilith flew over fields and lakes, the master kept trying to win her over. He kept bombarding her with sneering remarks and threats. Trees and hills rushed past below her. She had been following the river, but whenever it bore off to find its way through the lowland, Lilith kept heading straight for the north to pick up the course of the river again farther on.

"Leave me alone!"

"What makes you think I will? Jakob has a purpose for you. You can't escape His will. I'll make sure that you'll follow His path."

"Let me choose my own path," she begged.

"You, Lilith, are incapable of making your own decisions. I made you into who you are! And that's why I'll get you back!"

Ferhdessar patted Lilith's neck. It helped her to drive out her master's voice for a short while. She became aware of the fact that her wings hit the crowns of the trees with every beat. She was losing height. Lilith regained height and searched the landscape for something she could focus on. It wasn't long, however, before the master took full control of her thoughts again.

"You belong to Jakob, and since I'm His messenger, you are mine."

She shivered and started to pray to Jakob. She begged Him to save her from her master. Kasimirh laughed.

"Do you really think that He will help you? It was Jakob who gave me these gifts. He gave me the task to unite the people under His rule. It pleases me that you haven't turned your back on Him yet, but your prayers won't help you. You're going to have to come to terms with your destiny."

"Maybe Jakob is sending me to you to fight against you!" Lilith was trying to sound convincing, but her words were littered with doubt, because she didn't know if she believed them herself.

Kasimirh's laugh cut through her mind. "Has Ferhdessar told you that nonsense? Jakob did indeed see you as a weapon, but not to defeat me. He gave me power over you, so we could fight the heathens together."

"There might have been a time when you controlled me, but not any more," Lilith stammered. If only she could rely on the things that Ferhdessar had told her. If she could truly believe, heart and soul, that Jakob hadn't deserted her yet, it probably wouldn't be this hard to withstand Kasimirh.

"Do you really believe that? My power over you has never waned. It's as strong as when you used to live with me."

The master spoke the incantation to change her back into human form. Lilith flapped her wings, but the membranes were already disappearing, making it impossible to catch the wind. Ferhdessar fell down, giving her a look of horror. That helped her regain control over her body. She accelerated her descent and grabbed hold of Ferhdessar. Branches hit her body before she was able to change back into a dragon. With powerful wingbeats she managed to regain height. Her heart was in her throat. She was looking for a good place to land, but all she could see below her were trees.

"See, Lilith, I taught you everything you know. I will get you back, and I'll keep controlling your mind until I do. You renewed the ties between us, and this time I won't let you get away. That's a promise."

He kept talking and talking. At long last she spotted a lake. She landed on the shore.

"I'm sorry, Ferhdessar, I can't go on."

They sat in silence for a while. Her headache was killing her. Lilith pressed the palms of her hands against her temples. She closed her eyes and let the spring sun warm her. She tried to relax by thinking of other things, but the master hadn't lied. He controlled her thoughts and there wasn't so much as a corner in her mind where she could find shelter against him.

"What happened?" Ferhdessar asked cautiously, rubbing his arm. Lilith had clenched her claw too tightly around his body.

"It feels as if he's slowly drawing me towards him. I don't know if I can even fight him any more. So much has happened..." She fell silent again. "The incantations also work when my master speaks them. I've known that for a very long time."

She could tell that Ferhdessar instantly understood what had happened. He looked at her with great concern. She pulled up her knees and shivered uncontrollably. She hid her head in her arms. Now and again, she uttered soft, plaintive noises.

"Are you in pain?"

"It's a memory," she answered. Lilith remained quiet for a while. She rested her arms on her knees and stared into the distance. "My first flight..." she began. "I was allowed to fly for the first time. I didn't even know that I could fly. It was wonderful. The wind whirled around my body, and every beat of my wings made me go faster. Full of amazement, I looked down at my shadow gliding over the ground. In spite of my enormous body, I felt weightless."

She smiled. That was the good part of her memory. She could, however, never have suspected what her master was about to do to her.

"I flew over the mountains and the plains. Zebras bolted in front of me, but when I saw a village looming up in the distance, I decided to turn back. I was afraid of the people, my master had warned me about them, after all. But I was also getting tired, which made it harder to flap my wings. When I reached the mountains, I rose one last time."

She pressed her hands against her temples again and her eyes were squeezed closed. She gasped, "That was when my master made me change. I saw how the rocks rapidly came closer and I screamed for him to change me back. The wind whooshed past my body and it felt like I was falling forever. There was nothing I could do but wait for the impact." She sighed. "All the air was pressed from my lungs when I hit the rocks. I heard the bones in my arms splinter, and I felt excruciating pain in my entire body. Back then, I wasn't used to pain yet. Defeated, I didn't get up. I couldn't understand why he had done this to me. I felt so lonely."

There was a prolonged silence. Finally Ferhdessar said, "That alone should be enough to hate him…"

He couldn't hide the anger in his voice. Lilith, however, shrugged indecisively. She knew why Ferhdessar came to that conclusion, but it wasn't as simple as that.

"I'll tell you what happened next. Maybe it will help you understand that hating him isn't as self-evident as you think.

When the evening fell, I got up to fly back home. I was immediately summoned to my master's room. I was so confused; feelings of grief and anger took turns. But the strongest emotion was fear. Fear of the man I was dependent on and who I had trusted all my life. He asked me why I was angry and explained to me that it was my own fault that I had fallen."

"What!" Ferhdessar shouted infuriated.

Lilith raised her hand. "I could have changed myself back into a dragon. After all, I knew the incantation too. It had been a lesson to prepare me for what might happen if I encountered humans."

"What a bunch of lies," the sorcerer hissed.

Vexed, Lilith looked up. "Of course they were, but I didn't know that back then. He seemed so sincere. I could see the sorrow in his eyes and started to doubt myself. He told me to lie down on his bed. He took my pain away and I fell asleep. The following days he helped me eat and taught me how to read. Every time I moaned, I saw pity in his eyes. Since he took such good care of me, I couldn't but think that he truly had meant to teach me an important lesson and that he had my best interests at heart. I trusted him even more than before."

Ferhdessar grumbled but didn't say anything.

"I'm sure you think it's crazy, but sometimes I really see him as a caring man. Not as the tyrant that you see and who I decided to run away from."

"You ought to fight, offer resistance, set everything straight…" He fell silent and looked at her. Then he shook his head. "I'm sorry, Lilith, this is the last thing you need right now. I'm not good at these things…" He was fumbling for words. "I can imagine why you see it like that. It's been your life for such a long time, and the only way for you to survive. It must all be extremely confusing to you. Believe me when I say that I just want to help you see things clearly."

"I have to discover these things myself."

"You're right. And I'm confident that you'll make the right decision."

Lilith tried to smile bravely. "I already made this decision, didn't I? Why would you doubt me?" Sure enough, Ferhdessar seemed ill at ease. "Because I haven't shown much perseverance over the past few hours," she added understandingly.

Ferhdessar looked relieved. "You do still seem to have doubts, but I can't say that you lack perseverance. I don't think you were ever lacking in that department."

"It's tempting to give in," Lilith confessed. "It might have been better if I had met my master face to face. Because then I could have fought him. How can I guard myself from his words? It's almost physically painful to have to listen to him. Unfortunately, he still has tremendous power over me. As soon as I change into a dragon, I feel the desire to return to him. I know that I don't want to, but he draws me in regardless. Perseverance isn't enough to accomplish this task. I'm sorry."

Because there was no response, she looked at Ferhdessar. The sorcerer was staring out over the water. Then he said, "There is a way in which I can make sure that he can't reach you any more. Then you can fly to Havv'n and do what you set out to do. But I don't know if you'll allow me to do this. Whether you trust me enough."

"Ferhdessar..." she protested.

He smiled. "I won't hold it against you, Lilith. I know we're not the best of friends. I might not even let anyone do it to me, even if it was a friend."

"What is it?" Lilith asked reluctantly. Ferhdessar's words sounded ominous, but it was tempting to be out of the master's reach for a while.

Ferhdessar produced a silver box. It was shaped like a snail's shell. He handed it to Lilith. Her fingers traced the ridges. The box felt warm and soft. When her fingers reached the cap, she looked up at the sorcerer. He gave her a nod of encouragement. When she opened the box, she felt something starting to pull on her, as if whatever it was that was in the box was trying to suck her in.

"This", Ferhdessar said, "is a soul box. Your soul can regard this object as its body, but only if you want it to. As soon as your soul is in the box, I will lock it. From that moment on, I can do anything I want with your body. I'll also be the only person who can release your soul by opening the box." Lilith started to shiver. "Which, of course, I will do. When we arrive at Havv'n, I'll reunite your soul with your body. Up until that time, Kasimirh won't be able to reach you, not even when you're a dragon."

Ferhdessar looked at her expectantly.

"I'll be at the mercy of one sorcerer to escape the other."

"I have no desire to be your new master. I hope you know that. I just want to make sure that you're able to do what you really want to do."

"How do I know that I can trust you? You never made a secret of the fact that you think I'm dangerous. If you trap my soul, you can rest assured that I won't ever attack anyone again unless you want me to."

Ferhdessar nodded. "I give you my word, and that's worth a lot. But I understand your doubts."

"Your word..." Lilith said indecisively.

"Lilith, I've changed my mind about you. You're not as dangerous as I first thought. You've had ample opportunity to hurt me, but you haven't even tried. Quite the contrary, you saved my life. I know how badly you want to go north and this is how I want to help you."

He hesitantly put a hand on her shoulder. It was the first time he touched her this gently. After she had recovered from the surprise, Lilith realized how much this meant to her. Nevertheless, her aversion to the ritual was too strong.

"I don't know, Ferhdessar. Let's just continue our journey."

Lilith changed. As if he'd been waiting for her, Kasimirh immediately entered her mind again. Lilith instantly changed back.

She heaved a deep sigh and stared north. Clouds were drifting by, travelling north at great speed. How much farther would it be? Lilith shook her head and kicked a stone a few dozen yards away, growling loudly. Why couldn't she be stronger? Then she wouldn't have to decide whether she could trust Ferhdessar right now.

The sorcerer was still waiting on the shore. His facial expression had become unreadable again. Except for his short hair and clothes, which were moving in the wind, he was standing motionless. The decision was up to her. A decision that she had to make even though she didn't want to. Staying here was not an option, because there were people waiting for them. They needed help.

"Do you promise to release me as soon as we reach Havv'n?" she whispered.

Ferhdessar put his right hand on his heart. "As Jakob is my witness, I swear that I will only let you fly to Havv'n, nothing else."

Lilith looked to the north once more. *Just you wait, Kasimirh. I might not be able to fight against your words, but just wait until we meet face to face.*

"All right, let's use the soul box."

Ferhdessar opened the box and put it in front of her. He was curious to see what was going to happen. Even though he had owned the object for a long time, he had never found anyone willing to play guinea pig. Ferhdessar hadn't expected Lilith to agree to it either. The fact that she had, told him how awful the flight had been until now. Or maybe she finally trusted him. It hadn't been easy to find the right words to comfort her, but apparently he had done well enough.

Lilith looked insecure. "What do I have to do?"

"All you have to do is imagine sliding into the box."

Ferhdessar watched how she let her soul flow into the box. Her eyes glazed over and her breathing became shallow. She stood perfectly still in front of him. Ferhdessar waited a little while longer before he walked up to her. He pushed against her shoulder, but Lilith didn't respond.

"Turn around."

Lilith immediately did as she was told. Next, Ferhdessar wanted to order her to change, but then he thought again. He got out a notebook and a pen.

"Tell me the shapeshifting incantation word for word."

He wrote down the words as Lilith pronounced them clearly. It might come in handy one day to know them. He put the notebook away and wrapped his hand around her amulet. Her skin was cold to the touch. Hard, not human. All the while, Lilith was staring right through him with her glassy eyes, waiting for the moment he gave her an order.

"Qi ga ullar brut i-qi libèr qi ouander i-a drag."

Tiny jolts of electricity went through his skin and Ferhdessar pulled his hand away. Pleased, he watched how his words made her change.

"Kneel!"

The dragon slowly sagged through her legs, and Ferhdessar climbed on her shoulders.

"Fly!"

It was strange to see Lilith this obedient; she mechanically did everything her told her.

"Lilith isn't here any more," he muttered when her master's voice entered his thoughts.

"Is that you, Ferhdessar? I have a bone to pick with you as well, so we'll see each other in Havv'n. I'm looking forward to our reunion."

For a moment, Ferhdessar was tempted to ask the prophet what he was talking about, but he decided to shield himself from the other sorcerer. The remark kept haunting him, though. Kasimirh had talked about a reunion, but Ferhdessar still couldn't remember where they knew each other from.

The question kept weighing on his mind as he flew north at high speed. The dragon immediately responded to any order he gave her, as if she were the airplane that he had built. A plan slowly started to take shape in his head. It seemed increasingly unlikely that Lilith would willingly fight against Kasimirh. The way she had fought against the prophet during the flight made that abundantly clear.

She herself had admitted that the prophet was drawing her in. It was hard to believe that she still was this vulnerable, but Ferhdessar knew that if he wanted to bring her into action during the upcoming battle, he'd have to do it without her permission.

It was getting dark when Ferhdessar noticed a bright beam of light moving back and forth along the clouds. That had to be one of Havv'n's lighthouses. It was a sign that he was nearing his destination.

Far below him, other lights drew his attention: the swinging lanterns of the soldiers that had been sent to Havv'n from the nearest army camp. Only a few men looked up at him. Ferhdessar peered at the horizon again and tried to assess the distance to the seaport town.

"We'll be there in half an hour," he mumbled, patting Lilith contentedly on the neck.

At first glance, the damage to the town seemed less than Ferhdessar had expected. Havv'n was built on a cliff near the estuary of a river. Sheer rock cliffs rose up from the water, and the only opening was the place where the river discharged into the bay. A gate had been built in that spot. It was the entrance into Merzia that would benefit the servi the most, because the river would lead them straight to Nadesh. But so far, they hadn't been successful in breaching the gate.

Relieved that he had reached Havv'n on time, Ferhdessar let the dragon skim over the rooftops. In most houses, the lights on the ground floors were on. This showed that people didn't dare go to sleep for fear of another attack.

Lilith flew over the temples of the Gods. The lights were on in the temples as well, and Ferhdessar heard mumbled prayers everywhere. Imploring hymns rose up out of the roof of Wigg's temple. Ferhdessar hoped that they would help to put a stop to Kasimirh and caught himself praying as well.

The silence hanging over Jakob's temple was ironic, but hardly surprising. Jakob didn't play a big part in the faith of the Merzians, especially not where war was concerned. Perhaps the people of Havv'n would have been praying to Jakob right now if they had known the motivation of their enemy. But then again, they might have set the temple afire, Ferhdessar thought as they left the building behind them.

Ferhdessar set course for the fort that lay on the other side of the river. His eye soon spotted a building where birds of prey were flying in and out. That had to be the command post. Ferhdessar told the dragon to land on a nearby square. Everything was deathly quiet.

"Wait there for me."

Lilith, who had changed back into human form, walked to the alley at which he had pointed. The darkness swallowed her up. Ferhdessar caressed the soul box, turned around and started to walk. At the end of the street stood the building that he had spotted from the air. He saw Anukasan rushing inside, but he himself was blocked at the entrance by two soldiers.

"Who are you and what's your business?"

Ferhdessar showed them his signet ring as he introduced himself.

"The king sent me."

Before the soldiers could step aside, a voice behind Ferhdessar said, "I'll show him the way."

The soldiers saluted and let him through.

Ferhdessar recognized the man as Yorben. He was Purified, but the scar of his baptism was hardly visible between all the other scars he had sustained during the many battles he had fought in. Nevertheless, he wore a veil. Ferhdessar had met him a few times during meetings.

"It's good that the king has sent help this quickly, lord Ferhdessar. The situation is getting worse with every passing minute."

Yorben led him through a long corridor with doors on either side, but even without a guide, Ferhdessar would have known that he needed the last door. Lots of noise could be heard coming from the room behind it, and people kept walking in and out.

A bright light was burning in the room. People were crowded around a table that was placed underneath the lamp. Yorben coughed.

"Lord Ferhdessar has arrived."

A hush descended over the room. The people made way, so that the sorcerer could walk up to the table. General Kiril looked at him with a mixture of gratitude and impatience in his eyes.

"You managed to get here fast," Anukasan noted. He had been bent over the map, but now he was looking up.

"Lilith brought me."

"That explains a lot. Where is she?"

"Somewhere out of sight. It didn't seem wise to have people see her. They would be scared of her."

Kiril gave him a questioningly look. It was impossible not to notice that he was a wolf shifter and that wasn't just because of the symbol on his chest. Kiril had thick, dark-brown hair and a beard. His orange eyes glowed, and nothing escaped his notice.

"Lilith's a dragon," Ferhdessar explained. "She has agreed to help us in this battle."

"So you managed to win her over after all?" Anukasan asked. His disapproval could clearly be heard in his voice.

Ferhdessar decided not to respond. "Tell me, what have you discovered?" The eagle man served as a scout, and the commanders made their decisions based on the information they got from him and the other bird shifters.

Anukasan tapped on the map showing the area of Havv'n. "This is where I spotted a large number of servi in the water. It didn't look as though they were getting ready to join the other warriors. They might try to come ashore here."

Ferhdessar glimpsed at the map. Anukasan's finger was resting on a spot several miles to the north of the town. Ferhdessar knew that the cliffs were a bit lower there, but they still towered dozens of feet over the water. The woods extended as far as the edge of the cliff.

"The servi are trying to make an enveloping movement so they can access the river farther inland. Kasimirh knows that time is running out." Ferhdessar addressed Kiril, "Can you send troops to that place?"

The man studied the map again and nodded. "But that will be at the expense of the defences in town."

"There are a few hundred soldiers coming this way. They'll be here in less than two hours," Ferhdessar said.

"That's good news. We might be able to hold the servi back until reinforcements arrive." He looked at the man standing to his left. "Yorben, take your men to the place that Anukasan just pointed out." Yorben hurried out of the room as Kiril addressed Ferhdessar again. "You and your dragon are needed at the gate. The servi haven't breached it yet, but they've been trying to make a hole in the metal for quite some time now. I won't be long before…"

An owl flew in through a window and changed while still in flight. As the woman crashed to the floor, she called out, "They've breached the gate!"

"I'm on my way," Ferhdessar yelled, running outside.

He immediately called Lilith.

Spurred on by his commands, Lilith skimmed over the river not much later. They approached the three hundred feet high gate at great speed. One of the walls that filled the space between the gate and the cliff face had collapsed. The hole in the wall was so high above water level, however, that it was useless to the servi. Therefore, they had made a big hole in the open-work metal of the gate with a cutting torch. Ferhdessar suddenly spotted a woman who was fighting the servi with fierce stabs of her spear on the near side of the gate. She was hovering above the water.

It wasn't really surprising that this sorceress was fighting here. Afifa was known for seeking out wars and turning up to fight in the places where help was needed most. Ferhdessar didn't know her well enough to know what her motives were. It was as if she enjoyed pushing her luck time and again, but whether she did that out of a general contempt for life or sheer recklessness, he didn't know. He didn't really have time to think about that right now, anyway.

Lilith gained some height to fly over the gate. For the first time, Ferhdessar had a view of the destruction caused by the enemy. The poorest townspeople had lived on the narrow beaches of the river's estuary. The streets were still wet from the water that had washed away their wooden houses. Pieces of roofs ware scattered about. Household goods had been washed up against the few remaining walls. Ferhdessar knew that there had also been houses on pontoons on the water, but there didn't seem to be anything left of them.

In the surf, Merzians were fighting the servi. The sea quickly deepened here and huge waves were rolling in, so the people couldn't do much to stop the servi from swimming through the hole in the gate. It was up to Afifa to stop them.

The sounds Ferhdessar heard below him, weren't the sounds he expected to hear on a battlefield. There was no clanging of arms, and hardly any shots were fired because the water had rendered most rifles useless. It was the sounds of the warriors themselves that predominated. The curses that accompanied each sword blow were evidence of the Merzians' ferocious resistance. The servi growled as they threw themselves on their enemies and tried to kill them with their claws. On the beach, bodies belonging to warriors of both sides lay beside or on top of each other. The bulk of the bodies, however, was human.

Ferhdessar told Lilith to slow down. The water was swirling because of her wingbeats. There was a hush of anticipation when the people and the servi spotted Lilith. Nobody was sure what the dragon was going to do and whose side it was on. Fear prevailed among the Merzians, but the Muircadhi exchanged hopeful looks. Had Lilith come to fight on their side as she always had?

For a second it seemed as if Lilith was hanging still in the air, but then she stretched her legs and landed gracefully in the water. Waves pushed the servi onto the beach where they were killed by the soldiers. The dragon tilted her head back and flared her nostrils. Ferhdessar wondered if she smelled the servi or something else. Blood, perhaps?

"Attack!"

Ferhdessar released two fireballs. Lilith breathed fire. It immediately became clear to the servi that the dragon was fighting against them. Some dived under water and swam away from her. Lilith grabbed a Muircadh by his legs and pulled him back up. She let him dangle in front of her face. The creature was grabbing for her, but Lilith wasn't impressed. She broke the servus in two as though he were a twig and then she threw him aside.

Ferhdessar felt euphoric. It took a while before he realized that he was partly sharing Lilith's emotions. He had an overwhelming feeling of power, a sense that nobody was stronger than the two of them together.

"Get them, Lilith!"

The dragon slammed the water with such force that the servi came floating to the surface. Lilith grabbed hold of the creatures and crushed them with her claws. Feelings of rage and intense happiness took turns. Ferhdessar felt as one with Lilith. He gave her orders and she immediately carried them out. This was fantastic.

He praised the dragon, which apparently only encouraged her to fight even more violently. The scent of sulphur entered Ferhdessar's nostrils. This was characteristic of Lilith during her fits of anger. Shaking her head furiously, she was throwing flames everywhere. Not all the people watching on the beach ducked away on time. Some jumped into the water to extinguish the flames, others screamed and moved around wildly until the fire silenced them. Several houses went up in flames as well. The people tried to extinguish the fire with buckets of water, but to no avail. Lilith shook her head again.

"Whoa, Lilith. Easy!"

She restrained herself.

Meanwhile, the Muircadhi were carrying out counterattacks. They drove their claws into Lilith's legs. The dragon roared and lashed out at them. Ferhdessar launched some fireballs to help her. A Muircadh was trying to climb up along her belly. Blood, diluted with water, streamed from the wounds he left behind. Lilith clawed at him, but he tore open the flesh between her thumb and index finger with his six-inch nails. Lilith howled, but then she pulled him off her with her other claw. She slowly squeezed the life out of him. Dark blood dripped through her fingers. After she had dropped the body, she moved her claw through the water to rinse off the blood and briefly stroked her belly.

The rage that Lilith passed on to Ferhdessar was sickening. The dragon reared on her hind legs and subsequently landed her front paws on the servi with such force that the water spurted up in the air. Ferhdessar grabbed hold of her spikes to keep from sliding off her back. He tried to restrain her again.

"Easy, Lilith. A bit less power is more than enough to eliminate the servi."

Lilith calmed down somewhat but she wasn't any less destructive. There wasn't much left of the euphoric feeling. All she felt now was coldness. Lilith was fighting because she was trained to do so. There was an indifferent void inside her, and therefore also inside Ferhdessar.

At long last, the servi realized that they couldn't win against Lilith, so they fled. Ferhdessar received the cheers of the people of Havv'n with a proud smile. This was his accomplishment.

As he made Lilith fly up again, a protracted trumpet-call sounded across the town. The beam of the lighthouse passed over the hills, illuminating hundreds of soldiers. Almost at the same time, Ferhdessar's attention was drawn by something else. Farther to the north he saw a red flash of light. It had been visible only briefly, but Ferhdessar knew that he hadn't been imagining things. Mist immediately started to rise from the water. It was a signal! Kasimirh had realized that it was useless to keep fighting and he was ordering the servi to retreat.

Ferhdessar ordered Lilith to fly faster. He was peering into the darkness, but the mist was spreading so fast that pretty soon Ferhdessar couldn't see anything any more. Even his lightballs weren't of any help, so there was nothing for it but to return to the town. He wasn't worried; he would deal with Kasimirh tomorrow.

Ferhdessar made Lilith land on top of the debris of the ruined lighthouse and then he made them some light. He tried to dress her wounds as well as he could. The dragon moaned when he applied ointments on them, and she threateningly moved her head towards him. He tried to put her at ease.

"Calm down, Lilith. I don't want to hurt you, but I have to do this. It's for your own good."

The dragon sniffed at the stuff that he was rubbing on her stomach. Then she averted her head. Ferhdessar saw that her lips were stretched tight against her teeth because she was fighting off the pain. He caressed her paw. "I'm almost done."

A little while later, Ferhdessar gave her the order to stay vigilant and he went to sit down next to her. He pulled some food out of his bag and took a bite. Then he realized that Lilith had gone without food even longer than he had, so he started to feed her pieces of meat. Lilith kept pushing Ferhdessar's hand with her lips.

"I'm sorry, Lilith, there's nothing left."

He showed her his empty hands. She gave him a look of indignation. He suddenly realized that she was looking him over to see if he would make a nice meal.

"Watch the sea!"

Lilith immediately sat up straight. Ferhdessar lay down contentedly. He didn't have to fear the dragon because she did exactly what he told her. He slowly drifted off.

Every time that the dragon growled, however, he was roused from his sleep. Ferhdessar suspected that she was responding to servi swimming by without showing themselves, so he dozed off again.

He suddenly jolted awake, because Lilith had started hissing angrily.

"Who could have thought that a sorcerer like you would manage to catch a dragon," Afifa said as she rubbed Lilith's scales with her hand.

The dragon wanted to attack, but Ferhdessar stopped her. So Lilith went back to staring into the dark.

Ferhdessar would never get used to the contempt that the other sorcerers felt for him, but that wasn't the only reason why he suddenly felt ill at ease. Afifa was a stunningly beautiful woman. She was wearing a wide, green dress, but with every movement the red ribbons on the pleats became visible. The woman had plaited her long hair, and her green eyes were void of emotions.

The fact that the staff that Afifa was carrying was a powerful weapon, added to Ferhdessar's discomfort. The stone that she had been given at birth was attached to the top of the staff. And on top of the stone there was a long spearhead that was gleaming dangerously. She looked ready to use it.

"She was very useful during the battle," Afifa continued.

"Nevertheless, without your help it would all have been in vain," Ferhdessar answered. "The servi had already breached the gate."

Afifa smiled confidently. She glanced at Lilith again and sat down next to Ferhdessar. The dragon didn't respond and continued doing what she had been told.

"Where did you get this dragon?"

Ferhdessar explained who Lilith was.

"So she doesn't know anything about what happened today?" Afifa asked when he had told her about the soul box.

"There was no time to confer, but this is what she would have wanted."

"I doubt that."

Afifa grabbed her spear and jumped up. Anukasan appeared from behind Lilith. The dragon brought her head down to him and closed her eyes in satisfaction when he caressed her jaw. "It hurts me to see her like this," he said in a tone of reproach.

"This is for her own good. You have no idea what happened during our journey. I would never have done this if it hadn't been necessary."

"Her own good? If she ever finds out about this, it'll destroy her."

"Kasimirh will destroy her when she meets him face to face. She assured me that she wants to fight him, but she can't do it on her own. I know what I'm talking about. She'll hesitate, and that will give him enough time to kill her. Unless I'm with her to guide her."

"Does that logic truly ease your conscience? Does it help you sleep at night?"

"This was the only solution that was right for Merzia and for Lilith! It won't be long before we find Kasimirh. Once he's dead, I'll reunite her body and soul."

Anukasan shook his head in disapproval. Afifa had been observing them from a distance, but now she asked, "Who is this Kasimirh you're talking about?"

"I had hoped you could tell me more about him," Ferhdessar answered. "He's a sorcerer as well."

"I've never heard of him."

228

Ferhdessar gave her a brief update of what he knew. Afifa listened attentively. Anukasan was sitting a bit farther away. His entire posture showed that he didn't agree with Ferhdessar's choices.

The next morning, Ferhdessar climbed back on the dragon's shoulders. He vowed that – should he ever get another chance to fly with her after today – he would first make a saddle. His backside was bruised all over.

Ferhdessar let Lilith skim over the water again. The sun was just rising above the cliffs to the right and shone on the trees on the other side of the bay. Below him, Ferhdessar saw dolphins, who followed them for a little while. Some of the dolphins jumped out of the clear-blue water before the entire school disappeared far below the surface.

There were several little islands in the bay, but Ferhdessar didn't find what he was looking for on any of them. But then he discovered a rock a bit farther away from the town. After Ferhdessar had lowered himself down from Lilith's shoulders, he immediately discovered the tracks that led him to the top of the rock. The ground had been cleared of its growth and someone had laid out stones in a magical pattern. Ferhdessar walked around a bit, took his notebook from his pouch and leafed through it. The symbol represented the power of water. There was no doubt in his mind that Kasimirh had orchestrated the attack from this rock.

Ferhdessar looked around warily. When he had reassured himself that the island was deserted, he went to stand in the middle of the pattern. He reread the words that he had written down in his notebook a long time ago, raised his hands and started to chant. This was an opportunity he couldn't pass up, even though there was a good chance that he wouldn't be able to control this magic.

When he had said the last word, the water started to accumulate around the island. The water rose slowly. Ferhdessar was no longer in control of the water, the magical forces he had summoned were now in control of him. Ferhdessar knew what was happening, but he couldn't stop it. He didn't even want to. He felt the power pulsating as it flowed through his veins with every heartbeat. It made each and every hair on his body stand on end. Ferhdessar had never felt this full of life.

In the meantime the water had reached his feet. He felt every drop that crawled up his leg. The cold water made him even more alert. He whooped with euphoria.

His yell was smothered by the water that had now reached his lips. Ferhdessar was beginning to realize that he had lost all control over the situation. He didn't have the power to make this stop. He was going to drown.

Suddenly Lilith appeared above him. She swooped down, grabbed hold of him and slowly pulled him upwards, but the water didn't seem to want to let him go. Long, blue tongues reached out, trying to pull him back down, knowing that they couldn't exist without him. The water was feeding on Ferhdessar's magic and it pulled him down even more forcefully, not wanting to let him go.

Suddenly the ties snapped. The water let go of Ferhdessar and streamed back into the sea. The pattern of stones was washed away.

Lilith landed in the spot where Ferhdessar had been standing moments before. Ferhdessar lay on the ground, exhausted. He was even more worried than before. Kasimirh's magic was thousands of years old and was hardly ever used because it was so difficult to control. His experiment had made that abundantly clear. It showed him how powerful the prophet was.

At the same time, it explained why Kasimirh had retreated: the battle had been exhausting. Ferhdessar was surprised that the other sorcerer had been able to use the magic for such a long period of time. He himself had been worn out after only a few minutes. Or had it been longer? Ferhdessar looked at the position of the sun but he was too tired to calculate how much time the ritual had taken.

The dragon leaned forwards and shook her head. Then she very carefully breathed some hot air on him. Ferhdessar closed his eyes. It wasn't long before he was dry again. He slowly sat up and remained seated for a while. His body felt heavy and painful. He tried to ignore it as he let his gaze travel across the water.

Ferhdessar was convinced that the prophet was still around. He might not have been able to conquer Havv'n, but Kasimirh had also said that he still had a score to settle with Ferhdessar. He had sounded rather determined and Ferhdessar didn't think he would have changed his mind. Kasimirh had found himself a place to regain his strength and would surely return. For Lilith, but also for Ferhdessar.

Holding on to Lilith, he got to his feet. He patted the dragon on her neck.

"Thank you, Lilith, for saving me."

There was nothing else to discover here, so Ferhdessar climbed back onto Lilith's shoulders. He let her explore the surrounding area, but all the places where Kasimirh could have retreated to with the servi were deserted. Ferhdessar decided to return to Havv'n. There were many caves in the cliffs, but it would take too much time to search all of them on his own.

He made the dragon change at a clearing in the woods. Ferhdessar took the cord from his neck and put the open soul box on the ground in front of Lilith. He nervously watched how her eyes started to glow again and how her cheeks regained some colour.

Confused, Lilith looked around. "What happened?"

Ferhdessar heaved a sigh of relief. Lilith had been completely oblivious to what had happened during the battle.

"We've arrived at Havv'n. Can't you remember the last part of our journey?"

Lilith shook her head. "I only remember that everything went dark and an emptiness enveloped me." Then her eye fell on the little box. She picked it up and handed it to Ferhdessar, smiling. "You've kept your word."

He decided not to respond.

Lilith stretched herself and rubbed her stomach. Her expression grew worried when she discovered the wound on her hand. She gave Ferhdessar a questioning look. "How did this happen?"

He came closer and studied the wound. The flesh between her thumb and index finger was lacerated, just like her dragon claw. While bandaging her hand, he was looking for an explanation. "Maybe you hurt yourself when Kasimirh made you change. Maybe you got caught on a branch or something."

"But I hadn't noticed it before," Lilith protested.

Ferhdessar put a hand on her shoulder. "You had other things on your mind."

Lilith nodded and accepted his explanation. Ferhdessar took out his notebook. As he opened it he asked, "So you don't remember anything of what happened while you were in the box?"

She shook her head and Ferhdessar wrote her answer down.

"How are you feeling now?"

"Tired and stiff. My muscles are hurting, especially the ones in my arms."

"Could that be because you have flown such a long distance?"

"What's with the interrogation? But no, I've flown long distances often enough and my muscles never really bothered me before."

"I just want to know how the box works and what it does to you."

"Apparently it drains your energy."

"It's only logical that it has some side effects."

Nevertheless, Ferhdessar would sooner ascribe her complaints to the fight than to the box. He wrote down that the box probably didn't have any unintended effects on the subject, but that further research was required.

At that moment, general Kiril appeared from the woods with Afifa and Anukasan in his wake. Before the eagle man could say anything to Lilith, Ferhdessar took him aside. "Could you fly around to see whether Kasimirh is still in the neighbourhood? Take the other bird shifters with you and search each and every cave. It's important."

"So you haven't found him yet?" Anukasan sneered.

"Unfortunately not, but he should still be around."

"And Lilith? Does she know what you did?"

Ferhdessar shook his head.

"If she finds out..." Anukasan sighed. "You're driving her straight back into his arms, I've told you this before."

"Well, that only makes it even more important for her to remain ignorant. At least until we've defeated Kasimirh. Once that's over and done with, I'll tell her."

Anukasan hesitated. He glanced at Lilith.

"This is an order, Anukasan."

The man gave him a scornful look. "Is this how we're going to treat each other from now on?"

"This is a military issue. I outrank you, so you have to follow my orders."

Grudgingly, Anukasan agreed. Then he walked up to Lilith. "Have you been able to cope with everything that's happened?" he asked her after he had greeted her.

Lilith shrugged. "When I think about what happened to my parents, it still hurts. But pain isn't the only emotion, I also feel guilt and loneliness. I'd rather suppress all these emotions by focussing on what I can do here."

"I have to go now, but come find me if you ever want to talk."

She nodded gratefully.

Anukasan turned to face Kiril. With his hand on his heart he made a small bow. Then he addressed Ferhdessar.

"Kasimirh won't be able to hide much longer, lord Ferhdessar. I *will* succeed in finding him." He went down on his knee and kissed Ferhdessar's ring with a look of derision on his face.

Ferhdessar pulled his hand back. He wanted to tell Anukasan to act normal, but that was impossible now that he had pulled rank. By kneeling, however, the eagle man had undermined his authority. Only the king was honoured in this way. Anukasan was testing him to see if Ferhdessar would punish him as his superior. The sorcerer shook his head.

Anukasan rose to his feet with a sly smile and flew away.

Ferhdessar now introduced Lilith to Kiril and Afifa. They regarded her with interest, but to Ferhdessar's great relief, they didn't say anything.

"It was a fierce battle last night," the general began. "Fortunately, the enemy is gone now. The dr..."

"Yes, the troops chased them off. They arrived just in time," Ferhdessar cut him short.

Afifa glanced at Lilith again and went to walk next to Ferhdessar. She leaned in and whispered, "I thought you were convinced that she would agree with your actions? So why do you go to all this trouble to hide the truth from her?"

Lilith was walking in front of them. She threw suspicious glances over her shoulder at the sorcerers, but she didn't ask anything. She turned back to Kiril and asked him to tell her more about the attack.

"She's vulnerable and I'm not sure how she'll respond right now when she hears what happened. I hope you won't tell her anything." Ferhdessar answered quietly.

"It's none of my business," Afifa answered.

Fortunately, she wasn't being as difficult about is as Anukasan was. The eagle man didn't understand what was at stake, this was a matter that concerned all of Merzia, and perhaps even the entire world. How could he worry about the well-being of one single person at a time like this? Annoyed, Ferhdessar shook his head and looked around.

As they walked along the edge of the cliff, they had a clear view of the beach. Kiril was telling Lilith what had happened.

"I've never experienced anything like it," he said, shaking his head.

Lilith looked down. People were searching the ghostly emptiness of the coastline for anything that was still recognizable. There was nothing left. Everyone was keeping a fearful eye on the sea, but they were perhaps also hoping against better judgement that the missing people would suddenly come walking out of the water.

"The sea drew back many yards, and fish were lying all over the place. We thought it was an omen of the Gods. We thought that the Goddess Phoibos was going to reveal herself to us." The man shook his head again. "Then we saw the mountainous wave. At first, everyone was rooted to the spot, but then panic broke out and everybody started running. The wave overtook them with a thundering roar..."

Kiril was quiet for a while, and Lilith let her gaze travel along the cliff face.

There was no way to escape. These people had been trapped between the cliffs and the water.

"After that, it all happened again. The sea drew back a second time, and a wall of water came at us. The houses vanished into the sea, pontoons and all, without leaving a trace. Thousands of people disappeared. All this happened before the fish creatures showed up."

Lilith shivered, because she understood that he was talking about the servi.

Suddenly someone clung on to her. "Have you seen Séyda?"

Lilith shook her head. "I'm sorry."

The woman started to cry. Lilith wrapped her arms around her and held her tight. It seemed to calm the woman down a little bit.

"I'll look out for her," Lilith whispered, even though she didn't know who to look out for.

The woman freed herself from Lilith's grip and almost immediately turned around and started yelling again. The incident kept haunting Lilith as they walked on.

"There's hardly any chance of Jadea finding her daughter alive. Most people are hoping to at least find the bodies of their loved ones, so they can say goodbye. But there's not much chance of that either," Kiril said.

"Why did the enemy suddenly retreat?" Lilith asked curiously.

Ferhdessar immediately pushed himself between them.

"Hey, you could just ask, you know," Lilith called out indignantly as she was shoved aside by the sorcerer.

Ferhdessar, however, was already deep in conversation with Kiril and didn't respond. So Lilith decided to go walk beside Afifa.

"I know what you are, Lilith."

Lilith looked away.

"Don't worry, I won't tell anyone."

"How do you know?" Lilith asked, studying Afifa's face. The woman shrugged. They walked on in silence.

They passed the dead bodies that had been laid out in long rows. Family members who recognized their loved ones were hysterical. At the end of one of the rows, a young man was kneeling beside a body. He kept reaching out but every time he pulled his hands back before they touched the body.

Lilith was trying not to look at it. But scenes like that were playing out everywhere. Soldiers were laying the bodies on wagons to transport them. The dead servi were taken away as well, but they were simply thrown on the wagons.

"Where will you burn the bodies?" Ferhdessar asked the Governor of Havv'n, who had joined their company.

The man looked shocked. "Burn? I gave orders to bury them, just like we always do with our dead. The burial ground is behind that line of trees."

He was pointing at a row of birch trees. There was an opening in the middle. Ferhdessar sped towards it. Lilith rushed after him. She caught up with him near the trees. In front of her and to the right were the older graves. Slanting headstones indicated the oldest ones. Off to the left, men were busy digging new graves and placing the bodies in them.

"This is unbelievable," Ferhdessar sighed. Then he turned around to face the Governor. "I had hoped that you were at least digging one hole for all the bodies. It's madness to bury everyone separately."

"It's important that the dead keep their bodies. They can't exist in the hereafter without them. You know that. This is the only thing that we can do for the next of kin."

"By doing this, you're making sure that those next of kin will join the dead a lot sooner than they would like. The bodies need to be burned."

The man protested, "The people are irritable, and the situation is highly explosive. The tiniest issue can set the whole thing off. And burning the bodies isn't a tiny issue."

"When you bury the corpses the bodies will decay as well. They will get eaten by worms. People are stupid not to acknowledge that!"

This was the second time since they had arrived here that Lilith noticed that Ferhdessar had lost his self-control. When she asked him about it, he said, "I haven't been given a rewarding task. Nevertheless, I'll do what's good for this town and its inhabitants. Unfortunately, my decisions won't make me popular. If I let them bury the bodies, people will eventually die because of epidemics, but it will make me popular. Choosing to protect them, however, makes me the bad guy."

Lilith felt for him. She didn't understand why the Merzians had problems with burning those bodies anyway. In Naftalia that was common practice. She didn't really care either way. Maybe it was for the best if she didn't have a body any more once she was dead. At least there would be nothing left for God to punish.

"I do want to be cremated when I'm dead," she therefore told Ferhdessar.

He frowned at her and turned his attention back to the Governor. "Have the bodies piled up, so that they can be burned."

"There will be a massive uproar."

The sorcerer put his hand on the man's shoulder. "There's no alternative."

"People are going to try to steal the bodies of their loved ones to bury them somewhere else."

"Collect the bodies first. The soldiers will guard them. The cremation can take place on the beach, it's too dangerous to transport the decomposing bodies through town."

The man wanted to raise another objection, but then he saw the king's signet ring on Ferhdessar's finger. He quickly bowed.

"After that, you inform the people," Ferhdessar continued.

"Find men who agree with the cremation. They can build a platform. I want all bodies burned by nightfall."

The Governor sighed. His reluctance was showing on his face.

Ferhdessar, however, wasn't impressed. He turned towards Kiril and ordered him to gather enough soldiers to keep the angry citizens at bay. The general saluted and took off.

The news that Ferhdessar had ordered the bodies to be burned travelled fast. Lilith could tell from the crowds of people being held at bay by the soldiers during the erection of the platform that there was much resistance. The men she was helping build the platform were the ones who hadn't turned against the authorities for having failed to protect the town. These were the kind of men who clung to their leaders in times of need, in the conviction that they knew what was good for them. It was hard work and the muscles in Lilith's arms started to hurt more and more, but she ignored the pain.

At the beginning of the evening, the platform was finished and they could start piling up the bodies. Ferhdessar had been able to keep the people reasonably calm during the day, but now onlookers started to scream and elbow their way to the front of the crowd. A group of civilians managed to break through a line of soldiers. They grabbed the bodies they could get a hold of and dragged them away. The soldiers had to resort to violence to get the situation under control, which of course induced even more resistance.

Lilith tried to block out the shouting of the bereaved as much as possible. She was standing on top of the platform, hauling up the bodies that others handed to her. Some of the people that Lilith got hold of had been dead for almost three days. She had tied a cloth over her nose and mouth to block the stench of the decomposing bodies. Flies were buzzing around her head, but she hardly noticed that either. She sympathized with the bereaved, who were visibly shaken by the fact that these victims were going to be cremated.

Suddenly something did manage to break through the barrier that she had put up.

"Séyda! Séyda!"

Was that woman still looking for her child? As Lilith hauled up the next body, she let her gaze travel along the crowd of people. There was Jadea. She was clasping her hands to her mouth and she was screaming. Then she pointed. Lilith looked at the body in her arms, it was a little girl. She looked back at the woman.

Now that Jadea had finally found her daughter, she threw herself between the soldiers. Ferhdessar grabbed hold of her. The mother scratched at the sorcerer, screaming for her child. She struggled in vain.

Lilith turned around and laid the girl down with the other bodies. When she looked at Jadea again, she saw that the woman had fallen on her knees. She was still screaming her daughter's name. Her screams were heart rendering. Ferhdessar only seemed annoyed and motioned for some soldiers to remove the woman.

"Just give her a chance to say goodbye to her daughter," Lilith yelled at him. Her compassion for Jadea was growing.

"If we let her do that, everybody else will want to do the same," Ferhdessar answered unflinchingly. He didn't even take the effort to turn around and face her.

"Some compassion might not go awry. It's hard enough on these people as it is."

Two soldiers had pulled Jadea to her feet, but Lilith extended her hand to her. She expected Ferhdessar to interfere, but he was distracted by other disturbances. The soldiers were confused. Jadea seized the opportunity. She pulled free and grabbed Lilith's hand. Lilith hauled her onto the platform. Then she put an arm around the woman's shoulders and accompanied her to her child.

"Jadea?"

The woman stared at her with glassy eyes. They were swollen from her tears.

"I don't know anything about your customs, Jadea, so you have to tell me what to do."

Lilith supported her as she went down on her knees.

"Will you pray with me?" the woman asked.

Lilith nodded and folded her hands like Jadea did.

"Gaia, have mercy upon my daughter. I beg You, if You can, please let her live on in the hereafter." She bowed her head and started crying again.

Lilith put an arm around her shoulders and whispered her own prayer. "Rest in peace, Séyda. You'll be missed in this world from which you were taken so abruptly. I hope you'll find peace."

Lilith looked at the child's mother again. Her shoulders were shaking. She looked Lilith straight in the eye and gave her a grateful nod. Nevertheless, Lilith was taken aback by the enormous sorrow in her eyes. Defeat seemed etched on her face forever.

"I hope you can reconcile yourself with the fact that your daughter is going to be cremated," Lilith whispered.

Jadea's gaze travelled along the partly decayed bodies. "I do understand, but I'm glad I got to say goodbye. And I have you to thank for that."

"In my country, the dead are burned as well. The bereaved make figurines out of clay as a body for the soul." It all sounded so silly that Lilith started to blush. "Maybe it's an idea," she whispered, ashamed.

Jadea, however, smiled through her tears. "Thank you. I can always try."

They hugged each other.

"Could you tell the others that I'll pray for every body that passes through my hands? I understand how difficult Ferhdessar's decision is for everyone, but maybe it will soften the pain a little bit."

Jadea nodded, and Lilith helped her down the platform. As the mother was reunited with her husband, Lilith hauled the body of a soldier onto the platform. This man's body was burned for the greater part. He must have fought near the gate, because that was the only place where Lilith had seen traces of fire. She fought the urge to throw up when she dragged him away. His flesh was charred in several places and yellowish slabs of skin hung down his body. She tried not to think about how this could have been one of her victims. She hadn't come to Havv'n to hurt people. This man had been murdered by the servi.

A few hours later they were finished. Accompanied by the singing of Gaia's priest, Lilith walked onto the beach. The funeral pile was lit when she reached the surf. Lilith avoided looking at it as she undressed. The memories hurt too much.

She closed her eyes and lowered herself down into the water. When the water washed over her, Lilith felt a stinging pain. She jumped back up. The water rippled at her feet as Lilith looked at her body in bewilderment. There were little wounds everywhere on her arms and legs. There were wounds on her stomach as well. This couldn't have been caused by the branches she had hit during her fall.

A woman walked up to Lilith.

"I'll take you to your room."

She unfolded a blanket. Lilith quickly wrapped it around herself. She left her dirty clothes behind in the surf. They were going to be burned later on.

Lilith followed the woman along the narrow path to the top of the cliff. An encampment had been erected next to the fortress that day. The woman guided her past the tents until they reached a one-storey building.

When Lilith was alone again, she lit a lantern. She dropped the blanket to the floor and studied her stomach. The wounds were uncannily regular. They went up from her belly button in two rows and followed a staggered pattern. When Lilith looked even closer, she discovered that the wounds didn't consist of one big hole, but of five smaller ones. It was really difficult to see, because they were so close to each other.

The door opened. Ferhdessar came in. He immediately turned his back to her and apologized. Lilith quickly threw on some clean underwear.

"You can turn around now. I have to show you something. The soul box has left some more traces." Lilith showed him her arms. "It's everywhere. Also on my legs and my stomach."

Without saying a word, Ferhdessar let his gaze travel along the red dots on her stomach. Lilith had wanted him to come up with a reassuring explanation, but the sorcerer didn't say anything. When she was fully dressed she asked, "Shouldn't you write this down?"

Ferhdessar looked puzzled at first, but then he took out his notebook. "Of course, of course. Why don't you go ahead and have diner?"

He pointed at the serving tray that he had put down on the table. Lilith looked at it, feeling uncertain. There were two bowls of soup, but one was bigger than the other. The same was true for the plates. She decided to take the small bowl.

"That one's mine. I presumed that you would be hungry after all your hard work, so I brought larger servings for you."

With the large bowl of soup in her hand, Lilith lowered herself down into a chair. With the first mouthful she realized how hungry she really was.

"Thank you for being so considerate," she said in between mouthfuls when Ferhdessar came to sit next to her. He regarded her closely. Lilith started to blush. "What's wrong?'

"I was wondering if you're sorry that we arrived too late, and if you would have wanted to fight against the servi."

Lilith thought for a moment. Then she nodded. "Yes, I would have wanted to do that."

Ferhdessar smiled.

"I don't know if I would have been able to," Lilith continued, "but I like the idea of it."

"I'm impressed by you. Ever since we left Nadesh, I've begun to understand you better. You're on the right track, Lilith."

"Do you really think so? It's nice to hear you say that." Lilith yawned.

"You must be tired. Do you have a preference for either bed?" He gestured at the two camp beds.

"Will you sleep here as well?" The thought made Lilith uncomfortable.

"There might still be servi around. Therefore, I thought it best to share a room."

Lilith nodded. Without caring either way, she pointed at the left bed. The sorcerer took the lantern with him to the other bed and waited until she was lying down before he turned off the light. The bed creaked when he lay down.

"See you tomorrow, Lilith."

"Good night, Ferhdessar."

16

The next morning, Lilith and Ferhdessar paid a visit to the encampment. This was where the people who had lost their houses were being brought together. There was a disarray of improvised tents, constructed out of poles and tarpaulins. It was mainly women and children who were sitting in front of the tents. The men had either died defending the town or were busy helping with the reconstruction. It was a miracle that so many people living close to the sea had survived the waves.

Everywhere they went, people stared at them. Some people were just curious, but others seemed full of hate. Lilith understood why the people felt that way about Ferhdessar, but sometimes the suspicious looks were specifically directed at her. It made her feel uncomfortable.

"Why are they staring at us like that?" she asked the sorcerer.

He briefly glanced around him. "They don't trust strangers any more now that they've been attacked out of nowhere. But you don't have to be afraid. Seeing you with me is enough reason for them to leave you alone. You're under the protection of the king."

The largest crowds of people had gathered around the tents where the wounded had been brought. People were screaming the names of missing family members that were said to have been seen here. Nevertheless, there were only few reunions and the cries of joy couldn't drown out the cries of despair. So, most of these moments of joy went by unnoticed.

Lilith was relieved to leave the encampment and the cries of the people behind her. That feeling, however, didn't last long. The Governor had brought them to a place where the bodies of dead servi were gathered. The soldiers had defeated them in the woods that morning, and afterwards they had been brought here.

Filled with fear and loathing, Lilith stared into the big, dark eyes and started to shiver. "Are they really dead? They sleep with their eyes open, you know."

Ferhdessar walked along the row of bodies and kicked them all. None of the servi moaned or moved of its own accord. "Convinced?"

Lilith nodded and walked away. Leaning against a tree, she threw up. Ferhdessar and the Governor stared after her.

"It seems to affect her a lot," the man said nosily.

Ferhdessar shrugged and didn't reveal anything. He only nodded.

"The soldiers also captured a servus alive."

Ferhdessar turned around with a jolt. "Where is he?"

The man pointed at the prison. Two men were guarding the door. The Governor continued, "We haven't been able to talk to him. He either doesn't understand our language or he's refusing to talk to us."

"A bit of both, I think."

Ferhdessar looked at Lilith again. He was wondering if there was any harm in taking her to the servus. Seeing that she was the only one who could communicate with the creature, he decided to call her. She raised her head and when he told her he needed her, she got up. She joined him outside the prison. Ferhdessar explained to her what the man had just told him.

"I don't want to see him," Lilith said, shaking her head.

"Could you at least try? He might have valuable information about Kasimirh's current hiding place."

"You told me he was gone."

"Because I believe he is, but that doesn't mean he has gone all the way back to Naftalia."

The Governor was following the conversation with interest. He wanted to join in, but Ferhdessar raised his hand, causing the man to remain silent. Lilith glanced at him before she addressed the sorcerer again, "Why don't you talk with the servus yourself?"

"I don't speak their language."

"I hardly speak their language either."

"But I also don't know much Naftalian, and from what I understand from your stories, the servi do."

"Not much, just a few words."

Even so, Lilith took a few steps forwards and nodded at one of the guards. Ferhdessar followed her as fast as he could.

The servus was lying motionless on a couple of straw mattresses. His eyes were open, but nothing indicated that he had noticed them coming in. Lilith looked at his hands. His nails had been clipped, which meant that he was a slave. She wasn't sure if that set her mind at ease. It had always been the slaves who'd had it in for her.

"He's sleeping," Lilith explained. "But I know a way to wake him up."

Lilith snapped a few words at him, and the creature immediately started to move, giving off a salty stench. That scent, combined with the darkness of the cell, brought back many memories of the caves. If she couldn't push those memories aside, she would never be able to have a conversation with him.

"Can someone turn on the light?" Lilith asked, gesturing at the lantern. She waited for someone to do as she asked before she yelled in Naftalian, "Get up!"

The servus got up. Full of surprise he looked at Lilith and smiled. "New master, ynfytyn?"

Lilith flinched at the sound of the insult, but the rest of his words confused her. The servus looked over her shoulder and Lilith turned around. It became clear to her that he was talking about Ferhdessar.

"What do you mean?"

"Dragon has fought. He gave order."

Lilith cast down her eyes and bit her lip, thinking. "You're lying."

"Why I lie if truth is better?"

The creature was right. If this was true, it hurt more than the most terrible lie the servus could make up. *If it was true.* Lilith glanced back at Ferhdessar. He gave her a questioning look, but she decided not to tell him what the servus had just said. She had to think about this first.

"Where's Kasimirh?"

The creature laughed.

"He doesn't want to say anything," Lilith told Ferhdessar. She walked to the door to escape the servus. The sorcerer, however, stopped her. "I'm sure they prearranged a meeting point."

Lilith translated the words. The servus scrutinized the sorcerer before he got up to walk towards Lilith. She had to look up at him because of his height. Lilith swallowed and hoped that the creature wouldn't pick up on her fear. Then he leaned forwards and said into her ear, "Master wants you."

His breath touched her cheek. Lilith translated the words. The servus said something else and Lilith turned around to face Ferhdessar.

"He's coming back for me."

The servus brushed her hair back with his sticky hand. His lips touched her ear. "Ynfytyn can't run."

Ferhdessar dragged him away and threw him onto the straw mattress. Next, he pushed Lilith outside. The sunlight blinded her. When Ferhdessar came out, she turned towards him. "Will he really come back for me?"

Ferhdessar's gaze travelled the landscape. She had noticed before that he was nervous. She repeated her question.

"You're probably very valuable to him," he admitted reluctantly. "So, yes, I think he's going to try something. But you're not the only reason for him to come back."

"Why else would he come?" Lilith asked anxiously.

"He told me that he has unfinished business with me."

Ferhdessar stopped talking when the Governor joined them again.

"Why is it that you know these creatures so well?" the man asked Lilith.

She didn't respond. The servus's words haunted her. Had Ferhdessar really made her fight. She jumped when the sorcerer put a hand on her shoulder.

"You did well back there. Your fear was barely visible. I'm proud of you."

With a crooked smile Lilith said, "Thank you, but I'm glad that I could leave again."

She held his gaze for a few seconds. His face had become expressionless again, but Lilith thought that she could see more and more emotions in his eyes.

"What are you worried about?"

Lilith knew that her question had taken him by surprise, because he briefly lifted his eyebrows. "About Havv'n, Merzia and lord Yvar. I'm worried because I don't know when Kasimirh will turn up again." His eyes shone. "And even though I have faith in you, I'm also worried about you. I don't want to see you get hurt again, by him or by anyone else." He squeezed her shoulder. "You wouldn't deserve that after all the good things you've done of late."

The doubts planted by the servus faded into the background. Who was she going to believe: a creature that had always tormented her or the man who had promised to protect her from her master? Ferhdessar had kept his word before. Lilith shook her head. How could she have doubted him, even for a second...

She was startled by screams coming from a bit farther down. Lilith quickly followed Ferhdessar to the group of people that had gathered at the sickbay. They were throwing stones and they were jeering, cursing and raging. While the Governor was trying to calm down the mob, Lilith elbowed her way to the front. Afifa stood in the middle of the circle, parrying the stones by spinning her staff at high speed. There was a woman lying on the ground. She had curled herself up into a ball and was protecting her head with her arms.

"Filthy witch!" the people shouted. "You're in league with the enemy!"

The woman cautiously peered between her arms. It was Ébha.

Ferhdessar tried to stop Lilith as she ran to the front, but Lilith tore herself free. She knelt down beside the healeress.

"Step aside, woman!" someone yelled. "We're going to kill her and we won't be able to guarantee your safety if you get in our way."

"What has she done to you?" Lilith asked.

"The devil has sent her to help Kasimirh."

"What a load of rubbish. This woman has nothing to do with him, trust me. I bet that Ébha came here to help you. She can heal the wounded. She wants to fight against Kasimirh by undoing what he did."

Ébha softly moaned affirmatively. Lilith bent over her. "We'll get you out of here. You're not alone any more."

"We don't want anything to do with her diabolical tricks," a woman shouted.

Somebody else called, "We don't want strangers in our town!"

Lilith understood their fear of strangers, but it was madness that they were taking everything out on a woman like Ébha. Lilith was suddenly hit by a few stones. She rubbed her forehead and stared at the blood on her fingers with growing anger. Afifa got hit as well.

Lilith jumped up.

"We warned you, woman. Step aside or you'll die too." A woman stepped forwards and lashed out with a stick. Lilith received the blow for Ébha.

"Ferhdessar, do something!" she screamed. "How can you just stand there?"

At long last he stepped into the circle and raised his hands. The people hesitated. Afifa and Lilith were strangers to them, so it wasn't a problem if they got hurt in the process. But the king's counsellor… that changed everything. Lilith didn't wait to hear what he was going to say. She saw an opportunity to escape, so she picked Ébha up and carried her to the edge of the woods. Nobody followed her, except Afifa.

"Follow me," the sorceress said as she changed direction.

Lilith followed Afifa deeper into the woods until they reached a clearing. This apparently was the place where Afifa spent the night, because a hammock hung high between the trees. Woodblocks were smouldering on the campfire. Lilith laid Ébha down on the ground next to the fire. She caressed Ébha's forehead.

"Give me a bit more space," Afifa ordered as she undid a pouch and sat down next to the healeress as well.

"Let her stay," Ébha whispered, giving Afifa a nod of encouragement. The sorceress raised her eyebrows and smiled.

"Fine, Lilith, you can stay."

"Is there something I can do?"

"Keep doing what you were doing," was Afifa's resolute answer.

Lilith caressed the healeress while Afifa treated her. Ébha recovered before Lilith's eyes. Not much later Lilith helped Ébha back to her feet.

"Thank you so much for coming to my aid. I should have known that this was going to happen, it wasn't the first time. But I was in the neighbourhood and felt that I should offer my help."

"Why won't people just let you do your job?"

"Well, I don't understand that either. The Merzians are so extremely stubborn. I, and others like me, could have done so much good." Afifa nodded in agreement and Ébha laid her hand on the wound on Lilith's forehead. "But how are you? Have the wounds on your back and legs healed properly?"

Lilith nodded. "I've always wondered if you got in trouble for helping me that day."

Ébha shook her head. "Unlike Ferhdessar, lord Yvar wasn't very strict. I was just ordered to leave Nadesh immediately. So I did."

"I'm glad to hear that and I'm still very grateful for what you did for me that day. It's such a shame that the Governor won't let you help here. I've seen so many people who would benefit from your treatments."

The healeress heaved a deep sigh.

"Shouldn't we tell her?" Afifa cut into the conversation.

"No, it's best if we didn't. As long as she's with Ferhdessar, it will only get her into trouble. She'll find out herself, when the time is right."

Lilith looked at both women. "Do you know him well?" she asked Afifa.

"No, I normally don't associate with his kind of sorcerer."

"His kind?"

"Yes, there are sorcerers by birth, like Rochard and me, and probably Kasimirh as well. And sorcerers who have acquired magic, like Ferhdessar."

Now Lilith understood why the sorcerer used objects for all his magic. She had asked him about that once. Ferhdessar had explained that using magic cost much energy, so it was easier to use talismans. She had concluded under her breath that sorcerers apparently were very weak. He hadn't appreciated that. It still made Lilith smile. Nevertheless, she also felt ashamed for having said that out loud. She had deeply insulted him. Now she understood that there had been truth in her remark, which was probably why it had irked Ferhdessar so much.

"Do you think that Kasimirh is still around somewhere? Ferhdessar seems to be working under the assumption that he is."

Afifa looked around watchfully and nodded. "I don't think his work is completely finished here yet. What are you going to do once this is all over."

"What do you mean?"

"I was told that you came here to defeat Kasimirh. What are your plans after you've done that?"

Lilith shrugged and there was a long silence. "To be honest, I don't think I can defeat him. The journey to Havv'n was horrible and I was hoping that I'd feel more secure once I had arrived here. I was clinging to the thought that I'd meet him face to face and that seeing him would infuriate me enough to kill him. Especially with Ferhdessar by my side." Lilith bit her lip and bowed her head. The two other women came closer to be able to hear her. "But I saw a servus today and I was nearly paralysed with fear. Ferhdessar was there as well, but that didn't give me extra strength. I don't think it will be any different with Kasimirh."

She clawed at her hair.

"Maybe you should teach her some fighting moves, so that she's able to defend herself," Ébha suggested. "I'm sure they will come in handy in the future as well."

"All right, you're probably going to need to know these things. I'll teach you how to dance."

Lilith looked confused. "Dance?"

She watched as Afifa got up and picked up her staff. Her steps became more elegant. She started to slowly spin the spear. Her circles soon became wider and the spear was moving through the air at greater speed. When Afifa had reached Lilith again she added a turn to her steps and started to dance around her in a circle. The pleats of her dress fell open and the red ribbons whirled around Afifa's body. Everything melted together into one single motion. It was beautiful and frightening at once. The staff swished through the air. Whenever the blade of the spear caught the sunlight, there was a flash of light. Afifa's circles alternately became wider and narrower. Then, she suddenly stopped. The ribbons fell down and it was deathly quiet.

Lilith's laughter broke the silence. "Brilliant! I sure want to learn that."

Then she fell silent. She only now realized that the blade of the spear had stopped a millimetre from her throat. No matter how fast she had been moving, Afifa had stopped her movements and her weapon exactly on time. Lilith moved backwards. With a quick turn, the sorceress withdrew her weapon.

Afifa walked to a tree and chopped off a branch with her spear. The weapon cut through the wood with the greatest of ease. It was as if Afifa wanted to demonstrated how dangerous the weapon really was. Lilith shivered. With a few quick movements, Afifa rid the branch of its side branches and handed it to Lilith.

She hesitantly grabbed hold of the stick, but then she was seized by a feeling of excitement. She was eager to learn this form of fighting. Lilith wanted to make her staff spin. The stick hit her arm and she dropped it. But after a few pointers from Afifa she managed to make the staff spin slowly.

"You just have to keep practising, then you'll automatically get faster."

Afifa showed Lilith how to deal forceful blows. They moved forwards side by side as both staffs cut through the air. After they had done that for a while, Afifa sat down on the ground and motioned that Lilith should take place across from her.

"Now that you have a reasonable command of the movements, I'll tell you how to best use them. I'll first teach you how to eliminate an opponent without taking his life.

By spinning the staff you can defend yourself or, when you get lucky, disarm someone. When you want to flee, you direct your blows at the legs. When you break someone's knee or ankle, it's easy to escape them. Only really tough enemies will be able to tolerate the pain. If someone attacks you with a sword or another weapon, you try to break his arm so he can no longer wield the weapon. The bones of the lower arm are thinner, but with your strength you can easily shatter someone's upper arm. I saw you at work yesterday."

Afifa kept on talking and talking. She used her spear to indicate on Lilith's body what she was talking about. Lilith tried to take everything in. It gave her ominous premonitions to have to think about these things, especially when the sorceress started to explain how she could kill someone.

Ébha started to fidget uncomfortably. "This might be taking a bit too far, Afifa."

"Why? Lilith is smart enough to know that death is not the answer in most cases. But if this is supposed to also prepare her for a confrontation with Kasimirh, she's going to need to know more than the best defence against some random rapist."

Ébha reluctantly agreed. Lilith got up and started spinning the stick again. It demanded her full concentration. Therefore, she was startled when Ferhdessar suddenly stopped her.

"How can you be teaching her this? I've told you who she is, haven't I?" he said in annoyance.

"You're only scaring her with your stories about Kasimirh. I thought it would be more useful if I taught her something she could actually use when she comes face to face with him."

"She's strong enough as a dragon, she doesn't need to fight as a woman," Ferhdessar replied.

Afifa threw her hands up in the air. "You can't be serious. How can you know so little about her after all the time you spent with her?"

Ébha was keeping aloof, but Ferhdessar threw her a contemptuous glare as he dragged Lilith along. "Come, this woman is only putting weird ideas into your head."

"I like her and I don't understand why there's anything wrong with what she's doing. You should be talking to the Governor so she can start helping the wounded." Lilith dug her heels in the sand, making it impossible for Ferhdessar to keep dragging her along.

"These women get their power from the devil. Every time she touches someone, she infects that person with the poisonous filth of the evil one."

Lilith looked at Ébha. The woman was clenching her teeth and she had turned red in the face. She was shaking her head vigorously in response to Ferhdessar's allegations. But she didn't say anything.

"I don't believe that Jakob thinks that the healeresses are evil," Lilith whispered. She could still vividly remember the feeling that had flowed through her body each time Ébha had put her hands on her. How could something like that be wrong?

"You shouldn't believe in Jakob any more," Ferhdessar grumbled.

"But you said you believed in him as well!"

Ferhdessar hesitated briefly. Then he muttered that he was having doubts again now that he had seen what Kasimirh was capable of. "Why doesn't Jakob put a stop to him Himself? He should be able to!"

He did have a point, so when Ferhdessar started dragging her along again, Lilith obediently followed him.

Afifa stepped in. "Could you for once let her make up her own mind! Why do you think that you have any say in what she thinks or does? She's a free person, isn't she?"

Ferhdessar briefly loosened the grip on Lilith's upper arm, but then he thought better of it. He pulled at her arm with such force that Lilith stumbled. "This is for your own good, Lilith. One day you'll understand that."

Lilith glanced over her shoulder. Afifa was shaking her head disapprovingly.

"Always listen to your heart, Lilith," Ébha called after her. "It contains all the answers that you're looking for. Trust your instincts!"

17

With combined efforts they lifted the long beam. Lilith was holding the tail end and laid it down on the wagon. Next, the men pushed the beam farther onto the wagon. The wood had been severely damaged by the fire, but the biggest part was still usable for the reconstruction of the houses.

That morning, Lilith had gone looking for Ferhdessar. When she hadn't been able to find him, she had found something useful to do herself. A group of men was clearing away the debris of the burned houses, so she had joined them. It gave her much satisfaction that she'd been helping the people of Havv'n for several days now. It was something she could be proud of. Unfortunately, there also was a downside to this job, because every now and then bodies were found underneath the rubble.

Lilith was watching how the men removed what remained of a wooden wall. They were covered in soot and dirt. Lilith smiled, because she probable didn't look any better herself. Her eye suddenly spotted a glittering object. She was riveted to the spot. This couldn't be right, her eyes were deceiving her. Lilith shook her head and blinked. The image, however, didn't disappear.

"There's someone lying there," a man yelled.

Please, don't let this be true. Warily, Lilith came closer. She didn't want to see it, but at the same time she needed to know. *It can't be,* she kept telling herself. *He isn't here, he went to the south.*

A hand was sticking out from under the rubble. It was the only body part that was visible, but it clearly belonged to a man. There was a silver bracelet around his wrist.

As the men uncovered the body, Lilith fell down on her knees next to the hand. She still didn't want to believe it and kept hoping that it was somebody else, but at the same time she knew that it wasn't.

"Chrys." Her voice trembled

She carefully took his hand in hers and kissed it. After the men had pulled him out from under the rubble, she looked at his face. All hope of it being somebody else evaporated.

Lilith didn't stop screaming until she felt a hand on her shoulder.

"Did you know him?" Yorben asked.

Everywhere around her, grimy faces were giving her compassionate looks. Lilith slowly nodded and looked back at Chrys. The fire had devoured his long hair and his clothes, and it had left huge burns all over his body. Lilith could only hope that he had died quickly and that he hadn't felt the pain.

"Filthy servi!" she ranted as she jumped up and turned around to face the sea. The tide was out, so there was a wide strip of beach between her and the water. "Wait till I get my hands on you! You will suffer for what you did to him!"

Her anger was flaring so high that she wanted to run to get rid of some excess energy, but she couldn't move a muscle. Her breathing came in gasps. Whoever had done this was going to pay. "I swear to you that I'll take revenge, Chrys," she panted and growled, raising her fist in the air.

"The fish creatures weren't responsible for this," someone said.

"Shut your mouth," Yorben hissed.

Lilith turned around with a jolt. A cold shiver ran down her spine. "Not the servi? But who was?"

The men exchanged glances. Yorben shook his head in warning, but to no avail.

"The dragon did it."

"The dragon?" Lilith stammered. "What do you mean?"

"You're with Ferhdessar, aren't you? Then you should know this. During the last night of the attack he brought a dragon into the fight." It was as if Lilith was jolted awake. The man didn't notice her dismay. "If it weren't for the dragon, Havv'n would have been occupied by the enemy."

The man's story explained so much: Ferhdessar's strange behaviour whenever someone spoke about the attack, her physical complaints. Even his thoughtfulness. Lilith now understood that he had been trying to make something up to her. *He had given her his word!* She clenched her fists and pressed them against her temples.

"We thought you knew."

Lilith slumped to her knees and started to scream. She had once again killed someone she loved. First her parents and know her beloved. "Oh, Chrys, I'm so sorry. Forgive me!" But how could he, or anyone else, ever forgive her?

She caressed Chrys's cheek, then she fell forwards and rested her head on his chest. He was the reason why she had wanted to fight here in the first place, and now he had become a victim. He had always been full of admiration for her dragon side. What had he been thinking when she attacked? How much time had he had to realize that she was a monster. Had he died hating her?

The recollections of their last day together evoked memories of the scent of eucalyptus that had always hung around Chrys. Lilith hid her face in his shoulder and inhaled deeply. A sickening, sweet stench of rotting flesh drove away the memory.

"Maybe you'd like to have this?" Yorben knelt before her, holding the bracelet in his hand.

"I'm not entitled to it," Lilith said. But she did clasp the piece of jewellery around her wrist. It would serve as a reminder of what she had done. This way, she would carry the pain with her. This bracelet was more powerful than the wristbands that Ferhdessar put on prisoners. *He'll find that out soon enough.* A stab of pain went through her arm. *Filthy liar, I'll get you for this.* Her arm tensed up. The pain surged to her head.

"I'm sorry that you had to find out like this," Yorben whispered. "And I'm sorry about him." He pointed at Chrys's body.

"Does everybody know… about me?"

The man shook his head. "Only a few people from the army. The men who are working here don't know anything."

"What are the people saying about the dragon?" Lilith asked. "Are they angry?"

"Most people speak highly of you. Just after the enemy had breached the gate, you suddenly turned up. Ferhdessar was sat on your shoulders. You made a good team together: he gave instructions and you immediately carried them out. You burned the servi and crushed them."

Lilith bowed her head and clenched her fists. Crushed, what an awful word. But she knew all too well what Yorben meant. She had killed the servi with her bare hands. She had squeezed and squashed them. Images took shape in her head. At long last she had fought against the servi, but she couldn't be happy with the vengeance she had been given. Anger dominated all other feelings. A burning hatred, not directed at the servi this time, but at the sorcerer who had made her do this.

"Do you want to stay with him a little while longer, or shall we carry him away?"

Lilith shook her head and nodded. As soon as the men had lifted Chrys up, she walked towards him and kissed him. On the mouth, just like he had kissed her at the Fountain of Origin. It was one of the few undamaged parts of his body.

"Will he be cremated as well?" she asked quietly. She suddenly understood the aversion that the people of Havv'n had felt. It was inconceivable that Chrys would be exposed to the flames a second time. Yorben shrugged and motioned for the men to take the body away.

Lilith felt the urge to go to Ferhdessar at once to confront him with what she had learned, but she had no idea where she could find him. It was better to stay here and continue working. After all, she was to blame for the destruction of these buildings. And she didn't even want to think about the rest of her sins.

Lilith stooped down to pick up a piece of wood and hurled it into the wagon with all her might. Some of the men looked up in surprise when the wood slammed loudly against the back of the coach-box. The horses whinnied in fear. Seconds later, the next piece of wood landed in the wagon.

"Why don't you call it a day?" one of the men asked. "You've had quite a shock."

You don't even know half of it.

"Just let her be," Yorben said, giving her a look of worry.

Lilith worked harder then she had before. It felt good to let off steam. So when the men all took a break, she stubbornly kept on working.

But then Ferhdessar walked by. "Shouldn't you take a rest?" he asked in a friendly tone.

Panting, Lilith looked up. The mere sight of the sorcerer infuriated her. There wasn't anything in the world she wanted more than to fly at his throat. Her wristband was hurting her more than ever, but that wasn't what was stopping her.

Lilith spat right in front of his feet and wanted to go back to work. But Ferhdessar grabbed hold of her arm.

"Lilith?" He looked worried. His eyes were begging for an explanation.

"I don't think you want to have this conversation here," she snapped at him.

"Let's go somewhere else then."

He wanted to drag her along, but Lilith pushed him away. "Why should I obey you? I have more important things to do than to follow you around. You don't control me right now," she said with a snort of derision.

Ferhdessar looked bewildered. Then he apparently decided that she was right, because he stormed off without saying another word.

Lilith lowered herself down to her knees and held her clenched fists to her eyes. It had been extremely hard to control herself, but she had wanted to avoid having an argument in front of everyone else. Because then they would all see her as a murderer again. Everybody would know that she had burned Chrys and the other victims. She banged her fist on the ground and got back up. A bit farther down, she saw a big beam lying on the ground. When she wanted to lift it, someone called out, "Wait, let me help you!"

Lilith didn't wait. She lifted the wood as if it weighed nothing and hurled it away. The wagon wasn't full yet but the horses took off at great speed.

When the day ended, Lilith went back to her room. She washed the dirt off her face and fell down on the bed. She was still furious with Ferhdessar, but now that she was alone, her grief for Chrys took the upper hand. She thought back to the last day that they had been together. Despite her grief, she smiled. They had lain in each other's arm for hours, staring at the dome. And in the mean time they had talked about all kinds of things.

Ferhdessar entered the room. His eyes were full of worry and without saying anything he grabbed a chair. Lilith decided that she wasn't going to say anything either. He owed *her* an explanation, not the other way around.

When the silence dragged out too long, she grabbed a book from her bag and started reading.

"What's going on?" Ferhdessar finally asked.

Lilith slammed the book shut and sat up straight. She thought about what she was going to say. "We found Chrys's body today."

Ferhdessar went to sit next to her and wrapped his arm around her. It felt so insincere that Lilith slapped his arm away.

"The men told me who was responsible."

"The servi…"

"No, not the servi. Me!" Lilith couldn't control herself any more. She had been practising this conversation all day, but now the words wouldn't come out. She was too angry. She jumped off the bed and started pacing the room.

"I'm sorry that it had to happen this way, but Merzia was in danger and I had to do something," Ferhdessar said.

"Sorry?! I… I don't believe a w-w-word you say." Lilith despised herself for stuttering, but her emotions overwhelmed her. She was searching for the right words to express her feelings, while fighting the effects of the wristband at the same time. "You told me that this was the way to redeem my sins, but in the meantime you just went ahead and made them even bigger."

"I didn't know that he was here."

"Does that make any difference? Would you have stopped me if you had known? Are you really trying to tell me that it isn't so bad if it concerns people that I don't know? If it hadn't been my boyfriend it would have been somebody else's."

"I never meant for any of this to happen. I didn't tell you to burn those houses down. You did that off your own accord. I only wanted you to drive off the servi."

She growled and wanted to take another swing at him, but Ferhdessar caught her hands. "You wanted this too, didn't you? I felt your emotions during the fight, you were euphoric. Afterwards I asked you if you had wanted to fight the servi. You said yes."

"That's not the point. You promised me that you wouldn't do this. I trusted you. But you used me and the consequences are terrible."

"I understand that it's difficult for you and I'm sorry that Chrys was killed, but look at the result. Merzia is safe and you got to take revenge on the servi."

Lilith mustered all her strength to jerk her hands free and knock him over. "Why are you being so indifferent? You knew that I ran away from Kasimirh to never have to kill another human being again. And then you make me do something like this!" She had wanted to say more, but she had to pause because she wasn't getting enough air. "Couldn't you have thought of something else?" she panted. There was contempt in her voice. "A powerful sorcerer like you... But no, you probably enjoyed being able to make me do whatever you wanted. Maybe you wanted to experience what Kasimirh must have felt all these years."

"I'm not like him," Ferhdessar said in defence as he got back up and smoothed down his clothes. That made her even angrier.

"No, you're worse. Kasimirh at least gave me a choice. It often wasn't much of a choice, but it was more than you gave me."

She searched for the switch on her amulet. The two ends of the necklace dangled between her fingers when she moved her clenched fist in his direction. "If you want to have my dragon side so badly, then take it..." Lilith hurled the necklace at him. The head of the gold dragon hit his cheek and left a scratch. "It's no use to me anyway." Ferhdessar opened his mouth to say something in response, but Lilith wasn't interested any more. "I want you to leave my room."

She lay back down on her bed and opened her book. She was staring at the letters, but the words didn't register. Ferhdessar lingered.

"Why doesn't anyone understand that this was an absolute necessity?" he muttered before he left.

Lilith let the book slide out of her hands and turned onto her back. Thoughts filled her head until there were so many of them that she couldn't tell them apart any more. She had a headache. If only Ghalatea were here, she would be able to comfort her.

The Ancilla Princeps had tried to warn her, but Lilith hadn't wanted to listen. Amid all turbulence and uncertainty she had clung to the first tree stump to come floating by. Only to discover too late that it was a crocodile.

Lilith placed her feet on the floor next to her bed. She felt the rough floorboards beneath her soles. She had been staring into the dark for hours, but now she had resigned to the fact that she wouldn't be able to sleep. Too many thoughts were haunting her. It seemed as if everyone she had ever killed was screaming at her. "Murderer, spawn of the devil, ynfytyn!" They all demanded justice. Amid the chaos, she sometimes recognized Chrys's voice. That hurt even more, because he had never said anything like that to her before.

Lilith purposefully started to make some noise. Just to be annoying, even though she was certain that Ferhdessar hadn't returned. The thought of him made her anger flare up again, so she walked to his bed. She put the lantern down, picked up his rucksack and threw its contents on the floor. In a small box she found the splinter he had used to control the prisoner. Lilith conceived the plan to burn it, but almost immediately dismissed the idea. It wouldn't have much of an impact.

Then she found a letter. It was a brief, but sweet message from a proud mother. The woman had written it after Ferhdessar had endured a tough test which had completed his tuition. "I've always had faith in you," it said.

"Of course you have," Lilith sneered. "But would you still be so proud if you knew what he's using his powers for? Your son is as much a murderer as I am."

Embittered, Lilith tore up the piece of paper. She wanted to rip it apart into a thousand pieces, but then she realized how childish she was being. Instead, she dropped the two halves of the letter to the floor.

Then she spotted a knife. When she tested how sharp it was, it effortlessly cut through her skin. The voices in her head grew silent, and Lilith smiled. The fact that the voices immediately returned even more vicious than before, didn't matter. Lilith now knew what she had to do.

Knife in hand, she left the room. She left her cloak behind on the bed, because the night was warm enough to do without. Especially since she was dressed in woollen clothes.

The full moon illuminated the world around her. In the distance, the sea glistened. Lilith stole past the tents and followed the path down the cliff and onto the beach. The waves rolled over the beach peacefully, but Lilith needed something else to calm her down. She took off her boots and trousers and sat down in the surf. The salt water would intensify the pain. That was a good thing, because she deserved it.

Lilith confidently stabbed the knife into her upper leg. The pain immediately calmed her down. As she moved the knife in the direction of her knee, all other feelings were pushed aside, and the abusive voices disappeared along with the warm blood that was flowing out of the gash. Lilith closed her eyes. She drove the knife a little bit deeper into her leg before she pulled it out. A wave washed away the blood. The salt stung the wound.

Taken by surprise, Lilith bit down hard on her lip. She didn't manage to suppress a moan and that got her angry again. She had no right to give expression to her pain. What she was doing to herself right now was nothing compared to what Chrys had gone through. Fire was infinitely more painful than a sharp knife cutting through flesh. She had experienced that herself.

Lilith started to make a second cut, parallel to the first. She took even more time to make this wound. Teeth clenched, she drew marks into her leg. Right now, the pain was the only thing that was real. That was good.

Ever since the attack on Tewarsum, Lilith punished herself like this. Ever since she had completely shut down her emotions, she often felt like a walking corpse and wondered if she hadn't actually died when she had slit her wrist. Maybe this was the hell that her master had spoken of. That was why she had started hurting herself: if she could feel the pain, she knew that she was still alive.

Later on, it had become a form of punishment as well. For the things that she had done, and as an act of penance for the people she had killed. But first and foremost to counterbalance the rewards she was given for killing those people. At the same time, she also harmed herself when her master was mad with her, because that meant she hadn't tried hard enough to keep him satisfied. In truth, she'd had no trouble finding reasons to do it and it had turned into an addiction. This was the only thing she had any control over. If other people were allowed to hurt her, why couldn't she? But the fact that she did this to herself, gave others the right to hurt her as well. It was the axis that her life revolved around.

"Wait!"

Lilith turned around. A servus had been ready to throw himself on her, but now he was holding back. Kasimirh appeared behind him. In passing, he put his hand on the creature's shoulder. "Good boy."

When Kasimirh had reached Lilith, he glanced at her legs. Then he rested his gaze on the knife.

"What's going on?"

Lilith stared at the red traces on her legs that kept getting washed away by the water, only to return as quickly as they had disappeared. She felt ashamed now that someone had discovered her secret.

"Why are you doing that?"

"I have to do something with the emotions that nobody wants to see," she answered sharply, getting up.

"So, this helped you to stay strong? I'm sorry that I never knew." He scrutinized her as he brushed her hair out of her face. A fresh scent – eucalyptus – entered her nose. It was confusing that he smelled the same as the man she was mourning. "What's your reason for doing this right now?"

Lilith told him what Ferhdessar had done. She was so upset about it that the words just poured out after she had uttered the first syllable.

Kasimirh was livid. "The bastard! He had no right."

Lilith bowed her head. She had been so wrong about Ferhdessar. How could she have been so blind to what had been so obvious. What had he ever done to win her trust anyway?

Kasimirh's hand touched her jaw and moved down to her neck. "Where's your amulet. Has Ferhdessar taken it from you?"

"I gave it to him. That's what he wanted, wasn't it?"

Kasimirh pushed her chin up so that he could look into her eyes. He slowly shook his head disapprovingly. Lilith backed away. She was convinced he was going to punish her.

"Fine, I'll make you a new amulet later. The servus will take you home."

He indicated that he wanted her to hand over the knife, but Lilith didn't see that. All she could think about was that everything was going wrong. Now Kasimirh was assuming control over her again.

Ferhdessar had thought it best to leave Lilith alone, so he had found himself an empty tent. Despite his fatigue, he didn't manage to fall into a deep sleep. When a scream cut through the silence of the night, he immediately jolted upright. Ferhdessar listened motionlessly to the sounds on the other side of the tent. Someone ran by, and a bit farther down men were yelling something at each other.

He jumped up and rushed out of his tent. More soldiers were running by.

"What happened?" he asked someone.

"There's something going on at the prison."

When they arrived, it immediately became clear that the servus had escaped. It wasn't difficult to guess who had helped the creature escape. There was a small burn mark on the foreheads of the two men who had been guarding the cell. Exactly where Kasimirh had touched them with his finger.

"We have to go to the beach!" Ferhdessar yelled.

The servus would surely try to escape via the water, but if he was quick, he might still be able to stop him. Ferhdessar ran as fast as he could. He was clenching a magical fighting stone in his fist.

He held still at the top of the cliff. There were three people standing in the surf. Lilith was one of them. Ferhdessar could tell that Kasimirh was talking to her. A knife glittered in Lilith's hands.

Do it, Lilith, kill him.

He motioned for the soldiers to calmly walk on. When he was less than ten yards away from Lilith he said, "It's all right Lilith, you can do it. This is your chance to take revenge."

She turned around to face him. Doubt was written on her face. As soon as she recognized him, her face turned angry.

"Give me the knife, Lilith," Kasimirh commanded. "You shouldn't do this to yourself because of what he did."

Lilith closed her eyes and toyed around with the knife. She growled something and stamped her feet. Then she turned around and handed the knife to Kasimirh.

Ferhdessar was utterly astonished. "Lilith, what are you doing?"

"She's mine, Ferhdessar. Take your loss and leave."

Lilith stood in the surf with her head bowed. Ferhdessar took that as a confirmation of Kasimirh's words. She hardly even resisted when the servus started dragging her into the sea.

Ferhdessar released the magic that he was still clenching in his fist. Kasimirh, however, was too fast. He caught the attack before it could hit Lilith and he let the energy spin around his hands as he examined it.

"Bring her here," Kasimirh said to the servus. Then he took a drop of Ferhdessar's magic. "Hold out your hand."

After Lilith had obeyed him, he let the drop fall into her hand. She screamed as the drop ate away her flesh. She gave Kasimirh a startled look.

"Yes, Lilith, this is exactly what you think it is," the prophet whispered. "Ferhdessar wants to kill you. I take it that Yvar ordered him to do so."

"Is that true?" she asked Ferhdessar.

"You're an enemy of Merzia."

Lilith shook her head. "I want…"

"They never trusted you, my child," Kasimirh interrupted her. "It was useful to have you on their side, but now that you no longer are, they want you out of the way. I'm sorry that I have to tell you this, but I want you to understand."

Lilith hid her face in her hands. Kasimirh patted her on the shoulder.

"You feel bad, don't you?" he asked kindly.

Lilith nodded. "You were right, master, when you warned me about the humans. Only now do I understand. That makes me sad."

The glance that Lilith cast at him made Ferhdessar flinch.

"I can understand that. It's so unfair what Ferhdessar has done to you. But now it's over, my child."

Kasimirh glanced at Ferhdessar before he handed the knife back to Lilith. Her knuckles turned white because she was holding it so tightly. "He's the one who killed Chrys, Lilith, not you," Kasimirh whispered.

Ferhdessar fixed his gaze on Lilith before he walked up to her. "Don't let him talk you around, Lilith. We had a deal. We were going to fight him together. Side by side."

"Yes, we had a deal," Lilith screamed. "And you broke it!"

She jumped at him. Ferhdessar threw her off, but Lilith quickly recovered her footing and hurled herself at him again. A fight ensued during which Ferhdessar wasn't always able to avoid the knife. He tried to kill Lilith with magic, but Kasimirh kept coming to Lilith's defence.

At long last, Ferhdessar managed to pin Lilith to the ground. She struggled to free herself, but Ferhdessar tightened his grip on her wrists and used his weight to push her body into the mud. She cast furious glances at him. With every wave that washed over her face, the hatred in her eyes grew.

"Lilith, you have one last chance to turn your back on him. You know that I'll do anything for Merzia. The only way you'll be safe is if you join me again."

Lilith shook her head.

"I'm offering her the same. I've protected her her entire life. Lilith knows this." Kasimirh pushed Ferhdessar off Lilith with a simple wave of his hand and pulled her up. "I need to take care of him, sweetheart, but I'll see you soon."

He bent forwards and planted a kiss on her cheek. Lilith responded by pressing her lips against his jaw. Then Kasimirh addressed the servus, "Take her to the place that we agreed upon. I'll come after you once I'm done here."

Ferhdessar made another attempt to stop Lilith, but Kasimirh defended her again.

When Lilith was out of earshot, Kasimirh said to Ferhdessar, "You're a fool. Lilith hadn't returned to me. I came here to abduct her and I most likely would have needed to resort to violence to force her to come with me if you hadn't tried to kill her." He shook his head contemptuously. "But I'm grateful to you. She's like a faithful dog now. She'll obey me, no matter what I ask of her. Jakob apparently wishes me well." The sorcerer folded his hands and looked up at the sky.

"Attack!" Ferhdessar ordered the soldiers. When they threw themselves at the prophet, however, Kasimirh disappeared into thin air.

Ferhdessar suspiciously searched the beach with his eyes. He had gathered some energy in his fist, just in case Kasimirh turned up somewhere else. Then he heard his voice.

"I'm sorry, Ferhdessar, that I can't stay longer. It's a bit too crowded for me and I had planned a different welcome for you. I'll wait for you in the woods."

Undecided, Ferhdessar stood in the surf. He understood why the prophet wanted to lure him to another place. Would he be strong enough to escape Kasimirh's trap? The prophet was very powerful, he had already proven that. Ferhdessar threw off his doubts and started walking.

Today he was given a chance to prove himself. Some sorcerers thought he was inferior because he wasn't a sorcerer by birth. An incompetent wannabe is what they called him! Just thinking about it already galled him. He had worked so hard to be able to take the test. It hadn't come easy to him, but he had passed it. For that reason alone, he deserved more credit. *I'll show them what I'm worth.* Today he was going to make history. Ferhdessar chuckled. Who had ever thought that a sorcerer with acquired powers would save the world?

He followed the paths through the woods. Suddenly he detected a huge magical force field. Kasimirh was waiting for him behind the tall bushes. A few more steps and Ferhdessar would be beyond the point of no return. He hesitated briefly, but then he walked on.

Kasimirh was sitting in the middle of a clearing. Dishes with burning oil illuminated the trees and the sorcerer. Ferhdessar regarded him closely. Everything about the man's appearance was grey. His skin and his short-cropped hair were almost the same colour, and his dark robes accentuated the paleness of his skin. Nevertheless, the sorcerer didn't look unhealthy. His posture was dignified and his eyes sparkled, obsessed by the task that God had given him. Ferhdessar had no idea where he was supposed to know the man from.

Getting up, Kasimirh eyed him inquisitively as well. "You've grown tall, Ferhdessar. And you've become older. But not so old that you're becoming forgetful, right?"

Ferhdessar decided to answer by launching a fireball at the prophet. For a second it looked as if it hit its target, but it veered at the last moment. The fireball fluttered about briefly as if it had lost its way and then it was extinguished. Kasimirh didn't even respond. Ferhdessar attempted another attack, but to no avail.

"Keep it up, Ferhdessar. Waste your energy on useless attacks. This labyrinth makes anything that enters it lose its way."

Kasimirh made a gesture, causing the stones that he had laid out in the pattern of a maze to light up briefly. The prophet laughed haughtily and launched a fireball. Ferhdessar grasped at his shoulder. His clothes were singed to his skin.

"Except when you know your way in the maze, of course. I can go wherever I want. My attacks *will* find their mark," the prophet said triumphantly.

Ferhdessar realized that he was powerless unless he could manoeuvre himself into a fight at arm's length. He drew his sword and stepped across the outer stone circle. Determined, he walked towards Kasimirh. When he was halfway, he raised his sword. Kasimirh didn't so much as flinch. He was waiting with his arms folded in front of his chest. Ferhdessar made his final step and brought down his sword. He lost his balance because, unlike what he expected, the sword didn't meet with any resistance.

"Are you even listening to what I'm saying, Ferhdessar?"

The voice came from behind him. Surprised, he turned around. Kasimirh was still standing in the middle of the maze, but Ferhdessar was back at the outer edge.

"Who are you?" Ferhdessar was trying to buy time. How was he going to fight Kasimirh if nothing could reach him?

"So you never really listened to me at all. Ever since we were young I've tried to show people the right path. I was already preaching the word of Jakob back then. You must remember that, don't you?"

Ferhdessar slowly shook his head, but suddenly it started to dawn on him. When the full realization hit him, it felt like a punch in the stomach. He had always thought that he'd never see this man again. Appalled, he looked at the prophet. Kasimirh smiled at him.

Ferhdessar's memories took him back to the town where Kasimirh and he had grown up. Images flashed before his eyes of the other sorcerer walking through the streets yelling, "I am the messenger of the True God. It's time for everyone to start following Jakob again, so that we can reach the Golden Era once more. It's not too late. But if people keep ignoring God's will, the world will be destroyed. I foresee horrible events, and nobody will be able to escape."

They had both still been teenagers, and not much later the boy had disappeared. Because his drenched cape had been found on the riverbank, people had assumed that the sorcerer had been drowned. Life went on, and soon nobody ever thought about the young man any more. Ferhdessar had repressed the memory out of shame.

"I thought you were dead," Ferhdessar stammered. Why hadn't he realized this before?

"Brilliant. That was exactly my intention. Back then, I wasn't strong enough to fulfil Jakob's assignment yet, so I thought it wise to disappear."

Kasimirh's laughter cut through the night when another of his attacks hit its target. Ferhdessar was thrown back and landed against a tree. The air was knocked out of his lungs. Down on all fours, Ferhdessar was fighting to catch his breath. At the same time he racked his brain, trying to come up with a plan, but he doubted if there was anything he could do. His desperation didn't escape the prophet.

"I know how you're feeling, Ferhdessar. And you were right all along: it's wonderful to be on the other side and experience what it's like to have so much power over somebody else." His voice oozed with vengeance.

Ferhdessar tried to get up, but he fell back to the ground because Kasimirh launched an energy wave at him.

"I've always known that your magical abilities were substandard," Kasimirh sneered. "But I'm warning you, I'm capable of a lot more than levitation these days. Do you remember that day in the rain?"

Ferhdessar indeed remembered that day. He remembered everything. The streets had been deserted on the day that Kasimirh was referring to. Ferhdessar and a group of his friends had come across the other sorcerer when he was taking shelter from the rain in a doorway.

"You and your flock of sheep," Kasimirh hissed. "They were just scared of becoming your next victim if they didn't follow you. I've always know that you would make a powerful ally. Unfortunately, we weren't on the same side."

Ferhdessar didn't know how to respond. He'd had a happy childhood, with loving parents and many friends. The only thing that could have ruined everything was the fact that there was another sorcerer in town.

Ferhdessar's powers had been acquired, but Kasimirh's powers had manifested themselves all at once at a very early age. In the beginning he hadn't had much control over his powers, which had led to accidents, making him the object of derision. Ferhdessar had only too gladly taken the lead. He had felt threatened by a second sorcerer in town with the same – or perhaps even more – powers as him. Years later, he had started to regret his actions, but back then he had been young. By teasing and challenging the clumsy sorcerer, he had made the others look up to him. Ferhdessar had enjoyed the feeling of power.

"Is that why you made me come out here? To take revenge for what happened when we were boys?"

Kasimirh sent a fireball at him, but this time Ferhdessar managed to avoid it. His brains were working at full speed. How could he save himself from this predicament? This hadn't been the plan. He didn't want to die without so much as injuring Kasimirh. That was no way to impress other people.

"Of course not. That would be childish. You are, however, still my enemy, so it's best to eliminate you."

"Well then, what's taking you so long?" Ferhdessar had pulled himself together again. He put his arms akimbo and straightened his shoulders.

A quick attack from Kasimirh swept him off his feet again. "I want to savour the moment. And I want to tell you how grateful I am. Thanks to you, Jakob crossed my path."

As Kasimirh started to relate his story, Ferhdessar crawled back up. He walked around the outer circle until he reached the entrance to the maze.

"Chased by your taunts, I fled the town and reached the catacombs. I knew you guys wouldn't dare to follow me, so I had built myself a hiding place there. That's what you had condemned me to: a life among stinking bones. But still, it was better than falling into your hands again."

Ferhdessar came to a fork and tried the left path. Kasimirh went on. The tone of his voice became more gentle as he remembered the good things. When Ferhdessar quickly glanced at him, he noticed that the prophet had his eyes closed.

"Suddenly a bright light filled the room full of graves. For a tiny second I thought that you had followed me after all. But it was someone else who asked me to come forth. He had a soothing voice. Carefully, I stepped out from behind a pillar. In the middle of the room – surrounded by a circle of light – stood a man who I had never seen before. He stood with his back straight and hardly leaned on the staff that He was holding in His hand. The bright light was coming from a stone in the staff. His clothes were plain but well matched, and they added to His confident appearance. There was a smile on His lips, but at the same time His eyes looked worried. He introduced Himself as Jakob and asked if I was all right.

We sat down in a corner of the cave. Jakob put fresh heart into me. He acknowledged the powers hidden within me. He told me to never doubt myself. I asked Him if He was a sorcerer and He laughed. I'll never forget what he said in response, 'Some will call me a sorcerer, others will call me a fraud. But I am neither. I am God. The only God, even though many would claim differently. I created the earth and its inhabitants. I took care of my children until they turned their backs on me. I understand how you're feeling, my son.' All that time He had His arm wrapped protectively around my shoulders. He promised me that He would be my teacher."

Kasimirh looked up at Ferhdessar, who had progressed halfway through the maze by now. With a wave of his hand the prophet lifted him up and dropped him outside the labyrinth. Ferhdessar cursed.

"Listen to me, Ferhdessar. I want you to understand what I'm offering Merzia. Maybe it will help you to die peacefully. I'll take good care of the country, I promise."

"Merzia doesn't wish to be ruled by you."

"No, not by me. But how can they refuse Jakob? Don't the people know what God has to offer them? I'll lay odds on it that Yvar made the decision for his subjects all by himself, but that's not the right way. Everybody should consider Jakob's offer themselves. If the people would realize what He has to offer, they won't have to think twice."

"Jakob's gift is death."

"No, it is not!" Kasimirh's voice became fierce. "Jakob's gifts are peace and knowledge. Listen to me!" Ferhdessar only barely managed to dodge a fireball. "Jakob is disappointed in mankind. He taught them during the Golden Era and He gave them the world, but by way of thanks they turned away from Him. He had resolved to never return to the earth again, but He made an exception for me. He descended from heaven to teach me.

Those lessons were overwhelming. I suddenly had the whole world at my feet. My head was overflowing with information that

I could only partly comprehend. Just the idea of having all this knowledge gave me a fantastic feeling. Jakob also told me about the history of the universe and how the people caused the divide between the heavenly and the worldly during the Second Era. With all the knowledge that Jakob had given me, I couldn't understand why the people had done such a thing. I did, however, understand Jakob's feelings of powerlessness and anger, which strengthened the ties between us.

I so badly wanted the people to have access again to all the knowledge that He had given me. So I begged him to give all the inhabitants of the earth a second chance. At long last, Jakob agreed and gave me my assignment. If I can see to it that unity is restored to the world, God will bring about a new Golden Era. He will give everybody the knowledge that He gave me. How can lord Yvar refuse such an offer? Why are you so opposed to this idea, Ferhdessar?"

"I don't want to follow a madman who strives for world domination in the name of a God that doesn't exist," Ferhdessar said provocatively. In order to take part in the fight again, he had to make Kasimirh lose his temper. "Jakob is nothing but an assistant to the other Gods. A glorified nobody, just like you!"

His plan seemed to be working. Kasimirh flew into a rage. The stones that he had laid out so carefully, started to float. "Jakob also gave me a warning. If I were to fail and the people would turn their backs on Him again, He would make the world end. Water has created the world, but it can just as easily destroy everything. Do you want to be responsible for that?"

The prophet was making the stones circle around the two sorcerers faster and faster. Then he pointed at Ferhdessar. The stones attacked him as if they were fired at him. Ferhdessar tried to defend himself but was only partly successful. He fell flat on the ground. Kasimirh lowered his hands and the stones fell down from the sky like hail, pummelling Ferhdessar's body.

"I have no choice but to kill you Ferhdessar, and I'm going to do the same to your king. I know that you'll never pledge your allegiance to Jakob. As long as you're both alive, I cannot fulfil my assignment."

Ferhdessar charged energy into his fist. The prophet had made a mistake by destroying the labyrinth. Now Ferhdessar was no longer powerless. The magic in his hand was almost too much to hold on to any longer, but he boosted it up a little more regardless. His fist was throbbing. When he extended his fingers, the magic shot away. Kasimirh screamed when he was smashed into the ground.

Ferhdessar released two more fireballs. Only one hit its target. Kasimirh got back up. He fended off Ferhdessar's attacks and immediately struck back. Several trees caught fire, giving the clearance a spooky atmosphere. The prophet threw Ferhdessar backwards. With his hands on his knees, Kasimirh tried to catch his breath.

Ferhdessar rummaged around in his pouch. His hand touched a cold, metal disc. It was but small and there was a hole in the middle so that it could be worn on a lace around one's neck. It had been in Ferhdessar's possession for a very long time. The man he had bought it from had told him that it contained the power of all the Gods. Ferhdessar had never really believed that. So he contemplated looking for another object.

He was roused from his thoughts by an attack from Kasimirh, which was immediately followed by another attack. He was out of time, he had no choice but to trust in this object. In his mind, Ferhdessar called upon all Gods save one. At the same time he gathered energy into his hands. His body was tingling. The object was working after all! He released the power. It crashed with great force into the shield that Kasimirh had put up.

Panting, Ferhdessar remained lying on the ground. This spell had required almost all of his energy, but it wasn't enough. It wasn't enough! Ferhdessar sobbed.

Do it again. But do it right this time!

At first, Ferhdessar didn't understand the order. Like most magical items, this disc hadn't come with a manual. How was he to know what he had done wrong? But it slowly started to dawn on him.

"But I've used up all my powers!"

Do it again! But right this time!

He clenched the disc firmly in his fist again, willing to die if that was what it took to defeat Kasimirh right here and now.

"Wigg, Gaia, Ischa, Trudh, Phoibos, Gunnan, Wardan, Anleifer, Kyl, Alos, Felcita," he hesitated for a second, "Jakob!"

Magic shot through his veins like fire. Each and every hair on his body stood on end. The fire around him had gone out, but the clearing seemed to be illuminated even brighter than before. Everything felt even more intense than when Ferhdessar had called upon the power of the water. The magic accumulated in his arms. Ferhdessar's breathing became shallow, because the magic was drawing upon his life force as well. It was both frightening and overwhelming. What little survival instinct he had left screamed at Ferhdessar to let go of the magic. But at the same time there was nothing he wanted more than to hold on to it. He wanted to feel the power of the Gods inside his body forever.

Suddenly the magic let go of *him*. Ferhdessar stumbled forwards, reaching out for the magic that was moving away from him. He fell headlong. Kasimirh's shield was destroyed with a loud bang. There was a scream. Ferhdessar lifted himself up a little bit, but there was no trace of the other sorcerer. Exhausted, he fell down again. Almost immediately somebody kneeled beside him. For a moment, Ferhdessar feared that it was Kasimirh, but the person spoke with a woman's voice.

"That was quite an attack, sorcerer."

It was Afifa.

"Did you see it?" Ferhdessar whispered. He looked at her through his eyelashes. It cost too much effort to lift his head.

She nodded.

"Did you see what happened to him? Have I beaten him?"

Afifa shrugged. "We'll look for traces of what happened to him later."

She put her hands on his temples. The warmth of her touch spread in waves through his body. It was overwhelmingly intense and he felt how the energy immediately started to heal him.

"You're a healeress?" He tried to push her away.

"Yes, so what? I'm just trying to help you," Afifa grumbled as she kept doing what she was doing. "You'll die if I don't do something."

Ferhdessar tried to get up, but he couldn't. Then everything went black.

18

Lilith tilted her head back so that she would be able to breathe the second the servus pushed her above water. As she sucked in the air, her gaze travelled the horizon. In every direction she looked, she saw nothing but the sea. A wave washed over her and Lilith swallowed a large gulp of water.

"Please, stay on the surface a little while longer so that I have more time to breathe," she gasped. The servus usually didn't let her draw more than three breaths of air, but that was barely enough.

The servus said something and pulled her under again. Lilith noticed it too late. She swallowed down another gulp of salt water. She hadn't heard what he had said, but she was beginning to understand what he had meant. It was clear that he wasn't going to let her die. Lilith closed her eyes and hung on to the creature's waistband. She had to hold on to him, otherwise she would surely drown.

Only when something grazed her body, did Lilith open her eyes again. She propped herself up to see where she was. She was on a pebble beach that transformed into bare rocks farther down. The servus followed her gaze.

"Wait here for master."

Lilith nodded and looked for a place where she could sit. The servus went back into the water and disappeared. For a moment Lilith thought that he was leaving her behind, but then he reappeared and walked onto the beach. She noticed that his skin had a more greyish colour than she had seen on any of these creatures before. He also kept scratching himself.

The servus gave her a fish to eat. The animal's dead eyes were staring at her. Lilith, however, was too hungry to let that spoil her appetite, so she took a big bite. The scales crunched between her teeth. It tasted awful, but nevertheless she took a second bite. Then she threw the fish away and picked some bones from her teeth. She'd rather go hungry than eat the entire fish. The servus, on the other hand, was eating his meal with relish.

Lilith asked the servus for something to drink. The creature gestured that there was no fresh water around. He didn't seem worried about it, but Lilith was.

"Do you have a name?" she asked him.

Since she was stuck with a creature that she hated, she'd better try to make the most of it. She was dependent on him, after all.

"Call me meistri."

At first Lilith thought that she hadn't heard right, but his conceited grin told her otherwise.

"Meistri," she whispered. She knew that the servi used that word to address the Muircadhi they served. Then she shook her head. "No, I won't call you that."

He got up and struck her temple. "Disobedient slave."

"I'm not a slave."

The servus hit her again, but now Lilith got up and hit him back. She managed to strike him once before he clasped his hands around her wrists. Then she resorted to kicking him. He groaned and loosened his grip. Lilith pulled her hands free and took another swing at him. The servus jumped at her, pulled at her arm and placed his leg in front of hers. Before she knew it, Lilith was down on the ground. The servus went to sit on her, making it impossible for her to move.

"I meistri, you slave."

Lilith twisted and writhed to break free. He pushed her arms and legs even harder against the rocks. The sharp stones pressed deeper into her stomach. The servus bent over and whispered the same words into her ear.

"No," Lilith screamed.

Before she had even noticed that the servus had let go of her hand, she received a blow to her head. The servus immediately grabbed her arm again, so she couldn't even react.

"Say it," he hissed. Spit splattered against her cheek.

Lilith shook her head and looked hard at him from the corners of her eyes.

Totally unexpectedly, the servus let go of her. Lilith didn't understand. Did this mean that she had won? The creature turned around and ignored her.

For the first couple of hours, Lilith was glad, but that feeling soon disappeared. The servus ate without sharing with her. Nor did he offer her the fresh water he had found somewhere. Even though her good mood had vanished, Lilith didn't give in.

At least, not until the next morning, when she had searched the entire island without finding anything to eat or drink. Lilith longingly looked at the sea, but she knew that the water wasn't drinkable. The servus walked onto the beach and sat down on a stone across from her. He ate a couple of fishes with lots of background noises. He washed them down with water from a waterskin. It suddenly hit Lilith: he got the water somewhere else. From some island where she couldn't go because she couldn't swim. Until then, she had hoped to find the spring sooner or later, but now all hope went up in smoke.

Lilith waited until the servus disappeared behind some bigger rocks and sneaked to the place where he had been sitting. She carefully pulled the waterskin towards her. A shove in her back made her fall headfirst.

"Let me drink something."

"What?"

"I'm thirsty."

He shook his head. "What?"

Lilith hesitated but then she whispered, "I beg you to let me drink something, meistri."

He knelt down beside her and pulled her head back by her hair to pour water into her mouth. Lilith swallowed as fast as she could. It was delicious, but the servus kept pouring water into her mouth. Lilith tried to turn her head away.

At long last, the servus took the waterskin away. Lilith wanted to get up, but he pushed her back down. She looked up at him, afraid. He looked at her expectantly. Lilith closed her eyes and bowed her head.

"Thank you, meistri." It was hard for her to utter the words, but the servus had won.

The creature grinned and took his foot off her shoulder. Suddenly his face became grave. He stooped down and in one and the same motion he straightened himself and flung a stone. A bird squealed and fell to the earth. The servus was immediately there when the bird hit the ground. He made sure that it was dead before he threw it into Lilith's lap.

"Ferhdessar send spy," the servus explained.

Lilith stared at the animal in her hands before she looked at the horizon. Was this a sign that Ferhdessar was still alive and that he was coming after her? If that was true, it also meant that Kasimirh was dead. The fight between the two sorcerers must have left either one dead.

The longer Lilith thought about, the more credible it sounded. She sighed, neither disappointed nor relieved. She didn't know what to think. Until one of the sorcerers showed up, it would be unclear what her future was going to be like.

Then she started. What if nobody came? Then she would be stuck on this island with a servus who could make her do anything he liked.

"Jakob, please help me," Lilith sighed. "Help me out of this mess."

www.ingramcontent.com/pod-product-compliance
Lightning Source LLC
Chambersburg PA
CBHW052035240626
47153CB00006B/2094